RIVALS FOR THE CROWN

Kathleen Givens

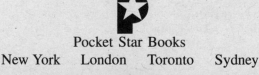

Pocket Star Books

New York　London　Toronto　Sydney

Pocket Star Books
A Division of Simon & Schuster, Inc.
1230 Avenue of the Americas,
New York, NY 10020

This book is a work of fiction. Names, characters, places, and incidents either are products of the author's imagination or are used fictitiously. Any resemblance to actual events or locales or persons, living or dead, is entirely coincidental.

First Pocket Star Books paperback edition June 2008

POCKET STAR and colophon are registered trademarks of Simon & Schuster, Inc.

For information regarding special discounts for bulk purchases, please contact Simon & Schuster Special Sales at 1-800-456-6798 or business@simonandschuster.com.

Illustration by Robert Hunt
Handlettering by Dave Gatti
Map by Paul J. Pugliese

Manufactured in the United States of America

10 9 8 7 6 5 4 3 2 1

ISBN-13: 978-1-4165-0993-6
ISBN-10:   1-4165-0993-3

To my sisters — by blood, marriage, and choice —
I treasure you all.

and

To Lily, Kate, Mikayla, Gavin, Michael, John, Patty,
Kerry, and Russ, always Russ, for making life so very grand

LIST OF MAJOR CHARACTERS

IN ENGLAND

Isabel de Burke—great-granddaughter of a king, lady-in-waiting to Queen Eleanor of England

Isabel's Grandmother—illegitimate daughter of a king

Rachel de Anjou—Isabel's best friend

Sarah de Anjou—Rachel's sister

Jacob de Anjou—Rachel's father

Edward Plantagenet—King of England, also known as Longshanks and Edward of England

Walter Langton—Bishop and Steward of the Wardrobe

Alis de Braun—lady-in-waiting to Queen Eleanor

Lady Dickleburough—lady-in-waiting to Queen Eleanor

Henry de Boyer—one of King Edward's household knights

IN SCOTLAND

Margaret MacDonald MacMagnus—lady of Loch Gannon, married to Gannon MacMagnus

Gannon MacMagnus—half-Irish, half-Norse warrior, now a clan leader and laird of Loch Gannon, married to Margaret

Rory MacGannon—younger son of Margaret and Gannon

Magnus MacGannon—older son of Margaret and Gannon

Drason Anderson—Orkneyman and friend of Margaret and Gannon

Nell Crawford—Margaret's sister, married to Liam Crawford

Liam Crawford—Nell's husband, nephew to Ranald Crawford, and cousin to William Wallace

William Wallace—Liam's cousin, destined to become Scotland's Guardian and leader of its army

Ranald Crawford—Liam and William's uncle, Sheriff of Ayr

Davey MacDonald—Margaret and Nell's younger brother

Kieran MacDonald—Davey's oldest son and Rory's cousin

Robert Bruce, the younger—grandson to Robert, the Competitor for the Throne of Scotland, later Robert I of Scotland

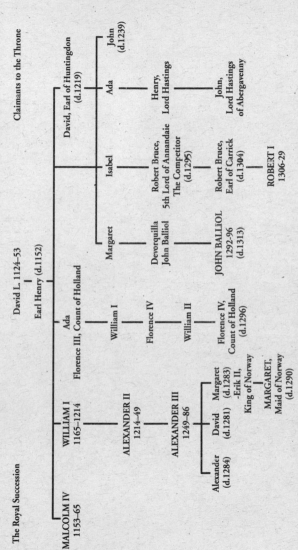

The Scottish Royal Succession and Claimants to the Throne

The Royal Succession

David I. 1124–53
Earl Henry (d.1152)

MALCOLM IV
1153–65

WILLIAM I
1165–1214

Ada
Florence III, Count of Holland

ALEXANDER II
1214–49

William I

ALEXANDER III
1249–86

Florence IV

David (d.1281)
Margaret (d.1283)
-Erik II, King of Norway

William II

Alexander (d.1284)

MARGARET, Maid of Norway (d.1290)

Florence IV, Count of Holland (d.1296)

Claimants to the Throne

David, Earl of Huntingdon (d.1219)

Margaret

Isabel

Ada

John (d.1239)

Devorquilla
John Balliol

Robert Bruce, 5th Lord of Annandale The Competitor (d.1295)

Henry, Lord Hastings

JOHN BALLIOL
1292–96 (d.1313)

Robert Bruce, Earl of Carrick (d.1304)

John, Lord Hastings of Abergavenny

ROBERT I
1306–29

BRITAIN

Atlantic
Ocean

Orkney
Islands

N
W · E
S

Skye
Loch
Gannon

SCOTLAND

Perth

Stirling
Edinburgh
Glasgow
Berwick

North
Sea

AYRSHIRE

Newcastle upon Tyne
Durham

York

Irish Sea

IRELAND

Dublin

ENGLAND

Norwich
EAST ANGLIA

WALES

London
Canterbury

Calais

English Channel

FRANCE

0   50   100 miles
0   50   100 kilometers

RIVALS
FOR THE
CROWN

PART I

The holly and the ivy
Are plants that are well known
Of all the trees that grow in the woods
The holly bears the crown.

ANONYMOUS
TRADITIONAL FOLK SONG
ENGLAND

PROLOGUE

LONDON, JULY 1290

R achel! Rachel, wake up!"

At first Sarah's whispered words blended into her dream. Rachel turned her head away from the fear in her sister's voice. She'd been dreaming of winter, of snow falling softly from a bright sky. She and Sarah, little girls, had been dancing, laughing as they collected the flakes in their small hands. Then Sarah's mouth had opened in a wail and the sky had darkened and the snow had turned to rain. Rachel climbed her way back to the world, her mind resisting, for whatever had frightened Sarah would frighten her as well.

"Wake up!" Sarah shook Rachel's shoulder.

Rachel opened her eyes. It was still dark. And although it was summer, there was a chill in the air. Outside the rain drummed on the roof just above their heads and the shutters clattered as the wind shook them against the wooden frame. She heard it then too—a terrible pounding on the door, male voices raised in anger.

"They're here," Sarah whispered.

Rachel sat up, fully awake now. She knew who they were: the king's men, here to drive them from their home. Just as Mama had predicted. Just as Mama had prepared for. Papa, ever optimistic, had argued that his family would remain untouched, no matter what King Edward's proclamation had said.

She could hear her father's voice now from her parents' room below. The pounding on the door stopped. The rain was too loud for her to hear their words, but Papa talked for a moment before she heard hurried footsteps on the stairs. The door to their bedroom was flung open and Mama rushed in.

"Get dressed, girls," she said, still fastening her own clothes as she spoke in a near whisper. "Remember the bundles under your clothes. Say nothing. No matter what happens, do not argue with them. And if . . . if there is violence . . . run. Remember the plan."

Sarah nodded, already out of bed and pulling her skirts on over the chemise in which she'd slept.

"Mama," Rachel said, but her mother shook her head rapidly.

"Get dressed. Say nothing. Do it, Rachel! For once in your life do not argue. Just do what I say." And then she was gone.

It was a blur then, as Rachel and Sarah dressed and stuffed the bundles they'd prepared under their clothing, attaching smaller ones to each knee, where they would be hidden under their skirts. The satchels they carried held only clothes and a few keepsakes that would alarm no one: ribbons for their hair, a lucky stone, a lace collar, a cloak pin. Nothing to raise suspicion. They had been tutored well. But Rachel had never believed this would happen.

Despite all their preparations, all Mama's instructions, Rachel had not believed they would have to leave.

King Edward had announced his edict on July 18, expelling the sixteen thousand Jews resident in England from his kingdom. Within days, the streets of London had been full of those who had already begun their exodus. Some had simply left everything they could not carry, and walked away from homes and shops and all they'd contained. Others had tried to sell their businesses and houses, and of those, some had been able to receive fair prices, but most had gotten only a pittance of the value. They'd scattered, neighborhoods and families separated, perhaps forever.

Many of the Jews had said they would not leave, declaring that King Edward had been their protector in the past. Just a few years ago had he not brought them within the walls of the Tower of London and kept them safe? He would not abandon them now. The edict, they'd said, was to soothe the feelings of those who had raised their voices against them, a political move on Edward's part. Nothing more. But others remembered that Edward had imprisoned the moneylenders in the Tower. Hundreds had died.

At first there had been no mass routing of Jews, no massacre of those who had not left immediately. But for others, it had been different. Several families had already been roused in the middle of the night, and removed from their homes, escorted to the gate of London, and cast out to fend for themselves. There did not seem to be a pattern to it, but it had happened every day for almost a fortnight. And now, on the thirtieth of July, it was their turn. Her father had been so sure they would be spared.

This is not real. This is my dream and I will wake to find myself in a snowstorm with Sarah. This is not real.

"Hurry!" Sarah said. "Faster! I can hear them on the stairs."

They were barely dressed when the first soldier appeared outside their bedchamber. He was older, his gray, grizzled hair refusing to stay under the helmet of the king's guard that he wore. He touched the brim with a sharp gesture.

"Mistresses. You have been given until daybreak to pack your belongings." He glanced outside at the dark. "Not long now."

"And if we're not ready to leave by then?" Rachel asked.

"Rachel!" Sarah exclaimed.

"My orders are that you are to leave. If you want to live. . . ." He shrugged, as though it were of no matter to him.

Rachel nodded tightly. There would be no mercy, no small kindnesses, from this man. He watched with a stony expression as they stripped the bed and tied the linens together. Sarah, her head bent over the bundle of linens, picked up her satchel. Keeping her eyes lowered, she squeezed past the man and made her way down the stairs.

Rachel took one last look at the room she'd slept in her whole life, at the empty bedframe, the mattress sagging against the ropes, the empty hooks on the wooden wall that had held their clothing. At the iron candlestick on the small table in the corner, which held the one precious candle they'd been allowed on winter nights. She reached for the candlestick and heard the guard clear his throat. She glanced over her shoulder. He met her gaze and shook his head, she pulled her hand away as though the candlestick would burn her, feeling her face flush. For one mad moment she wanted to shout at him that the candlestick was a paltry thing for him to take from her when he was already taking her home and her past, but instead she kept silent and followed her sister.

Downstairs her father was packing his books in an oiled cloth bag with his siddur, the prayerbook, and the Tanach, the Bible of the Old Testament, given to him by his grandfather. The menorah and the tallit, the prayer shawl he used on the Sabbath, lay in a small wooden chest at his feet. Outside she heard the rattle of the cart her mother had reserved, just in case. She could see the tears in her father's eyes as he worked, but he would not look at her. Neither would the two younger guards, both just a few years older than she and Sarah. One, without meeting her gaze, gestured for her to go into the back room. Rachel stood frozen, staring at him. He wanted her to go into the empty dark room. With him. Alone. She felt a hand on her shoulder and turned to look into Mama's eyes, seeing banked anger there.

"The cart is here," Mama said softly, in a diffident tone that Rachel had never heard her use. "May we load it, please, sir?"

The guard must have nodded, for Mama picked up a box and carried it out the front door. Rachel did the same, glad to be out of doors, where the rain had abated to a drizzle. The carter stopped them with an upraised hand.

"Payment first," he growled.

"We will pay you when we're out of the city," Mama said. "That's what we agreed."

The carter laughed low in his throat. "Then carry your own goods, madam. You have until daybreak."

Mama stiffened, but relented with a nod and handed

the man the coins from the pocket at her waist. He shook his head and named an exorbitant price.

"That's not what we agreed!" Mama said, an edge of fear in her voice now.

"Daybreak," the carter said. "Decide."

"We'll take it," Papa said and reached past Mama to hand the man the rest of the money. The carter bit each coin in turn, then grunted.

"Load it yourself. Only two ride. The others walk."

It took less than an hour to load everything. Mama and Sarah rode on the back of the cart as they made their way through the dank streets. When the sky brightened Rachel could see the fear in her parents' eyes. Daybreak was almost here and they still had much of the city to cross.

She hadn't looked back at their house, refused to think, even to herself, that she would never be back. She had not acknowledged the few faces at the windows above the street as they'd left. She'd known those people since she was a child, but not one of them had lent them assistance, not one had raised a cry of dismay. Not one had said a word, not even farewell. It was as though she and her family had never known these people.

Her family had left much behind—their furniture, except for a few stools—but they'd taken her father's books, her mother's precious plate, her sister's dowry box, and three chests holding their possessions. Her mother had sighed as she'd looked around her kitchen, running her hand one last time over the wooden table she'd used daily. Rachel had turned away from the sight, her anger threatening to erupt. What had she and her family done to deserve this? They'd been good citizens of London, good subjects of the king. Their customs and beliefs might be different from those of the Christians, but they prayed to the same Father God, obeyed the same rules. What sins against society had made them outcasts now?

And what of the Jews who stayed despite all the warnings, those who watched them now—would they pay dearly for their decision? Would soldiers truly kill all those who remained? She would not think of it, would not remember their names. She would not think of the boy who had promised to woo her when they were older, who had watched silently as she and her family left. Would not think of Isabel, her dearest friend, who would never know what had happened to her, only that Rachel had left with no farewell.

The light was brighter now and the rain had stopped. But still they were in London. There were other Jewish families departing too, people carrying bundles and babies, hurrying toward the city walls. Carts like theirs fought for places in line to pass through Aldgate, and their carter swore and whipped his horse to push forward. Rachel, like her father, kept one hand on the cart, unsettled now by those around them and the fear that suddenly filled the air.

Boys pelted them with rotten fruit from overhead, but no one complained. Everyone was intent on the imminent sunrise and the slow-moving line passing through the gate. And then her mother was hit with refuse, the dark stain spreading on the shoulder of her gown. Her father whirled, his face a mask of rage.

"No!" Mama cried. "Jacob, no! Ignore it."

Papa was hit next, and his face went scarlet. "Is it not enough that we are forced from our homes? Is it not enough that we are running like cattle? Must we endure this humiliation as well? It is beyond bearing!"

Mama grabbed his arm. "Jacob, think! They are nothing, those boys throwing this at us. They want you to get angry. They want you to go after them! And then what? We will still be here at dawn. And what will happen to you, to us? Ignore it. They are nothing. This is nothing. We will survive this."

They stared into each other's eyes. And then Papa nodded.

There was a sudden commotion behind them, and a troop of the king's cavalry burst through the throng, coming forward with a great show of weapons and armor, and lining the path to the gate, the horses' breath looking like smoke from a foul fire in the unseasonably cool morning air. Rachel looked at the faces of the king's men, at the glances they gave each other and the sky. Would the soldiers be given orders to fall upon those who were still in London at daybreak? She began to pray, for her family, for those behind them. Ten people ahead of them, then six.

And then she heard Isabel's voice.

"Rachel! Rachel!"

Only Isabel de Burke would have braved this madness, Rachel thought, her heart lifting. One person in all of London still cared whether she lived or died. "Isabel!" she cried, standing on her toes, trying to find her friend. "Isabel!"

The line moved forward and Papa grabbed her arm. "Do not stop, Rachel!"

"But, Papa, it's Isabel! How did she know?"

"She lives at court," he said. "They all know."

"Rachel!" Isabel's voice was louder now.

A slim hand with long fingers waved madly above the fray, and Rachel finally saw her. Isabel's light brown hair was in disarray, tumbling around her shoulders as though she'd risen hastily from her bed. She was dressed as a servant, her clothing simple and drab, but not convincing. Servant girls did not have Isabel's fine bone structure or her rare beauty. Rachel's eyes welled with tears of gratitude that her friend had found her.

"Here! Isabel, here!"

"We have no time for this, Rachel!" Papa said.

Rachel stayed where she was, waving her arm high. The group in front of her family was arguing with the guards at the gate, and it became clear why the wait was so long. They would have to pay to leave! The word spread to those behind them, and she could smell their fear and anger. The king's men let their horses paw at the ground, as though impatient to start their tasks.

"I thought I would not find you!" Isabel darted through the crowd and embraced Rachel.

"I could not send word to you! Soldiers came—"

"I heard what was happening and ran to your house," Isabel gasped, "but you were not there. Oh, Rachel! Where will you go? Sir, where will you go?"

Papa's expression softened. "I don't know, Isabel. I don't know."

"I did not believe the king would enforce his proclamation!" Isabel's eyes were wide with worry. "You'll have no safe passage. You'll have no protection! It will be dangerous. You know how treacherous the roads are!"

"We have no choice," Papa said.

"I wish I had money or the power to send men with you! Be careful, be so careful!" Isabel cried and hugged Rachel tighter. "I cannot bear it! It will be so long until we see each other again!"

"Isabel, we will never see each other again!"

"No, no, do not even say that!" Isabel said. "We *will* meet again. You must believe it! We must both believe it! We will always be friends. Nothing, not even this, will change that!"

"Rachel, come!" Papa said as their turn came to pass through the gate. He handed the gatekeeper coins and turned to Rachel. "Farewell, Isabel. Thank you for being a friend to my daughter. Come."

Rachel tore herself out of Isabel's arms, both girls sobbing.

"Stay safe, dear friend," Isabel said. "Rachel, oh dear God, take care! I will pray for you every day! I will pray for you all!"

"And I you, Isabel! I will think of you in your new life at court!"

"Rachel, come!"

Rachel passed with her family through the gate. She turned to look for Isabel but could not see past the frenzied throng pushing through behind them. The sun's rays touched the tops of London's buildings, and her father turned her away from the sight, hurrying her along the road behind the cart. Her tears, unleashed by Isabel's appearance, continued to flow.

"Rachel," Papa said, his voice comforting. "We are out of London, and we have much ahead of us. Dry your eyes. We'll face the future together."

Rachel sniffed. Now they faced the dangers of the road. She hugged her arms and looked at the stain on her mother's shoulder. Part of her would never feel safe again.

ONE

Margaret MacDonald MacMagnus lifted her head and let the wind blow through her hair while she caught her breath. Even after all these years, she still climbed to the top of this headland to wait for her man to come home. Two ships today, and neither of them his, but there were still hours of daylight left. She was not worried, for Gannon MacMagnus was a man to trust. He'd said he'd be home this day, and home he would be.

She'd missed him. Wasn't that absurd, to live with a man for nigh on thirty years, then miss him terribly when he'd only been gone a few days? He'd not gone anywhere unusual or dangerous, only to Skye to visit her brother Davey, then down to Ayrshire to visit their oldest son, Magnus, who lived on the lands the king had granted to Gannon so many years ago.

And there it was, the sail she'd expected and had hoped to see. Gannon's ship was approaching rapidly from the south, its rail almost under water, its white sail mirroring the foam at its bow as the black hull sliced through the dark blue water. But it was not alone on the sea, for there, in the north, was a second sail, one that made her draw her breath in sharply. A dragon ship. A longship, of Viking design, its wide beam and shallow hull bringing back a flood of unwelcome memories. Dark storm clouds billowed behind it, putting the square sail, red with yellow stripes, into high relief. She clasped her arms and ignored the chill that swept through her, reminding herself that it was not a warship— those days were over forever. It would be a messenger from the north, nothing more. Still . . . She looked south, where Gannon's ship was nearing the entrance to the sea loch, and was comforted. Whatever the news the dragon ship brought, she and Gannon would face it together, as they had everything else life had brought them.

She turned to start down the slope, then took a moment to look over the glen that was her home, where she and Gannon had built a life together, binding the remnants of her family and clan into a thriving community. The sea loch was now known as Loch Gannon, which never failed to amuse her husband. But the honor was appropriate, for without him, none of them would be here. Across the usually placid waters, ruffled now by the wind, the mountains rose to the north and the east, protecting them from the world beyond. Below her the fortress grew out of the rocky promontory on which it rested, and to which she now hurried, hearing the horns sounding twice, first with the familiar notes that let all below know that the laird of the glen was coming home, then again, with the message that a ship was approaching and that it was not one of their own. Gannon had the men of the clan well trained, and her staff would know to prepare a meal to welcome him and his men home. But she would greet him—and the visitors—herself.

Rory, her younger son, tall, strong, and ready for the world, met her on the path to the postern gate, his blond hair catching the light, the same pale shade as his father's. He was so like his father. He had Gannon's chin, Gannon's blue eyes, his wide shoulders. And his impatience.

"Mother! Do ye ken who it is? Da and who else?"

She shook her head, not wanting to betray how breathless her headlong dash had made her. She often forgot that she was no longer young, but her body never did. "Aye, yer father's coming. But the other is a dragon ship."

Rory's eyebrows drew together, just as his father's always did when he turned thoughtful. "From Orkney? Perhaps with news of the queen's progress?"

Margaret's mood lifted at once. Margaret, Maid of Norway, only seven years old, was on her way to accept the throne of Scotland that she had held since she was three. "Of course. That's what it is. Drason did say he'd let us ken when she stopped in Orkney on her way to London. I'll just—"

"Go to meet Da," Rory finished with a laugh. "As if ye dinna always do that?"

"And someday, my lad, if ye are as fortunate as yer father, yer own wife will do the same."

"Ye'll have to teach her to adore me, as ye do Da."

"Adore! He's been spreading rumors again, has he?"

She laughed with him and led the way into the fortress that Gannon had built to keep them all safe. Wooden walls at first, replaced over the years with thick stone walls, filled with rubble to withstand siege machines. And unable to be burnt to the ground, as both Inverstrath and Somerstrath had been. But she would not remember that now, any of it. Those memories belonged to a time past, when she and her sister Nell and young Davey had faced horrors no one should have to endure. When Gannon had entered her life and changed it forever.

She'd been Gannon MacMagnus's wife for twenty-seven years, had borne five children and seen two live to be grown men. Magnus, already married, was learning how to manage lands and people. And Rory was young, but Rory would do well, for Rory excelled at everything he attempted. All he needed—eventually—was a home of his own, and a woman to love and, yes, to adore him, for he deserved it. But that would come in time.

Gannon's Lady sailed into Loch Gannon under full sail, her husband at the helm. Margaret stood, as she always did, at the end of the dock, waiting for him, Rory at her side. The sky was darkening and the wind rising, bringing the smell of the storm with it. This one would be more than simple showers, for already the mountaintops across the loch were obscured, and the seabirds were flying inland, seeking shelter. The autumnal equinox often brought fierce storms, and this one, coming nine days later, looked to be no exception. Rory's hair was whipping around his head, and he brushed it back with a gesture that was so like his father's that she smiled.

And then Gannon himself was calling to her, his tall form alive with movement. As always, she saw nothing else. He wore the clothes of a Scotsman, plaided trews, knit leggings, and a saffron overtunic. He'd abandoned his Irish clothing long ago. Sometimes she herself forgot that he was of Ireland and not a native of the western shore of Scotland that had always been her home. But the painted carvings along the railing of his ship, Celtic symbols and Norse runes painted gold against the black of the rail, reminded her that he was her gift from the sea, Ireland's loss and Scotland's gain.

She waved in return, her smile wide. Her man was home and all was well . . . for a moment at least, for there, rounding the last turn through the barren entrance that hid Loch Gannon from the world, came the dragon ship. She recognized it as Drason's at once. The Orkneyman had been their friend since their fateful meeting that long-ago summer of 1263. Their friendship had begun strangely. They'd been enemies who quickly discovered that they were united in their hatred of Nor Thorkelson, Drason's uncle and the man who had murdered her family. They'd joined forces and had finally defeated Nor in a mighty battle on the Isle of Skye that was still talked about all over Scotland. Drason waved, but not with his customary exuberance, and her heart lurched. Whatever news he brought was not good. She was certain it did not concern Magnus, or her brother Davey and his family, for Gannon had just come from them. And surely not Nell, who was in Stirling to greet the child queen, nowhere near the Orkneys nor the sea.

But something had happened.

"Lass," Gannon called, as his ship neared the dock. "Ye do see Drason, aye? Send word to bar the door to the wine cellar. He'll drink us out of house and home."

She smiled, but saw Gannon's eyes narrow as he looked at the dragon ship and knew he saw the same tension in Drason's stance that she did. Drason was wearing leather armor and a leather helmet that hid his blond hair. Not the garb of a man simply visiting friends, but what a prudent man might wear in uncertain times. She kept her silence, waiting while the clansmen caught the ropes and secured

Gannon's Lady. She wrapped her arms around Gannon when he caught her in his embrace and kissed her for all the clan to see, his ardor never failing to please her.

He smiled down at her. "I missed ye, Margaret. How are ye?"

"Wonderful now that ye're here," she said.

She laid her hand along his cheek and kissed him again. He was no longer young, this splendid man of hers. There were lines around his sea blue eyes and gray at his temples now, but he still moved quickly and his back was still straight. He was still the most handsome man she'd ever seen, and she was the most fortunate of women to love this fierce warrior and have him love her in return. She smiled again as Gannon embraced Rory, clapping the boy on his shoulder.

"Tell me it's ye growing and not me shrinking," Gannon said to his son.

"It's me growing, Da," Rory said, and they both laughed.

"All is well here, love," she said. "It's good to have ye home. How is everyone?"

"Well. Everyone's well," Gannon said. "Magnus is learning how to run his own home, and Jocelyn is the same as she always is."

Which meant, Margaret thought, that their daughter-in-law, difficult at best, was as prickly and spoiled as ever. Magnus was a good man, but serious and cautious, and Margaret had hoped he would marry a woman with laughter in her soul, rather than a woman like Jocelyn. Still, she pleased Magnus, and what else could a mother want for her son?

"Yer brother sends his love," Gannon told her. "His pile of rocks is beginning to look like a castle instead of a rubble heap. It'll be a good fortress when it's finished. Davey wants ye to come and see it soon. Everyone there is fine." He looked at Drason's ship and his tone deepened. "We'll see what news he brings. Ye've heard nothing?"

Margaret shook her head. "No. Rory thinks it must be about the queen's journey from Norway. She was to stop in the Orkneys."

Gannon wrapped an arm around her. "That must be it."

"Drason himself," Rory said. "Must be important."

"We've not seen him here for four years," Margaret said quietly. "Since we lost King Alexander."

Gannon met her gaze. "Aye, since we lost the king."

The longship slid alongside the wooden dock, and Drason leaned forward over the rail. He yanked off his helmet. His gaze swept across them.

"She's dead," Drason said. "Your queen is dead in Orkney."

Margaret gasped. "Are ye sure? The wee lass is dead?"

"I came as soon as I heard," Drason said. "The word is just getting out. I knew you'd want to hear it at once."

"Oh, the poor child!" Margaret cried.

Gannon reached to clasp Drason's hand. "Aye, ye're right. And I thank ye for bringing word yerself, my friend. Now come inside and tell us all the rest of it."

"What does it mean?" Rory asked. "What will her death mean?"

"There will be a struggle for the crown," Margaret told her son, shaking her head. "And there's no assurance that the winner will be the best leader for our people."

"It means," Gannon said, "that the wolves will be coming out of their lairs. And the leopard in the south will wait to see who wins. God help Scotland now."

There was not much more for Drason Anderson to tell than the stark news of the child queen's death on her journey to claim her throne. She'd been called the Maid of Norway because her father had been King Erik of that land, but her grandfather had been Scotland's King Alexander III, and she had been the queen of Scotland since she was three. The Maid, the daughter of Alexander's daughter, had been the last of his line. And now she, too, was dead, and the succession was left unclear.

Margaret sat with Gannon and Rory near the huge stone fireplace in their Great Hall, listening to Drason. The years since she'd last seen the Norseman from Orkney had changed him. Drason was younger than Gannon, but his blond hair was ribboned with gray. He looked weary beyond words, and she felt a wave of affection for their staunch friend. Drason had left his own wife and family to bring the news to them. There were good men in the world—even in Orkney.

"It's said she became ill on the voyage," Drason said. "Some say, of course, that she was poisoned, but I've heard she was sickly. And in truth, there is no reason for the Norse—nor us Orcadians—to have the child die on their watch."

"Nor does it benefit Edward of England," Gannon said. "This will change his plans."

"A child should not be a pawn in games of power," Margaret said. "What was her father thinking to let her leave him? She's just a wee lass." She paused. "She was just a wee lass, poor soul."

"Her father was thinking that he'd signed the treaty with Edward of England, pledging her to his son," Gannon said. "And King Erik's a mere lad, only twenty, I think. Edward is a force to be reckoned with. Lesser men have crumbled before him. I'm not surprised that Erik let Edward have his way."

"Foul thing, that," Drason said, "to wed your son to your sister's granddaughter."

"And as foul to have the Pope approve it," Gannon said. "But approve it he did. And now there is no clear heir."

"It'll have to go back generations," Margaret said. "The Balliols will claim the crown is theirs. So will the Bruces. And my Comyn cousins certainly will have opinions." She sighed, thinking of the measures her cousins might take to assure that their position of power was not diluted. "And there are a host of illegitimate royal children who could make claims."

Drason frowned. "Surely they'll have no success? I'm no expert on Scottish politics, but I cannot remember a bastard taking the throne."

"Actually," Gannon said with a laugh, "many a bastard has taken the throne. But no, I canna see one of the earlier kings' bastards getting the crown. What's the talk in Orkney? What are yer people thinking?"

Drason smiled ruefully. "That they wish she'd died elsewhere. Some are thinking this will bring Erik of Norway's wrath on Orkney, although Erik's men were with her. Others are afraid that the Scots will blame us and take revenge, or that Edward of England will. And although no one's saying it straight out, some are wondering if she was as ill as she was made out to be."

Gannon's brows furrowed. "Murder?"

"Unlikely, but not impossible," Drason said. "Show me a country where men cannot be bought or frightened into betraying someone who trusted them. There are evil men in every land. As we know."

Gannon nodded. "There is a kingdom at stake. That will bring out the greedy ones, and Scotland, like everywhere, has its share."

"What will Nell do?" Margaret asked, turning to Drason. "Nell and her oldest, Meg, were to serve the queen. They're at Stirling, waiting for her arrival."

"Well," Gannon said to Margaret, "yer sister willna be going to London with the queen. Despite the reason for it, that should please ye, lass."

"Aye," Margaret said, comforted by the thought. The Maid was to have stopped in Stirling and Edinburgh to greet many of Scotland's nobles, then travel to London, to live at Edward's court and await her marriage to Edward's son. Nell was to have accompanied her, with her daughters. "I wonder if Nell will stay at Stirling while the king is chosen. What if she hasna heard yet? We must get word to her."

"I'll go," Rory said eagerly, drawing her gaze. "I'll go to Stirling and tell her."

Her son's face was alight with the possibility of the journey, and Margaret felt a stab of fear. She would lose him. She'd always known they could not keep Rory at Loch Gannon forever, that its peaceful life was not enough to hold him. They'd taken him on their travels to Ireland and throughout Scotland and he had accompanied Gannon to the Continent and to London. But Rory was ready now for more. Or thought he was.

Gannon looked at his son thoughtfully. "They'll be hearing before we can get ye or anyone there, but it might be a good idea to send ye. I'd like to know what is being said at court."

"I could leave in the morning," Rory said.

"Ye'd need others to go with ye."

"Not many," Rory said, naming a few young men.

Margaret listened to them discussing the journey. Rory's manner betrayed his growing excitement, and she hid her own dismay. Why could Rory not have ventured into a peaceful Scotland, as his brother had? Why now was he hearing the call to join the world, when once again Scotland was about to plunge into turmoil? Or was she being ridiculous? She leaned close to her husband.

"Gannon, I fear this," she whispered. "Am I wrong, love, to worry so?"

Gannon kissed the top of her head. But he did not answer.

OCTOBER 1290, LONDON

"There will be men," Isabel de Burke's mother said, bending to examine the hem of Isabel's skirts. "They will test you, you know. They are the hunters."

"Yes, Mother," Isabel said.

She had heard this lecture many times before. The men whom her mother called "the hunters," preyed upon young girls foolish enough to exchange their virginity for a few baubles. Invisible in her demure clothing, she'd watched these men lean over a shoulder, caress a cheek, kiss a neck. And never notice her watching. But those days were over. Now she would be one of those pursued.

"Most of the men are married," her mother said, adjusting the fall of the silk gown Isabel wore. "But even those who are not do not have honorable intentions. Some of the girls are foolish enough to think what they're being offered is true affection. They do not see it for the game of hunter and prey that it is." She straightened and looked into Isabel's eyes. "Those girls do not realize that they are nothing more than a prize, a name for these men to brandish before their friends and then be forgotten. Many a young girl has mistaken lust for love and bartered away her only value. You will not be one of them."

"No, Mother."

She knew the answer her mother wanted to hear. And truly, she had listened and learned, knew the price of such foolishness. She was taking the place of a girl from a good family who had suddenly left the royal household after weeks of vomiting at strange times, obviously with child. Isabel would not be so foolish.

"Remember this day," her mother said. "Nothing will ever be the same. You have been invited to serve Eleanor of Castile, by God's mercy the Queen of England and Ireland and Aquitaine. Over all the others, she chose you, an English girl, instead of one from her own land. It is a high honor. And an unexpected one, given who we are."

And while the honor could not be declined, neither could it be explained. Her mother was convinced it was because of their ties to the throne, but that had been generations ago, and the family had been all but ignored in the years since. Isabel's great-grandmother had been seduced by a king who had never acknowledged the child—her grandmother—and who had been disowned by her family, left to fend for herself. Happily, the king had given her great-grandmother a house of her own in the City of London, where she had raised her daughter alone, and done it well.

It had helped, of course, that Isabel's great-grandmother had been a beauty and had passed those traits down. Isabel was fortunate to have inherited her mother's clear skin and green eyes and thick brown hair. She had her mother's long fingers and, her mother told her, her father's height. Her mother's expression softened, and she turned Isabel to face their luxury, the long mirror from the Continent that had been a gift from her grandfather.

"Look at yourself."

Isabel looked at her image, wavy in the glass, and saw a young girl who put on a brave face. She was ready for this new part of her life, but she was terrified of it as well. She was not afraid of the work, although she knew she would be asked to do the least pleasant tasks, those things that the queen's older and far more powerful ladies would not deign to do. What terrified her was that, after all these years of being unseen, she would suddenly be highly visible, a topic of discussion, of speculation. There would be many who would question why she, of all those at court or in the nobility, had been chosen by the queen.

"I wish your father were here to see this," her mother said fiercely.

"And I as well. He would have been so pleased."

Her mother raised an eyebrow. Her mother did not mourn the loss of her father as she did. Mother rarely spoke of him, and never with fondness. Isabel had only dim memories of a man lifting her into his arms, his laughter merry, his embrace comforting. She missed him, even after all these years.

"You must never trust any of them," Mother said. "Listen, learn, laugh. Flirt. But never, never trust."

Isabel nodded again. She knew what the court was. She'd been born in the shadow of a royal palace, where her father had been a clerk of the Wardrobe. Despite its name, the entity had little to do with clothing. The Wardrobe handled all the financial dealings of the king's household. The servants, garments, and accoutrements of the king and queen, of course, but much more, for the Wardrobe equipped not only the royal household but the king's armies as well. The Wardrobe was responsible for purchasing, dispensing and storing large supplies of armor, bows, swords, spears, lances, and other weapons, as well as the horses and the servants to care for it all.

Her mother was head seamstress for the queen, with a staff of five, and rooms at Windsor and here at Westminster. Isabel had spent most of her young years roaming the halls of royal palaces, invisible to the royal family and the nobles who frequented those halls. She had watched them with fascination, as a child mimicking their accents and manners for her mother's and grandmother's amusement. But all of that had changed now, for she would be one of them.

Eleanor of Castile was wife to King Edward, a lion of a man. Once Isabel had admired him. Now she hated him. Edward was a pitiless king, one year a champion of the Jews, another year expelling them from their homes. She would never forgive him for his casual cruelty. Eleanor, on the other hand, had taken the time occasionally to talk with her seamstress's daughter. Isabel had heard stories that with others—especially the tenants on her lands—Eleanor was not so pleasant, and she certainly was not a popular queen with the people.

"What I do not understand," Isabel said, "is why I was chosen. The queen has always been kind to me, but we've not spoken a great deal, and I would not have thought she could even remember my name."

"There was a sudden opening, remember. She has known you all your life."

"Mother, Queen Eleanor certainly does not know me."

"Are you questioning your good fortune, Isabel? Most young girls would be delighted to have been offered this position. Most women in England would be delighted! You have the chance to reclaim our family's name, and perhaps to make a brilliant marriage. Why do you have to examine everything? If the queen does not know you well, time will remedy that."

"When I have become settled," Isabel said, "when the queen does know me, I will talk to her about King Edward expelling the Jews. Surely, if I explain it well, that the king was too harsh, that they did nothing wrong and have lost everything simply because a handful of Londoners complained about them, surely she will talk to King Edward. He could easily rescind his expulsion order."

Mother straightened, her eyes blazing. "You will not!"

"But I will, Mother. The king is only looking at it from one point of view. Christians are forbidden to lend money, and that's why the Jews were brought to London. A few years ago the king himself defended them, and now this!"

"The king had them put into the Tower and demanded they pay a fine to be released, Isabel! You will be silent on this."

"Rachel's family was driven out of London like cattle.

You did not see it. I did. And what did they do—prosper? Is that their sin?"

"They refuse to acknowledge Christ."

"As do the Moors, but they are allowed to stay."

"There are not so many of them."

"They have not the wealth that the Jews have. Had. Do you not see this as an injustice, Mother? How can you not see this? I have lost my dearest friend—because of money!"

"It was time for that friendship to end, Isabel. It was unnatural."

"Unnatural! We were little girls together. There is nothing unnatural about that. She was my friend when others scorned us. She did not care that Grandmother was illegitimate and I did not care that she was a Jew."

"You must tell no one that you were friends with Rachel de Anjou! No one! And you will not approach the queen with any complaint, let alone this one. You risk more than a rebuke, Isabel, you risk your very life. And mine. And your grandmother's. Do you understand who you are, who the queen is? With one word she could have us all imprisoned or put to death. Your grandmother could be punished for allowing your friendship—encouraging it, even, and keeping it from me. You know I never approved of you being friends with her. I would lose my station, at the very least. You risk our lives!"

"If she is so harsh a queen that no one can talk to her, then why do I want to serve her at all? What loyalty do I have to King Edward, whose grandfather chose not to acknowledge his own child? How easy it would have been to acknowledge her!"

"You speak treason, Isabel!" Mother took a step

back from her. "It is not for us to question the dealings of kings. I know you are young, and losing Rachel has wounded you, but you cannot ever speak of these things again. Ever! We have no choice in this. This is your grandmother's fault, letting you roam and mix with all sorts of people." Her expression softened. "I know how steadfast you are, and that this has been difficult, being neither here nor there. I ask you now to be loyal to me, and to your grandmother. You have been chosen to be elevated. It is a great honor, and God's plan for you. Do not question it. I pray you, child, keep your silence. Promise me that you will not confront the queen on this! You hold our very lives in your hands."

"Do you really believe that, Mother? That for merely questioning the king's expulsion of the Jews, we could all die?"

"Have you learned nothing in all your years at court? Why would you think that the queen would not agree with her husband in this? They are in accord on everything else. And if she were to complain to Edward of you, what think you of our chances then? Does he seem the kind of king who would enjoy being questioned? Do you think he would hesitate to have us removed from his presence? Do not question this, Isabel. Dislike it if you will, but say nothing. Promise me that you will say nothing."

"Mother—"

"Promise me!" Her mother burst into tears. "Go, then! Go. I cannot do more with this hanging between us." She wept into her hands.

Isabel sighed. Her mother never took the middle road on anything. All was perfect or it was unsalvageable. There was no other choice. She'd become accustomed to her mother's swings, the suddenness with which her moods changed. People once considered friends had been cut out of her life forever, but Isabel had never understood it. She could not imagine abandoning Rachel—who had laughed at Isabel serving the queen. Isabel sighed, missing her friend even more and knowing she would not speak of this to the queen. Yet. She was sure there would come a day, when she and Eleanor were alone, when she could talk of all this.

"Promise me at least that you will not risk our lives, Isabel."

"No, Mother. I will not risk your and grandmother's lives."

"Or yours. Promise me!"

"I promise to be cautious."

Mother wiped her tears away. "Good. When the Court is at Westminster, you will live with the queen's ladies and I will see you every day. Where the queen goes, you will go, of course. When she travels, you will travel. You will take an escort with you when you visit your grandmother. Remember to ask for it and don't go dashing off by yourself."

"I don't need an escort. I've been walking London's streets all my life."

"Not alone at night you haven't. Promise that if it is late and there is no one to escort you, you will stay in the Tower."

Isabel nodded. That would be no hardship; she liked the Tower, with its two hundred years of history. She wondered what it would have been like to have lived then, when William of Normandy, Conqueror of the Saxons, had built the magnificent structure and surrounding walls to protect his men and court from the hostile local population. Her mother hated the Tower, and although she'd never said why, Isabel thought she knew. Her father's office had been there. The very buildings must be a painful reminder of her loss.

She watched her mother sew and thought of all the years her mother had served the queen, all the years she had been invisible at court, all the years she had cared for Isabel alone. And now, by a twist of fortune, Isabel had been given this golden chance. Somehow, she told herself, she would find a way to reconcile the two, to talk with the queen and still not endanger her family. She was sure she could. Somehow, strange as it seemed to her, she had caught the eye and the favor of the queen. She would be a fool not to make use of that.

"Name the queen's ladies," Mother said.

Isabel did, their faces coming to her mind with their names. Important women from important families, wives and daughters of important men. And Isabel, of no importance at all. But every one of them would know why Isabel had been included, and once again her great-grandmother's one sin would be recognized, but never discussed.

"Lady Dickleburough," her mother said. "You forgot her."

"Oh, yes," Isabel said, nodding, thinking of the aging courtier with distaste. Lady Dickleburough behaved as though she were young and desirable, but those days, and years, were long past, although she gave no sign of recognizing that.

She wore clothing appropriate to a much younger woman, her very low necklines revealing deep wrinkles on her neck and décolletage, her sunken breasts no longer able to hold the bodice in the correct position. During the day sunlight cast shadows in the deep wrinkles around her mouth and eyes, and made the kohl she used to hide the gray in her hair all too visible. Isabel's mother often said that Lady Dickleburough pulled the coils of her hair tightly to the top of her head to draw her skin up to hide some of her wrinkles, but the attempt failed. Her skin, surrounded as it was by the white silk wimple she wore, was pasty. Her small brown eyes looked beady behind the folds of skins that threatened to hide them altogether. Her husband, a baron of little note from East Anglia, was neither influential nor wealthy, and his family was certainly not noteworthy. Isabel thought her repulsive.

"Why is she still at court? Does she have some importance I don't know?"

Mother laughed. "In her youth she was attractive enough, in a sly and furtive sort of way. She was a . . . very willing companion."

"Is it true that she was mistress to several important men? Several!"

"It is. And some were willing to pay to have her stay at court rather than risk her talking of all she knew. They gave her rooms in which to live, bought her clothing and jewels to keep her quiet."

"What does her husband think of all that? Did he know?"

"Do the waves on the shore recede and return? Of course he knew. He prospered because of it, was content to look aside and take other men's leavings. There may be no one willing to pay for her favors now, but there are those who are willing to pay for her silence. She can smell a secret miles away. Never trust her with anything you do not want all of London to know. She can be an interesting ally, for she knows everything about everyone. Now, you will need to be alert when you travel with the queen. The roads are not safe, and even with the king's men guarding you, you must be careful."

Isabel nodded, thinking of Rachel and her family. No word since they'd left. Isabel had not truly expected to hear from her friend, but it was so hard not to know what had happened to them. She sighed.

"I wonder where Rachel—"

"Yes, yes," Mother said. "I know you still worry. But we may never know what happened to them. Her father will have thought of somewhere to go. It's been but three months. Rachel and her family have no doubt found a haven somewhere."

"But where would they go? They had to leave England!"

"There is a world outside England. There are many places where a man like Jacob de Anjou could find a position."

"I should ask Lady Dickleburough," Isabel said with a laugh. "If, as you say, she knows everything, she'll know where they are. Or know who knows."

Mother did not answer but looked at her with a strange expression. Then she put her needle down and stared at Isabel's skirts. Isabel watched her uneasily.

"It was a jest, Mother. I will not ask her about Rachel."

"Isabel," Mother said, an odd note in her voice.

"And I promise to stop talking about Rachel. I know it's not wise even to acknowledge that we were friends. I do love her, but I will stop talking of her."

"Isabel." Mother did not look up from the hem. "There is something you need to know." She stood, then sighed and walked across the room. "I would rather you never knew, but you need to know the truth, and I would have you hear it from me than from Lady Dickleburough, or someone else at court. They would never mention it in front of me, but now that you will be among them, someone is sure to tell you." She sighed again.

"Mother, I know all about great-grandmother's . . . folly. I know that Grandmother is illegitimate. I've known that for years."

Her mother shook her head. "It is not that, Isabel. I know you've known about that. But . . . there is more that you need to know. And I do not know how to tell you." She turned to the window, tracing a finger along the leaded glass.

Isabel waited, her heart beginning to pound. What could it be? Was Grandmother ill? Was that why Mother wanted her to visit her more often? Another possibility occurred to her.

"Are you ill, Mother? You look well, but are you . . . ?"

"No, no. It is not me. Or rather, it is. You see, your father . . . I . . ." Mother turned from the window, her chin raised. "I was very young, not much older than you are now. He was so handsome and charming, and I believed everything he told me, that I was beautiful and that he loved me and that he would always love me and always be with me. He won my heart. I thought he loved me. And so I . . . I became his lover. And you came from that union."

"But there is no shame in that, Mother! Men and women always declare their love and marry and have children. It is the way of the world."

"The way of the world." Mother's laugh was unpleasant.

"I should have known better, Isabel. I knew the stigma of being a bastard. I knew the things said about my grandmother, that she was a king's whore. I knew that my mother suffered for her mother's mistake and that her family disowned her. And still I learned nothing from knowing all that."

"But, Mother—"

"Hush! You need to hear this, and if I do not tell you now, I may never tell you. I am throwing you into a pit of wolves and I have just realized how ill-prepared you are." She took a deep breath. "I have misled you. Your father is not dead. He is alive."

TWO

His name is Lord Lonsby now," Mother said. "He was the son of a younger brother when I met him, but he inherited his uncle's title. He was never a clerk of the Wardrobe; that was a fabrication and I wish I'd never invented it, for it's made you far too fond of the Tower. He did not marry me. He was already married, long before we . . . before you were born. He did not die. I am sorry that I let you believe that all these years. He has a home and a wife and children in the north, in Northumbria, near the Scottish border."

She paused, then continued, her hands pressed together at her waist.

"You, Isabel, like your grandmother, are illegitimate. You must be wiser than I was. Do not trust the hunters. Never trust men."

Her mother turned her face away. Isabel rushed to embrace her, assuring her it made no difference. But of course it did. She was hurt that the truth had been kept from her for so long, and excited to discover that her father was still alive. Perhaps she could travel to meet him. But would he want to meet her? He'd abandoned them, after all. But still . . . her father was alive. And for years she had not known. Her emotions were tempered by the pain in her mother's eyes.

"Why did you not tell me?" she asked at last.

"At first you were too young to understand. And when you were old enough, I knew it would change the way you thought of me. What young girl wants to hear that her mother was a wanton?"

"Mother! You are hardly a wanton! It doesn't change how I think of you." But even as she said the words, she knew they were not true. All these years of being lectured to, of the repeated demands that her behavior be above reproach, and now to discover that her mother had been . . . what? Foolish? Wanton? Surely her mother had never been a wanton, Isabel told herself. But she also knew that her mother never considered the consequences of her actions. Perhaps she'd been like that as a young girl, plunging into situations without heed to the results, her emotions flaring and dying, hot and cold, as they still did now. And now she was bitter. But all those years . . . and to discover now, just as she was about to be thrust into the court, that she herself was illegitimate. That she was, like her grandmother, a bastard.

"It doesn't," she said again, knowing that, like her mother, she was capable of dissembling. It was an unquieting realization.

Her mother's eyes blazed. "But of course it does! It should! You need to be more careful, less trusting, than I was. And your great-grandmother before me, though hers was the lesser sin, for how does one say no to a king? She had no choice and no family to protect her. But I did . . . I should have known better, Isabel. I should never have believed him. I brought on my own ruin with my unseemly behavior. I was wanton."

"You were young. You were foolish."

"I was indeed young, and far more a fool. And that is why I warn you, why I have always warned you about men. They cannot be trusted."

"Would you ever have told me if I'd not been chosen as one of the queen's ladies? If you were not fearful now that someone like Lady Dickleburough would have told me . . . would you ever have told me yourself?"

"I always meant to tell you. When the time was right. When you were old enough. I meant to tell you. But . . ." Mother straightened her shoulders. "But perhaps not, Isabel. It's not something I ever wanted you to know."

"Are you . . . does he . . . do you hear from him?"

"Occasionally. At first he sent money, but in the last ten years . . . nothing."

"He has a wife, you said. And children."

"Seven, last I heard."

"Seven." Isabel was dumbfounded. "I have sisters . . . or brothers."

"Yes. He has two sons older than you. And a daughter . . . just your age. And younger ones. I know nothing of them other than how many there are. Isabel, can you forgive me?"

"Oh, Mother!" Isabel rushed to embrace her, then stepped away and gave her a tremulous smile. "Of course, Mother. It changes nothing. Of course I understand."

"No, you do not. You cannot. Until a man blinds you so completely that you forget yourself, you will never understand. My prayer for you is that that day never comes. Never let down your guard. Trust no one."

The first three days that Isabel served Eleanor of Castile were gray and cold. The fourth was brighter and the fifth clear and brilliantly warm. Isabel's mood matched the weather—gloomy and uncertain at first, then eventually clearing as she became more familiar with her new life and learned the tasks required of her. She'd been chosen to serve the queen. Of course she was delighted. She told herself that daily. Her resentment against the king still burned within her, but she kept her silence, biding her time. When she had been at the court longer, when the queen, with whom she'd not yet had a private conversation, knew her, when she had proved her loyalty, then she would broach the subject of Rachel's people.

In the meantime, she had enough to deal with, learning her new responsibilities. And coming to terms with the truth of her birth. She tried not to wonder why her mother had waited so long to tell her the truth about her father's abandoning them. It would have fit so well in one of her mother's lectures about predatory men. She was sure that her mother had simply meant to caution her against being promiscuous. Or had her mother's motive in not telling her been less pure? She should be more generous, she told herself, less judgmental of her mother. Her mother was fragile, she knew that. And bitter, which was understandable after having been tossed aside.

Her father had seven children, two daughters and two sons who were older than she. She, who had longed for a sister all her life, had one. And at least two brothers.

And she would never know any of them. She'd not asked her mother more—the questions that had occurred to her later, during the hours when she'd sat idle in the service of the queen.

"At last I understand why I am called a lady-in-waiting," she told her grandmother when she was able to visit her, "for that's truly what I do."

She had been given the day to herself, asked only to return to Westminster by dark, and in the clear morning had taken a boat down the river to see her grandmother, who greeted her with a wide smile and a sadness behind her eyes, which let Isabel know her mother had visited and told Grandmother that Isabel now knew that she was illegitimate. They did not speak of it at first, talking instead of Isabel's new life.

"I spend most of my time waiting. I thought I would be sitting in court, or walking in the gardens with the queen. And I do both. But I had no idea that a lady-in-waiting meant just that."

Grandmother laughed with her and pushed a plate of figs closer to Isabel.

"What are your duties? What is the queen's day like?"

"We must rise first, of course, and ready her clothing and tidy the rooms and clear the chamber pots if they need cleaning, and receive messages. Most mornings—listen to me, in her service five days and already an expert!" Isabel laughed at herself. "The king visits every day, sometimes with his counselors. And the children are often there as well."

"The children each have their own household, do they not? How many are still at home? Queen Eleanor had, what, fourteen?"

"Fifteen, but only six are still alive. Can you imagine, only six?"

"It's common, sweet. They were fortunate. Princess Eleanor is married and lives in Aragon, is that right? And Joan, the one they call Joan of Acre—she's the one who married Gilbert de Clare in May?"

"Yes! I wish I'd been with the queen then. I'm told it was a magnificent ceremony at Westminster Abbey. Surely you heard all about it?"

Grandmother laughed. "Surely I did. And just as surely I've forgotten. Unlike the rest of London, I do not spend my day discussing what the king's family does. Princesses are expected to marry well, and she did. And the other children?"

Isabel counted on her fingers. "Margaret is fifteen, Mary is eleven, Elizabeth is eight and Prince Edward is six. Lady Dickleburough says they've all inherited their father's willfulness."

"Lady Dickleburough? She is still at court? No one's murdered her yet?"

"Grandmother! Why ever would they?"

"She knows far too much. They must be paying her well to keep her silence. Do not trust her, sweet."

"Oh, I don't, but she's ever so amusing. And I'm starting to know Alis de Braun. She's been very kind to me."

"Alis de Braun?" Grandmother sniffed. "Her grandfather was a merchant!"

Isabel laughed. "So was mine."

"Your grandfather," Grandmother said archly, "was a successful merchant, who became a knight. He gave me a very comfortable life. Her grandfather sold fish on the docks and then was able to buy a fish stall."

"Then how did she end up at court?"

"Alis is lovely, which helped. And she had a benefactor. Alis's mother married an old fool of a baron, who conveniently died shortly after Alis and her sister were born. Now there was a woman who knew how to manage her life."

There was a pause. Isabel took a bite of fig. "Did you know him? My father? Did you ever meet him?"

Her grandmother sat back against the wall and watched her for a moment. "Lonsby? Many times. I despised him. Still do. He lied. From the first day, he lied, and my girl was foolish enough to believe him. There are men, Isabel, who cannot resist a pretty face or a willing lass, and he is one. I daresay you are not the only child he fathered while he was here. The king fathered fifteen. I'm sure Lord Lonsby fathered as many. He could not keep his . . . he has no restraint."

"He was married before he met Mother?"

"For several years."

"And this was widely known? No one told her?"

"He was of little importance. It never entered my mind that she would find him attractive. He was furtive in his pursuit. I knew there was someone who had caught your mother's interest, but I thought it was the lad down the street. I knew he would not harm her. He loved her. Still does, if you ask me, but he's been married for years now, and he's not the kind to break his vows."

"My mother says she was a wanton."

Grandmother sighed. "No, although there is a wanton streak in our blood. Certainly my mother had it, but certainly yours did not. My mother never truly regretted her fall from grace. She told me all my life that I should be proud I was the daughter of a king, for all the good that ever came of it. Although, this house was given to her and one cannot sneeze at that. The wages of sin, I suppose, are not always as paltry as one might think. But, sweet, you need to be wiser than my mother, and yours. You see how bitter she is. It is always the woman who pays the price, never the men. Be wiser, my dear."

"Why did you never tell me?" Isabel tried to keep accusation out of her tone. "Why did neither of you ever tell me?"

"It was not my place to tell you; it was your mother's. I had hoped you would never know. Now you are mourning the death of your vision of your father, not the real man. Why did you need to know that your vision was far from the truth?"

"Did he know—my father—did he know about me? He must have, Grandmother. I remember him . . ."

"Of course he knew. His uncle was a powerful man and through him Lonsby got your mother appointed to the queen's staff. He would not care for her, but at least he made sure she would eat, although you know I would never have let you starve. But your mother was proud and would not accept my help. I begged her to come here, but she was determined to pay the price for her mistake."

"Me."

"No, Isabel, you were not a mistake. He was. A charming, handsome mistake. He would have left her broken-hearted and ruined. You gave her a reason to get up each day, and she needed that after he left her. Bastard!"

"That would be me, not him, Grandmother." Isabel smiled weakly, feeling tears threatening.

They stood instead in her grandmother's eyes for a

moment. "I apologize, sweet. I spoke without thought."

"But that's what I am, is it not? A bastard."

"No. A well-loved child."

"A love child, you mean. She hates men, Mother does. She hates them."

Grandmother sighed. "Aye. But there are good men as well as the liars. Listen to her, but temper your caution with wisdom of your own, Isabel. There are few more wondrous things than a good man who loves you, child. Your grandfather loved me, and your mother. And he loved you. He was a good and faithful man. They do exist. I only wish he had lived to see you grown."

"What did he think of my father?"

"It was a good thing that Lonsby left London before your grandfather heard the news. But enough of Lonsby. Is it true that the Scots have asked King Edward to decide who will rule them?"

"That is what I've heard. There are thirteen competitors, including King Erik of Norway and even Edward."

"Thirteen! Why not a hundred? What foolishness this is." Grandmother shook her head in disgust. "The Scots will never agree among themselves. It will be their downfall, their inability to come together. It would be better if they simply recognized Edward as king and let the whole island be united under his rule. It would have happened eventually anyway when the Maid married Prince Edward. We all know the king would have been the real ruler until they were grown. And the world would be a better place for it, if you ask me. Look how much better off Wales is now that it is under the king's aegis. So, will the king go to Scotland? Will the queen?"

"I'm not sure. The parliament that he held in Nottinghamshire, at Clipstone, has concluded. I'm told that the king will stay in the north and that the queen will travel to meet him in Lincoln. Lincoln! Think of all I'll get to see!"

"Perhaps even Scotland, although why anyone would want to see Scotland is beyond me. Even the Romans knew there is nothing up there. But enough of Scotland. Tell me, what do you wear these days?"

Isabel laughed and told her grandmother about the marvelous new clothing she wore in her new position.

Her grandmother loaded a basket with fruit and treats for Isabel to take to her mother and sent a lad to accompany Isabel back to the river dock, where she would take one of the many ferries that ran passengers from the City to Westminster and beyond. A light rain was falling as Isabel gave the lad a coin, then paid the ferryman and stepped onto the boat. Her arms were around the basket, and when the wind lifted her hair into her face, she could not brush it aside.

"Careful, demoiselle," said a male voice. "Here, I'll assist you."

She felt her hand taken and tossed her hair out of her face. He was tall, the young man who held her hand, and dressed in the garb of one of the king's household knights. She thought she knew all the knights of the king's household, but she'd never seen this one before. She would have remembered him. His hair was brown, brushed back from an arresting face, dark brows over darker eyes, the shadow of a beard on his jaw. His cheekbones were sharp, his chin sharp as well. His smile was wide. French, she thought.

"Thank you, sir," she said crisply, stepping into the hull of the boat and withdrawing her hand from his.

She placed the basket next to her and folded her hands in her lap, looking across the river. The rain began to fall harder. Passengers around her began to pull hoods over their heads and grumble to each other, but the craft was not even half full and she knew they'd have a wait before the boat would leave.

She was wrong. The knight leaned to talk with the ferryman, and she saw coins exchanged. As the ferry pulled away from the dock, the knight settled on the bench, her basket between them, and gave her another smile.

"I did not think you would wish to wait for the rain to soak us all through."

"No."

She could think of nothing else to say and sat there like a fool. Had he really paid the boatman to leave at once? She looked at him out of the corner of her eye. He gazed placidly out over the water as the boatman steered them into the center of the river. He must be one of the knights who had returned with King Edward from Gascony, where he had spent much time in the last few years, overseeing his French lands. He'd brought many knights back with him, granting them lands and titles. This man was younger than most, but his accent was unmistakable.

"You are one of the queen's ladies?" he asked, his tone mild.

"Yes," she said, surprised.

"You must be the new one."

"How did you know, sir?"

"It was not difficult to guess. Everyone in London knows the queen has a new attendant. You must become accustomed to being recognized. And approached to talk with the queen for people's causes and requests."

She'd been warned of that, that she would be asked to plead cases for others, and she knew ladies-in-waiting who had done just that. And been richly rewarded for it.

His smile was wide. And charming. Isabel ignored the echo of her mother's words. What harm could there be in being polite on their short voyage? The other passengers were watching them openly, some with obvious disapproval, some with apathy, a few with smiles.

"And you are, sir?"

"Henry de Boyer."

She gestured to his clothing. "Sir Henry de Boyer? One of the king's men?"

"Oui. I am. And your name, demoiselle lady-in-waiting?"

"I am Isabel de Burke."

"I am pleased to have met you, demoiselle."

"And I you, sir."

"Coming from a tryst with a lover?" he asked.

"No! I was visiting my grandmother."

They were silent for a moment.

"Are you?" she asked.

"Coming from a tryst with a lover?" He laughed. "I am. I am in love with this city. When I have time to myself, I roam the streets and learn every inch of her." He leaned closer. "She will soon have no secrets from me. I'll warrant I know her better than you do."

"I'll warrant you do not, sir. I have lived here all my life. I used to play on the very street where we caught this boat."

"Did you?" His smile was slow. "Last year?"

"I am not so young as that, sir."

"Ah, but you are, sweet Isabel de Burke. Innocence is shining from those lovely eyes of yours. In a few years you will be jaded and bored, but now you still have that fresh shine of youth. It is quite appealing."

She gave him a sidelong glance, unsure of what to say. He chuckled to himself, but he did not speak again. At the dock at Westminster he lifted her basket and carried it up the stairs from the river, reaching back for her hand, as though they had taken this journey together before. She let him assist her, then dropped his hand once they were on level ground.

"You are going to the palace?" he asked.

She nodded.

"As I am. I will escort you there."

They did not speak as they made their way through the crowd and past the guards, who nodded at them both. Once inside, Isabel shook the rain from her cloak and pushed her hood off, reaching for the basket. Henry handed it to her, bowed low, and gave her a smile as he strode away. She watched him until he rounded the corner, then smiled to herself. Henry de Boyer, king's knight.

There will be men . . .

"Oh, please! Surely you do not believe any of that?" Isabel laughed as she brushed her hair over her collar. "It's all rumor."

"Rumors can be true, you know," Lady Dickleburough said.

"That Langton is in league with the devil? That he murdered his mistress rather than paying her to leave him? Surely these are the inventions of fertile minds rather than truths."

"And surely you are very young."

"But he is the Steward of the Wardrobe, and a companion of the king's."

"Which must demonstrate his virtue, no? Look now, there they are," Lady Dickleburough said, leaning forward to watch the knights of Edward's household prepare to ride out. "Which one is this handsome knight you admire?"

Isabel leaned over the stone railing. "That one. See, he turns his head."

"To look at a woman. He told you he was coming from a tryst with a lover and you chose not to believe him. When a young man says such things, it gives you a window into his mind. I believe he had just left a lover. I have heard that he is the father of the child that the girl you replaced is carrying."

"And I have heard it was Bishop Langton," Isabel said.

"Which is why I told you the things said about him. You've not met Walter Langton yet, have you?"

"No."

"I am surprised. With all your mother's dealings with the queen's household I would have thought you had. No matter. Have you not seen him at least?"

"No."

"You will find him memorable. We all do."

Isabel turned to look at the older woman. In the daylight the wrinkles around her eyes and mouth were highly visible. She was elaborately dressed for daytime, her girdle laden with jewels, her wimple made of the finest white

silk. Most of the queen's ladies wore only the finest mate-
rials and jewels, but the styles were more subtle, for Edward's court was far from ostentatious. The king himself
seemed not to notice what he wore, and his courtiers followed suit. Lady Dickleburough ignored the rules, wore
what she chose, and somehow had managed to stay at
court.

It was difficult to see in her now the woman everyone claimed she had been, a siren who'd lured men to
her and kept their interest. And yet, there were moments,
when Lady Dickleburough flirted with a younger man as
though she, too, were young and attractive, when Isabel
could imagine what she had been like in her youth. Alis.

The two were very alike. Alis was lovely and knew it.
Everything from the sway of her hips—always more pro-
nounced when there was a man around, whether a servant or a lord—was calculated to attract attention. The
practiced moves she made, the pretty tilt of her head, the
lilting laugh over a tired joke, the slow, curving smile that
promised so much more—all were designed to make men
watch her. No wonder the other ladies avoided her. They
might have titles and excellent marriages, and be laden
with gold and silver and jewels, but none of them had her
youth or beauty.

"Langton will find you, Isabel. And you will decide."

"Decide what?"

Lady Dickleburough smiled. "There are many paths
available to us here at court. Many men. A word of advice: if you give your favors, make it be for something
valuable in return." She fingered a ruby on one of her
many rings. "Do not mistake how precious—and rare—
virtue is at court. If you are trading it, bargain for the

highest price. Henry de Boyer may tempt you. Certainly you are not alone in that. But is he the best recipient of your interest? Look for an older man, Isabel. Snare him before he even knows you are hunting. Get an offer of marriage, not simply an offer of an afternoon in a room in London."

"Are you instructing Isabel on life?" Alis asked as she joined them. She leaned to see the knights below. "Ah, look how they shine."

"Am I so ignorant that she could not learn from me?" Lady Dickleburough asked. "I do have some stories she might find interesting."

"Oh, yes, Isabel, she has stories enough to fill a treasure house. Listen carefully. You may hear some that sound familiar."

Isabel looked from Alis to Lady Dickleburough.

"She might learn something, dear Alis. I have a husband."

"And I, dear Lady Dickleburough, have a lover. Who I am off to meet."

Alis gave the knights one last look, then tossed her hair and left them. Isabel looked after her, then down at the knights. But she was too late. Henry was gone, ridden through the gate into the city of Westminster.

"Who is it?" Isabel asked. "Alis's lover. Do you know who he is?"

Lady Dickleburough merely smiled.

It was a week before she saw him—a week filled with learning her new duties, part of which was accompanying the queen wherever and whenever she chose. And today she chose to ride through the streets of Westminster, then on to London, not far away. There had been a time, Isabel had been told, when the two cities had been separated by farmland, but those days were gone. They would ride through the crowded, narrow streets, which was why the king's knights would accompany them.

"Demoiselle! Are you ready to brave the world?"

Isabel recognized the cheerful voice at once. She smiled at Henry de Boyer. She had looked for him everywhere she'd gone, but had not seen him once. He was seated on a magnificent warhorse, bedecked with the king's colors and the royal crest. He wore a breastplate of shining metal and long gloves with chain mail that extended to his elbow. His helmet was cradled in the crook of his arm. His companions leaned to see who he was speaking with.

"May I present the queen's newest lady, good sirs? Demoiselle Isabel de Burke. We will be traveling with you today, my ladies, protecting your travel through London."

"My thanks, sir," she answered, echoing his light tone. "I feel safer already."

"No woman is ever safe around de Boyer," called one of the younger knights.

"I will keep that in mind," she said, laughing with them.

"We will see you anon, demoiselles." He leaned toward her from the saddle. "I look forward to it."

"As do I," Isabel said. She sighed as the knights rode forward.

"Is he not the most handsome man you've ever seen?"

"Is that de Boyer?" Alis asked. "I've heard of him."

"You do not know him?"

"No," Alis said softly, watching Henry ride through the gate.

"What have you heard?"

"That he is as delicious as he looks. I wonder."

Isabel gave her a startled glance, then hid her surprise. She'd been at court long enough to know courtiers talked like this—though never before to her.

Alis smiled slowly. "You will learn, Isabel, to take your pleasures where they lay. So to speak."

"Don't you always take your pleasures, Alis?" Lady Dickleburough asked.

"A wise woman does. As Isabel will learn eventually. She has excellent taste in men, does she not? Ah, our horses. Now we can be the ones doing the mounting instead of being mounted. Isabel, you'll learn what that means as well."

Isabel smothered her annoyance. She was weary of Alis's treating her like an ignorant child. She fell into place. The queen's retinue was long, and some of the streets were so narrow that they had to ride in a single file. Not everyone, it seemed, loved the queen, for several called insults as she passed. One imprudent soul even threw refuse from a window above, but it hit no one. Isabel saw the queen's guards burst through the door of the house; the man would pay dearly for that transgression. No one dared approach the queen, but the knights, including Henry, were kept busy riding along the procession in a show of force. When at last they turned onto the wider western road that led back to Westminster, Isabel was glad of it, and gladder still when Henry fell into step with her.

"Demoiselle, did you enjoy your ride?"

"Sir! How could I? I was filled with fear that the queen would be attacked at any moment. I am so glad we are out of the city."

"She is not a popular monarch, is she? But that is why we are with you, demoiselle, to protect you. And for the sheer joy of your company."

"Well said, sir," Alis said, bringing her horse alongside his. "You have a pretty way with words."

Henry bowed with a smile. "Pretty words are plentiful with such inspiration as you two, demoiselle."

Alis smiled and tilted her head. "How the women must love you, Sir de Boyer. Are you as good at everything as you are at flattery?"

"It is not flattery, demoiselle, simply saying what I see."

"Would you say more if you saw more?" Alis asked.

"I would see first, then say," he answered, laughing.

"Then let us see," Alis said, and she spurred her horse forward to engage Lady Dickleburough in conversation.

Henry watched her leave. "Who is she, demoiselle?"

"Alis de Braun," Isabel said sullenly.

"I have heard of her. Now I will remember her."

Isabel was taken aback by his remark.

Henry laughed. "Jealous, sweet? Do not be. She is lovely, yes, but you are beautiful. In ten years she will be bitter and haggard and you will still be beautiful. Hers is a beauty that fades with time. And use. Now, tell me, have you been visiting your grandmother?"

"Yes, often."

"I shall look for you on the river then."

He touched the brim of his helmet and left her, riding forward along the procession. He paused for a moment, leaning to say something to Alis. She smiled at him, seemed to hesitate, then nodded. Henry's smile was wide as he left her.

THREE

H ere we are," her father said cheerfully.

Rachel Angenhoff, formerly Rachel de Anjou, stared in dismay at the building that was to be her new home, trying to find something good about it. It was standing. She could see no other virtue in it. She spared her father Jacob a glance, seeing the strain in his eyes that belied his jovial manner. But she dared not meet her sister Sarah's gaze, for Sarah was no doubt feeling the same horror she was.

The building was more than old; it was ancient. Its walls leaned precariously, its roof tiles were cracked and covered with mold. The wood of the doorjambs was riddled with wormholes; the steps that led up from the street were gray and sagging with age. Her father, she knew, would see none of that. He'd see the tall leaded glass windows that faced the street, the ones on the first floor above them, which leaned out over the street, letting lots of light into those rooms. He'd see the bustling street itself and the many travelers who had already let him know they would welcome a new place to stay in Berwick. He'd see the freshly painted sign that looked so out of place above the grimy door. He would see the future, and she could not see anything now but an old building that needed years of work. Her father ran up the steps and pushed open the door, ignoring the creak of protest it made as it swung inward.

"Come in, come in," he said, as though he were inviting them into the royal apartments in London rather than this filthy and empty inn in Scotland that would now be their livelihood as well as their home.

That's one good thing about the inn, Rachel thought, not moving. *It is not in England.*

Mama walked gingerly up the stairs, holding her skirts high above her boots, then stepped into the gloom.

"Well," she said, her voice echoing out the door to where Sarah and Rachel stood waiting. "Well," she said again, in the tone that Rachel knew meant that Mama was not pleased. But she knew, as they all did, that the inn had already been purchased and that there was no sense in protesting.

"Yes, Jacob," Mama said, "we can make this work. Girls, come in and see. We need your ideas for our new home."

Sarah glanced at Rachel with raised eyebrows, lifted her skirts high, and entered the inn. Rachel paused, turning to look over her shoulder at the men who patiently waited to carry in their possessions, then behind them, at the town of Berwick. Home, she thought, trying out the word. *Never, although I may live here the rest of my life.* Berwick was their refuge and where they would now live, but it would never be home.

It was not a dreadful place, this busy port town on

the Tweed. None of them wanted to be here, but after two months of traveling and then a week waiting across the river while Papa searched for a place for them to live, they were all grateful that their journey was over. They'd arrived this morning on one of the ferries that constantly crossed the Tweedmouth estuary. She'd gripped the rail of the shallow ferryboat as they'd neared the city, studying it, hoping to find something to admire. She'd found little.

"Rachel . . ." She heard her mother calling her from the doorway to the inn. Still she did not move. Below her, Berwick's wooden walls rose from the peninsula on which it was built, Berwick Castle rising higher still above the houses and shops that clustered around the welcoming harbor. The city faced the river rather than the sea, which sheltered its harbor from the harsh storms and tidal flows of the open ocean. Legend said Berwick had been founded by St. Boisel, a Saxon saint, for whom the cathedral presently being constructed had been dedicated 150 years before, but there was little that was saintly about the port that hosted ships from all over the world. How ironic it was that St. Boisel's Day was July 18, the very day that Edward of England had expelled them. The same day King Edward had signed the treaty that bound his son to his sister's granddaughter. But the child queen had died, and while that was sad, Rachel found some solace in Edward's plan being thwarted.

"Rachel, come in," Mama said.

Rachel lifted her skirts but paused a moment longer in the street. She told herself not to be so melancholy. They'd survived being ousted from their home, and the journey here, with their possessions intact. Her family had been fortunate. Jacob had been to Berwick years before, had stayed at the inn and talked with the innkeeper, who had no family and worried about keeping a roof over his head as he aged. The innkeeper had been on the brink of closing the inn and had welcomed Jacob's offer to buy it.

"Gilbert will stay on and help us in exchange for his room and board," Papa had told them last night.

Rachel had frowned.

"Do you want to continue traveling?" Mama had asked sharply. "Have you already forgotten what we went through to get here?"

"No," Rachel had said, thinking of the harrowing journey, of the many moments they'd lived in fear of their lives. She was ready to find a new home.

"But what about Shabbat?" she'd asked. "We cannot run an inn in a Christian manner and still observe Shabbat."

"We talked about that as well," Papa had replied. "Gilbert will work on Friday evenings and Saturdays when necessary. And we'll have to hire help. We will handle the rest of the week."

"Which means we do the extra work before Shabbat, or after it," Mama had said with a warning glance at Rachel. "Just as we always have."

Rachel had nodded, not at all convinced that the plan would work. Her father had never worked with his hands; it had been his mind that had fed them.

"It will be good, Jacob," Mama had said, with another stern look at her daughters. "We will make it all work. We'll learn how to run an inn. And even if we fail . . . ," Mama had said, waving the hem of her skirt, "all is not lost."

Rachel had been comforted at that. Her mother, on

the day of King Edward's edict, had sewn her jewelry and gold coins into the hems of their clothing. It was their buffer against starvation. None of it had seen daylight yet, but it was good to know they would not starve even if the inn failed.

"We will learn," Papa had said. "Now let us pray together."

Rachel had said the words of the prayer by rote. Her father prayed three times a day, as every devout Jewish man did, but she could not concentrate on prayer while their future was so unsettled. They would learn to change in order to survive. Now she stared at the inn, wondering what her father thought they could make of it.

At least here in Berwick they would blend in with the other immigrants. The city was full of Dutch and Flemish traders, and Scottish and English sheep farmers and wool merchants. The French, while tolerated, had never been welcomed in the city, so the de Anjou family had become the Angenhoff family, and Jacob of Anjou had ceased to exist. But what matter? Names were not that important.

There were other Jews in Berwick, merchants and tailors and those who had fled north as they had at least one rabbi among them, which would mean there would be temple. Berwick, full of people from every part of the world, took them in with barely a notice. Sarah would blend with the Scots—her hair was fair, her eyes light blue. She could be from anywhere. Rachel, on the other hand, had the blackest of hair and pale skin. Her looks and her name would give her heritage away every time.

"Rachel!" Mama's tone brooked no argument now.

Rachel quickly climbed the steps and went inside. She tried to ignore the filthy rushes on the floor and the mice scuffling in the corners of the room. Not to be sickened by the smell of mold and mildew, of decay and disuse, of urine, and worse.

Mama gave her a brittle smile. "We'll get settled and start cleaning at once. Shouldn't take us long," she said as she moved to the back of the inn. "I think we can be open within a fortnight."

Sarah and Rachel exchanged a look.

"Look," Mama said, pointing to the tables and benches. "They're sturdy enough. All this place needs is a good cleaning and a new coat of plaster. The floor is firm and the walls may lean, but they don't move. Jacob, tell them to bring our things in. We're ready to be home."

Home, Rachel thought. At least in Scotland they would be well out of King Edward's reach. They would be safe.

Rachel surprised herself, and no doubt her parents, by quickly learning the tasks required of her. They served their first meals in the tavern room a fortnight after their arrival, and a week after that the rooms upstairs were ready for visitors.

Since the Maid of Norway's death, the talk had been of nothing but who would succeed her. The clamor of rivalry filled Berwick's streets as the townspeople debated the merits of the competitors vying for the throne of Scotland. Thirteen of them there were, but the Scots narrowed it quickly to two rivals: Robert the Bruce, the elder, and John Balliol. Rachel listened to the bloodline arguments and decided that the choice was simple: anyone but Edward of England.

Strangely enough, her mother's mood had improved with their misfortune. She had not complained once on the voyage here, had not even mentioned their changed circumstances except in the most matter-of-fact manner. Her mother, Rachel had discovered, had inner strength that had seen them all through this transition. In London her mother had had servants, worn furs and gold jewelry, and managed a large household. Here she was learning to run an inn, keep the rooms clean, make sure the travelers paid in advance, and see that every cup of ale was counted. And doing it well. Already the inn was prospering, but some of that had nothing to do with them, for all of Scotland seemed to be on the move.

Almost at the end of October, on a rainy gray day, Sarah burst into the kitchen, where Rachel and their mother were preparing the evening meal.

"I've just heard some news from England," Sarah said. "The Jews, the ones who stayed behind in London, when we left . . . nothing has happened to most of them. Some were forced out, like we were, but some were left alone. But now . . . they were collected, all of them, and forced out of London, onto ships that sailed from the Cinque Ports. Everything they left behind has been taken. Some refused to leave." She lowered her voice. "And they died for it. We were right to leave last summer. And there's worse news. A letter has been sent to King Edward in England, asking him to decide who should rule Scotland."

Mama looked up, then quickly down, but Rachel had seen the flash of fear in her eyes. Rachel put the knife down.

"Some say the Bruces sent the letter," Sarah said, hurrying on breathlessly. "But others are saying it was a bishop who did it to keep Scotland from falling into war over the throne."

Mama put a hand to her breast. "Tell me King Edward is not coming here."

"I've heard that he's staying in England, at least for now."

Mama slowly rose to her feet. "England's not distant enough, but at least he is not here. I'll go and tell your father." At the doorway she stopped and turned to look at Sarah. "Who told you all this?"

Sarah blushed. "That merchant. His name is . . ." She waved her hand airily, and Rachel knew she was lying. "Edgar Keith, I think it is. Something like that."

"Edgar Keith," Mama said. "The one who's been here for three days?"

Sarah nodded. "Yes."

"Ah," Mama said and left them.

"Do you think it's true?" Rachel asked Sarah when they were alone.

"Of course it's true! Edgar wouldn't lie to me!"

"I mean," Rachel said, trying to keep the edge out of her tone, "was he told the truth? King Edward having a say in Scotland? This cannot be good for us."

"It will be fine, Rachel. Don't worry yourself so much."

Rachel tried, but as the day passed, filled with rain and travelers seeking shelter from it, the news was confirmed. Edward of England would help decide who would rule Scotland. Rachel worked long hours, falling into her bed at night, too weary to talk with Sarah. Which was just as well, for all of them knew but none said the obvious that should Edward's rule extend to Berwick, their livelihood—and perhaps even their lives—would again be in jeopardy.

How strange, she thought, that her dear friend Isabel would be hearing the same news in England as one of the English queen's ladies. Would she think of Rachel when she heard it? But of course not. Isabel did not know where they'd gone, was probably imagining her living somewhere on the Continent. Rachel sighed. London might as well be on the far side of the world. Would that it were, for then the hand of Edward of England might not reach her family. How strange that Isabel now saw Edward daily and Rachel not at all.

Rory MacGannon wiped the rain out of his face and shifted his weight. He made no pretense at patience while he waited before the gate at Stirling castle, nor did his cousin Kieran MacDonald, who walked his horse back and forth.

"MacGannon, is it?" the guard asked for the third time.

"Aye. Rory MacGannon. Here to see Liam Crawford."

"MacGannon." The guard's eyebrows lifted. He slammed the small window in the gate.

"I should have said MacDonald," Rory told his cousin Kieran. "Ye MacDonalds are welcome here. We'd be sitting in front of a fire right now instead of standing in the rain wondering if we'll be sent away in the dark."

"Aye," Kieran said. "It's a better name. My father and your mother would agree, not doubt," Kieran added with a laugh. "Ye should let me do all the talking."

Rory snorted. But perhaps Kieran was right. He half-expected not to be allowed to enter at all. He'd been to Stirling several times before, with his parents, but he'd never come on his own. And Kieran, younger by two years than Rory, had never been on a journey of any length without his father or Rory's.

"What will we do if they dinna let us in?" Kieran asked.

"We'll find somewhere dry to sleep, and curse them over a cup of ale."

"Which will not be necessary," said a voice from the dark.

Rory's worry left him in an instant. His uncle Liam's voice was followed by the man himself as the guard pushed open the small door in the gate. Liam Crawford grinned at Rory and Kieran, then looked behind them.

"Ye'll be sleeping in a dry and warm bed with a bellyful of good wine. How many d'ye have with ye?"

"Just the two of us," Rory answered. "And horses."

"Aye. I'll send word to get some hot food ready for ye. Give us a moment to get the larger gate open," Liam said and ducked back inside.

As Rory backed his horse away from the gatehouse, he could hear Liam's commanding voice, then a deeper voice answering. At last the gate swung wide, and Liam gestured them through.

The gate was closed by a team of armed men, which surprised Rory. He'd imagined that some of Stirling's guards had deserted in the uncertain times, that perhaps the castle was undermanned. But a quick glance around, even in the dim light of the torches in the wall niches, made him realize that the opposite was the case. Stirling Castle, and the village that shared the crest of the mount, was alive with soldiers. Some wore the royal garb, obviously still loyal to the crown, whoever held it, but the rest were a mix of Highlanders wearing the clothing traditional to their clan, Border men who dressed in their notable leather armor, and, from their accents, men from the south and the southwest. Rory and Kieran dismounted, leading their horses up the pathway slowly, for the rain made the stones slick.

"Why the delay?" Rory asked Liam.

"Ye're lucky it wasna much longer. No one here can decide who's in charge."

"I thought perhaps the MacGannon name caused a problem."

Liam threw him a sharp glance. "It did."

"Aye, everyone seems to have heard of my da."

"They have. And yers as well," Liam said to Kieran. "Notorious, the both of them."

Rory nodded. All of Scotland knew of his father and his uncle Davey, his mother's brother. It was Davey's abduction by Norsemen and his being sold into slavery that people talked of. His parents, Margaret and Gannon, had found Davey after years of searching in Jutland, in Denmark, owned by a Danish miller who had been reluctant to release him. Gold—and the threat of violence—convinced him to let Davey go.

But Gannon was not remembered for his courage and brilliant military tactics in defeating the Norsemen, nor for his persistence in his search for Davey, but for being accused of murder and being banished from King Alexander's court, where for years he had been such a favorite. Few remembered the injustice of that accusation, for Lachlan Ross had not been murdered but killed in a fight that Lachlan had instigated with Gannon. Gannon's lack of remorse and his fierce refusal to apologize for killing the king's cousin had led to his banishment. And fewer remembered why Gannon had come to court to confront Lachlan: the brutal battering Lachlan had given Nell that had almost killed her. But Nell, and Liam, who had loved Nell even then, remembered, and that was enough for Gannon.

"But it wasn't yer da's name this time, Rory. It was yers."

"Mine?"

"Aye. What the hell is this I hear about ye, lad? A blood feud? They're calling for yer death."

"I told ye he would have heard," Kieran said. "Everyone has."

Two men approached them on the narrow pathway, looking intently at Rory. "MacGannon," one said to the other. As they came abreast, the man bumped Rory's shoulder hard, but kept walking. Rory looked after them.

"Do ye ken them?" Liam asked.

"No."

Liam swore. "We'll talk on it, but not here. Delay, that's what I was saying. There's enough confusion here to have made ye wait no matter who ye are. We have no queen, no king. Every decision, no matter how small, seems to need half a day and twenty men to discuss it. Fortunately one of the lads kent I was yer uncle and came to get me, otherwise we'd be waiting for a meeting of the Guardians."

"So obviously ye've heard about the Maid's death?"

"Aye, and sent word to yer parents. Ye no doubt passed my messenger going west on yer way east. Let's get ye inside."

Rory nodded his agreement and followed Liam through

the next gatehouse and into Stirling's inner ward. The rain increased again. There would not be a spot on him that wasn't wet through, Rory thought, but at least they'd been given entry, and eventually they'd be dry. They left their horses in the stables with a groom, then followed Liam across the courtyard, up a flight of stairs, and through a tall wooden door. Once inside, they pulled the hoods from their heads. Walls built of stone were replacing the wooden ones, but that was hardly surprising. Rory had never been to Stirling without seeing some part of it under construction. The latest work was only partly finished and looked as though it had been stopped abruptly.

"Aye," Liam said, following their gaze. "Who kens when this will all be done now? Or if the new king will ever come here." He nodded to the guards, who looked at Rory and Kieran without expression. Liam led them around a corner and up another flight of stairs. "I dinna ken if Stirling will remain. I've heard it's to be abandoned and heard it's to be enlarged."

"But it's the gateway to the Highlands," Rory said. "It's too important to be left unmanned."

"Ye ken that and I ken that, but do John Balliol or Robert Bruce?"

"So ye think it'll be one of them?" Kieran asked.

"Who else?" Liam answered. "No one is going to let one of the bastards, royal bastards though they are, become king. And who else has put in a claim? Erik of Norway? D'ye think the Scots will go under the yoke of Norway after all we did to free ourselves from the Norsemen, and that only twenty-some years ago? The whole of Scotland lived in fear that summer. There's many a village or family that no longer exists, but I hardly need tell the two of ye that, do I? Think it's been forgotten? Erik's too weak to push his claim, and that's good for all of us."

"What of Edward of England's claim?" Rory asked.

Liam put a finger to his lips. They climbed the next set of stairs in silence.

"Here we are," Liam said, throwing open a door and ushering them inside a large, well-appointed room, comfortably furnished with chairs and a box bed in the corner. A table stood against the far wall with bottles of wine and ale.

"We can talk here, but quietly. And we willna say anything of importance outside this room, aye? I'm sorry, lads, but things are unsettled, and everyone talks. Edward of England's claim—that's the most interesting one of them all, isn't it? Edward's not asking for the throne outright. He's saying he already is Scotland's sovereign overlord. It's an old argument, but it's a sham."

"I dinna understand that one at all," Kieran said.

"Aye, well," Liam answered, "ye ken that our King Alexander married King Edward's sister?"

"Aye."

"After that, Alexander went to England and paid homage to Edward. Alexander made it clear, then and later, both in his words and writings, that the homage he paid was only for his English lands, that he recognized Edward as overlord of those properties, but not of Scotland. He affirmed that he was still Scotland's king and that Scotland was its own sovereign land. Of course, if the wee queen had lived it would have been a moot point, wouldn't it? Edward's son would have been married to the queen of Scotland, and when their children inherited, the thrones would have been united. But the Maid has died and that plan is gone."

"What d'ye think Edward will do?" Kieran asked.

"The leopard of the south? D'ye think Edward will pass up a chance to choose who will rule us? Not likely. Food will be here soon. Get those wet clothes off and get yerself warm. Yer aunt Nell is not here, or she would have been fussing over ye already."

"Nell's not here?" Rory asked, pulling off his boots. Fine leather and well made, but his feet were still glad to feel the warm woolen rug underfoot. "Where is she?"

The light from the fire illuminated Liam's copper hair and his face, letting Rory see the shadows in Liam's eyes. His uncle was worried.

"I sent her and our lasses down to Ayrshire when the word came that the Maid had died. I'm weary of my wife being in danger because the throne of Scotland is unsettled again."

He strode across, grabbing a bottle of wine and pouring three cups, then handing two to Rory and Kieran. "The Comyns were at her already, wanting her to stay, pulling at her for their own ambitions, and the Balliols were sending her messages. I wanted her out of the fray, at least until we ken who will be on the throne. Or whether there will be war over this. Ye'll notice most of the women are gone from Stirling."

Rory and Kieran exchanged a glance while Liam crossed the room again, throwing up the lid of a chest that lay before the window, and pulling two woolen shirts from its depths.

"D'ye think it'll come to war?" Rory asked, pulling his wet tunic over his head and tossing it on the floor.

"Look at the two of ye, half hoping it will," Liam said. "Dinna hope it, not even for a moment. I've seen war and ye dinna want to be part of it. Here," he said, handing the shirts to them. "We have a good fire, and these will keep ye warm while yer own clothes are drying. Now tell me why ye're here and why the hell is everyone talking about Rory MacGannon killing a man over a lass."

"I told ye he'd have heard," Kieran said. "And it's only two days ago."

"My da asked us to come see ye and Nell and hear what was being said," Rory told his uncle. "And to be sure ye'd heard about the Maid, although none of us could think that ye hadn't. After this we're to go to Edinburgh and listen to what's talked about there."

"And then down to Berwick," Kieran said.

"Where ye'll hear what's being said there as well," Liam said, answering the knock at the door. He returned with a tray of food and put it on a table. "Come and eat, lads, and tell me why there's a blood feud with ye at the center. What happened?"

"We were in Onich, on the bank of Loch Linnhe," Rory said.

"Aye, I ken it. And?"

"And a man was trying to rape a lass."

"And?"

"And I stopped him. And we fought. And I killed him."

"I heard ye cut him into pieces."

"No."

"His head was almost off, but not quite," Kieran said. "There were four of them. Rory killed the one and we wounded another and the others ran."

"The lass lived to tell the tale," Rory said.

"That's not the rumor that's being spread. I heard ye were the one doing the raping and ye attacked the others."

"How could that be?" Rory asked. "If I'm busy raping a lass, would I take the time to start a fight with the onlookers?"

Liam nodded and took another sip of wine. "But isn't that just what ye're saying the other man did?"

"No. We came upon them, him tearing her clothes off and two of them holding her down and another watching. We stopped it. I dinna mean to kill him, but he fought back, and after that there wasna a choice. I dinna regret it."

"Ye may. Ye've made enemies out there. Think they're telling the tale that they were the wrongdoers? Not likely."

"The lass will tell the truth."

"And be raped for it, or worse? She'll keep her mouth shut if she's wise. Who were they?"

"MacDonnells."

"Och! Making enemies from the clan whose land ye have to pass through every time ye come here. Cousins of yer mother's."

Rory took a long drink of wine and put his cup down. "I dinna choose the fight, Liam, but neither did I shrink from it. Given the same choice, I'd do it again. And if the MacDonells shelter men like those, we need to ken that about them."

"They're not like that." Liam leaned back and gave Rory a long, appraising look. "How old are ye now?"

"Twenty-one. Last Lammas."

"Ye have a lot to learn."

"What was I supposed to do?"

"Just what ye did, lad, just what ye did. But ye need to be a bit wiser."

Rory bristled, but Liam continued.

"Kill them all next time. Dinna leave anyone to tell false tales. Now, tell me what's being said in the west and on the islands."

They told Liam the news they'd brought while they ate warm beef slices with dark bread, a cheese that complemented the red wine, and a compote of apples and oranges. Liam sliced the meat with a dagger engraved with a language Rory could not read. Liam, he thought, must have bought it on one of his many journeys, for Liam had traveled almost everywhere. Liam's past was shadowy, and seldom discussed, but Rory had pieced together that Liam had been an ambassador for King Alexander, spending much time on his behalf in other countries' courts. Liam had been in France when Davey had been rescued, when Nell had been forced to marry Lachlan. And in Flanders when Gannon had killed Lachlan and been banished from court. But all that was ancient news.

"D'ye really think it'll come to war?" Rory asked.

"D'ye really think the Bruces will back down from their claim? Balliol's closer to the throne and we all ken it, but the Bruces are an ambitious lot."

"Ye dinna care for the Bruces?" Kieran asked.

Liam snorted. "Ye could say that. Ye ken my uncle is the Sheriff of Ayr, and as such, in command of yer da's lands. And Carrick is just south. The Bruces have caused enough trouble down there, haven't they? They've made many enemies. But only a fool would discount them. Robert the elder may be an old man, but he's a vicious one still. And look what his son did, kidnapping Marjory of Carrick and forcing her to marry him."

"I heard it was the other way round," Kieran said.

Liam shrugged. "Does it matter? They're well matched, those two. And all of them are tied to the English throne and probably hoping Edward will lend his weight to their cause. Three Roberts, all looking out for themselves first."

"And Balliol?" Rory asked. "Is he looking out for himself, or tied to England?"

"Both, of course. But he also has yer cousins, the Comyns, guarding his back. And ye need to guard yers, lads. When they hear ye're abroad, they'll try to recruit ye to gather news for them as well, and will make vast promises for the future. Ye'll do well to be cautious of everyone. Ye see what happened on our way in here. Ye've got some vowing to kill ye and everyone willing to take sides. It's an interesting time for ye to be traveling. Ye'll stop back here on yer way home?"

"Aye."

"Good. Who kens, maybe we'll have a king by then."

They talked for a while longer, then found their beds, Liam in his comfortable room, Rory and Kieran down the hall in less sumptuous surroundings. Liam had handed them a wine bag as they'd left, and Rory shared it with Kieran now.

"D'ye think there will be a war?" Kieran asked, then took a mouthful of wine.

"Could be," Rory said, stretching out on the cot he'd been given. Outside, the rain drummed on the tile roof of the hall, and he pulled the cover over his shoulder, glad to be inside.

"Who will we fight for?" Kieran asked.

"Balliol, I guess. Ye heard Liam. He has no use for the Bruces. Neither does my da, so I'm thinking we'd fight for Balliol."

"I'm ready!"

Rory laughed. "Drink a bit more wine and ye'll be starting a war of yer own."

"Are ye not ready to fight for a good cause?"

"I am for the right cause."

Kieran slept then, but Rory lay awake in the dark, wondering what lay ahead. He felt as though he stood on the threshold of something, but he had no idea whether it was wise or foolish to step forward. Or if he had a choice. His father, he knew, often had dreams that foretold the future. Not for the first time, Rory wished he'd inherited the gift.

The morning was clear and bright, with the promise of warmth later, and they were anxious to get on the road while the weather held. They had breakfast with Liam in the large hall teeming with soldiers and men from all parts of Scotland, then set out, heading east to Edinburgh.

When they went to the stable to collect their horses, the lad greeted them, asking their names.

"MacDonald," Kieran said.

"MacGannon."

The lad's eyes widened. He pointed down the line of stalls and fled.

Kieran and Liam exchanged a look as Rory walked slowly past the other stalls, some empty, some containing horses that watched him pass. There was Kieran's horse, but not his. The stall at the end was empty. Or so he thought at first, but then he caught a glimpse of something dark on the floor. He leaned closer.

"Jesu!" Kieran, at his shoulder, covered his mouth and turned away.

The horse's throat had been cut. It had bled to death on the floor of the stable, the blood spreading through the hay to stain the whole space.

"They ken ye're here, lad," Liam said quietly.

FOUR

Rory bought another horse in Stirling village, ignoring the glances thrown his way as they left. The day seemed colder than before, and he found himself looking over his shoulder much too often. Liam accompanied them for an hour, leaving them at a crossroad, but not before lecturing them again.

"Berwick's a bit rough, ye ken. Not all of it, of course. The Flemish are all over and the Dutch are there now, too, and God kens a host of English. Ye'll be sending messengers home with news?"

"Aye. If we hear of anything important, we'll send them to ye as well."

"Stay alert." Liam paused, frowning. "Shall I see ye to Falkirk?"

"And tuck us in our beds?" Rory asked. "I'm thinking no."

Liam held out a hand to each of them. "Remember, they ken who ye are, but ye dinna ken who they are. It looks like a whole bunch of MacDonnells have decided to go after ye. There's no law right now in Scotland. Dinna depend on the goodness of man. Safe journey, lads. Guard yer backs, aye?"

"We'll do that," Rory said.

In Falkirk they learned little new information, hearing the same discussions about the rivals for the crown repeated endlessly. They also heard the story of the murderous Rory MacGannon, who had killed four men with his bare hands, then raped a family of women. He fought the urge to defend himself and his name. He kept his head down and said nothing, but he wondered how high the tally would go before people stopped believing it.

In Edinburgh, where many of the Eastern Highlanders and Border families had men stationed, they heard no more about Rory MacGannon—only political talk. And here they heard some news from the Continent, and that King Edward, and the forces that had accompanied him, were lingering in the English Midlands.

They did not stay in Edinburgh long and soon were on the road again, far from alone. They rode south with a steady stream of travelers, arriving on the bank of the River Tweed opposite Berwick late on the afternoon of a gray November day. The city had an interesting history. It had originally been Scottish, then had been granted to England's Henry II as part of the ransom paid by Scotland's imprisoned King William the Lion for his freedom. Richard I of England sold it back to the Scots to raise money for his Crusade, and England's King John destroyed it in 1216. Berwick had survived the changes and had thrived despite them.

Rory had no trouble finding a ferryman to take them across the estuary to the city itself, and before long he and Kieran were on the flat barge, looking around them with interest as the ferryman navigated the current. Berwick harbor was filled with watercraft of all sorts, small fishing boats moored alongside merchant ships from the Continent. English galleys bobbed next to long-ships. Coracles and ferries competed for passengers who crossed the estuary like insects on new growth. There did not seem to be any pattern: there were as many leaving as arriving. Rory's first task was finding a place for them to sleep.

"D'ye ken a good inn for us, sir?" Rory asked the ferryman.

The man snorted. "For the two of ye? Down by the water, just within the city, there are places that will house ye. And women willing enough there to serve ye whatever ye desire. Even Highlanders."

"What?" Kieran asked indignantly.

"Even Highlanders?" Rory asked the ferryman mildly. "They're that undemanding?"

The man laughed. "Your kind is not always welcome in the south, but Berwick has very few scruples about its visitors. If ye stay peaceful ye'll do well."

"We're here to do business, not cause trouble."

"Then ye'll do just fine. Berwick understands making money." He slanted a look at Kieran, then at Rory. "Young to be merchants."

"We're not merchants. Any advice for dealing with them?"

"Don't let them know you're Highlanders. Change out of your Highland clothing and talk proper Scots, not Gaelic, and ye won't be taken advantage of."

"We're not idiots," Kieran said.

The ferryman gave him a long, appraising look. "Ye asked for advice. I gave it. If ye act like that ye'll just convince everyone that what they've heard, that Highlanders are akin to savages, is correct."

"Is that what ye think?" Rory asked.

"I don't think. If the coin is genuine, I ferry them across. If not, I don't."

"Fair enough," Rory said, and the ferryman laughed.

They were silent the rest of the trip, but as they climbed the hill, Kieran complained about the ferryman's remarks. Rory shook his head.

"Let it go. Ye'll be starting that war we were discussing all by yerself."

"Did ye hear what he said about Highlanders?"

"Aye. They think we're barbarians. They ken us for what we are as soon as they look at us. See anyone dressed as we are?"

The differences were notable. The citizens of Berwick wore long, dark tunics and leggings, or long, dark robes with under robes of a contrasting color. Their cloaks were often unlined, or lined with the softest wool. Rory and Kieran wore saffron-colored heavy linen tunics over knitted trews. Their cloaks were long, dark and lined with fur, and over that, tossed over a shoulder, was the plaid length of wool every Highlander knew, dyed with the plants of their homes. Their hair was different as well, braided away from their faces and loose down their backs, whereas the townsmen's hair was cut shorter or hidden under felt caps. The only similarity was their boots, all of leather, most with a low heel.

"Aye, but look around us," Kieran said. "There are people here from all over, and far more outlandishly dressed than we are."

He was right. There were visitors from many places—Italians wearing silk and brighter colors, Norsemen bedecked with furs and gold, dark-skinned Spanish moors, soberly but finely dressed burghers from the Continent.

"Maybe they think everyone not from here is a barbarian."

"Then maybe we need to show them that we're not barbarians," Kieran said.

"What we need are beds and a meal," Rory said, looking up at the darkening sky. "We're here to listen. We'll change their minds another time. There's just ye and me and I'd rather we were better equipped than that when we try to change their opinion of Highlanders."

Kieran grinned back at him. "Ye're right. But we could prevail if we had to fight them. I hear Rory MacGannon killed twenty men with one hand."

"I heard it was forty."

They found an inn, The Oak and The Ash, on a small street below the castle hill, the tavern room lively, loud with conversation, and every table filled. Rory stood in the doorway, getting his bearings and enjoying the delicious aromas. Serving girls pushed past him, carrying trays loaded with plates of food, and he realized how hungry he was.

He turned to Kieran to say just that, but his cousin was across the foyer, talking to a girl. Rory could not see her face, for her back was turned to him, but he could tell she was young and lithe and, from his cousin's expression, comely enough. Her hair was very dark, and when she laughed it fell down her back in lustrous waves. Kieran, it seemed, was well on his way to charming her.

Rory was able to negotiate a decent rate for rooms and meals with the tall, lanky man who greeted him, then found a small table at the side of the room and called to his cousin. Kieran's smile was wide as he sat on the wooden bench.

Rory grinned. "Not a moment in the door and ye're after a lass. Who is she?"

"I dinna ken her name, but she says she'll bring us some ale, so I suspect she works here."

"Ye're that brilliant, ye are."

"Whoa. Which of us has already talked to a lass?"

"Which of us has found beds for this night?"

"Ah, but which of us has ale on the way?"

"There is that."

Rory laughed, then studied the other patrons while he waited. Most were men, but there were women interspersed among them, some dressed very finely. Not surprising. Berwick was the richest city in all of Scotland, the port from which most of Scotland's, and much of northernmost England's, goods were exported to the Continent. If the wealthy visitors to Berwick ate here, it meant the food was good. The voices around them spoke in many different languages. There was Scots, the language of the south of Scotland, and French, from the Scotsmen and Englishmen who frequented the royal courts. A smattering of Gaelic was heard, not the Gaelic that was spoken in the west but the northeastern Highland Gaelic. He heard English, Flemish and

Dutch, and a couple of languages he did not recognize.

And, of course, there were the usual sorts to be found in a port tavern, rough sailors who looked like they'd spent far too much time at sea. A tall, skeletal-thin man whose head jutted forward on a neck knotted with blood vessels watched the serving girls with his mouth hanging open. A small man sat with his cloak pulled close to him, his head hidden in the hood. Two burly men cavorted in a corner with a woman who looked like a whore. A huge and very happy man from the Orient, his dark hair pulled tightly into a queue atop his head, laughed raucously and drank heavily. A man with a vivid scar that ran from his temple to his collarbone clutched a bottle from which amber liquid dribbled. Now there, Rory thought, was a story.

They waited only a few moments before the dark-haired lass came to them, placing tall metal cups of local ale before them and telling them their choices of food. He listened, looking up and into a lovely face, her features even and soft, her gray, thickly lashed eyes filled with curiosity as she looked from him to Kieran, who was grinning like a fool. Her voice was soft, her accent refined.

And English, he realized with surprise, taking a better look at her. She was quite lovely. Her face was thin, or perhaps just seemed so with her dark hair framing it, putting the angles of her cheeks into stark relief. She was dressed modestly, her clothing clean and fresh, her hands well-tended. What was a lass like this doing at an inn in Berwick?

Kieran, obviously pleased with himself, sat back against the wall and watched her avidly as they ordered their food. She looked at Kieran, then away, then back

RIVALS FOR THE CROWN

again. And again. Amused, Rory, asked her to repeat the meal choices.

If she was annoyed, it did not show in her expression. As she told them the choices again, she and Kieran continuing to glance at each other. Rory grinned at her and chose the venison. Kieran chose the fish, and she nodded.

"It's good tonight."

"I'm sure everything you serve is good," Kieran said.

Rory rolled his eyes. "Thank ye, mistress."

"You're welcome, sir."

"Dinna be too polite to him, lass," Kieran said. "Just call him Rory or he'll get ideas above himself. And call me Kieran. And ye are . . . ?"

"Pleased that you're here with us, sir." She smiled and moved to the next table, where three sailors sat, and told them their choices of food.

"And what of the fish?" one asked.

"It's good tonight," she said.

One of them leered at her. "It could be good every night."

She smiled tightly and asked if they would like ale or wine.

"Neither. I've something else in mind altogether," one said. He reached for her, but she slid out of his reach.

"I am not one of your choices," she said.

He rose to his feet and grabbed her waist, pulling her next to him. "And if I want you to be my choice?"

She struggled, but he held her fast, then leaned to put his lips on her neck.

"Let me go! Let me go!" Her voice held an edge of panic.

Rory and Kieran rose as one. Rory held his dirk to the

man's throat. Kieran removed the man's hand from the girl's waist.

"Ye'll let her go, lad, and apologize, aye?" Kieran said softly.

The man turned his head, his eyes far to the side, trying to see the dirk. Rory pressed it a bit harder against his skin. The sailor pulled his head back and released the girl.

"Good idea," said a new voice. Scottish, but no Highlander.

Rory looked into the blue eyes of a man he'd seen across the room earlier, brown-haired, young, his knife now pressing into the sailor's stomach.

"I think," the new man said, "that you're not hungry after all and that you'll leave a generous amount for the insult. And I think you're ready to leave now."

"The hell he is!" the sailor's companion cried, leaping to his feet.

He raised a bottle and swung it at the young Scot, who ducked and punched the second sailor in the stomach. A third sailor jumped up, shouting.

It was a short-lived melee, ending with Rory and Kieran and the other Scot throwing the sailors out the door into the rain.

"We'll burn the tavern down!" one shouted as he climbed to his feet.

"If ye do, we'll find ye," Rory called after them. "Trust me, ye'll regret it."

"Damn Highlanders!"

Rory took a step forward and watched the three break into a run. He stood, laughing with the others on the step, until the sailors were out of sight.

Then he turned to Kieran and the other Scot. "Well done!"

The other patrons cheered them as they returned to the tavern room, and the innkeeper thanked them effusively.

"You never know what the night will hold," the innkeeper said, shaking his head. "Some nights it's quiet. And others . . . We cannot choose who walks through that door. I thank you, sirs. I'll send more ale to your table."

"Many thanks, sir," Rory said.

The other Scot grinned. "Scared the devil out of them, didn't we?"

"That we did," Rory said.

The serving girl hurried over to them. "Thank you so very much," she said, breathlessly. "Sirs. Edgar. Thank you! I was terrified."

"With good reason," the other Scot said. "He meant trouble."

"It was our pleasure, lass," Kieran said. "How could we let anyone harm a beauty like ye?"

"Thank you for your help." She hurried away, her face scarlet.

"A good team, lads," Rory said as they sat down. "Now come and join us, sir. I am Rory MacGannon." He raised his cup in salute to the other Scot.

"Edgar Keith," he said, extending his hand. "You are Highlanders."

"How could ye tell?" Rory said with a grin, pointing to Keith's clothing. "Ye think we look different than ye?"

"A bit, sir."

"That we are. Ye all look a bit strange to us, dressed improperly as ye are."

Keith laughed. "Look around us. Who's dressed the same here?"

"Aye," Kieran said. "Kieran MacDonald. From Skye."

"Skye? Do you know Davey MacDonald? The one who was—"

"Abducted by Norsemen," Kieran said. "Ye've heard the story?"

"Who has not? And was rescued by a man named Gannon. Same man?"

Kieran laughed. "Aye, and this is his son sitting here with us."

"I heard something about this Gannon . . . ," Edgar Keith said and shook his head. He raised a hand and the serving girl hurried over. "It'll come to me. Another round," he said to her, "if you would."

Edgar Keith was the younger son of a cloth merchant in Lothian, he told them, and often came to Berwick. They talked of the death of the Maid and what those here were saying about Scotland losing its queen. He talked earnestly, expressing his concern about their country's future. His lank brown hair fell across his face as he talked, and he pushed it out of his eyes absently. Then suddenly his expression changed. He stared at someone behind Rory so intently, and for so long, his face ruddy now, that Rory turned to see who it was.

As he'd expected, it was a lass, and a fine-looking one, with golden hair and a worried look directed at Mr. Keith. She was young, dressed modestly, but Rory could see the curves of her waist and hips.

"Excuse me for a moment, sirs," Keith said and rose

clumsily to his feet, hurrying away from the table before either of them had a chance to answer.

"I wonder if all the lasses in Berwick are this bonnie?" Rory asked.

"They seem to be," Kieran said, watching the dark-haired girl serving ale to a large group of men. "She looks a'right now, doesn't she?"

Rory followed his gaze. The lass seemed to have recovered from the scuffle with the sailors. And for the most part, she was skilled at evading those who tried to touch her or hold her with conversation.

"Ye mean her manner, or do I find her pleasing?"

"I saw her first, lad," Kieran said.

Rory held up both hands. "I willna infringe on yer territory. Just thinking she's worth watching."

He turned to see how Edgar Keith was faring. The young Scot and the lass were deep in conversation, oblivious to those who moved past them. Rory finished his ale, put the cup on the table, and studied it.

"More ale, sir?" the dark-haired lass asked, suddenly next to their table. "More for both of ye?"

"Aye, and thank ye," Kieran said. "Miss . . . ?"

"And for Mr. Keith? Or has he left?"

"No, he's there, talking with the lass," Rory said.

The girl looked over at Edgar Keith and paled noticeably. "Excuse me," she said and hurried away toward the foyer.

"Ye're wasting yer time," Rory told Kieran. "She won't even give ye her name."

"I'll find it out." At Rory's laugh, Kieran held out a coin. "Wager? Match it?"

"Wager," Rory said. "Before morning ye have to discover her name."

"Done," Kieran said.

They watched as the dark-haired girl approached Edgar Keith and the blond lass, the dark-haired girl's gestures agitated, the glances she threw over her shoulder almost fearful. The blond girl listened, then shook her head and smiled serenely, saying something that stopped the other girl's stream of words. The two girls stared at each other, then at Edgar Keith, who nodded. The dark-haired girl took a step backward, spun on her heel, and disappeared.

"Grand," Rory said. He was hungry and thirsty, and had a feeling he'd stay that way for a while.

"I am sorry, sirs," Edgar Keith said as he slid back into his seat. "Your cup is empty. Let's have another and finish our talk."

"I ordered another," Rory said, "but she ran off to join ye. Are ye pleased with yer talk?"

Edgar Keith's smile was wide. "Very. Ah, here's Jacob."

The innkeeper arrived with a pitcher in his hand. "Here we are, good sirs."

"Gentlemen," Edgar said, "meet our host, Jacob Angenhoff. Been here not even two months and has already turned a decaying building into a comfortable inn. I stay nowhere else when I am in Berwick. Jacob, Rory MacGannon and Kieran MacDonald."

"I am pleased to have you with us, sirs," Angenhoff said.

"And we to be here," Rory answered, thinking that the attraction of Angenhoff's inn for Keith had more to do with the blond lass than any improvements the innkeeper had made. "Where did ye come from, sir?"

Jacob paused, then smiled. "London."

"What would make ye leave grand London for Berwick?" Kieran asked.

Jacob's smile froze. "Have you been to London, sir?"

"No," Kieran said. "But I'd like to see it someday." He spilled a few coins on the table. "For our meal and ale, sir."

"No, sir. Keep your money," Jacob said. "You'll pay for nothing while you stay with us. I'm grateful for your protecting my daughter Rachel. Ah, here she is with the food. I'll see to your rooms." He left them with another smile.

Kieran nudged Rory. "Rachel Angenhoff. I dinna even have to ask."

Rachel served the food quickly, not looking at any of them, her manner pleasant but subdued.

Kieran smiled up at her. "Are ye a'right, lass? Still feeling shaky?"

"No, sir, I am well now, thanks to you."

She glanced at Edgar Keith and walked away. Kieran watched her.

"She's angry with me," Keith said. "That's her sister I was talking to, and Rachel does not approve."

"Why not?" Kieran asked.

"I'm not . . . She's a . . ." He stopped. "I'd be grateful if you said nothing to Jacob. He doesn't know, and he certainly will not approve."

"Ye're not what?" Kieran asked, draining his cup. "So her father willna approve of a younger son wooing her, or is it the smell of wool about ye?"

Edgar grinned. "That's it, I'm sure. I tell the world I come to Berwick to talk about wool with the merchants here, but the truth of it is I come to see Sarah."

"From London, are they?" Rory asked.

"Aye," Edgar said. "Newly arrived. I thank ye for yer help earlier."

"Canna let a man do that," Rory said.

Kieran flashed him a grin. "My cousin has appointed himself champion of all women, it seems. He rescues them regularly."

Edgar blinked. "That's it. I've just remembered where I recently heard the name MacGannon." He lowered his voice and looked at Rory. "There are men here in Berwick, asking for a Highlander by that name. I was told you had raped a lass and killed her husband."

Rory made a disgusted sound and shook his head.

"It was the other way 'round," Kieran said. "Rory saved the lass, then killed the man attacking her."

"Then you need to get that word out."

"Who were they?" Rory asked. "The men asking about me. Who were they?"

"Hired thugs, I'm thinking. Not Highlanders, certainly," Keith said. "Look, everyone's on edge already with different factions lining up to claim the throne. There's lots of men just looking for a reason to fight someone. Your name is being bandied around, and I heard there's a reward for your head. You stand out here, sir. I would suggest you at least change into less conspicuous clothing. You saw what happened here tonight. Look around you. It could erupt again at any moment."

Rory scanned the room. "The men here look ordinary enough, for a port town."

"Then let me explain. See the man there, with his wife and two children?"

"Aye?"

"And the woman and her maid at the table next to

them? That's his mistress. He never travels without her. Jacob puts her in one wing, the wife in the other. His last mistress was poisoned. So who's to blame? And the strange-looking man with the long neck, the one that slides his head like a snake? He's a French marquis, drummed out of his home for crimes no one will speak of. And that one, the fat man with all the rings on his hands? A wool merchant who cheats all those who work for him. Two have tried to kill him. One died, one disappeared. And the tall, thin man, with the five sailors? Captain of a ship that preys on smaller vessels, runs them aground, and splits the proceeds with those waiting on shore to strip it clean. Mind yourselves here, sirs. Our noisy companions from earlier are not the only dangerous ones here."

He took a long draught of his ale. Rory looked around the room again. And he'd thought they all had looked so innocuous. He felt very green. Their food arrived then, hot and delicious, their plates filled twice without comment. Not by Rachel, nor her sister, but by another woman, who seemed to be more comfortable serving in a tavern.

Rory and Keith talked for an hour or so, drinking Angenhoff's fine ale, talking of the queen's death and all it might mean for Scotland. Kieran left them after a while, joining a dice game and drinking far too much. And in a corner of the room, a man watched Rory. He'd not moved all evening but had sat, slowly sipping from a wooden cup, watching Rory's every move.

"Claret is the answer," Keith said. "The nobles love their wine, and claret's the favorite. I'm convinced that there's a fortune to be made."

"Claret?" Rory asked, watching Kieran sink lower in his seat. His cousin must be losing badly, hardly surprising, given the amount he'd drunk.

"In England," Keith said, "the king takes a tun of wine before the mast from every ship that lands from the Continent, and another from behind the mast. Every ship. Two tuns. We need to be paying attention, for if Edward decides who rules Scotland, will he also decide our laws?"

"So what do ye think will happen?"

Keith shook his head. "I think we'll be sold to the highest bidder."

"A dismal prediction."

"And one I hope will be proved wrong. I bid you a good night, sir."

Rory finished his ale. The tavern room, he realized, was almost empty now. Kieran sat with one last dice player. The man in the corner had gone about the same time Edgar Keith had left. Perhaps he'd been wrong about that one after all.

From the doorway, the dark-haired lass—Rachel—watched them. She'd not looked at Keith as he'd passed her, nor answered whatever it was he'd said to her. Obviously Rachel did not approve of Edgar Keith's suit at all.

Rory shrugged. None of that was his concern. It was time for him and Kieran to find their beds. And bar the door.

Rachel leaned against the doorjamb and watched Rory MacGannon help his cousin to his feet. Kieran MacDonald swayed but stayed upright, which was surprising, considering how much ale he'd imbibed. Highlanders, both of them, tall men wearing the strangely patterned clothing that their kind favored. She'd seen a few in Berwick, most of them big men, and, until tonight, she'd thought them as uncouth and barbaric as they were reputed to be.

These two had changed her opinion. Kieran had made her laugh from the first moment, introducing himself and bowing like a courtier, telling her his appearance did not reflect the refinement of his heart. And they'd been the only ones—along with Edgar—who had stepped forward to help her. It did not happen often that a patron overstepped himself, but when it did the situation often turned ugly quickly.

She was more than grateful that they'd rescued her—she was delighted, for it gave her another reason to speak with Kieran MacDonald. She was not sure she'd ever seen anyone so wonderful looking, even in London. He was so tall. His eyes were so blue, his dark hair thick and wavy. And his cousin Rory was also a fine-looking man. Highlanders, she thought with a smile, and suddenly she missed Isabel, who would have spent hours discussing them with her.

Rory had spent the evening with Edgar, whom she had ignored when he had bid her good night. He'd told her their names and had said he'd tell her more if she stopped lecturing him about trying to see her sister secretly. She'd not answered him, for she would not speak to him about Sarah again. Tonight she'd learned that she was already far too late to stop whatever tender feelings had sprung up between them.

The most bruising part was that she'd had no idea of their relationship until this evening, when she'd found

Sarah and Edgar Keith, heads bent together, whispering in the foyer like lovers. She was shocked that her sister had not told her that there was something between them.

Her sister had kept her secret well. Sarah was most fortunate that it was she who had seen them, and not Papa. And not Mama, who lectured her daughters daily on the evils of offering anything more than food and drink to their customers. Edgar Keith's attentions seemed genuine, but no future was possible between them, and Sarah should know that as well as Rachel did.

When they'd moved into the inn, she and Sarah had been forbidden to even enter the tavern area and had been confined to the kitchen, performing the countless menial tasks required to run an inn. But Mama was a far better cook than either of them and Papa a far worse server than they, so they'd begun to take the travelers orders and serve them food, at first only during the day. But gradually their time as servers had increased, and now they did little else.

On nights like this, when the tavern was full and it took all of them to serve their guests, she almost did not mind the work, for she was too busy to think and the customers did not expect more than the food she was offering. But on the days when few entered their door and those that did wanted to talk—or more—she truly hated her new life.

From the start her parents had established the inn as the kind of place where women were welcome, and a sizable number of the travelers who passed through Berwick were wives or mistresses. Berwick's port was always busy, and it seemed that every sort of person imaginable had walked its streets.

For the most part the men were content to eat and drink and flirt a little. It was serving the women that Rachel hated the most. She was ignored by them sometimes, or saw pity in their eyes, or kindness mixed with their knowledge that she was the serving girl and they the customers. She hated that most of all, and the pride that she could not seem to suppress. She knew there was no going back, that her former life was over and this was now her lot. And that she'd better learn to make the best of it. But she hated it.

And now Berwick was drawing more travelers and was already changing from the Berwick they'd first discovered. Since the Maid had died, the mood of the town had grown more restive, and every week brought more Englishmen to the port. If the rumors were true, Edward of England would be coming to Scotland himself to decide who would be king. Her father brushed away her fears, saying that Edward had not forbidden them to go to Scotland, and the Scots were unlikely to welcome English rule or laws. But Mama checked the coins that were still in the hems of their clothing and reminded Rachel that they could always move on again. Of course they could, but her parents were no longer young. And so she worried.

They'd changed their name, and now they worked hard to acquire a local accent. Rachel worked less hard than her family at perfecting a Scots accent for she was loathe to give up all her ties to London. But occasionally, as Rory MacGannon had done tonight, someone paused at the sound of her voice to study her. And that was dangerous. To look as she did, and to be identified as English, might give them away. They were not hiding who they were, but neither were they announcing it.

Which led her back to Sarah. What was her sister thinking, to dally with Edgar Keith? He did not seem like a man who would trifle with her, but it might be better if he were. What were they thinking, to look at each other like that?

"Pardon us, Mistress Angenhoff."

Rachel started, looking up into Rory MacGannon's blue eyes. He nodded at his cousin, half-asleep and leaning precariously despite Rory's grip on him.

"I dinna think we'll fit through the doorway with ye there. If ye could? . . ."

She jumped to the side. "Oh, I am so sorry! Do you need help?"

He smiled down at her. "Ye, lass? He's twice yer size. No, I'll manage."

"I meant my father, or one of our men."

"Aye, ye're Jacob's daughter, are ye not?" His look was long and appraising.

"Yes . . ."

His cousin lifted his head and squinted at Rachel, then turned to Rory, his head bobbing loosely and his dark hair falling over his forehead. Even in this condition he was as handsome as she had thought him to be earlier.

"Look at her, Rory!" he said now, his accent heavy. "Look at the lass. She's beautiful! A bonnie lass, standing here before us. Rachel. Her name is Rachel and ye owe me my wager. We should say something to Rachel. What should we say? Just tell her that she's a bonnie lass. We should tell her, aye?"

"We should say good night. Sorry, mistress, he means no harm."

"Here," her father said, hurrying in from the kitchen, "I'll help you, sir."

She stepped back, watching while her father helped the Highlander carry his cousin up to the room that they would share with the others. She waited until the sounds of their struggle to maneuver on the narrow stairway were faint, but then she heard him sing, a ribald song that lasted only for a moment or two before being silenced. He had a lovely voice, if not a proper choice of songs. She laughed softly.

And then she went to find her sister.

FIVE

It's not as if I planned it," Sarah said, an edge of irritation creeping into her voice. "I've told you. And told you. We just starting talking, and—"

"I still cannot believe you said nothing to me about him."

"He's been here at least five times in two months! Did you not notice that?"

Rachel tried not to cry. She felt betrayed by Sarah's silence. How could she not have seen this happening? "Yes, I noticed that he was here often."

"And he always asks for me. Did you not notice that?"

"No. And you didn't tell me."

Sarah shrugged. "I thought you knew. And there was nothing to say."

"You didn't tell me."

They stared at each other for a moment, and Rachel knew her world had just changed yet again. "Do Mama and Papa know about this?"

"Mama knows. Papa doesn't. But . . . Edgar will talk to him. Not just yet, but eventually."

"And ask permission to court you? You cannot be serious!"

Her sister crossed her arms. "And why not? Is it so far-fetched that a man would find me attractive? Is it so impossible to believe?"

"No! It's not that. But he's—"

"A good man, Rachel. Does anything else matter?"

"Does anything else matter? Have you lost your mind? Does he know? . . ."

"That I'm a Jew?" Sarah spat the words. "Yes, he knows. And he still wants me, Rachel."

"What does his family say?"

"They don't know."

"Sarah! They will never approve this! Papa will never agree! Sarah, what are you thinking?"

"We're not in London anymore, Rachel! I do not have the choices I had there. I will not spend my life serving men in a tavern! If I must empty chamber pots, they will be my own, not a strangers! Edgar Keith is interested in me. And nothing has happened yet. But it will, Rachel. I will see that it does. I will make him love me. I will make him need me. I will make him happy and he will keep me safe. Our children will never have to leave their home in the middle of the night. It is not a bad bargain for either of us. Can you not be happy for me?"

"But, Sarah . . ."

Sarah turned her back. "If you are not generous enough to be happy for me, Rachel, then there is nothing to say."

Rachel stared at her sister's back for a long time. Then she blew out the candle and stared into the dark, missing Isabel more than ever.

"Mistress Angenhoff."

Rachel heard his voice but did not turn. It was not until he said it a second time that she realized that he was talking to her. She was Rachel Angenhoff now, the innkeeper's daughter. She straightened from the basket of clothing she was folding, suddenly aware of her unkempt hair and worn clothing, and faced him.

Kieran MacDonald, the dark Highlander, stood before her now, this man whose very blue eyes and wide shoulders she had noticed when she'd first met him in the foyer. He'd been witty then and had made her laugh. And later, when he had been too drunk to stand, when all his reticence had left with his sobriety, he had remembered her name and complimented her beauty. His eyes were a bit red this late morning, his cheeks a bit pale, but he seemed none the worse for it.

"Sir?"

He clasped his hands before him, his expression so earnest that she fought the urge to laugh. But there was no humor in his eyes now—just, she realized with a start, embarrassment.

"I have come to apologize to ye."

"For?"

He unclasped his hands then clasped them again. She took pity on him.

"There is no need to apologize, sir. You have done nothing that merits it."

"I was drunk."

"You were."

"I was loud."

"Yes."

"I sang?"

"Briefly."

"Did I keep ye awake then?"

"No. You went to sleep yourself, I believe."

"I dinna do that as a rule."

"Sleep?"

He grinned at her, and she caught her breath.

"Nay, lass, I sleep well as a rule. I meant that as a rule I dinna get drunk and make a fool of myself."

"You did no harm, sir. You lost your money and drank too much ale, but believe me, you did nothing dreadful."

"I'm told I was too forward with ye. I am sorry for that."

"There is no need. You saved me earlier, and I am remembering that. You did nothing wrong."

"What did I say to ye?"

"You don't remember?"

He shook his head.

"Your cousin—"

"My cousin says I was a blithering idiot. What did I say to ye, lass?"

She ignored the sudden heat in her cheeks. "I . . ."

"Come, lass, what did I tell ye to make ye blush so now?"

"You said I was beautiful."

His smile was slow, and she felt a fool. He cocked his head and studied her, and she thought she would die.

"It seems," he said, "that I have good taste in women whether I'm drunk or sober. I was right. Ye are beautiful."

She could not speak. His smile grew wider, and he laughed quietly.

"Ye are a beautiful lass, Mistress Rachel Angenhoff, and I hope ye willna think worse of me for saying it to ye again. There's not a drop of liquor in me now, so ye'll ken I mean what I say."

He left her there, staring at the door through which he'd gone.

A week passed without incident. The Highlanders stayed, but Rachel begged off waiting on them, leaving the task to Sarah and the woman they'd hired to help, a coarse but likable and hardworking woman who did the serving on Friday nights and Saturday. Rachel had heard Highlanders were dangerous, but Kieran MacDonald was a hazard she'd not anticipated. He would leave. And she would forget him.

She and Sarah had spoken very little. It was as though Sarah had passed through a door to another land and Rachel was left behind, watching and unable to follow. She watched with new insight as Edgar talked to Sarah, and as Mama watched them. Mama had known, Rachel realized, and had not stopped it. But surely this could not go on. Papa would be horrified and would never give his permission for Edgar Keith to court Sarah. What would come of this?

It was never far from her mind, but she kept herself busy, spending her days in the kitchen or cleaning the rooms. The former owner, Gilbert Macken, was a comfort to her, teaching her little tricks to make the work easier, and ways to tell who would be a good paying guest and whom to turn away. He never talked about her family except in the most vague terms, and she found his company comforting.

At times she would watch her parents in their new incarnations as innkeepers, and her sister, whom she'd thought she'd known so well. She wondered how they could have changed so much. She felt guilty about Sarah's clandestine activities and her own part in them as she distracted Papa when Edgar arrived so that he wouldn't see them, their heads together as they whispered in a corner. Or the looks they threw each other across the crowded tavern room, as though everyone else was blind.

She was miserable. And Kieran MacDonald, with his handsome looks and wide smiles and polite manner, did not help at all. She avoided him even though, to be fair, he'd done nothing more than smile at her, or wish her a good morrow, or good evening. She much preferred his cousin, for Rory simply talked with her as an equal, never flirting, never seeming even to notice that she was a young woman and he a young man. That was much better, she told herself, refusing to notice his well-defined jawline and blue eyes under that wealth of blond hair, refusing to notice his tall form and long fingers and his courtesy, his contagious laugh that would ring out in the tavern and make all around him smile. Much better, she told herself. They were guests of the inn, customers, nothing more.

The rain had kept the travelers within walls all day, and Papa joked, as the afternoon stretched toward evening, that he was hurrying to get all their guests drunk before dark so they would sleep through the Sabbath. Sarah laughed, but Rachel could do no more than smile tightly. Shabbat would begin at dusk, and she knew Papa would observe it whether the tavern was full or not.

She had always loved the rituals of the evening, the ancient ceremony that linked them with untold generations of her family before her, with its reminders of all that her people had experienced, their joys and their suffering, the connection that led them back to the dawn of time.

She'd thought her sister and mother felt the same. But how could Sarah share that feeling, how could she stand with them and pray, watch Papa put the prayer shawl on and read to them from the siddur or the Tanach when in her heart she'd already left them, and their religion, behind? How could Mama fold her hands, bow her head, and murmur the responses when she knew what her daughter planned, when she must know it would destroy Papa? Rachel was torn between her loyalty to her sister and hope that Sarah would come to her senses.

This night Mama hurried into the small room off the kitchen that they used for the Shabbat, carrying their meal, wiping her hands on her apron before sitting to receive the blessing. The door behind her rattled in the wind, but none of them paid it any attention, for it often shook when the wind was wild. Wearing the tallit, the prayer shawl, around his shoulders, Papa said the prayer of thanks for another week of health and good fortune. Mama, Sarah, and Rachel stepped forward to light the candles held in the silver candlesticks that had been passed from mother to daughter for generations. Papa said the second prayer.

And the door opened.

There were two men there, Kieran and Rory, standing in the small courtyard that served as the kitchen garden, their faces lit from the side by the light from the kitchen, their surprise obvious. It was Rory who moved first.

"I beg yer pardon," he said, reaching to pull the door closed. "It's crowded in the tavern and we were trying to help Gilbert. He sent us to the cellar, and we thought this might be it. Sorry to interrupt yer . . . service. I beg yer pardon."

He closed the door, but not before Kieran's gaze met Rachel's. The shock on his face made her wish she could sink to the bottom of the earth and never resurface. She felt a wave of embarrassment, almost shame, then anger at herself for the emotion. She was a Jew. How could he not have known that? Her name was Rachel, for heaven's sake. And she was not ashamed of who she was.

How could he not have known? She closed her eyes, forcing her tears away, then opened them to meet her sister's gaze. Sarah said nothing, but she didn't have to. "See?" her expression said. And to her eternal regret and shame, Rachel did.

"Stand still, Isabel! How can I finish this hem if you are jumping about like a rabbit?" Mother spoke through a mouthful of pins, but her annoyance was clear.

Isabel straightened, then stared forward at the wall, as anxious as her mother to have the fitting finished. The queen was leaving to join King Edward at Lincoln, where he still tarried, waiting for word from Scotland, and most of her ladies would accompany her. Isabel was thrilled.

She'd been out of London only once before, and then only for a few days.

She'd been given several discarded robes, and her mother had been ordered to alter them at once. Next she would hurry down to the furrier for a lining for the velvet cloak the queen had discarded and given to Isabel, along with the letter necessary to allow the young girl to wear the royal velvet. And shoes! She was to be fitted for another pair of exquisitely embroidered shoes, with heels so high that Isabel had to step carefully when she moved. But it was worth it, even to have to take mincing steps, to be able to lift her skirt and step forward, swinging her foot so even she could see the finely sewn design atop the leather shoes that were so soft that they felt like linen.

It was so heady, all the changes in her life, from her new position to her clothing and shoes. She had a difficult time staying still. She wanted to dance with joy. Had anyone ever been so fortunate as she?

"We have only two days," Mother said, gesturing for Isabel to take a quarter turn. "You must be ready to accompany the queen at dawn on the third day and you cannot be late."

"I will not be late, Mother," Isabel said. "It will all be done."

"Aye," Mother said. "But it's not you sewing by candlelight."

Isabel felt a wave of guilt. "Mother, I will sew with you! Or I can sew on the journey! Please do not fret over this!"

"And have my own child, the daughter of the queen's wardrobe mistress, be anything other than dressed perfectly? I think not! It will be done, Isabel. No doubt you will stop at one castle at least, if only to see if it can be bought. You know our queen. If a piece of land can be obtained, she will have it."

Isabel nodded. She was now well aware of the queen's rapacious appetite for land, and her habit of acquiring it however she might. Queen Eleanor's holdings were vast, and her stewards were said to be both harsh and greedy. Still, Isabel was willing to wait to discover for herself if the rumors were true. People, she had long ago discovered, were keen to spread falsehoods as though they were gospel.

"There!" Mother said, straightening and replacing the pins in the small cushion she wore at her belt. "Turn around and let me see."

Isabel twirled, then curtsied perfectly, and Mother laughed.

"I vow you are the fairest of all her ladies, child."

"Not such a difficult task, Mother. Most of them are much older than I. Some have served her since she and the king were on Crusade, and that was decades ago."

"Not so long as all that. Joan of Acre is but sixteen, younger than you by two years. Now take the robe off so I can sew this."

"An English princess born in Acre," Isabel said, unlacing her sleeves. "Imagine traveling all that way as a child."

"Imagine surviving the journey. You need to care for yourself on this journey, child. Keep yourself dry and warm. You'll not be in the carriage with the queen, I assume?"

"Did I not tell you, Mother? I have been given a horse of my own!"

"Which means you'll spend the day in whatever weather God provides and be the first to suffer if brigands attack."

"The king is sending some of his own knights to guard us, Mother." Isabel's cheeks flared at the thought that Henry de Boyer might be one of them, but her mother, busy putting Isabel's things away in the wooden chest, did not notice.

Isabel hugged herself. Her first journey with the queen! They would stop along the way at several of the queen's properties and some of the king's as well. They would visit with nobles, then head farther north, to meet the king at Lincoln. Rumors were everywhere, that the king was advancing with an army to invade Scotland, or that he'd been offered the crown and was traveling north to accept it. She did not believe any of it. She had been given a wonderful white mare and a saddle that was the envy of the queen's other ladies, who had had to provide their own. When they'd asked why she'd received such largess, she had only been able to shrug and say nothing, for truly she had not known.

Until yesterday.

She'd been told to visit the Wardrobe Tower within the Tower of London's walls, to sign for her robes and horse and wages. She'd taken a boat down the river, amused to discover that Henry had been correct, that the ferryman did know her name. She'd entered through the water gate that King Edward had built just a few years before, holding her skirts high as she'd hurried up the damp steps to the outer ward, then to the Wardrobe Tower.

She'd taken a moment to study it, the site of so many of her imaginings over the years, and she'd realized that she missed the father she'd invented. Part of her would always imagine him working here, climbing these very steps to the steward's office, spending his days writing the expenses of the crown into the large ledger books that lined the wall behind the steward's desk.

Walter Langton had not been in the room when she'd arrived. No one had been. The guard who had accompanied her had stayed with her, which had been comforting after all she'd heard about Langton and his nefarious habits. It was said that he was in league with the devil and had used strange powers to have his predecessor removed, so he could be placed in the position himself.

When the man himself had hurried in, three clerks at his heels, she'd found his appearance repulsive, but hardly that of a man who worshipped over pentagrams. He looked as though he should have been peddling fish on a wharf. His hair was dark, but graying. He was tall. And he had no neck. His head had gone straight into his shoulders, like the reptiles that the king kept. He'd walked with his stomach thrust forward, swaying slightly, almost like a woman. He had square hands and blunt fingers that had borne ink stains. He was dressed, as most of Edward's courtiers were, in simple clothing, abstaining from the gilt and jewels earlier courts had embraced. He'd leered at her with his moist brown eyes. She'd kept her face impassive.

"Ah. The lovely demoiselle de Burke. I am pleased to see you again."

She'd curtsied, not sure when they had met. "Sir."

He'd stepped closer, then circled her, and suddenly her skin had crept at his acquisitive expression. *There will be men* . . . His manner had changed abruptly and he'd sat at his desk, gesturing to one of the clerks to bring him one of the ledgers behind him. The clerk had scurried to pull the book from the shelf and set it before the steward, opening it to a page lined with signatures.

"I will need you to sign for your robes and horse, demoiselle. You do know how to write your name?"

"I do, sir," she'd said, and approached the table.

"No, come around this side," he'd said.

She had, pulling her skirts close, glancing at the guard, who'd watched with a stony expression. As she'd neared Langton, he'd put a hand on her waist and pulled her closer to him, but he'd not risen. Her breasts had been at his eye level.

"Do they meet with your approval?" he'd asked.

"Sir?"

"The horse." His hand had slid across the silk at her waist. "Your clothing. Such fine material. I can feel the warmth of your skin through it. Do they please you?"

"Greatly," she'd said, keeping her tone light.

His hand had slid lower, cupping her buttocks. She'd twisted out of his reach.

"Where do I sign, sir?"

"Here," he'd said, putting his hand atop hers. "Your skin is very soft. I imagine you are soft all over. Careful. The parchment is thin. Use a light touch. As you would with a lover. Stroke the ink onto the page. Draw the line slowly, let it enlarge under your touch."

She'd bent over the book, acutely aware of his hand remaining on her waist, and of his gaze on her breasts. She'd written her name as quickly as she'd been able, then she'd straightened and hurried back around the table to face him. His eyes had glinted. The guard had taken a half-step toward the door. Langton had come to her side, standing far too close. His gaze had once again been on her breasts. She'd taken a quick breath, seeing his eyes flicker.

"Would you like more?" he'd asked.

"Sir?"

"Clothing. Robes. Horses. Positions. Have you not asked yourself how it is that a seamstress's daughter should suddenly be elevated to a lady-in-waiting to the queen of England? Does that not seem strange to you? Have you powerful family ties? Enormous wealth? Are you an heiress, or the daughter of a noble?"

"I thought the queen liked me."

He'd looked over his shoulder at his clerks and laughed. "She thought the queen liked her! You thought you found favor with Queen Eleanor? That she actually even noticed you? Has she shown you any special favors? Has she sought your company above the others?"

"No," she'd whispered.

He'd moved closer, his stomach meeting hers, his chest just touching her breasts. "I make all things possible, demoiselle. For those who please me, wondrous things can happen." He'd traced a finger down the side of her neck, to her shoulder, then he'd followed the neckline lower, his fingernail rough on the skin of her breast. "Ask Mistress de Braun how she got her position. And ask your mother who pays her wages. And who could have her dismissed." He snapped his fingers. "Like that."

He'd stepped back from her. "Thank you, demoiselle. If there is anything else you . . . desire . . . I am here at your disposal. I make all things possible."

"Th-thank, thank you, sir," she'd stammered and hurried to the door, rushing through it when the guard had opened it.

"Isabel?" Langton's voice had been languid.

She'd stopped. "Sir?"

"I chose your horse and your saddle myself, thinking of you astride, your legs open, of your body touching the leather, only thin silk between your skin and the leather. I will continue to picture you there."

"I . . . I will ride palfrey, sir. But thank you, sir," she'd said and fled, hearing the male laughter behind her, cursing herself for a fool for thanking him. She'd lifted her skirts and run down the stairs, feeling like a whore. He had arranged for her clothing. Her horse. Her position with the queen. And now she knew his price.

The guard had followed more slowly, but at the foot of the stairs he'd caught her arm. "Demoiselle, a word of caution."

She'd nodded, unable to speak.

The guard had lowered his voice. "I have daughters of my own. Please, miss, do not go there alone. He is a powerful man, and accustomed to having his way. . . . You did not mistake his meaning." He'd opened the door to the Outer Ward. "Go, miss, and remember my words."

She had. She'd felt soiled. And later, as she'd tossed and turned in the small bed she shared with Alis.

"Isabel! Can you not keep still!" Alis had cried. "What is it? Nothing can be that dreadful! What are you thinking of that disquiets you so?"

"I went to see Walter Langton today."

"Ah." Alis had sat up. "And he frightened you."

"No. Yes. He is loathsome."

"You will become accustomed to him in time."

"He said he gave me my position with the queen and to ask you how you got your position."

Alis had laughed softly. "Oh, yes, he always picks the position. Did you not know? How do you suppose things are done at court? Are you that witty, that entertaining, that the queen had to have you among her ladies? That she chose you, the seamstress' daughter, over all other women in the land to serve her? Yes, Walter Langton arranged it, both yours and mine. And you'd be wise to be grateful."

"So it's true? He did arrange for you? . . ."

Alis had given a delicate shiver. "I am powerless against him." Her mood had shifted, and she'd given Isabel a cat-like smile. "Can you keep a secret? Can we be friends, Isabel de Burke? Can I trust you with my thoughts and my sorrows?"

"Oh, yes, Alis. My closest friend is gone from London and I would be happy if you and I were to become friends."

"And I as well. My own dear friend was the girl who was sent away. Poor silly chit, but I miss her so. Tell me of your friend. Is she also with child?"

"Oh, no, not at all! She is a Jew and was expelled."

"A Jew." Alis's expression had been thoughtful. "But many of them have not left London yet."

"Some were removed at once, and Rachel's family was among them. And you have heard that the rest are being removed to the Cinque Ports and sent to the Continent."

Alis had waved her hand. "Yes, I had heard something of it. We will be friends then, Isabel. Then we must tell each other everything. I never believe Lady Dickleburough, but how can I defend you when she tells me strange things, if you have not confided the truth in me?"

"What did she tell you?"

"Oh, nothing."

"Come, Alis, tell me!"

"Very well then. She says that you told her years ago that your father had been a clerk in the Wardrobe."

"Did she?"

"When you were a child and she asked you. But you have told me he lives in the north."

"Yes."

"So which is it?"

"I thought he was a clerk in the Wardrobe. For years. But I was wrong."

"How can you confuse such a thing? Either he lives in London, or he lives in the north. So which is it?"

Isabel had been silent.

Alis had sighed heavily. "I can see you do not wish to be friends after all."

"Tell me about Langton."

"Tell me about your father."

"I have only just found out myself."

"What?"

"It's—"

"It's what, shameful? How can you say that to me, when I acknowledged that I am also Walter Langton's victim? How can anything be more shameful?"

"He is vile!"

"Oh, yes. But powerful. Now tell me about your father."

"His name is Lord Lonsby," Isabel had said, then she'd poured out the rest.

By noon it had been repeated back to her twice.

First lesson, Isabel told herself. *I will keep my own counsel after this.* She did not tell her mother, not any of it, not the visit to Langton, nor the fact that she'd told Alis about her father, nor that Alis had told the world.

Both the gown and Isabel were ready to leave at dawn of the morning of the queen's departure. She waited, with the rest of the queen's ladies, in the shelter of the porch. None of the other ladies, save Lady Dickleburough and Alis, spoke to her. Now she knew why they did not, and why she had not been invited to share their coach, or their meals. She shivered in the cold, feeling that she was already on a very strange path and they'd not even left London. Once in the saddle, she remembered Langton's words, and her mood soured further.

The royal party traveled for a fortnight, but they were not on the roads every day. Some days were so filled with tasks that Isabel fell asleep as soon as she lay down in her bed. It was Isabel's responsibility to see that the queen's bed was assembled properly, that the linens were arranged just as she liked them, and when they were ready to move on, it was her responsibility to pack the linens carefully and oversee the dismantling of the bed and its delivery to the baggage carts. When they only stayed one night in a place she got little sleep, for she was expected to do all that and still attend the queen at every moment. And heaven help the fool who overslept and kept the royal train waiting, even for a moment.

There were other days, when they stayed in one place for several days, that were tedious. She and the other ladies would attend mass after mass at an abbey or monastery, sometimes with the queen, sometimes in her stead.

Or she simply sat, hands folded in her lap, listening to endless discussions of political matters, or, worst of all, petitions brought before the queen.

It was not all tedium. She saw much of the midlands, from castles such as Warwick and Kenilworth, to the great university at Oxford, and slept in monasteries and manor houses. She was fascinated to see the different ways in which the king's subjects lived, some in tiny cottages, others in large homes surrounded by out buildings, and still others in the fortresses and castles that dotted the landscape less frequently. The queen did not go everywhere she was invited but chose her stops carefully from a host of choices.

By listening rather than by being told, Isabel learned they would continue north, to Lincolnshire, and that the king would meet them on their journey. And by watching rather than by being told, she learned that Alis traded her favors for baubles, treats, and the occasional jewel from a grateful man in an outlying area. The bed she was supposed to share with Alis would often be hers alone, but they never discussed Alis's nocturnal absences, or the new clothing or ribbon that would suddenly appear in Alis's wardrobe.

A few of the queen's ladies had thawed in their treatment of Isabel; some were almost friendly as they got to know her better—and as she did her own job and often theirs as well. But all shied away from Lady Dickleburough's company. The older woman often sought Isabel out, as though she could smell Isabel's powerlessness to avoid her. Alis was also excluded from the queen's inner circle, and Isabel rode together with these two ladies-in-waiting behind the queen's carriage. In Nottinghamshire the weather grew colder, and mud made the roads difficult.

"My first husband had lands close by here," Lady Dickleburough said one afternoon. "Lovely lands. It's a shame he'd already had two sons, or I would be there now, counting my riches. If I had not been so young—younger than you are now—I would have made sure he changed his will before he died so suddenly." She laughed with a disquieting note.

Isabel was not sure what to believe, but truly, did she care if Lady Dickleburough's husband's death had been unnatural? She simply nodded.

"The queen's fever is worse," Lady Dickleburough said. "You weren't here when she was so ill earlier. Three years it's been, and I'm not sure she has ever fully recovered. This was a foolhardy journey, coming north in November. We could be trapped away from London for the winter."

"We're almost at Clipstone," Isabel said, "and the king is there. He will have doctors who can treat her."

"Doctors!" Lady Dickleburough snorted. "As if any doctor is worth his salt."

"Not all doctors are charlatans," Alis said.

"No," Lady Dickleburough said, "not all doctors are charlatans, are they, sweet Alis? You are grateful to one in particular, are you not?"

"I have no idea of what you mean," Alis said, but the bright spots on her cheeks belied her words.

"No idea." Lady Dickleburough's smile was smug. "Isabel, did you know that it is possible to rid yourself of the burden if you ever find yourself with child?"

"I have heard that," Isabel said carefully. "There are women who know potions."

"And witches who will cast spells," Lady Dickleburough said, slanting a look at Alis. "And doctors who will give you something to drink. And if that doesn't work, who will even cut the thing out. For a price. Wasn't it in Lincoln, sweet Alis, that you were taken so very ill?"

Alis's glance was impassive. "I was. But I was not with child, Lady Dickleburough, no matter what you've heard. Or imagined."

Lady Dickleburough chuckled again and spurred her horse forward, to talk in low tones to another of the queen's ladies. Alis stared at her back with hatred in her eyes.

"I loathe that vile creature!" she hissed. "It's not true! Not any of it!"

"She's hideous," Isabel agreed.

Lady Dickleburough turned then to look at Isabel with a knowing smile, and Isabel felt a chill down her spine. London seemed very far away.

The next few days were uneventful, although the queen was still feverish by the time they reached Clipstone and joined King Edward. Eleanor's illness, and the king's concern, filled the entire entourage with tension. They traveled slowly north, toward Lincoln, part of a much larger party now. There was little conversation among the travelers, whose mood grew more somber as word came each day that the queen was worsening. The king spent most of his time with Eleanor.

They lingered in Harby, near Grantham, just ten miles short of their goal of Lincoln, where the queen was housed in the home of Richard de Weston. And then word came that they would not travel farther.

Isabel and Alis spent many hours, as did most of the

queen's ladies, in the small parish church near de Weston's house, praying for the queen's recovery. Or in the corridor, outside the queen's rooms, where her women, the ladies-in-waiting, waited.

Isabel heard the queen cough so violently and so often that she wondered how her chest was still in place. The king was a madman, calling for unguents and potions, shouting for broth in the middle of the night and hovering over his queen. And somewhere in all of it, Isabel began to forgive King Edward for expelling the Jews from London. Perhaps he had been misled by his advisors. How could a man who loved his wife so well be so harsh with others? The doctors had been arriving daily, Egyptians with swarthy skin who looked deeply into Eleanor's eyes, doctors from London who bled her and left her weaker than before, doctors from the north who applied poultices. Astrologers who leaned over charts and muttered to each other, their expressions grim. She did not need to hear their pronouncements.

The hours seemed to slow, the moments seemed to drag by as they waited. Few spoke aloud, and none said what was obvious to all. In the evening of November 28 a priest was rushed in to give Queen Eleanor the last rites.

It was said that the king held her hand while she died.

The next days were a blur. The queen's body was brought to Lincoln for embalming, where prayers were said for her soul in elaborate masses that filled not only the cathedral but the entire town as well. Her viscera were buried there, but her heart, placed within a golden box, accompanied her body to London.

It took twelve days for the funeral procession to reach London. They stopped at Grantham, Stamford, and seven more times before reaching Charing, and Westminster Abbey at last.

Isabel, lost in the middle of the procession, wept almost the entire journey. She wept for Eleanor, the queen who might not have been loved by the English people but who had held a king enthralled for thirty-six years. She wept for Edward, whose suffering was tangible although his expression was stony. And she wept for herself and her mother, for what would their future hold now?

SIX

Rory took a bite, of the roasted chicken, savoring it. Then another, knowing he would miss the cooking at the inn. Berwick was an interesting place, but it was time to go home. They'd learned what they could here. They'd heard all the news the travelers had brought from the Continent, of Edward's disagreements with Philip of France, and the new alliances between city-states in Italy. And from England, where Queen Eleanor had died. King Edward, they'd been told, was bringing her home to London, where a royal funeral would be held for her. An Englishwoman had burst into tears when the news had come to the inn, but her husband had shushed her. "She was not a good queen, madam. Don't waste your tears on the likes of her," he'd said, and many others had agreed.

Rory and Kieran had kept their mouths shut. Two queens dead in two months was passing strange, but there was nothing to be done about it. It was time to go home. He watched Rachel take food to another table and glanced at his cousin. "Have ye talked to her about it?"

Kieran shook his head. "What do I say? 'I dinna ken ye were a Jew, and seeing ye at yer ceremony was a surprise, but I should ha' figured it out, kenning as I did that ye'd come suddenly from London, and yer name is Rachel and that should ha' been a hint, but I was too busy looking at ye and what does it matter anyway?' How do I work that into a conversation?"

"Why not say just that? Ye've not spoken to her since. D'ye think she hasna noticed that? We're leaving, Kieran. Say it, or ye'll wish later ye had. And stop watching her every movement."

"Aye." Kieran nodded but continued to watch her.

Rory made a disgusted sound in his throat and raised his arm, drawing Rachel's attention. He motioned her to them, ignoring Kieran's red face. Rachel moved slowly to stop at the end of their table, her hands folded before her.

"Ye ken we're leaving today?" Rory asked her.

"Yes. I heard you telling my father."

"Aye. And we wanted to tell ye thank ye for yer fine hospitality. It has been a pleasure meeting ye and yer family, Rachel Angenhoff. We wish ye well here in Berwick, and in all ye do. And if yer sister does marry Edgar Keith, as I think she might, I hope ye and yer father will forgive her in time."

Rachel nodded, pressing her lips together. She glanced at Kieran, then looked at Rory again. "We were pleased to have you stay with us. And we wish you safe journey home."

"Thank ye," Rory said.

There was an awkward moment of silence. Rachel smiled and left them.

Rory shook his head at Kieran again. "And ye said not a word. Have ye learned nothing from all I've taught ye about women, lad? It's this simple: say what's in yer heart. Ye may get slapped, or draw angry words. Hell, ye also may get kissed, but whichever it is, ye'll have no doubt about her feelings."

Kieran laughed sheepishly, then shrugged. "But likely I'll never see the lass again. What, if by saying it, I make her feel worse? Would I not regret that? I think silence is best, Rory."

"I'm sure ye do, but . . . I'd be thinking on it."

They packed their meager belongings and bid Jacob farewell, but Rachel was nowhere to be seen. Rory went out to the street. Kieran lingered a moment longer in the foyer, then came outside with a sigh.

They'd just begun to walk down the hill when Rachel burst through the door, rushing after them to stop next to Kieran. "Sirs. King Edward is taking Eleanor's body to London."

"Aye," Kieran said.

"Which means he won't be coming here," Rachel said. "It is good news."

Kieran looked into her eyes. "Aye, lass, it is good news for ye. For all of us."

"Yes. Safe journey. I . . . Safe journey." She took three steps away, then turned back. "Kieran, Rory . . . will you travel to London?"

"Ye mean, will we go to the English queen's funeral?" Rory asked. "I dinna think so, lass."

"Oh. Safe journey then."

Kieran caught her arm before she could leave. "Why? Is there something you need from London?"

Rachel shook her head quickly. "No. But . . . if you ever go there . . . if you do travel there, ever . . . Could you find a friend for me? She is . . . she was . . . one of the queen's ladies."

Rory raised his eyebrows.

"We . . . we were girls together," she said, rushing her words together and looking away from Kieran, who continued to watch her. "Her grandmother lived near my family and she and I would play when we were very young and we stayed friends as we grew older, even though we were different and our lives were very different." Her cheeks were scarlet. "I . . . we left London hurriedly. I would like her to know that I am well."

"Ye could write to her. Does she read?" Rory asked.

"Oh, yes." Rachel glanced at the inn doorway, where Jacob stood watching them, his arms folded. "But I am afraid . . . I would like her to know where I am, that we are well. But I would like no one else to know."

Rory glanced at Kieran, but his cousin stood silent. "It is unlikely that we'll ever go to London, but give me her name, lass. If I hear of anyone going, I'll ask them to find her and give her yer message."

"Isabel. Her name is Isabel de Burke. I would be so grateful." She smiled. "I thank you for everything, for your kindness . . . and understanding."

"Another smile like that," Kieran said, "would be worth the trip to London."

Rachel's mouth fell open.

"I kent ye were from London," Kieran said, "but I dinna ken why ye left. Now I do. I want ye to ken that I dinna care what god ye worship, nor what King Edward thinks of yer people. I'm glad to have met ye, Rachel

Angenhoff, and I wish ye safe journey as well. Wherever life takes ye, safe journey." He took her hand and brought it to his lips. "I will think of ye, lass. And I'll find a way to get yer message to yer friend. I vow it."

"Thank you." Rachel looked into Kieran's eyes, then fled.

"I dinna believe it," Rory said.

Kieran puffed out his chest. "Dinna worry, Rory, lad, I'll teach ye how to behave around women."

Rory laughed aloud. "Aye, ye do that."

They reached Stirling just before nightfall, and unlike the last time, they were shown through the gates at once. They sent word to Liam that they had arrived, then headed for the stables, where Rory left a generous sum and a warning that this horse was not to be harmed. The stable lad nodded with a terrified expression. And then they went to find Liam, but instead, it was their aunt Nell who rushed forward as they entered the castle, throwing her arms around each of them in turn, her smile wide.

"At last!" she cried. "We've been worried, wondering what had detained ye in Berwick. Come say hello to yer uncle, and get a bite to eat. We need to talk. We're all leaving in the morning."

"Are we?" Rory asked, laughing.

Nothing changed Nell, not time, nor being a mother, nor all that had happened to her. She still embraced life with open arms and a glad heart. She never seemed to age. Her brown hair was as thick and wavy as ever, her step as lively, her green eyes as clear. And she was, as always, in a hurry.

"Where are we going? Are ye coming to Loch Gannon with us?"

"Och, no, laddie," she said, her smile fading. "We're not going anywhere together. Ye're going to London to bury a queen."

Liam poured each of them another cup of wine. "She thinks it's a good thing, the two of ye going to London."

"It is a good thing," Nell said. "Ye will learn much, going to Queen Eleanor's funeral and discovering the mood in England. We need to ken whether Edward has the backing of his own people in trying to rule us. They were behind him when he invaded Wales, but I've heard they're weary of war."

"Weary of paying for it," Liam said.

"Which amounts to the same thing," Nell said. "Yer brother Magnus came to me, when he heard about ye killing the MacDonnell lad. And yer da came to Ayrshire to see him and discover what was happening. It's not something ye can take lightly, Rory, a blood feud being called against ye. So I came here, to tell Liam."

"Ye used it as an excuse to come see me," Liam said, "which was foolishness, since Rory's yer own blood, and a feud against him is one against ye as well."

"I had twenty Comyn men accompanying me, as ye well ken, since ye sent them down to see if we were a'right, love. And I'm only his aunt. And ye had already gone to talk with the MacDonells. Which yer da did as well, Rory. The MacDonnells dinna want this to get any bigger than it is and they're spreading the word of what really happened. Last thing this country needs is to have two western clans killing each other."

"Aye," Liam said. "They could be killing Balliols or Bruces instead."

"Bruces, if I'm asked," Nell said. "When I got here, John Comyn was here."

"He's taking a whole group of yer Comyn cousins to London for the funeral," Liam said. "He thinks ye should go with them. And so do yer parents. They sent word that ye need to go. And we agree."

"So drink up, lads," Nell said. "Ye'll go and see John Comyn tonight, and in the morning ye leave for London."

John Comyn had aged well, Rory thought as he waited to talk with his mother's cousin. The Comyns were the most powerful family in all of Scotland, and John, Earl of Buchan, and Lord of Badenoch, was their leader. He was one of the thirteen Competitors for the crown and had been—still was, for that matter—one of the six Guardians who ruled Scotland in the Maid's absence and now in her death. Black Comyn, he was known as, for his son was also named John, called Red Comyn to describe them by the color of their hair and distinguish between them.

William, the third Earl of Ross and uncle to Rory's mother, had married Jean Comyn, uniting the two families. His brother Magnus had further cemented the ties when he'd married Jocelyn Comyn. Black Comyn had extensive holdings in both the north and south of Scotland, especially around Lochaber. It was within the boundaries of his control that Rory had killed the MacDonnell. The web of Comyn power extended throughout the land, and Rory should have realized that he'd be called to task by John Comyn for starting a blood feud, inadvertent or no. There was enough unrest with the conflict between the rivals for the crown without adding to it.

Which is exactly what Black Comyn told him. Rory defended himself, explaining what had happened, trying to control his anger. He'd done what any decent man would have done and look what had come of it. Which is just what he said.

Comyn listened carefully, nodding when Rory was finished. "I have ensured that the other men who were party to it have been punished," he said. "They'll not be coming after ye, nor will their families. We've made sure of that. Make no mistake, I applaud ye for saving that lass, and had I been in yer position I would have done the same thing. But it's spread beyond the MacDonnells, and ye have become a target for anyone to aim at. There's a rumor that there's a large prize for yer head, and many are listening. We need to end this, and end it now. Ye need to be gone for a while and let the whole thing be forgotten. The Mac-Donells will deal with their hotheaded young men."

He handed Rory a bundle wrapped in scarlet silk, with a ribbon embroidered with gold wrapped around it. "From the MacDonnell's lady, to thank ye for saving the lass. She says ye're a champion of all women." He laughed. "That may be why some of the MacDonnells are ready to believe the worst of ye. Let a man's woman praise another man and he's not too pleased about it. It will pass. But it will take time, and the last thing I need is to have ye murdered on a dark night."

"Or any other," Rory said. "I'm not fond of the idea myself."

Comyn nodded. "Ye'll come to London with us. After the funeral we'll return home, but ye'll spend the winter there learning what ye can. Ye'll send regular messages back to us. And perhaps by spring this dispute with the MacDonnells will be forgotten."

"Have ye not yer own men in London already, my lord?" Rory asked.

"Of course I have, but it never hurts to confirm what I'm hearing. Look, lad, I know yer father well, and I know yer mother. I know what ye're made of. I need ye to do this. And ye'd be a fool to displease me. Do we understand each other?"

Rory nodded. "When do we leave?"

London might officially be in mourning, but one would never have known it from the behavior of its citizens. Each day looked like a feast day. Hawkers roamed the streets with trays of hot chestnuts and dumplings carried in iron pits, ladled out into wooden bowls that were emptied, then reused by the next customer. Innkeepers wore wide smiles as their rooms were filled, and butchers worked long hours, preparing the food for all those who would need a funeral feast.

The streets grew ever more crowded with new arrivals. Nobles on horseback jostled with farmers bringing the contents of their root cellars to sell. Fruit from Spain and Italy was sold for a premium. Stuffed figs and persimmons were piled on trays next to bright oranges, sold from open stalls set up in the squares. Every church was filled, whether because of the warmth from the pans of coals that were allowed for these few days to burn in braziers above the worshippers, or whether Londoners felt a sudden upsurge in piety at the news of Eleanor's death, Rory could not say.

Every building seemed to have people hanging from windows and doorways. The houses, dark wood or half-timbered plaster, stretched out toward each other over the narrow streets below. Walkers had to take care to step over refuse—and worse—as they pushed their way through the crowds. Whores invited Rory and Kieran inside brothels. The lads bantered with them but did not linger.

And then it was December 17, the day of the funeral. The ceremony itself would take place at Westminster Abbey, and all of London seemed to be heading there. Rory and Kieran would be among the many who would attend the mass within the Abbey's walls, their seats assured by their connection to the Comyns but far from the altar. Rory did not mind. He was too busy taking it all in, for everywhere he turned, London presented a display unlike anything he'd seen.

Westminster Abbey stood near the river, in the part of London once called Thorney. Edward the Confessor was buried there, as he'd planned before being driven into exile by the Danes. William the Conqueror had been crowned there on Christmas Day in 1066, and every monarch since had held important ceremonies in the Abbey. The building itself was fascinating, easily the most intricate Rory had ever seen. The sanctuary was raised and glorious. Someday he would like to walk through the abbey and see all the detail. But not today.

"The queen's ladies." He heard the murmur as the women were ushered past, the most important of the noblewomen first, wives and daughters of dukes and earls, begowned and bejeweled in amazing fashion. Behind them was another group, less lavishly costumed.

"What was her name?" Rory asked Kieran. "Rachel's

friend, the one we said we'd try to find? What was her name?"

Kieran thought for a moment. "Isabel de Burke. She must be one of them. But which? They all look older than I thought."

Rory nodded. Isabel de Burke. He could not guess what her connection to the queen might have been, but certainly none of these women looked like a possible friend of Rachel's.

And then he saw them, two younger women, one blond and pretty, her cupid's mouth pursed, her blue eyes anxious. And the other, taller, with a regal manner. Her lovely face was framed by a wimple of creamy white and topped by a headdress of the same material, brown hair curling softly around her temples. She had a very fine body, lithe, the curves of her breasts and waist revealed by the line of her gray gown, the same gray as her eyes. Her sleeves were a deep yellow, almost golden in color, a bright spot in this sea of somber hues. She turned her head, showing him her profile and the line of her jaw, smooth and feminine, then nodded at something said to her and hurried forward, propelled by the guards behind them.

He nudged Kieran and gestured to them.

"I'm thinking the blond one," Kieran said.

"Wager?" Rory asked, not from any conviction that the brown-haired lass was Isabel but more to see what Kieran would do.

"Wager."

The entire world, it seemed, would attend Queen Eleanor's funeral. Leaders from every known country had been invited. For weeks London had been filling with people eager to see history made, and now that the day was here, the streets had been almost impassable. Isabel had watched the crowds from her spot in one of the many royal carriages.

She had not expected to be here. She'd thought she would be dismissed upon their return to London, but instead, both she and her mother had been instructed to continue as they had been before. Her mother, distraught at the queen's death, had been astonished, and honored to be asked to help in the creation of the drapings of Eleanor's casket. They had been told to keep their rooms in Westminster. But all Isabel could think of was the price Walter Langton would demand.

Even more surprising, Isabel had been instructed to be in court every day. No one ever told her why, or what she was supposed to do there, but she had attended as told, most days doing nothing more than being present at the meals, sitting with the other courtiers as the more foolish jesters and minstrels tried to amuse the king, and the wiser ones simply performed. Every day she'd woken with the expectation of being called to the Wardrobe Tower. And each evening she'd sighed with relief. It would not last, she knew.

The king already had plans underway to construct twelve great crosses, one at each town where the funeral procession had spent the night, and the court was filled with architects and stone craftsmen, who met with Edward to plan them. Eleanor's tomb, bearing the same pose as her great seal, had been ordered years before, and until it was completed, her body would rest in a grave near the high altar at Westminster Abbey. But that was months, perhaps years, away.

Eleanor's heart had been removed in Lincoln, carried to London, and buried with a sumptuous ceremony at the Dominican priory at Blackfriars. Isabel had attended with the rest of the queen's ladies. Langton had been there, but he'd given no sign of having noticed her, and the band around her heart had loosened. Perhaps he had forgotten her. As Henry had seemed to do.

She saw him almost daily now, for he'd been moved to rooms near the queen's ladies' apartments. She would wave, and he would smile, and sometimes he'd even take a moment to chat with her. He was always friendly. He never failed to compliment her. But they said nothing of importance to each other, nor were they ever alone. Which was fitting, she thought, for both of them had to be mindful that the court was in deep mourning. She was sure he felt the same, and that when the mourning period had passed, they would see more of each other.

Until one rainy December day.

She had gone to visit her grandmother and was hurrying through the wet streets to the ferryboat that would take her back to Westminster when she saw them. Henry had his back to her, but she would know him anywhere, his dark hair just over the collar of his armor, for he was in uniform.

He held the reins to his horse in his right hand, but his left was pressed to Alis's back, holding her against him. Isabel stopped, seeing Alis's bright hair over his shoulder, and Henry's lowered head. She did not need to get closer to know he was kissing her. She stood rooted to the ground.

What a fool she had been! She'd told Alis where she was going this day, had told her the time she would return. Alis had planned this. And then all the other times Alis had asked her schedule, seemingly innocent questions about Isabel's comings and goings. And Henry.

They'd talked about Henry constantly, leaning together at meals and watching him with the other knights. Sitting at tournaments, cheering him when he'd defeated his opponent. Dancing with him at the royal festivities. She'd known Alis had been flirting with him, and he with her, but Alis flirted with everyone. And no one had told her anything of this. But then, who would have? Lady Dickleburough. She must have known. Of course she did. The entire court did.

She had been such a fool. How could she not have known that Alis found Henry as desirable and exquisitely male as she herself did? And of course Alis was pretty and flirtatious, and Henry had noticed it. He'd told her himself that he thought Alis was lovely. He'd told her she was beautiful, and she'd chosen to believe it. She'd also chosen to believe that his flirtation with Alis meant nothing. All the knights flirted with Alis. And many with Isabel, or any woman they met. It was a game, a faux wooing, that amused the court, something to pass the days. Courtly love. But not real. Not love. Or so she had thought.

Now it was time to face the truth. And them. She'd had no choice. She must pass them or stay where she was and let the boat go to Westminster without her. And somehow find her way back in the dark. Overhead, thunder rolled, and she had pulled her cloak hood tighter, bending her head and hoping that they would be too occupied to notice her.

They were lifting their heads and looking deeply in each other's eyes until just the moment she had reached them.

It was Henry who had seen her first, his cheeks staining with sudden color, his gaze sharpening as she passed. Alis had turned then, with Henry's arm still around her, and she smiled at Isabel, a self-satisfied smile that let Isabel know that Alis was well aware of shattering Isabel's foolish dreams.

"Isabel. Dear child, how are you?"

Isabel had ignored her, continuing on to the boat, giving the boatman her fare and climbing carefully aboard.

"I must go," Alis had said loudly, pulling away from Henry, then darting back to kiss him one last time. "You are delicious. As always."

Isabel had refused to look at them, did not want to see Henry's expression as his lover left him, or Alis's triumphant look. *"Coming from a lover's tryst?"* he had asked her that first day. She had cursed herself for being so easily taken in.

A moment later Alis had plumped herself beside Isabel, wiggling to be sure that she was noticed, then sighed contentedly. She had sighed again, the sound infuriating. Isabel had clenched her hands beneath her cloak.

"Some day you will understand," Alis had said.

Isabel had glared at her, then slowly turned away, as though she found Alis beneath her notice. "You did that intentionally."

"What, sit beside you? It's a small boat, Isabel, and we know each other."

"You know what I mean. Henry. You took him."

"You never had him, Isabel. You dreamed of him, but you never acted on those dreams. I did. You offered nothing but smiles. I offered him much more. And he took it. In time you will understand."

"I understand now, Alis. You had not noticed him

until I admired him. Of all the men at court, all those you could have picked, you chose to pursue him."

"He pursued me, Isabel."

"I know what you are. All of London recognizes you for what you are."

The boatman had snickered.

Alis's eyes had widened, then narrowed. "You are a fool to speak to me thus. You are no more than a spoiled child who has been denied a treat, Isabel."

"A child with tales to tell," Isabel had said, knowing she was creating an enemy. "And the will to do just that. The whole country will be gathering for this funeral. I will see many of those we visited on our journey. I am looking forward to renewing their acquaintances and perhaps introducing them to each other. And to Henry."

Alis had stared at her. "I have my own tale to tell. You are a bastard."

"I have made no secret of it. I am a bastard by birth. You are one by choice."

The boatman had laughed aloud.

It had been a moment Isabel had been paying for ever since. Her brave words had been only that—she'd not said anything to anyone about Alis. But Alis had spread tales about Isabel immediately, saying that it was not her grandmother Isabel went to visit in the City but a married man of low birth. Isabel held her head up, but she was ashamed of the bits of gossip about herself that Lady Dickleburough repeated to her, in great detail. Isabel had rarely been more miserable.

When she had visited her grandmother she had hated worrying that she would see Alis and Henry together again. She had gone often nevertheless. Her grandmother was grateful and laughed softly when Isabel poured out her story.

"He is a man, Isabel. And gentleman enough to know that you are not offering yourself to him. Alis de Braun is. There is an Alis in every woman's life, a woman who knows from her earliest day how to attract men and what to do to keep them. It will not last. He will tire of her, or she of him. And when he is ready for marriage, or a meeting of the minds rather than of bodies, he will look elsewhere. As will Alis de Braun. But she will be that much older. Soon she will have nothing to offer and she will become another Lady Dickleburough. Her days are numbered. When they are through, she has nothing. Beauty fades even for the most beautiful."

"Henry said she was lovely. And I was beautiful. It meant nothing."

"As you are. Do not hate him, sweet. He is but a man, and as your mother will tell you, they are all weak."

"I don't hate him," she had said. "I have tried. But I cannot."

Her grandmother had smiled. "There are other men, sweet. Find one."

She had avoided Alis. Difficult, since they slept in the same bed. And today they had shared a royal coach on the way to Eleanor's funeral.

They had sat silently in the coach for what seemed like hours, even longer during the interminable ceremony. She'd been relieved when the choir had begun to sing and then the trumpets outside blared to the world that the king had arrived.

Edward had made his way up the North Aisle, slowly. How strange this day must be for him, Isabel had thought, for Edward and Eleanor had been married in this abbey, and had been the first king and queen to be jointly crowned here. This was where Edward had raised a monument to his father, Henry III, and where his son Alphonso was buried.

Men from every part of Edward's life had followed him. His old friend Sir Otes de Grandison, who had been with Edward in the Holy Land. Gloucester, Lancaster and Warwick were there, with magnates from all over England and Scotland. Barons and knights and wealthy merchants who were among Edward's favorites. His six children, from the child prince Edward, to the newly married Joan on the arm of her husband Gilbert de Clare, to the eldest, Eleanor, who had traveled far to come to her mother's funeral.

Isabel had paid little attention to the ceremony itself, for the sights and sounds of it had been mixed with her sorrow—and her worry for what the future would hold. At the conclusion of the hours-long service, the king and his entourage had filed out first, then the nobles who had sat near him. And then Isabel and the rest of Queen Eleanor's ladies had walked down the North Aisle only to wait at the end of the Nave while the crowd outside dispersed. She looked at Alis, then away, and met the gaze of a man standing near the door. He was blond, Irish, perhaps, or Norse, for he was quite tall.

His eyes were very blue, his hair pale and drawn back from his striking face. His nose was straight, his cheekbones were sharp, his jawline well defined, his mouth wide, with lips pressed together as he examined those leaving. He looked like a warrior, but he was dressed as a noble, his wide shoulders covered by a beautifully woven cloak with a circular golden brooch set with jewels. He glanced at the others, then looked into Isabel's eyes. And smiled. And suddenly the noise of the people around her disappeared, the slow shuffling as they moved forward now unnoticed.

She smiled in return, and his smile widened. Handsome man. Golden-haired man who lit the dark space he stood in. And then he was gone, his face blocked by a tall man who moved between them. She was hurried forward by the guards, through the crowd, and into the coach. She peered through the open door until it was slammed, looking for him, but it was impossible to find one tall blond man in the crush.

The funeral meal was overlong, and all those who had not had a chance to talk to Edward before or at the funeral itself clamored for a moment now. He ignored most of them, sitting with his closest companions at the dais, speaking little and eating less. But none could leave until he did, and so they sat and waited.

"Are you in need of anything, demoiselles? Isabel?"

She recognized Langton's voice at once but pretended she did not hear.

"Isabel?" His tone was insistent. "Is there anything you need?"

She forced a smile. "Thank you, my lord. But I am in need of nothing."

"Be sure to visit me soon. I insist." Langton patted the hand of the woman whose arm rested on his, then continued to his seat with the other officers of Edward's household.

Isabel shivered, trying to mask her revulsion. The man terrified her.

"Langton, Isabel?" Lady Dickleburough asked. "Have you not been warned? He is a snake, and you would not be the first to be devoured by him."

"I am careful, madam," Isabel replied.

"Wise." Lady Dickleburough emptied her wine glass. "I have a weapon for you. It is an interesting tale about Alis to share. I give it to you as my gift. But a gift you must share." She pulled a piece of swan meat off the platter before them and chewed it, licking her fingers. "Did you know that Alis has a daughter?"

Isabel shook her head.

"She'd not want you to know. She thinks no one knows, but people talk, and there is no such thing as a secret. Yes, it's true. The girl must be six, or seven, perhaps now, for she was born not long before our Prince Edward's birth. Which is why Queen Eleanor's attention was distracted from Alis's absence."

"I've never heard her mention a child."

"Nor will you. Nor will you ever see the child. She is in Gascony, where Alis left her four years ago. Simply walked away and left the child with its nurse."

"And the child's father?"

"Dead, killed in the king's battles. Although some say it is Walter Langton."

"Did she not send for her daughter?"

"Oh, no. Nor does she visit her. She's not seen the child since the day she left." Lady Dickleburough leaned forward. "So when she spreads the tales she invents about you, you can respond with this one. The child's name is Miriam. I hear she's been sent to a convent now."

"How do you know this?"

Lady Dickleburough smiled slowly. "I hear everything, Isabel. Everything."

Isabel was miserable. Her days were long, and she either suffered Alis's presence or agonized in her absence, wondering if Alis and Henry were together. She visited her mother, who complained bitterly of having nothing to do. When she told her mother to be glad they had roofs over their head, her mother asked what she would know of earning a roof over her head. And Isabel bit her tongue before she shouted out her fear of Walter Langton.

The next time she visited her mother they argued again; her mother accusing her of being cosseted while she lived in one tiny room. Isabel thought of the bed she shared with Alis. And the apartment she shared with the rest of the queen's ladies. And said nothing.

Two days after the queen's funeral, a guard came to fetch her where she and Alis sat in their apartment, doing embroidery.

"There are men here to see you, Demoiselle de Burke," he said.

Isabel looked up. She was expecting no one. "Who are they?"

The guard's disdain for the visitors, or for her, was obvious. He examined his nails and waited for her reply. "Foreigners, but aren't they all these days? I could not understand their names."

She sighed with relief. It was not Walter Langton, or his men. She exchanged a glance with Alis, their uneasy truce since the funeral still untested.

"Don't bring them here," Alis said. "Go to them instead."

Isabel nodded, tempted for a moment to ask Alis to accompany her, then thinking better of it. "They asked for me by name?"

"Which is why I am here, demoiselle."

She stood, her irritation flaring. "Take me to them," she said, tossing her needlework onto the cushion, and wondering how quickly word would get to Lady Dickleburough.

The guard did not answer but led her down the stairs and through the corridors to one of the anterooms used by the queen's household for meeting with tradespeople. He paused outside the door, looking down at her, then thrust the door open and waved her inside.

There were two men waiting there, both tall, both outlandishly dressed, their cloaks well-tailored but of a fashion she knew was not from London. They wore high boots and long saffron shirts and tunics of finely woven wool, with a pattern that featured lines crossing themselves. Gaels, she thought, knowing them now for what they were. One was dark, his black hair well-brushed and just below his shoulders, his blue eyes curious. A handsome man. He bowed, smiling.

And the other was the blond man from Westminster Abbey.

SEVEN

Her heart jumped. Who was this man? She was certain she'd not seen him before the day of the funeral. She would have remembered a man who looked like this one. Did he think he knew her, on the basis of her smile? But how could she not have smiled at such a man? The two foreigners exchanged a glance.

"My lady," the blond man said, his accent telling her he was a Scot.

His voice was middle-timbred, his tone warm, his manner polite, nothing more. His face was even more striking at close range. His eyes were an amazing mixture of blues, banded at the edge with the deepest shade of all. His was a strong face, a masculine beauty that was arresting. His hair was very pale, drawn away from a wide brow and arched eyebrows. His jaw was firm. And his mouth. Dear Lord, look at his mouth. He wore the same cloak, pinned with the bejeweled brooch that she'd noticed before. She looked up at him, at his wide shoulders and tapering waistline, at his long fingers and strong legs. Something stirred within her, filled with yearning, something primitive. She felt like she needed to sit down.

"Please forgive our intrusion, mistress. We ken that ye dinna know us and that we may be overstepping ourselves. Are ye Isabel de Burke?"

She paused before answering. What difference did it make if they knew her name? A few well-placed coins would bring them the same information.

"I am," she said.

He bowed slightly. "I am Rory MacGannon. This is my cousin Kieran MacDonald. We bring you a message from Rachel Angenhoff."

"Rachel? You have seen Rachel?"

"Aye. In Berwick-Upon-Tweed, my lady. In Scotland."

"Scotland! I'd not thought of her there. Oh! But are you sure it's my Rachel? Her name . . ." Isabel stopped. She was being ridiculous. No other person named Rachel would have known to ask someone to find her. If Rachel and her family had changed their names, it must have been necessary, and she would keep their secret. The wonderful news was that Rachel was alive, and well enough to send these men with her message.

"Is she all right? Is her family well? How did you know to find me?"

"They are all well. Her family owns an inn in Berwick," Rory said.

"An inn? Rachel's family owns an inn?" That was difficult to imagine, Rachel's mother serving ale and cleaning rooms for strangers. Her father, always a scholar, collecting money for meals. How unexpected.

"We stayed there for a fortnight," Kieran said. "When the news came of yer queen's death, she asked us if we were going to London. We dinna ken that we were, but . . ." He spread his hands wide. "Here we are."

The door opened suddenly. Henry stood there, armed, three men behind him. He looked from her to the Scots, his gaze meeting Rory MacGannon's.

"Is all well, demoiselle?" he asked. "I was told you had visitors."

"Yes, as you can see," she said. "They brought me a message . . . from . . . from my cousins. In the north."

Henry stepped into the room. "Gentlemen, I am Henry de Boyer. Knight of King Edward's household, of which Mistress de Burke is a part. Your business here with her?"

Rory MacGannon stood taller. "Delivering a message. As she told ye."

"Your names?"

"Rory MacGannon. Kieran MacDonald." Rory turned to her. "Thank ye for yer time, mistress. Yer cousin will be pleased we were able to deliver her message."

"Yes. Thank you," she said. "I am so pleased to hear from her."

"It was our pleasure," Rory said and moved toward the door.

"Wait, please, sirs! Will you be returning there? May I send a message to her with you?"

Henry made an impatient gesture. "Surely you will have no need—"

"A letter!" she cried. "I could write her a letter. You could carry a letter north for me, could you not? I will pay for the messenger to take it to her."

"You can do that from here, demoiselle," Henry said. "You do not need them as intermediaries. The king's men would be happy to carry it for you. I will arrange for it."

She ignored him. "Sir. My lord MacGannon, how will I find you?"

"Ask for the Comyns. We are with them."

She saw the flicker in Henry's eyes. Everyone knew the Comyn name and the power the family held in Scotland. Rory MacGannon gave her a slight smile.

"Ye ken where to find us, demoiselle, should ye need us. Farewell. Sir."

He bowed and left, his cousin behind him. Henry gave her an appraising look.

"Who are they?" he asked.

She smiled. "Messengers. My cousin is faring well. Is that not wonderful?"

"How do you know they are who they say they are?" Grandmother asked the next afternoon. She crossed her arms over her chest. "You cannot visit them, sweet. You cannot. Do not even try to argue with me on this."

Isabel paced the floor. "But they will see my letter gets to Rachel."

"Send it with the king's men."

"It could be dangerous for her."

"Her family was expelled, not arrested. They have done nothing wrong."

"But it could be dangerous for her, and I cannot risk her safety. The Scotsmen have seen her. I know they will try to get my letter to her. Shall I go to them?"

"Of course not! Silly chit, you cannot appear at their lodgings like a woman of the streets." Grandmother shook her head, then sighed. "Send for them to come here. And if you tell your mother, we'll both regret it. Get the boy downstairs to fetch them. And ask him to stay here while we talk. I do not like this at all."

Isabel leaned to kiss her cheek, feeling how papery her grandmother's skin had become. "Thank you!" she cried.

She sent the boy off with her message, then waited impatiently for him to return. She pounced on him when he did. "Well? Will they come?"

"They are here with me," the boy said. "They're big!"

"Show them up," Grandmother said irritably. "Probably murder us both now. Isabel, I'm not pleased at this."

"They will not harm us, Grandmother. Truly. Wait and see."

Rory and Kieran walked into the room just as the church bells tolled, and stood, awkwardly, waiting until the last note sounded. They were armed and wary, but their manner relaxed a bit when they saw Grandmother.

"Thank you for coming," Isabel said, then introduced them.

Grandmother nodded. "Scots. Highlanders, both of you. Where are your homes?"

"The west of Scotland," Rory said. "I'm from Loch Gannon, and Kieran's from Skye."

"I see. And your purpose in London?"

"To attend the queen's funeral."

"But you bring a message from Rachel de Anjou."

Rory paused, and Isabel knew he was noting the change of name. "Aye, madam. She asked us to find your granddaughter and tell her that Rachel and her family are well. We are pleased to do so."

"Sit, gentlemen," Grandmother said, as though she

had just remembered her manners. "Bring some ale, Isabel, and my mead. Or would you prefer mead, sirs?"

"Och, no," Rory said.

Isabel almost laughed at his repugnance. "Ale, then."

"Ale is grand, madam," Kieran said. "Did ye attend the queen's funeral?"

Grandmother shook her head. "No, no. I spent the day safely here."

"It was very grand," Kieran said. "A fine funeral."

"Did you know the queen, sir?"

"No, but I feel like I did after hearing so much of her. Not all good."

Grandmother smiled. "She was not well liked. The king may have loved her, but his people did not. Still, she did her duty. We have a prince in line for the throne. Have you children, sirs?"

Isabel caught her breath at the abrupt change of topic.

Rory laughed. "No, madam, nor wives, nor any furtive motive. We are merely messengers between friends. Nothing more."

Grandmother smiled, and Isabel began to relax. They talked for almost an hour, about Scotland and England and the sea, which Grandmother talked of with a longing that surprised Isabel. And candles and Yuletide customs, and their siblings, the conversation easy and unforced. They made Grandmother laugh several times. When the church bells tolled again, the men rose to their feet. Grandmother extended her hand, and each of them bowed over it.

"I wish you a good time in London, sirs," she said. "And safe journey home."

"Thank you, madam," Rory said. "Demoiselle, do you have a letter for us?"

"I do," Isabel said. "I will see you out."

She led them down the stairs and opened the door to the street. "I thank you for your forbearance. My grandmother is very protective."

"She is very fond of ye, lass," Rory answered.

"And I of her." Isabel handed him her letter. "I am grateful to you for taking this with you. And thank you again for finding me. I am so pleased to know where Rachel and her family are, and to know that she's safe. She is safe there, isn't she?"

"Safe enough, aye. No one in Berwick cares that they were expelled. Her family is not alone in that. Many Jewish families came at the same time."

She looked at him with a startled expression. "And they were welcomed?"

"I canna say welcomed. Allowed to join the madness that is Berwick is more like it. It's a port town, mistress, with people from all over." He put the letter in his shirt. "I canna guarantee that it will get to her, but we'll do our best."

"And here," she said, holding out a handful of coins. "Money for the messenger to carry it from wherever you will have to leave it."

Rory shook his head. "I willna take yer money, Isabel de Burke. There is only one way ye can repay me."

Isabel stared into his eyes, wondering what he meant.

"I ask only one thing in return for carrying yer letter, lass."

She caught her breath as he leaned over her now with a gleam in his eyes and a smile flitting around the edge of his mouth. That mouth. A kiss, perhaps? Her heartbeat quickened. "Sir?"

"A walk, lass. Tomorrow. Nothing more. Ye can bring an army of chaperones, if ye wish. One walk in the sunshine."

She let out her breath and smiled. "You will have it."

His smile was wide and his eyes merry. He seemed to glow, and she thought, *That's it, it is as though he brings light with him.*

"Good. At the dock near the Tower, then?"

"Yes. At three."

"At three it is. I'll be there, lass, waiting for ye."

She watched them walk away, laughing with each other. *Rachel,* she thought, *another tie between us, these two men. I miss you so.* She closed the door and hurried upstairs, knowing Grandmother would be counting the moments she'd been away.

"Handsome man," Grandmother said as Isabel rejoined her. "Both handsome men. Young. The MacDonald one is nice enough. But the other . . . many women will be noticing that one. A very memorable man."

"Yes, isn't he, though?"

"Here only for a short time," Grandmother said. "But much can happen in a short time. I saw how you looked at him. Be careful, sweet. He's the kind of man who can turn a girl's head without even trying. And when he is trying . . . he could be dangerous."

"You sound like Mother."

"She may be bitter, Isabel, but she's not always wrong. Rory MacGannon is a man to be cautious of."

"I am sure he will not harm me."

"You're seeing him again, aren't you?"

Isabel looked at her, realizing how easily she'd let that slip.

"Enjoy his company, Isabel. Guard your heart and your body. He's the kind of man who could take both."

Isabel nodded, her mind now filled with new images.

Rory waited in the rain at the Tower landing, where the ferryboat would bring her from Westminster. Two boats arrived, then a third, with her on none of them. He felt like a fool and stepped back under the cover of the nearest shop, telling himself that if she was not on the next boat, he would leave.

When the next boat came, she was on it. But not alone.

Henry de Boyer leapt to the dock, reaching back to help her out instead of the ferryman, who watched them with a crooked grin. She smiled at de Boyer and let him lead her to the small square near the street, where she stood in a pool of sudden sunshine. She pushed the hood off her head and looked left, then right, her simple skirts swaying from her hips as she moved, her light brown hair gleaming in the sunlight. De Boyer said something to her that made her laugh, and Rory peeled himself from the shop wall, striding quickly forward.

He stopped before her and bowed. "Mistress de Burke, I thought perhaps ye had forgotten."

She whirled to face him, her face brightening as she saw him. "Oh! Good! I thought I was too late and that you had gone. Or perhaps not come at all."

"I would not have missed this, demoiselle."

"I am so very sorry to have been delayed," she said, her words rushed. "I was asked to do several tasks, and everything seemed to take forever. I came as quickly as I could."

"I'm glad of it, mistress. And dinna worry about yer letter. I'm sending it north with John Comyn. He assures me it will be delivered to your cousin in Berwick."

"Even better news," she said. "You here and my letter on its way."

"A cousin in Berwick, demoiselle?" de Boyer said. "One of your father's relations?"

She gave de Boyer a wary glance. "Yes," she said, then turned back to Rory. "You do remember Sir Henry de Boyer, sir?"

"No," Rory said. "Nice to meet ye, de Boyer."

Henry de Boyer nodded. "We met at the palace, Mac-Gannon. I would have thought you on your way north already. Scotland is very far from London."

"I'm staying all winter."

Isabel's smile was delighted. "Oh, wonderful! Henry, is that not lovely?"

"Yes, Henry," Rory said. "Are ye not surprised?"

De Boyer's smile was slow and appraising. "I admit I am. Why do you stay, MacGannon? Does John Comyn always keep his lackeys here in London?"

"I dinna ken. I'll ask him. I am here to see the sights, sir. And are they not grand?" He smiled at Isabel. "I dinna ken ye still would have duties."

"I do, which is very surprising. I thought I'd be dismissed."

"Speaking of dismissing . . . de Boyer, d'ye mean to spend the afternoon with us? I am delighted, of course, if ye are. Nothing would please me more than to spend my time with ye, sir. But I am surprised that ye keep seeking me out."

De Boyer laughed. "I assure you, sir, that it is not your

company I seek. No, I have an appointment elsewhere. Demoiselle, I will meet you here for your return as we agreed." He met Rory's gaze. "We see each other daily, of course, living as we do so close together at court."

"Do ye now?"

"We do." De Boyer bowed over Isabel's hand. "Until later."

She smiled. "Enjoy your tryst, sir."

De Boyer looked startled, then smiled. "Enjoy your walk, demoiselle."

"I am sure I will."

They stood together, Rory and Isabel, watching de Boyer walk briskly away. Rory wondered briefly if Isabel was using him to make de Boyer jealous. And how he could make the most of that. He turned to her with another smile.

"Good to see ye, lass. I was afraid ye'd been warned away from me."

"We made a bargain, sir, and I always keep my word."

"Do ye? Good to ken that. Ye look bonnie..I like yer hair loose like that."

"Thank you, sir. Now, tell me, why will you stay in London?"

"I'm being hunted in Scotland and am here for my health."

"I do not understand."

"Nor do I, to tell ye the truth. But tell me, lass, how is it Henry de Boyer appears every time I see ye? Ye seem to be well acquainted."

"Henry is one of the king's household knights, and I was one of the queen's ladies. There is nothing more between us."

"Ah. I'm glad of it. But he is escorting ye back to Westminster."

"There is nothing to that, sir. We were on the same boat coming here and he asked me what time I would be returning."

"And is he truly off to a tryst? Do the two of ye talk of such things?"

Her laugh was brittle. "It was my poor attempt at wit, sir. I have no idea of his plans, nor who he is meeting."

Rory nodded but was not convinced. He'd seen the looks thrown between the two of them, seen the surprise on de Boyer's face at her remark, the caustic note in her voice. There was something between them, perhaps something unrealized, but still there.

"Tell me," he said, "how can ye still have duties if the queen is dead?"

"I've been asked to do small things. To start packing her clothing. It won't last. One day I'll be told my services are no longer needed."

"And ye'll go home to yer family?"

"My family is here, my mother, and my grandmother."

"And yer father?"

"Dead. And you?"

"One brother, many cousins, of which Kieran is one. Two parents, two aunts, two uncles. That is my family. So what will ye do, when yer services are no longer needed?"

"I have no idea. Where shall we walk, sir?"

He smiled at her. "Ye ken the city and I'm the stranger. What should I see?"

"What have you seen already?"

"We were at Westminster Abbey for the funeral, as

ye ken. And we were at the funeral banquet afterward."

"Were you? I didn't see you there."

"Why would ye? Ye were dining with the king's party and we were among the invisible Scots."

"I'm still surprised I did not see you. You are . . . notable, sir."

"Am I? Trust me, lass, I am of no significance here in London."

"Nor I." She shivered at a sudden blast of wind. "Now, where shall we go?"

"Somewhere within walls? Could ye show me the Tower, at least from the outside? Then we'll find somewhere warm."

"Oh!" She seemed to consider something, then nodded. "Of course. But we'll go into the grounds. I'll be pleased to show it to you."

She led the way up the slight hill from the water, then along a narrow and cramped street, keeping under the shelter of the houses that leaned toward each other from either side, lifting her skirts high to step over a suspiciously colored puddle. He enjoyed the view of her leg above the short leather boots she wore, then took her arm to pull her against the wall while a cart laden with fish rumbled past them. He enjoyed the feel of her next to him. He looked down at her, at the curves of her body, soft and desirable. No wonder de Boyer was attentive.

"How is it," he asked, "that ye and Rachel Angenhoff are friends?"

"Her family lived near my grandmother. We met as small girls and played together, and we continued to be friends as we grew. What did she tell you?"

"The same thing. And that she had to leave London suddenly. They were expelled, aye?"

"Yes." Her face flushed with color. "How horrid is that, that they were driven from London because they are Jews! I was going to ask the queen for her help in rescinding the expulsion, but, of course, I cannot now."

"Probably wise that ye dinna, and I wouldna put it to the king, were I ye."

"No. Nor will I have the chance."

"I'll probably see him before ye do."

"Why, sir? Are you acquainted?"

"No. But I think yer king wants my country and I think he means to have it."

"Surely he simply means to help you find a king. And why is it that your people have not been able to do that?"

"We have two factions and everyone has chosen sides and willna relent. Neither side is willing to let the other rule, and can ye blame them? There's a throne at stake, and a great deal of money and power. And that's why yer king is 'helping.' He's put his own name on the list of Competitors, has he not? If he thought the Scots would accept him, he'd be ruling us now."

"Would that not at least bring peace to your country? I mean no insult, sir, but would it not be better for all if our countries were united?"

"Let me ask ye this, lass? What would happen to yer friend if England and Scotland were united? Would she and her family then be driven from Scotland as well?"

"I don't know," she said hesitantly. "But, sir, may I remind you that King Edward generally gets what he goes after?"

"Aye. Ask the Welsh, right?"

She nodded. They talked then of their families, of the differences between Scotland and London. She told him of her grandmother's illegitimacy, and of the lady-in-waiting named Alis, who had betrayed her trust. And her fears for the future, that she and her mother might be turned out into the street.

"For what need does a king have of a queen's lady or a queen's seamstress if there is no queen?" she asked.

"Now," he said. "Perhaps, King Edward is planning to marry again and he wants all of ye to stay to attend his new queen."

Her eyes widened. "Oh, no! Surely he won't remarry! I may despise what the king did, but he was devoted to Eleanor, and to his daughters. And he has a son and heir. He does not need to remarry. How could he? They were married for thirty-six years. He loved her. And she was devoted to him. You've heard the story of how she saved his life in the Holy Land?"

"No." Rory looked over her shoulder. Had he not seen that same man at the dock earlier? The man was of middle height, middle weight, and middle age. Rory almost laughed at himself, but what better person to spy on another than a man easily lost in a crowd? He would look for the man again later, he thought, and turned his attention to Isabel once again, enjoying her bright eyes and lively tone.

"It's such an amazing story! King Edward was struck by a poisoned arrow and he was dying. No one knew what to do, but Eleanor pulled the arrow out of him and sucked the poison from the wound and saved his life! Is that not the most romantic story?"

"Ye think it romantic when a woman sucks the poison out of a man? So would most men."

She took two steps, then stopped and faced him, her cheeks scarlet.

He felt coarse. "I'm sorry. That wasna a proper thing to say. I dinna mean to offend ye."

"I'm . . . I'm not offended. I've been at court all my life. There is not much that can be said that I've not heard."

"I'll wager ye're wrong, mistress. We men are base creatures."

"Not all, certainly."

"Most. But probably not yer Sir Henry."

"He is not my Sir Henry. If he belongs to anyone, it is Alis de Braun."

"The lady-in-waiting who betrayed yer trust?"

She nodded.

"Ah, so that was it then, she and he . . . I take it then that I am to be the instrument to bring his attention back to ye?"

"I never had his attention."

"But ye wanted it."

"I . . . admit I found him handsome at first. And charming. But . . ."

Her gaze went to his mouth, and he felt his body respond. God's blood she was beautiful. Her smile was admiring, and his body stirred again.

"I have discovered that there are men whose charms are equal to Sir Henry's. Or far exceed them. I would not use you as an instrument, sir."

"Not even if I begged?"

She laughed. "It depends upon how prettily you beg, I think."

"That could be difficult. We speak what we mean in the Highlands and not in riddles, nor with pretty language."

"You could put it in a poem perhaps."

"Me? Write a poem? Like one of the king's courtiers? Is that what they do all day, write poems and sing bawdy songs?"

She laughed again. "No, sir, it is far more serious than that. You forgot the scheming to get in the king's good graces and to eclipse all the others trying to do the same. Some, of course, do weightier things, like create songs or write poems or make up riddles for us to solve."

"And here I thought I understood courtly love."

"Courtly love is completely different. No one is scheming there."

"Ah, then I am mistaken. I thought courtly love was when a man wrote a poem to a woman he pretended to love but could never attain because she was wed to another."

"You are somewhat correct."

"So he's lying to get her to lay with him, aye?" he asked, keeping his tone light. "Or at least give him her kerchief, if not her body, depending on how good his poem is, aye? So he's scheming. And she's flirting and throwing her kerchief—or herself—on the floor. Or asking him to wear her color in a tournament, for her own reasons, which are female and therefore unfathomable to me. So she's scheming as well. And that's what ye all do all day."

"It sounds so sordid when you put it that way. It's not all like that, though some of that does exist. But what is wrong with a love poem?"

"It should be real. It should be a song of love, not artifice."

Her gaze drifted across his face, dropped to his shoulders, as though measuring their width, then returned to his eyes. "Would yours be, Mr. MacGannon?"

"Rory," he said, wanting to hear her say it.

"Rory, then. So your poem of love would be genuine?"

"I would not tell a lass I loved her if I dinna."

"Have you ever written a love poem?"

"No, and I dinna think I could. But if I were to, it would praise the beauty of her gray eyes, and talk of her lovely brown hair and the graceful way she moved through London's streets, and I would tell her that meeting her had been something I wouldna ever forget."

He met her gaze and smiled, watching the color mount in her cheeks.

"Do you fall in love often?"

"I've yet to. But I'm starting to think it might be enjoyable."

Her smile was embarrassed, but pleased. They walked in silence past another few houses, then she slanted a glance at him.

"So, if not a poem, do you tell riddles?" she asked. "I am fond of riddles."

"Are ye now? Then I have one for ye." He faced her and took a step forward.

She took a half-step backward and hit the wall of a house. "I'm ready."

"Oh, aye, ye are, lass. So, here it is. When is a thief not a thief?" He put a hand against the wall to her right, then did the same to her left.

"Are you confining me?"

"Och, no, lass. A woman's confinement is not a result of blocking her way."

"No," she said, her eyes merry. "It is the result of giving a man his way with her. I could scream and accuse you of attacking me."

"And watch while yer English guards skewer me?"

"And watch while the guards skewer you."

"But ye willna, will ye, lass?"

"And pray, sir, why should I not?"

"Because ye're dying to hear the answer to the riddle."

She sighed heavily, as though infinitely bored. "Then tell me, sir."

He leaned low over her, watching her breasts rise and fall. "A thief is not a thief when what he steals is freely given." He took his hand from the stone and trailed his fingers along her jawline, raising her chin higher, leaning even closer.

"And what is it you want to be freely given to you, my lord MacGannon?"

"A kiss, my lady." He rubbed two fingers across her cheek. "One kiss."

"No."

He sighed, glanced up as though pondering, then nodded quickly, returning his gaze to hers. "Aye. Ye're right. One is not enough. Three, then, at least. Or more, if ye insist. But I think three is good for the first time, aye?"

She shook her head. "None, sir, although I do admire your persistence."

"It's a beginning. And remember, we are at court. Which means we are required to engage in courtly love."

"We are not at court, sir."

"And may God be blessed for that. But England has been full of Normans and their Norman customs for two hundred years. And, of course, we also must do what God instructs us."

"God did not instruct us to engage in courtly love," she said tartly.

"But He did, madam. He told Moses to tell us to love our neighbors. Scotland and England are neighbors, lass. I am merely trying to follow God's laws."

She covered her laugh with her hand. "That's a blasphemous argument!"

"And amusing, apparently." He leaned low again, his mouth an inch from her throat. "But more importantly, is it a successful argument?" He took a long, deep breath, letting her scent fill his senses, letting his gaze drift from her white throat to the tops of her breasts, pressing now against her bodice. He watched, unable to look away, as her breasts rose and fell, then again. And then he kissed her.

She was sweet, her lips soft and welcoming. She opened to him and he leaned closer, feeling her breasts against his chest, her thighs along his, and her breaths matching his, their bodies moving in rhythm. And then she pulled away from him, covering her mouth with her hand and blushing prettily.

"I am not a wanton, sir," she said, hearing the catch in her voice.

He stepped back, letting his hands fall to his sides. "No. Nor did I think ye one, lass. It was but a kiss, and I a thief who could not resist ye. Ye are beautiful, Isabel, and I admire ye. And now, lass, another kiss?"

She shook her head. "No more."

"What, ever? Why not say no more kisses today, Rory, and leave the future to sort itself out?"

"No more kisses today," she said, but she smiled.

"I am bereft, but consoled by the promise of it in the future." He grinned at her and she laughed. "Ye're safe, demoiselle. I shall work on a new riddle." He looked around him for a few steps, then at her. "D'ye believe that story, of Eleanor saving the King's life?"

"Why would I not?"

"Well, let's look at it. Where was Edward wounded? On the battlefield?"

"I suppose so."

"And was Eleanor on the battlefield with him?"

"Most likely not."

"Ah. So Edward's men brought him off the field—to their tent, let's say—and she tended him there?"

"Perhaps," she said.

"But that would take some time. The poison would have begun to work. Edward looks none the worse for his wound. And Eleanor is dead."

"Edward has had many years to recover. And Eleanor bore sixteen children. Her body simply was worn out."

"Ah," he said, trying to ignore the image of lovers that came to mind.

"I believe the story," she said. "I think their love was that strong, that she risked death to keep him alive, and you scoffing at it will not change my mind."

She pointed at the church next to them. "That is All Hallow's. No one can say when it was first built, but there are Roman tiles in its floor. It is here that some prisoners are executed at the crest of this hill. And there, below us, is the Tower."

He looked at the church, then followed her gaze to the immense walls of the fortress called simply the Tower, which was surrounded by a moat linked to the River Thames. Above the walls, the large and impressive White Tower rose high to dominate the skyline. And ahead of them, built of heavy gray stone, lay the Lion Tower, the formidable entrance to the fortress. She moved toward it and he followed, throwing a glance over his shoulder. No man of middle height crossed the empty space behind them.

"William the Conqueror built The White Tower," she said, "after defeating Harold the Saxon at Hastings, in 1066, over two hundred years ago."

"Were yer people in England then?"

"My mother's people came over with William. When William stayed, so did they. We've been in London ever since. King Edward's father, Henry III, enlarged and improved the Tower, which was not popular with those who lived on the land he confiscated. And King Edward has done the same, only tenfold, pushing the outer walls into the city, and building new towers and creating the new entrance."

She moved forward to speak to the guard at the first barrier, who greeted her by name. "My companion is Rory MacGannon, of Loch Gannon, in London for the queen's funeral. We have business within."

"Of course, Mistress de Burke. Mind your step, there's still ice from last night on the stones."

Isabel thanked the man, leading the way across the first drawbridge. "There, you can see where the land gate was. And this," she said as they entered the first structure, "is the Lion Tower."

He jumped as the air was suddenly filled with a sound

he'd never heard, as though she'd conjured demons from hell. He reached for the sword at his hip.

"Lions, sir," she said with a smile. "Have you not heard lions before?"

He smiled at her, feeling foolish as he took his hand from the hilt of his sword. The lions roared again. And he might do the same, imprisoned in these dank stones rather than roaming free in Africa. "Nay, but it's a sound I will remember. I'd heard the king had a menagerie."

"Not a large one now. He did have elephants once. They died, but the lions have thrived. They remind visitors that this is the home of the lion of England."

"Outside of England your Edward is often called a leopard."

She arched an eyebrow. "And within England he is called king."

He laughed, following her across another drawbridge and within the walls of the tower themselves. She showed him the palace that Edward had built overlooking the river, where she'd slept when she'd stayed here with the queen. And the water gate Edward had constructed, and the rest of it.

But he did not retain all her words. He was too busy watching her, enjoying the graceful way she moved, the way her eyes lit when she looked at him, the soft curve of her smile. He was not the only one to notice her, he saw, as the king's household knights greeted her, and even the guards smiled at her on this cold, wintry day. The sun had stayed with them, but it was dank and chill within the Tower walls.

"And that building?" he asked her as they made their way to leave.

"The Wardrobe Tower," she said, an odd note in her voice as she glanced up at it. "Come, it grows late."

"Isabel."

The voice came from above them, and she stopped moving at Rory's side, her expression suddenly wary. He looked up to see a man leaning through a window, watching them. He was richly dressed, the gold on his fingers and clothing visible even in the dim winter light. Isabel sucked in her breath.

"My lord bishop," she said, bowing. "I had heard you were in Greenwich."

"You heard incorrectly," he said. "Bring your friend up to see me."

"I'm so sorry, my lord, but we must hurry. I must have him at Westminster before dark, and we have little time."

"Who do you take him to see at Westminster, Isabel?"

Rory put a hand on Isabel's arm. "Who is it who's asking, sir?"

"Your friend is a Scot, Isabel. Who do you take him to see at Westminster?"

"Bishop Bek, my lord," she said, naming the first powerful man she could think of.

"Are the Scots wooing Bek now, my dear?"

"This Scot prefers to woo women, sir," Rory answered.

The man's smile was not amused. "Bring him up, Isabel."

"I thank ye for the invitation," Rory said, then lowered his voice. "Do ye wish to see him, lass? I'll go if ye wish it."

"Oh, no! Please, let us leave."

"Aye, then we will," Rory said quietly. "Farewell, sir,"

he called and hurried her forward. The man withdrew, slamming the window behind him.

"Hurry!" She turned to look at him, her face now pale and fearful. "We need to leave before he comes down to find us!"

"Lass? Who is he? Why does he frighten ye so much?"

"Please! Let us leave here and I will tell you."

Rory followed her, through the large gate, past Edward's palace and water gate and through the Byward Tower. This time the lions were silent as they passed through that tower, and Rory was grateful for it. She hurried him across the drawbridge and through the first gatehouse. He let her lead them past All Hallow's Church and around the corner before he stopped her, grabbing her arm and turning her to face him.

"Far enough. Who is the man and why are ye so afraid of him?"

"He is Walter Langton, Bishop of Lichfield, Steward of the Wardrobe."

"He terrifies ye. Why?"

She looked close to tears. "He . . . he looks at me . . . he says things that make me . . . feel . . . soiled."

"Has he harmed ye? Has he touched ye?"

"No. But I fear . . . if I were to be close to him . . . I fear him."

"Can ye tell no one of this?"

"Who? He is among the king's closest advisors. I am alone in this."

He did not think then but pulled her into his arms, ignoring the glances and smiles of those who passed them. "No, ye're not, lass. Say the word and I swear I will protect ye."

She stayed in the circle of his arms, resting her forehead on his chest for the briefest of moments. Then she pulled away, smiling sheepishly. "I am fine. Thank you."

He held her gaze. "Are ye sure? Swear to me that ye'll not go there again."

"I won't. If I have a choice, I won't. I did not think he was there or I never would have gone." She shivered and moved away from him.

He let his arms drop and took a deep breath. "God's blood, but it's cold out here. Let's find a warm spot."

"I must go," she said, glancing up at the sky. "I must go."

He saw her to the boat to Westminster, where Henry de Boyer leaned against a building, waiting for her. De Boyer moved forward, offering her his arm.

"I will take her from you, MacGannon. Come, Isabel, let's go home."

She nodded. "Thank you again, Rory, for taking my letter. I am most grateful."

"My pleasure, lass. I'll be thinking of a new riddle."

Her smile was wan, and she let de Boyer walk her away and hand her into the boat. Before following her, de Boyer threw Rory a look of triumph and hurried to her side. She waved but soon was gone.

As rain darkened the sky, Rory walked back to his lodgings, his mood matching the weather. They'd made no plans to meet again. And a man of middle height surreptitiously followed him. He swore again and kept his hand on his sword hilt until he was within walls.

EIGHT

Isabel did not sleep well, troubled by dreams in which Walter Langton leaned over her bed, reaching for her, his smile full of promise of things to come. She woke twice, to stare into the dark, trying to dispel her nightmare. And a third time, in the wee hours, when the rain pounded on the roof and Alis was slipping into bed, letting icy air in as she raised the covers.

"Move over," Alis said, her voice thick, and a musty smell about her.

Isabel did not answer but moved closer to the other edge of the bed, where the sheets were cold. She knew where Alis had been and she hugged herself, forcing the images of Alis and Henry, intertwined and ardent, from her mind. At last she slept, to dream yet again, but this time of Rory MacGannon, naked, in her bed, his legs, long and lean, stretched atop hers. But no, her legs would be . . . she opened her eyes, astonished by her mind. Surely she was going to hell.

The day was no better than the night. She attended

mass with the others, shivering in the dank chapel. With the queen gone, their household rations of wood had been drastically reduced, leaving their rooms chill and damp. An omen for the future, Isabel thought, for why would the queen's ladies be kept on when there was no queen to serve? She was sent on numerous small errands, from the laundry to the kitchens, feeling as though she was now no more than the lowest servant.

In the afternoon it snowed, and she stood on the porch with Lady Dickleburough for a moment, watching the flakes descend, at first just a dusting, then with a fury that drove them inside. There she learned that the king would spend the Yule in Norham on Tweed, at the castle of Anthony Bek, the bishop of Durham, who had left London three days earlier. Which meant Rory MacGannon could not have been hurrying to meet him. And no doubt Walter Langton would discover the same. She told herself Langton would not remember, that although she remembered his every action clearly, he was an important man who had no doubt already forgotten her words. She also learned that all the queen's ladies would accompany the king north for the Yuletide. She sighed, thinking of the return to London with the queen's body, and the snow now falling outside.

That evening she went to tell her mother that she would be leaving for Durham. Her mother opened the door at Isabel's knock, pulled her inside the room, her eyes blazing. And slapped her face twice.

"You fool! I warned you! I told you! And what did you do?"

Isabel put her hand to her stinging cheek. "What have I done, Mother?"

"You know what you've done! The whole palace knows what you are!"

Isabel fought her anger. "And what am I, Mother? What is it that you've heard? And how is that you would believe the worst of me?"

"You spent yesterday afternoon with a man."

"Yes. I walked with Rory MacGannon, one of the Scots who brought me Rachel's message. I told you of them. He is taking my letter to Rachel."

"You told me you gave him your letter at your grandmother's. Why did you see him again?"

"Because he would take no money for the messenger he would give it to. He asked me to show him the Tower, Mother, and I did. We were never alone. And nothing happened!"

"You were seen in his embrace in the City."

Isabel blanched, remembering Rory pulling her into his arms to comfort her. "Briefly," she said. "I was cold. It meant nothing."

"Tell me you are not his whore!"

"What is the matter with you, Mother? I am no man's whore!" ·

"You told the world you find Henry de Boyer handsome."

"And I do. He is handsome."

"I hear he has a woman, that she sneaks out of the palace in the night to go to him."

"It's Alis, Mother!" Isabel rubbed her cheek. "Who is telling you all this?"

Mother's fury faded. She sank to sit on her bed. "Does it matter?"

"Yes! Whoever it is, is lying! I walked with Rory,

nothing more. Why would you believe lies about me?"

"I . . . I worry so, Isabel. You must be wiser than I was."

"You have told me that my whole life. I listened." Isabel hugged her arms to herself, miserable.

"I am sorry, child. But when I heard, I was so angry that you had not listened to me."

"I remember everything you've told me, Mother. I always have."

"Then how could you let this Scot touch you?"

"He was comforting me. I was frightened." She told her mother the whole story then, of her first visit to Walter Langton's offices, and what had happened the day before. "He terrifies me, Mother. The way he looks at me is . . . it makes me feel . . . I now believe all the stories I've heard of him."

"You should be terrified if he has noticed you. He is a powerful man, Isabel. You have no weapons to fight him."

"I will not go to the Tower again. And I will avoid him when we are at court. He will not do anything there. I will be very careful. And now I know what he is."

"Yes." Mother came to her and pulled her into an embrace. "You poor child."

Isabel stood stiffly in her arms for a moment, then relented and hugged her mother. "I did nothing wrong, Mother. You must believe that."

"I do. And I am sorry, child. I need to trust you to be sensible."

"Yes." Isabel nodded, then told her mother about the journey north. "I will not be here for Yuletide, Mother. And I am so sorry to have to miss celebrating it with you and Grandmother."

Her mother nodded. "Yes. It will be lonely without

Rivals for the Crown

you. But you must remember, on this journey, there will be men . . ."

Isabel let the words flow over her.

The next few days were full of preparations for the journey north. Isabel and Alis worked in companionable silence for the most part, but Lady Dickleburough seemed to have enough words for the three of them. Isabel was still wary of whoever it was who had carried tales to her mother, and she kept her thoughts to herself—what little time there was to think between Lady Dickleburough's outpourings.

At the midday meal, while most around them were quiet in recognition that the court was still in mourning, Lady Dickleburough was voluble. At first Isabel ignored her, paying attention instead to Henry, who today, of all days, sat near them. Far too near, for he and Alis were close enough to share glances. And once, a cup of wine. Isabel told herself she did not mind, but she could not look away from the two of them. She sipped one cup of wine, then another. And another, feeling herself relax.

"I've been told that the king is traveling north in case he is needed in Scotland," Lady Dickleburough said, when asked if she knew why the king would spend Yuletide at Durham Castle. "How tedious the Scots are. They cannot rule themselves. Never could. I don't know why King Edward doesn't simply take the cursed land and make it his own."

"As he did with Wales?" one of the ladies of the court asked, her words and tone reminding Isabel that she had Welsh relatives who had lost everything by resisting Edward's incursion.

"As he did with Wales," Lady Dickleburough said. "Think of all the masons and carpenters and stone carvers and haulers who have prospered. Your uncle has been there for years, has he not, Alis?"

"He has," Alis said.

"And no doubt earned much more money than he would have elsewhere. Everyone involved has. Traders have new ports to supply. All the new castles need fittings. It is a great boon for all of us. And Scotland could be the same. The Scots will thrive as well. And why, if they did not want King Edward's assistance, did they ask?"

"I'm told it was one man, Bishop Fraser, who wrote, asking the king's assistance," Isabel said. "And if Scotland is a cursed land, why would we want it?" She drained the last of her wine.

Lady Dickleburough gave Isabel a glance that clearly said she thought her an idiot. "Why would we not want Scotland? There is great wealth there. Berwick alone would be worth much to us. It is Scotland's busiest port— imagine the revenue it brings in. Many of our nobles own lands in Scotland as well as England, and most of their nobles own lands here. It would simplify things for everyone."

"I'm told parts of it are beautiful."

Lady Dickleburough shrugged. "The eastern half is arable, and there is much wealth there as a result. It is absurd that it is a separate country. We should rule the whole of the island."

"And perhaps Ireland as well," Isabel said. "We should make it a matched pair of islands. Isn't that what the king is trying to do? He's all but finished what Henry II began there. We could have both islands entirely to ourselves soon. Of course, the king would have to alter his crest. He's already called King of England, Lord of Ireland and Duke of Aquitaine. Why not Scotland as well? He could arrange everything to his tastes then, expel the Jews from every part of his kingdom and subdue all those who resist him. I think perhaps we could call him Potentate of Scotland. I quite like it. What do you think?"

The ladies laughed, but Henry gave Isabel a long, measuring look that made her pause. Isabel ignored him, looking instead at the dais, where King Edward sat with two of his favorites, John de Warenne and Robert Bruce.

"I wonder if Robert Bruce would agree with you, Lady Dickleburough," Isabel said, "for while his family has considerable holdings both here and in Scotland, his grandfather is one of the contenders for the Scottish throne. Of course, he stands to gain either way, does he not, for if his grandfather becomes Scotland's king, he will be in line for the throne. And if King Edward becomes king of Scotland, Robert might continue to be one of the king's favorites."

Lady Dickleburough nodded. "I've been told that the king has lent young Robert considerable coin to pay his debts. Robert would be wise to be loyal to the king, would he not? Or visit the same Italian moneylenders the king does now that he has expelled the Jews."

"Look," Henry said, pointing at the doorway. "The mummers have arrived."

The procession of the mummers through the hall distracted them from their conversation, their bright costumes and cheerful music drawing the attention of everyone in the hall. Isabel usually enjoyed their antics, finding the acrobatics, singing, and lively music a delight. But the mummers were muted this day, in recognition of the queen's passing, and she found it difficult to keep her gaze on them with Henry watching her so intently.

After the meal the court dispersed. Henry rose to his feet, as did the queen's ladies. Isabel sat where she was, not wanting to leave with Alis and Lady Dickleburough, content to be away from them for a time. The servants hurried to clear the tables, piling the soaked bread trenchers on boards to be carried outside and fed to the poor. The minstrels put their instruments aside and were finally able to eat themselves, and underfoot the dogs scrambled for the last of the scraps. Isabel turned her back to the others and watched a group of lords talk among themselves, their expressions serious. Which meant, she told herself, that the topic was some weighty matter of politics. Or money.

Henry's voice caught her off guard.

"Have a care, my lady," he said. "Heads have rolled for less."

She looked up into his eyes, his handsome face serious as he took a seat next to her. He glanced around them, then leaned close.

"Your words about what the king would call himself if he ruled Scotland."

"It was merely a jest, sir. No harm was meant by it."

"Only the king makes jests at Edward's court. I would have you remember that. And to imbibe less. Remember that next time, Isabel."

"I will, but surely—"

He put a finger to her lips. "Edward is not a happy man just now. Do not let his wrath fall upon you." He let his finger fall to her chin and stroked a line along her jawline. "Keep yourself safe, Isabel. I would see you more cautious. Those were foolish words and, if repeated, could be dangerous."

"I will be more careful in the future."

"Good." He let his hand drop and rose to his feet. He strode away without looking back.

She watched him until he was out of sight.

Rory had sent word to Isabel twice, with no reply. He went to Westminster twice, attempting to see her, but both times was told she was unavailable. The king was leaving soon, he knew, to travel to Norham for the Christmas festivities, muted though they would be this year. Edward would stay at the castle of Anthony Bek, the bishop of Durham, the man Isabel had told Langton he was going to see in Westminster. Norham was not far from Newcastle-Upon-Tyne, the largest city in the far north of England, conveniently close to the Scottish border.

He and Kieran had talked on what was best to do, whether it would be wiser to travel north as well, or to stay in London. There would be little to learn here while the king was gone, but certainly neither he nor Kieran would gain admittance to the bishop of Durham's castle, and lingering overlong in the nearby villages would bring unwanted attention to them. They concluded that the best thing to do was to go home, or at least to Stirling.

He'd done some investigating about Walter Langton and did not like any of what he'd discovered. The man might be a bishop, but he was far from a man of God. Wealthy, arrogant, rumored to have at least one mistress and a penchant for deflowering young and often unwilling women, Langton would be formidable enough without the armor of being the Steward of the Wardrobe. Langton was the man who oversaw the royal households, including the wages and living quarters of the queen's ladies. And he oversaw the king's wars and weapons and knights, of which Henry de Boyer was one. A powerful man. Little wonder Isabel feared him. He worried that she'd paid a price for lying to Langton, for he knew the man had plans for Isabel. And he was curious about Henry de Boyer. He'd asked about the man, but had been told little interesting information.

He also worried that Isabel would leave with the royal entourage without him having a chance to see her again. Kieran was out somewhere, pretending to be playing dice and drinking with young nobles, but actually gathering the latest news. Rory ate his midday meal, then made up his mind.

He was surprised when Isabel's grandmother received him, and even more surprised by how warmly she did so, inviting him to join her before the fire and offering him ale or mead. He took the ale and let her drink the honey mead that had always cloyed in his throat. She sipped the sticky liquid, then nodded at him.

"I thought you might come, sir," she said.

"Did ye, madam? I dinna ken it myself."

"Ah, but I am that much older than you. You have been a young man for only a few years. I have been watching them for decades. You are fond of my Isabel."

"I am, madam, and a bit worried as well. I've sent word and been to Westminster twice, but I've not been allowed to see her. Have ye talked with her?"

"She was here just yesterday."

"Oh." He sipped his ale, wondering how quickly he could leave.

"Someone carried the tale to her mother that Isabel let you embrace her."

"There was nothing wrong in it. Isabel was cold."

"She was frightened. She told me the whole story about Langton, and your afternoon." She sipped her mead. "I agree, I see nothing wrong with it."

"The mead, madam? Or my afternoon with Isabel?"

She laughed. "Both. Neither. Isabel's mother is wary of men. She has tried to fill Isabel with distrust of all men. I have tried to insert a measure of sense into it. There are men—and Walter Langton is one of them—of whom a woman should be wary. But there are others—and her grandfather was one of them—who can be not only trusted, but loved. I want my Isabel to find a man who will care for her as I was cared for. I know you are not here to propose marriage, but that you are here at all shows me you are not easily dissuaded from seeing her."

"But she has refused to see me."

"I do not think so. I think orders have been given to refuse you admittance. You do know Sir Henry de Boyer, sir?" At his nod she continued. "He has been making inquiries about you. He told Isabel that you murdered a man in Scotland and ran to London in fear of your life."

"I did kill a man, and there are those trying to harm me for it. But, madam, I dinna regret it." He told her the truth of the tale.

She listened without interruption, then nodded. "I do not think Isabel knew you were there, nor do I think she believed the worst of you. She complained to me that you had not called upon her again."

"I have been twice. How do I get word to her?"

"You don't." Isabel's grandmother took another sip of

mead, then wiped her mouth slowly with a handkerchief. "I do. Be here tomorrow at the same time, sir."

He grinned at her. "I will be here, madam!"

And he was, flowers from Spain in his hand, bought at great expense, for Isabel, and two bottles of the finest mead he could find for her grandmother. He brought almonds, and oranges shipped from Italy. He'd taken extra care with his clothing, brushed his hair until it flew about his head, scrubbed his teeth with salt, then shaved carefully.

He hurried around the corner next to her grandmother's home, in time to see a coach pull up before the house. Henry de Boyer leapt from the carriage, reaching up a hand to assist Isabel, the knight's cloak flying about him in the brisk wind. Isabel, her hand clasped in de Boyer's, climbed from the carriage. She smiled up at him, then laughed as the wind tossed her hair before her eyes. De Boyer gently helped her push the hair back from her face and said something that made her smile again. As they entered the building a church tolled the hour.

Rory stood there for a moment, debating whether to follow or leave, and wondering if her grandmother had arranged this. Then he squared his shoulders and crossed the muddy street. He might not wear the uniform of the king's own, might not be wealthy enough to bring her here in a carriage. And he might be nothing more than a younger son with little to his name, but he'd be damned if he would surrender the field without a fight.

"Almonds, and oranges too! Sir, what a treat!" Isabel's smile was bright as she placed Rory's gifts on the table. "And flowers in December, sir. You are extravagant and too generous!"

Rory grinned at her and bowed, delighted with her response. "Your smile far outshines my paltry offerings, demoiselle."

De Boyer groaned aloud, and Rory laughed. The knight had been polite enough when Rory had joined them on the stairs, but his courtesy had not hidden his displeasure at Rory's sudden appearance. Isabel's grandmother's surprise at seeing de Boyer had seemed genuine. When she said she'd not expected Isabel to be accompanied, de Boyer bowed low.

"How could I let such a young girl ride the riverboat on a December day?"

"She comes often to see me, sir," Isabel's grandmother said. "You will soon empty your purse of coin if you insist upon driving her each time."

"What better purpose could I have for it, madam?"

Rory groaned, and de Boyer laughed.

"By the time Isabel returns to London, madam," de Boyer said, "the weather may be milder and the boat trip more pleasant. Who knows how long we will be with the king in the north?"

Rory looked at Isabel. "You will accompany the king to Norham?"

"Yes," she said. "I'm told that all of the queen's ladies will go. We will stay as long as we are told."

"Do not worry for her safety, sir," de Boyer said. "I will be with her every step of the way, guarding her person closely."

"Will ye now?" Rory asked.

"Gentlemen," Isabel's grandmother interjected, "while my granddaughter has grown up with the court, she is not an experienced courtier. She will be keeping her own body safe."

Isabel's cheeks were scarlet. She picked up a piece of greenery from her grandmother's table.

"Well said, ma'am," de Boyer said. "And it will be my pleasure to guard that innocence."

"De Boyer," Rory said, "since ye've been learning so much about me, perhaps ye can tell me whether I'm going as well, or staying behind in London."

De Boyer's smile was more guarded this time. "You'll stay in London."

"Will I?" Rory asked. "Sorry, but ye're wrong. I'm thinking of riding north myself. Norham is almost to Scotland, is it not? I can assist ye in keeping Mistress de Burke safe."

"I welcome the help," de Boyer said. "You have a war-horse, MacGannon?"

"No."

"A squire?"

"I have a younger cousin, will he do?"

"Depends on how well he serves you."

"Then I'm lost."

"And armor?"

"Not with me. I thought I was attending a funeral, not a war."

"It's always wise to be well armed," de Boyer said.

"I quite agree," Rory said, nodding. "Some of us need warhorses and armor and squires. Some of us can survive simply on our own wits."

"Some can. May I suggest an armorer who can outfit you?"

Rory laughed and surprisingly, de Boyer did as well. "I will gladly take yer suggestion, sir. Ye've been in London much longer than I. No doubt ye've gained a great deal of experience in all yer years here."

"Four years is all. But you are correct, London is my home, and where I will reside when I marry."

"What? Still without a wife? Most men with your years have had five children by now. But then, it is not necessary to marry before producing children, is it, sir?"

De Boyer ignored the insinuation. "Had I a wife, I would not be here now."

"Are you seeking one?"

"I am content to guard the queen's ladies."

"So ye guard all the queen's ladies, do ye, not just demoiselle de Burke?"

"I do indeed."

"And you treat all alike, with the same attention paid to each?"

"Not at all. One could certainly not confuse demoiselle de Burke with Lady Dickleburough."

"I've not had the pleasure of meeting her."

"She is—how shall I say it?—quite unforgettable."

"As is demoiselle de Burke. And, I hear, demoiselle de Braun. Perhaps that quality is a requirement to become a queen's lady?"

"Gentlemen, enough!" Isabel's grandmother gestured for them to sit. "I have a large fire already. I do not need it any warmer in this chamber. Isabel, bring those almonds and oranges over here. They will distract us from the sparring. Now, sirs, tell me about your mothers."

Rory and de Boyer exchanged a glance.

"Our mothers, madam?" Rory asked.

"That is what I said."

"My mother," de Boyer said, "is gracious and kind. Her spirit is mild, yet she runs my father's household with ease."

"And you, Mister MacGannon?" Isabel's grandmother asked.

"My mother is courageous and loving. She runs her household with much laughter and allows my father to live there as well."

Isabel's grandmother nodded at Rory, her eyes shining. "You play the game well, young master MacGannon. Now, gentlemen, tell me about your fathers."

"My father is bold and fair to his people," de Boyer said.

"My father," Rory said, looking at Isabel, "is devoted to my mother."

"As is mine," de Boyer said.

"My father is a warrior," Rory answered.

"And mine—"

"Cease!" Isabel's grandmother laughed. "Thank you both for playing my game. Isabel, sweet, bring me some of that wonderful mead that Mister MacGannon brought to me. It is a wise man, Rory MacGannon, who remembers a girl's grandmother."

"And it is a wise grandmother, madam, who remembers the man who remembered the grandmother."

Isabel's grandmother laughed again. "You may rest assured, I will."

"What is it you're making, demoiselle?" De Boyer moved next to Isabel. He smiled down at her. "A wreath, perhaps?"

Rory gave him a sharp glance, then looked at Isabel. She was still holding the greenery she had taken from the table. She smiled at de Boyer and held up a circle made of thin pine branches.

"I was simply keeping my hands busy. It's a crown, I think." She leaned forward and placed it on de Boyer's head. "There! You look like a king! Very regal!"

"It's fortunate that it's made of pine, de Boyer, rather than holly," Rory said.

De Boyer met his gaze with a slow smile. "But at mid-summer I would be glad of it, would I not?"

Isabel looked from one to the other. "I don't understand."

"I do," her grandmother said. "They are both Celts, Isabel. One from France, one from Scotland, but united by a common bond. Do you not know the story of the Oak King and the Holly King?"

"I remember something of it," Isabel said, "but not clearly."

"In olden times," her grandmother said, "before Christ, our people celebrated two kings, the Oak King and the Holly King. Midsummer and midwinter marked the two halves of the year, each a beginning and an ending. The Oak King, who ruled the time of growth and light, would battle the Holly King, who ruled the time of harvest and death. The outcome of the battles was always the same: at Midsummer the Holly King was victorious, symbolizing the end of the growing season. At Midwinter, the Oak King would win, symbolizing the return of growth in the spring. Have you never seen the Green Man in a church, with oak leaves growing out of him? It is a symbol that spring will come and life will return to the world."

Isabel looked at Rory. "So you are the Oak King?"

Rory smiled. "Look at our coloring, lass. I am light. He is darkness."

De Boyer laughed and removed the crown from his head. "It is almost Midwinter, Oak King. I give you your crown rather than do battle with you."

Rory stood, rooted to the floor, unwilling to take the crown held out to him. He felt his skin rise, as though an unseen spirit had joined them, a whisper of premonition. "Ye do ken the rest, de Boyer?"

"Do you believe all that, MacGannon? That I must die so you will live?"

Rory did not answer.

"What do you mean?" Isabel asked.

"We kill each other, demoiselle," de Boyer said lightly. "In summer the Holly King slays the Oak King. At Midwinter, the Holly King dies."

"It is the rhythm of the year," Rory said. "In ancient times, I've heard it said, a king ruled for just one season, then was sacrificed for the good of his people. His blood fertilized the ground and his death ensured that they would live."

"Surely that is symbolic and not real?"

"If it were real," Rory said, "who would wish to be king?"

"He who would possess the world, if only for a season," de Boyer said, holding out the crown. "Here, MacGannon. If I am the Holly King, then my time is almost at its end and your time not yet come. Take the crown, sir."

"And all that goes with it?" Rory asked.

De Boyer's smile was slow and confident. "I have no doubt that our battles are far from over, nor that death always wins. The sun may shine for a season, but darkness comes every night and rules half the year."

Rory's answering smile was wide. "As does the light. I will take the crown, Holly King, and keep it for the day when the battles are over and the light has won the prize." He took the crown but did not put it on. He met de Boyer's gaze, and in it saw not simply a spirit of competition but respect, which surprised him.

"Will you not wear the crown, Rory?" Isabel asked.

"When it is time," Rory said. "When it is time."

Isabel's grandmother rose to her feet and let them know by her manner that the visit was over.

"I thank you both for your attendance upon my granddaughter. She is my treasure and my hope is that the man she marries treasures her as well. No, say nothing. This is my house. I have the last word. Go with God, sirs. Isabel, a word alone before you leave."

She gestured the men out and they left together, waiting outside for Isabel.

"There is no need for you to stay, MacGannon," de Boyer said. "I will see her safely home. And safely to Norham."

"Will Alis de Braun also be on the journey?"

"I believe she will."

Rory grinned at him. "Should be interesting for ye, then."

De Boyer nodded and held out a hand. "I expect so. I would invite you to join me for a cup of ale, sir, but I have Isabel to care for. When next you come to London, do come and visit us."

Isabel came through the door, and de Boyer waved the coach forward.

"Thank you, Rory," she said, "for the delightful gifts. We are most grateful. You are very kind."

Rory bowed. "My pleasure, demoiselle. I hope to see you before we all leave on our journey."

"I do hope so. But if not, I shall see you on the road." She smiled again.

"Farewell, sir," de Boyer said, opening the door of the coach as it stopped. He handed Isabel inside and extended his hand to Rory.

Rory took de Boyer's hand. "Not subtle. Nor, unfortunately, effective. Dinna think to start the game without me, sir."

De Boyer smiled. "The game is well begun, Oak King."

"That was meant as a warning."

"And taken as such. But I have the lady's company, as you can see."

He closed the door firmly. The coach lurched away.

Two days later Rory and Kieran were ready to leave London. They waited to follow the king north with hundreds of others—penitents, merchants, sycophants, and those simply trying to attach themselves to the royal party for safety. The king's entourage had taken over an hour to lumber out of the Aldgate on their way north. Rory and Kieran watched the king's knights parade past in three contingents—those forward; then the king himself and bands of courtiers, both on horseback and in coaches closed against the light snow that floated down upon them; then a second group of knights and another set of riders and coaches. Behind them was the baggage train and last, another group of knights. Finally, the waiting crowd was free to jostle their way through the gate.

"I dinna see her," Kieran said as they inched forward. "Did ye?"

Rory shook his head and pulled his hood forward. If it was snowing in London, what would they find farther north?

It was hours before the snow slowed enough for Rory to search among the travelers for Isabel. He found Henry de Boyer more than once as the knight rode alongside the entourage, but none of the queen's ladies. The next time he came along de Boyer, sitting astride his horse at the side of the road, watching the slow progress of the travelers, he stopped.

"MacGannon," de Boyer said, glancing up at the sky. "Looks like more foul weather ahead of us."

"De Boyer. How goes the nursemaiding?"

De Boyer grinned. "That's exactly what it feels like. It will be a long journey at this pace. We'll be fortunate to be in Norham by Candlemas, in February."

Rory laughed. "More time for ye to spend with the lasses, de Boyer. Where can I find Isabel?"

De Boyer gave him a sharp glance, then looked at the travelers. "I assume she's here, but I've not seen her today."

NINE

Isabel watched the snow blow off the porch of the church in whirling drifts, then started on her way home. She'd gone to light an advent candle as her grandmother had requested, and she'd lit another for herself. The day had been dreadful.

It had started so promisingly. The bustle and rush of the final preparations to travel north had taken hours. She had risen at dawn with the other queen's ladies, her leather satchel packed and placed with theirs to go in the baggage train, and she'd been waiting just inside the doors to hear whether they would ride in the small coaches or on horseback. She had chatted with the others, laughing about which was better, freezing to death outside or sitting atop each other in the cramped carriage. And then she and Lady Dickleburough had been called aside, but well within earshot of the others. The queen's household steward had told them that the two of them would stay behind while the rest of the royal party traveled north. The man had appeared a bit nervous as he'd imparted the change in plans but he'd provided no explanation.

She had endured the questions of the other ladies, had watched her satchel be pulled from the pile and placed alone near a wall, had seen the pitying glances the servants had thrown her way. But Alis's smug smile and gleeful whispers had pushed her beyond control. She'd run, like a small child, away from the palace, away from the excitement of the departure, and into the city. She'd wandered for a while through the small streets, looking at the shops and trying to match the cheerful mood of the Londoners as they'd slogged through the December cold. And then it had started to snow, and she'd made her way to her grandmother's house.

Grandmother had listened to her, sympathized, and fed her. And argued with her, begging Isabel not to return to the court.

"It could be dangerous," Grandmother had said.

Isabel had shaken her head. "Less so than before, Grandmother. Now I know where the dangers are. And who I am."

"But . . ."

Isabel interrupted. "I have no choice. I am contracted to serve the queen whether I accompany her or not. If I abandon my post, I can be thrown into jail. No, Grandmother, I will go back and be less of a fool than I was. I was left behind. It's not the worst that could happen."

Grandmother had nodded slowly. "I wish it were otherwise."

Isabel had given her a brave smile. "As I do."

Her grandmother sent her back to the palace with instructions to light an advent candle on the way home. Which she had done. But what now? None of it—not the long walk, not the church, not even Grandmother's kindness—had changed anything. She ached with the rejection. *Rachel,* she thought. *Where are you? You would understand. You would make me laugh.* But Rachel was so very far away, with worries of her own.

By now the royal party would be well away from the city. Alis would have already talked with Henry. And somewhere, not with the royal entourage itself, but nearby, with the hundreds who trailed the royal procession, Rory Mac-Gannon would be riding north with his cousin.

She walked quickly, pulling her cloak close to her body, glad of the fur lining and the thickness of the wool. She had been left behind. No matter, she told herself. She had been the last of the queen's ladies to be brought in and was the first to be left behind. There was no queen now; she had no official duties. She had no wealthy family nor husband to protect her, no ties of kinship to the king that had even been recognized. What had she expected? But . . . it hurt.

For a few months her future had seemed to be glittering. For a few months she had belonged with the shining people who made up the court instead of the invisible ones who watched them. For a few hours she had had two men dancing attendance on her. And then . . . but how could she complain, when she thought of those she passed sleeping in doorways or in crowded, unheated houses? Or Rachel, living in Berwick, instead of in her home here.

The guard at the palace let her through the gate without comment, and she was grateful to see her bag still waiting in the foyer. It looked forlorn and small against the high walls, as insignificant as she was, as unnoticeable as she herself must be to the nobles who had shared the same halls with her. She'd been a fool to think she could join them as an equal.

She picked up the bag and climbed the stairs, walked slowly through the corridors, and climbed again, and again, at last reaching the rooms the queen's ladies had shared. They were empty. Or so she thought at first. She tossed her bag on the floor and pulled off her cloak with a weary sigh.

"We are allowed to spend the night," Lady Dickleburough's voice came out of the dim doorway. "But in the morning we are to be out of these rooms. They will be closed, possibly forever. We have been dismissed entirely."

"And where are we to go?"

"'We'? 'We,' Isabel? You shunned me whenever possible. The only time you sought me out was when you needed information. 'We' are going nowhere. You will most probably go running to your mother. Who, by the way, came looking for you. I told her our happy news. I told her you had run away, probably to that Scotsman you've been with recently."

"I have not been 'with' him."

"Then you are truly a fool. He is young and virile and easy to gaze upon. You would do well to find him. He might feed you for a few months, before you bore him or he finds another more pleasing woman." She took two steps, then turned. "And the knight you long for, Isabel? Henry de Boyer? He is the father of the child carried by the girl you replaced. Had you not realized that by now? It is common knowledge in the court. We've all been wagering if you would become the next victim. Some say it will be Alis, but you and I know she is far too cunning to become his prey. I think it will be the reverse. Look at your face! You look as though I slapped you. How could you not know all this?" The older woman staggered away, her crackling laugh drifting back to Isabel.

She untied the sleeves of her bodice. Lady Dickleburough was quite correct. She was truly a fool.

The morning brought more snow, huge drifts of it that hid the shapes of buildings and blew across the open spaces around the palace, piling against the walls and gates. Isabel packed the last of her things in her leather satchel. The servants watched her with puzzled expressions, as though she were behaving strangely. Which no doubt she was, stopping as she did to wipe away her tears, or stand at the window and sigh, knowing she would never see this view again. She said nothing to them, not willing to face their sympathy, not able to answer if they asked why she had been let go. What could she say? She did not know what it was she had done to deserve disfavor, or how to rectify it.

She went to find her mother, only to discover that her mother was not at Westminster. She'd gone to Windsor. She'd been expected to return that day, but with this weather . . . , the woman said, spreading her hands wide. Isabel thanked her, then lifted her bag. She would go to Windsor and find her mother, and together they would plan the future. But not even that was possible, for the dock was empty and the ferryman gone; a man in the nearest tavern told her none of the boats would run this day. She had no way to get to Windsor, and her mother would have no way to return until the storm passed.

Isabel returned to the palace, mercifully unquestioned,

and spent the night alone in her mother's rooms, waking to brilliant sun and a world that was frigid but sparkling. She straightened the room and left, carrying her bag herself—a sign of how far her station had fallen—and paused at the outermost gate to look back.

A few more steps and she would be on the other side of the wall, never again to have entry to her former life. She swallowed, thinking of Alis, riding north with Henry, seeing him every day, having the moments with him Isabel would never have. Alis, she knew, would be quick to entertain him. And Rory MacGannon, who would attract his own retinue, she was sure. Both men, and Alis, going north. For months, perhaps.

She stepped forward, then again, walking through the gate with her head high and her step rapid. She might be dying inside, but no one needed to know that. This time the boats were running.

The trip down the river to Windsor was brutal. She arrived, half-frozen, only to discover that her mother had already returned to Westminster in a coach. The guard took pity on her and led her into the gatehouse, giving her a cup of warm wine and a spot by the fire. She waited as patiently as she could for the next westward boat, reminding herself that she was warm, and the boat would not be.

"Demoiselle," the guard said, leaning through the door. "I have secured a place in a coach going to Westminster for you. Come, please."

She thanked him and climbed into the sumptuous coach, wondering how much she would have to pay for the luxury of the ride. The door of the coach opened again, letting in a bright shaft of sun and a gust of wind carrying snow. She narrowed her eyes against the glare, seeing only the shape of a man lifting himself into the coach. He sat heavily on the seat opposite her, adjusting his cloak around him as the door was closed. The coach began to move at once, and as her eyes adjusted, she stared, her heart thudding, at the man who now smiled at her.

"Isabel. How lovely it is to find you now, with the king gone to the north." Walter Langton's smile grew wider. "Cold? Come, share my blanket."

"No," she whispered. "Thank you, my lord. I am fine here."

Langton leaned forward, bending down to touch something on the floor of the coach, then rising swiftly, his hand sliding up her leg beneath her skirts. She screamed and jumped away, but his hand followed her, rising to her thigh before she was able to squirm out of his grasp. He leaned back, laughing softly, then lunged forward, grabbed her wrists, and leaned forward, his eyes glinting.

His kiss was moist, fetid, and mercifully short. He withdrew, his lips still gleaming. He ran his tongue across them, and she shuddered.

"Isabel," he said softly. "Would you like your position restored? Would you like your wage portion to be increased? I alone can make both happen. You do not need to live on the street." He touched his lips and looked at hers. "You will come to me tomorrow at my office in the Wardrobe Tower. Just before midday."

"No."

He leaned forward as though to kiss her again, but instead his hand closed on her breast, then tightened. He thrust his mouth forward. She struck his face, then again. He caught her wrist, lowering her arm to her lap. His other hand went to her throat and squeezed. And then again, tightening his grasp until she could not breathe. Her vision darkened. She clawed at his hands and fought for breath, kicking at him and striking flesh. Then suddenly he released her and stared at her. Then slowly, deliberately, slapped both her cheeks. And again. And again. She screamed, but her throat could make no sound above a hoarse whisper.

"You are a madman," she said, fighting her tears. "You are mad."

"Tomorrow. Come alone. And do not think to evade me. I know where your mother is. I know where your grandmother lives. I will find you." He tucked his hands beneath the robe and smiled that repulsive smile again.

"What do you want with me?"

"Oh, please, do not play the innocent with me, madam. We both know you have been, how shall I put it, on the friendliest of terms with two men, Sir Henry de Boyer, and the Scotsman MacGannon, who you brought to the Tower to flaunt before me."

"No. I thought you were in Greenwich."

"Ah, so the truth at last. I have heard so much about you lately, my dear, that you are very sympathetic to our expelled Jews, so much so that you raised your voice in their defense at a meal at court. And that you ridiculed King Edward's actions in Ireland and Wales and Scotland. How angry he becomes when he hears of such disloyalty, such questioning of his motives and actions. It is almost as though you are speaking treason, is it not? And poor Edward, will he want to hear this, do you think, so shortly after putting his wife in the ground? And you, one of her own ladies. I do worry about you, Isabel, if he were to hear any of this. He is so short-tempered these days. Think of the betrayal he would feel, that a young woman his own departed Eleanor had trusted in her inner circle would, within a month of her death, mock her husband, and question such things as his expulsion of the Jews and his war in Wales. Alis de Braun says you frequently told her, in the queen's own chambers, that the king was cruel and heartless and unjust. And Lady Dickleburough tells me that you imitate the king to the queen's ladies, that they have asked you to stop, but you will not. You even suggest that he call himself 'Potentate of Scotland.' Now how, sweet Isabel, will you defend yourself when Edward asks you to explain?"

"I never meant—"

"It is not important what you meant. Nor what you said. Only what others will swear they overheard. You were unwise at the midday meal at court, Isabel. Many heard you, and some are willing to swear to it." He leaned forward to stroke her cheek. "I can make it all go away. I make all things possible. Come to me. Just before midday."

He settled back against the seat and closed his eyes. She calmed her breathing, ready to scream and kick if he touched her again, but he did not move. She would have thought he'd gone to sleep except for his hands, moving rhythmically beneath the robe. At last he groaned, bucked up from the seat, then sank back, opening his eyes and watching her. She felt her stomach heave and pressed as far back in the seat as she could. Could there be a man more foul?

The ride seemed interminable. She was determined to jump out as soon as the coach stopped, or even slowed. But when it did stop at last, the door was thrown open and she looked into the face of a Westminster Palace guard. Stifling her sob, she scrambled toward the door and reached for the guard's hand, letting him help her out.

"Tomorrow," Langton said languidly.

She stared, shivering, as the coach drove away.

"Are you all right, Mistress de Burke?" the guard asked, his tone kind.

"No." She knew she must look like a madwoman, but she shook her head. "No. No. No. I am not all right. I will never be all right again."

"You will not do it!" Mother's voice was shrill and rising. "You will not!"

Isabel wiped her eyes again. She'd managed not to cry as she'd made her way through the palace rooms, avoiding everyone who'd come near, refusing to meet anyone's eyes. But once within her mother's door, she'd burst into tears and poured out her story in a frenzy.

"I was so foolish, Mother! One meal, one time, I was foolish enough to say what I thought. They twisted everything I told them, Alis and Lady Dickleburough! They betrayed me!"

"You betrayed yourself, Isabel. I warned you not to trust anyone. I warned you that there would be men after you, but did you listen? No. You already knew everything, did you not? And now, you stupid chit, you have destroyed everything you were given. I will be tossed out into the street and we will starve together, if you are fortunate enough not to hang. I warned you about your friendship with Rachel! But you persisted. And this is the result, the destruction of everything we had hoped for. You have taken it all from us."

"The queen's death took it all from us, Mother. And I would never have been a queen's lady if not for Langton. It was all an illusion. What do you wish me to do now, Mother? Do you want me to go to him? Is that what you want, so all of this can continue to be yours?"

"I forbid it!" Mother cried. "You will not!"

Isabel burst into hysterical laughter. "I am not arguing with you, Mother! The man terrifies me. I will not go! I will kill myself first!"

Mother paced the room while Isabel cried. "We must think of something. First, we must get you out of here. Gather your things. You will go to your grandmother's. Hurry, Isabel. Hurry!"

"He said tomorrow, Mother."

"Do you want to risk him changing his mind?"

Grandmother's maid opened the door, her eyes widening when she saw Isabel's face. "Jesu, Mary and Joseph, Mistress Isabel, what happened?"

Isabel shook her head, unable to speak of it, and let the woman pull her through the door. Her grandmother cried out in dismay, then hurried her to a chair before the fire.

"Isabel? Sweet? Tell me what happened. Where is your mother?"

"She sent me to you," Isabel said, her tears falling again. "Oh, Grandmother! It was so horrid!"

She told her grandmother all of it, sobbing through the telling and unable to stop shivering. "There is something so dark, so foul about the man! As if—"

"He's said to be in league with the devil," Grandmother said. "Perhaps that's what you sensed. I've never met the man, but I have heard stories enough."

"I will not go to him! He is evil!"

Grandmother nodded. "That's what I've heard. Here, drink this."

Isabel drank the wine she was handed, sipping slowly, willing the warm liquid to calm her. Someone knocked on the door below, and Isabel leapt to her feet.

Grandmother waved her back from the window, peering out the tiny diamond-shaped panes at the street. "It is no one," she told Isabel and slipped out to the landing, where she spoke softly to her maid.

A moment later the door downstairs opened and closed, then Grandmother was back with her, handing her another cup of wine. Isabel could not stop her tears. How had her life changed so quickly? The second cup of wine calmed her considerably. She still cried constantly, but more than anything, she wanted to go to sleep. She nodded off, and when her grandmother suggested a nap in her bed, Isabel gratefully agreed.

She woke hours later to find Grandmother asleep in her chair and her maid stirring the fire back to life. It was dark, which meant she'd slept the afternoon away. And Mother was not here.

Nor did she come until very late that night, waking them with quiet knocks on the door. She embraced Grandmother and Isabel, then sank into a chair, accepting a cup of warm wine with grateful thanks.

"I have solved it," she said. "You are safe. No one will look for you now."

"He will find me," Isabel said. "He told me he knows where Grandmother lives. I will not go to him! I will kill myself first!"

"There is no need," Mother said. She sipped her

wine and looked into the fire. "You are already dead."

Isabel and Grandmother exchanged a look.

"That is what I told everyone, that you killed yourself after you were released from the queen's service. Everyone I told believed it. They talked of how distraught you were when you heard the news. Lady Dickleburough will gleefully spread the word everywhere. And except for Langton, who will question it?"

"But how? . . ." Isabel asked.

"There was an old woman pulled from the river this morning," Mother said wearily, sipping the wine before she continued. "No one knows who she was. I paid the man who found her . . . I had him bring the wrapped body to the palace, and I wept as though it were you. There was a bad moment when Lady Dickleburough wanted to see your face, but I wept like a madwoman and she backed away. She talked of how volatile you were, how unpredictable. There are a few servants who might not swallow this, but most will accept it, or know it for what it is and keep their silence." She sipped the wine, then looked up at Isabel. "What I want to know is what you did to get yourself dismissed."

"I do not know. I tried to be good." She thought how foolish she had been to trust Alis and Lady Dickleburough, of her careless words about the king and Scotland and Ireland, and she cursed herself. How had she been so unwise as to say all that in front of others? Henry had warned her.

"I was imprudent. I talked about the king's policies and I should not have."

"Fool!"

"But Lady Dickleburough was also let go."

Mother shook her head. "No. She was not. She told me she asked to stay behind. The rooms have not been closed permanently, only until the other ladies return. You had it all wrong."

"No," Isabel said, looking from her mother to her grandmother. "That is what Lady Dickleburough told me. She lied to me."

"You did something, Isabel," Mother said. "You were told to stay behind. Something changed."

"What changed," Grandmother said, "is that she caught the eye of Walter Langton. Do you really think there are not other women that Langton has approached? I'm sure he arranged all of this, your dismissal and then his offer to you. There was no word of you staying behind until the morning you were to leave. And it would not be the first time Lady Dickleburough lied—or laid—for a price."

Isabel's mouth fell open. She closed it and nodded. She was indeed a fool. She should have been more suspicious. Langton had confessed that he'd gotten her the position in the first place, but still she had not imagined that he would be so despicable. But even if she had suspected, who was she to have questioned the queen's household's steward, who had told her to stay behind? In retrospect, the man had seemed unaccountably nervous, but she had attributed his odd behavior to his dislike of the task given him. It looked different now.

"What can I do to remedy this?" she asked her mother.

"I told everyone you were dead, Isabel. Would you show me to be a liar?" Her voice rose. "No. Your life at court is over. I have written to your father. I bought you passage on a ship going up the coast. You leave with the morning tide. You will sail to Newcastle and await your father's arrival. It's time he shared the responsibility of you. You may have a long wait, I am afraid, for he lives quite close to the Scottish border, and it is December." She held out a coin purse. "Here. It is enough to see you through until he finds you. You must be frugal."

"No! Surely there is someone in London who could shield her?" Grandmother cried. "She can stay here. I have friends. They will help."

Mother's smile was pitiless. "They are old women, Mother, as you are. And Langton would find her here with you. No, she must leave London."

"Look at her!" Grandmother cried. "She might have been unwise, but you have been hasty. And now you send her away, to a man who hasn't seen her in a decade? What are you thinking? At least go with her, to be sure she is safe."

"I cannot leave London. I am still engaged by the king. And would it not seem strange if I were suddenly to leave? No, it's better that I stay here and repeat my story." She looked at Isabel with narrowed eyes. "You need to ask yourself one thing, Isabel. How did you cause this? What were your actions that led Langton to believe you would welcome his attentions?"

Isabel stared at her mother.

"Damn cold. Tell me why we dinna live somewhere that's warm all the time."

Kieran pulled his cloak hood back over his dark head after the wind tossed it from him. His face was pinched with cold, but his expression was cheerful.

Rory was grateful for that, and that his cousin had not argued when Rory had told him they were returning to London. Nor when Rory had suggested they sail to Leith rather than make the long trip overland. And all because Isabel had not been with the king's party. Nor had she been at the palace, where no one seemed to know why she was not with the king. But something had happened, for when he'd asked for her, the servants had exchanged looks, then nodded to each other, as though they'd agreed to keep their silence. He'd gone to her grandmother's house then, but the maid had refused to admit him.

They'd been fortunate to have a night in their former lodgings, and in a day or so would book passage on one of the ships that plied the eastern coastal ports. The weather had grown worse with every hour, the snow and cold promising to make a December voyage uncomfortable. But before he left London, he would find out what had happened to Isabel.

She must be ill. He could think of no other reason why she'd not been with the royal party. De Boyer had been as surprised as he when, at the midday meal stop, they'd discovered that Isabel had not been among the queen's ladies. Alis de Braun had walked away from the others, and, lowering her voice almost to a whisper, had said none of them knew why Isabel had refused to accompany them. And that the king was very displeased with Isabel for all she had said against him.

"Why would she have refused to go?" he asked Kieran.

"She must be ill," Kieran said, sidestepping the refuse in the road. "But if she's ill, then why is her grandmother asking us to come to her house after turning us away yesterday? Makes no sense. The lass is bonnie, aye, but ye hardly ken her. Why the fuss over one lass ye dinna even ken?"

Rory shrugged. "I like her."

"She's the only lass who's looked at ye in London is more like it. I'm telling ye, ye need to watch me and learn."

"The only lass. Ye're forgetting . . ." He couldn't remember her name, the barmaid who had brought their meals every night and made it obvious she was willing to serve much more.

Kieran laughed. "Ah, her. The memorable one. Here we are, in one of the largest cities in the world, and ye see only one lass." His eyes narrowed. "Are ye sure ye dinna have some of yer da's second sight? Are ye having dreams that tell the future?"

"No. Well, a few, perhaps. But I canna remember them later."

"But ye have a sense of them?"

"Aye."

"And Isabel is in these dreams?"

Rory grinned. "Would I be the first man to have a woman in his dreams?"

"No. And not the last. A'right, we're here. Which house is it?"

The boy who had brought them the message from Isabel's grandmother looked relieved to see them. "They're up there," he said, darting up the stairs and throwing open the door to the room they'd visited before.

Isabel's grandmother rose from her chair, her stern expression lightening as she saw Rory and Kieran. "I thank you for coming, good sirs."

There was a woman standing near the window, her

face angry, her arms folded across her chest. She looked at Rory, then Kieran behind him, and sniffed, turning her back to them.

"Thank you for coming," Isabel said quietly.

He whirled to find her in the dim corner behind the door. She stepped forward into the light, and he caught his breath. Her face was battered, her cheeks swollen and bruised. Her throat was multicolored, and there, at the side of her slender neck, startlingly clear against her pale skin, was the mark of a finger, the bruise where someone had held her in a stranglehold. He took her chin and looked at her bruises, then into her eyes.

"Who did this? Who did this to ye, Isabel?"

Her lip trembled and he fought his anger, telling himself she was alive. He'd been ready to mourn her, surprised at the grief that had caused. "Who did this?"

The woman at the window turned. "Does it matter? Her grandmother has asked your help and you have come running. I might have expected no less of men who are always prowling. But for my mother to play procurer—"

"Enough!" Isabel's grandmother cried. "My daughter, sirs. Isabel's mother, though one would hardly know it from her behavior now."

"I solved the problem!" Isabel's mother said heatedly.

"You caused a far greater one!" Isabel's grandmother replied. "You did not denounce him, did you? No, you blamed Isabel for his behavior and then you told the world she was dead instead of demanding that she be protected."

"You are a fool if you believe anyone at Westminster will condemn Walter Langton. They would have listened, and repeated the story until all of London had heard it, but no one would stop him. Alis de Braun and Lady Dickleburough would swear that Isabel made those treasonous statements. And perhaps she did."

The two women glared at each other.

"Langton!" Rory looked into Isabel's eyes. "It was Langton who did this?"

Isabel nodded.

"I will kill the bastard!"

She laid her hand on his arm. "No. Please, do nothing. It doesn't matter now. My mother is correct. No matter how loudly we protest, no one will stop him. Certainly not now. Part of it is my fault. I said too much. And was unwise to trust certain people at court."

"Which you were well warned about. Now there is nothing that can be done," Isabel's mother said. "No one can reprimand Walter Langton but the king, and the king has far greater matters to deal with now. Think what you want, all of you. I protected my daughter. I removed her forever from his grasp."

"We canna just let this go unanswered," Rory protested. "Did he . . . ?" He stopped, unable to put into words the images that filled his head, of Isabel, helpless in Langton's grip. "What else did he do to ye?"

"Who are you, sir, that you talk so intimately with my daughter?" Isabel's mother cried, then turned her gaze to Isabel. "He is the one you were seen embracing, is he not? You said there was nothing between you, but here he is again, asking whether Langton raped you as though he has a right to ask that, and calling you by your Christian name. You are obviously well acquainted, or he hopes you will be. What man assists a woman without expecting something in return?"

Rory stepped forward, his temper flaring, but his cousin answered first.

"We do, madam." Kieran stepped forward, bowing low. "We've not introduced ourselves. Kieran MacDonald, madam. And my cousin, Rory MacGannon. Scots, as ye no doubt can tell. We brought yer daughter news from Berwick of her friend Rachel, and were charmed by yer daughter's beauty and manner. Ye speak the truth—we dinna ken her well, nor she us. But, madam, we are Scotsmen and as such always help any who need our assistance. As for Rory, my cousin is both a gentleman and a warrior. He would assist anyone in need, and has done so more times than I can count. I would hope that Englishmen would do the same were one of our lasses in distress here."

Isabel's mother stared at Kieran, and the others watched her. She raised her chin and nodded, her expression softening. "Well said, sir. I am overwrought perhaps. My daughter has been attacked by a creature so foul as to make my skin crawl. My life these last few hours has been hellish. And now my very livelihood is threatened! What will happen to me if Langton has me turned out?"

There was silence while Isabel and her grandmother stared at her mother, then Isabel's grandmother spoke in an icy tone.

"I am sure you mean to say that you are worried about your daughter and heartsore that now you must bid farewell to your only child in order to save her. Is it not?"

Isabel's mother nodded. "Of course."

"Of course," Isabel's grandmother said. "And that, gentlemen, is why I asked you here. When you called earlier, Mr. MacGannon, and left the message that you were once again in London, but sailing north soon, I was glad to hear of it. But I could not speak with you then, for we did not yet know what we would do. But now my daughter has arranged for Isabel to sail north, on a ship that sounds as though it might be the same one you have booked passage upon. I beg your assistance, for which I am prepared to pay handsomely. It appears that my granddaughter must leave London, and I am loath to have her travel to Newcastle alone. May I hire you to accompany her? She will travel on the *Leslie B,* which will leave with the morning tide."

Rory gave Kieran a look, pleased that his cousin nodded.

"We will be traveling on the *Leslie B* as well, madam," Rory said, hoping they could find the captain and make it so. "It would be our honor to accompany ye, demoiselle, if that is yer wish. But do ye really need to leave London?"

"There is nothing for me here," Isabel said. "I have been dismissed from service, and somehow I am responsible for Langton's attack upon me."

"Isabel, enough!" Isabel's grandmother said. "No one believes you are anything but the victim here."

Isabel's mother sniffed loudly and turned back to the window.

Isabel met Rory's gaze. "I am more than ready to leave London. I wish we could leave now, this night. And I will never return."

Her grandmother put a hand to her throat. "Sweet, do not say that!"

Tears stood in Isabel's eyes. "I will miss you terribly, Grandmother! And I know you will miss me. But you will be the only one in all of this city who will."

Her mother whirled from the window. "Oh, poor

Isabel. You said you were terrified of the man, but you got into the coach with him, did you not? Even knowing what he was, you let yourself be alone with him!"

"I told you!" Isabel cried. "He got in after me! I did not choose this!"

"You did not ask whose coach it was, did you? Or did you?"

"No. I did not ask whose coach it was, you're right. And that part is my fault. But not the rest, Mother! I did nothing to warrant this, and I will not be made to feel I did!"

"I warned you! I told you what men are, and you pretended to listen, but you did not. Now you turn upon me with ungratefulness."

"No more! No more!" Isabel's grandmother stepped between them, then turned to Rory and Kieran. "I pray you forgive us for what you have seen and heard here this day. Isabel will be at the dock in the morning, sirs. I thank you for your assistance."

Rory bowed. Kieran did the same and they left the room, closing the door behind them. They did not speak as they descended the stairs, but once outside, they exchanged a look. Rory let his breath out in a huff of air.

"Well," Kieran said. "Let's go find the barmaid whose name we dinna remember and see what she's serving tonight."

TEN

The morning was clear, but very cold. Isabel stood near the end of the dock, her fingers numb and her heart sore. They'd argued for hours after Rory and Kieran had left, but at last she and her mother had made a kind of peace between them. Her mother had gone back to Westminster then, and Isabel and her grandmother had talked the rest of the night, aided by not a little wine. Her grandmother's open unhappiness with her mother had soothed Isabel's wounds somewhat, but Isabel knew that she and her mother would always have this between them.

Not that it would matter. She could not return to London, or at least not until Walter Langton had lost his influence at court, or died. Her more immediate problem was how she would now live. She knew no trade, had no skills.

She could read and write in French, and Latin, and the English that the common people spoke. She could recite lovely poems, even some in Greek—none of which would have any value in her new life. Her needlework was exceptionally good, thanks to years of her mother's training.

Perhaps that was it, how she would earn her bread, for she would do just that. She had sold, for a good price, the horse given to her by the queen. The money was in a small purse under her skirts. She would use that to live on until she was settled. Her mother might have written to her father, asking him to take her in—at best a desperate plan—but who knew if he would ever get her letter, let alone come to Newcastle to find Isabel? Which did not matter either. She would not be there.

"Good morrow, demoiselle."

She turned to find Rory and Kieran, bags in hand. They were dressed in those strange plaided knit stockings that the Scots wore, which hugged the taut muscles of their legs. Tunics above, and heavy cloaks over all. She wondered for the first time whether her clothing would look as strange to those in her new home. Certainly the silk and embroidered gowns and headdresses she'd been given to wear at court, and even the clothes she now wore, dark and practical for the rigors of travel, would mark her as an outsider. No matter. There was neither time nor coin to remedy that.

"Good morrow, sirs. I am so sorry for all you witnessed last night." Her cheeks flushed with embarrassment at the memory.

Rory waved her words away, glancing up at the sky, then back at her. "Have ye spoken with the captain, lass? D'ye wish me to do that?"

"No, thank you. I have talked with him and my passage is assured. He tells me the voyage could be stormy and rough."

"I'm thinking the same thing," Rory said. "The wind is strong, even this early, and look at those clouds, the long ones there. Snow. And we're heading north. It could be uncomfortable."

She laughed ruefully. "Nothing could be more uncomfortable than yesterday and last night. I apologize for all of it, for me, and my mother—"

"Och, lass, please dinna. It's over and done with. Yer face looks a bit better this morning. How d'ye feel?"

"As though I am standing at the edge of a cliff and thinking of jumping."

"Dinna even say that," Rory said, his manner grave.

She forced a smile, trying to lighten her tone. "I will reconsider then."

There was no time then for talk, as they were shown aboard the ship with the six other passengers—a young family, and two men who seemed to be traveling alone—and the ship's sails were raised. The ship inched away from the dock and into the middle of the Thames. The sailors showed them to the large cabin in which they would all stay, but Isabel begged just a moment more on deck, and the captain agreed.

Rory and Kieran stayed with her while the others went below. She fought her panic as the ship began to move toward the sea. For one mad moment she clutched the rail, wondering if she should throw herself from the ship and return to land. What had possessed her to agree to be here, with two men she'd only just met, traveling into the unknown? And what had possessed her mother to arrange it?

"What made ye refuse to go north with the king?" Rory asked, his tone mild.

She stared at him for a moment. "I didn't. I was told to stay behind."

"But . . . we talked with Alis de Braun. She said ye refused. De Boyer was as surprised as we were. So we came back to London to find ye."

"You came back to London because I wasn't with the king? You rode all the way back to London to find me?"

"Aye. I was worried about ye. I thought ye must be ill."

"Rory, you rode back to London to find me?"

"Aye. I told ye that we did. D'ye not believe me?"

She put her hand over her mouth, not sure whether she would laugh or cry, then took a deep breath to calm herself. "I do. It is what has happened in the last days that I cannot believe! I have been let go by the king and I do not know what I have done to cause it, and my mother accuses me of the vilest behavior. My own mother! And yet you, who I do not know at all, was worried on my behalf? I am overwhelmed."

She wiped a tear from her cheek. "You are most kind. I feel so alone. I know my grandmother loves me, and she is distraught that I am leaving. This morning she wanted to come with me, but how could I let her, when she can hardly climb her own stairs? I had to argue with her and tell her I would be fine. But I don't know how I can be. I feel set adrift in a sea full of serpents, and I don't know what I did to cause this. And you are kind to me!" She put her hands over her face and sobbed.

Rory wrapped his arm around her and pulled her to his side. "Whist, lass, ye are set adrift. Ye're on a ship, remember?"

She laughed against his shoulder, then sobbed more. At last she pulled away from him, mopping her eyes and nose with her handkerchief and trying to be calm. The sailors around them watched her with wide eyes and glances at Rory. Kieran stared into the distance, pretending to ignore them. And Rory smiled at her.

"Think of it this way. Ye're off to see a part of the world ye've never seen before. Now look, lass, London's already behind us. When was the last time ye sailed out to sea this way?"

"Never. I've been on the ferryboats on the river, but never on a ship, and never at sea. I've never even seen the sea."

"Not seen the sea?" His smile widened. "Then ye have a grand adventure before ye, Isabel. Ye'll love it, I'm sure of it. Ye'll love the roll of the ship and the feeling of the wind in yer hair. We grew up onboard ship, Kieran and me, and my brother Magnus, and all five of Kieran's sisters. I dinna think I've ever met anyone who's not been on a ship. So, first lesson. Stay on deck as much as ye can." He glanced at the sky. "And dinna travel in the winter, when the storms come. At least ye'll not have as far to go as we will. We'll be going all the way to Leith and ye'll get off at Newcastle."

She brushed aside the hair the wind had blown about her face, meeting his gaze. "I won't get off at Newcastle. I'm going to Berwick."

She lost track of the stops the ship made. Southend, Harwich, Hull, Yarmouth, Scarborough, Whitby. She did not even know in which order they'd been where, for she'd spent most of the voyage hanging over a wooden bucket, losing each meal she'd forced herself to eat. And she was not alone. They'd been battered by storms the entire journey, and all of the passengers, save Rory and Kieran, had been ill, leaving the cabin they all shared noxious and almost unbearable. She had no idea how long she'd been aboard, whether it was days or years. She settled into a mood of endurance. She would live through this—and never in her life would she go aboard a ship again.

"I told ye that ye'd love the roll of the ship," Rory teased her while they waited in one of the ports.

"Aye, ye've seemed to be enjoying yerself grandly," Kieran said.

She threw him a baleful glance, then smiled. "You have been very kind. I do not know how you both have managed to stay so cheerful with all of us so ill."

"Ye'll notice," Rory said, "that we do slip out now and then. The captain doesna mind. If we fall overboard, what's one less Scot?" He studied her face. "I've not seen ye in the light since we left. Yer face and neck look much better."

"They feel better. It's like a dream," she said softly. "All that happened in London . . . it's as though it happened to someone else, not me."

"And here ye are, an experienced sailor now," Kieran said, smiling.

She laughed. "I can think of nothing worse than being on a ship again." She ached all over; not a part of her did not feel pummeled. "I'm dreaming of a bath and putting on clothing that is not damp."

"What are ye thinking?" Rory asked. "Ye're going to Scotland in the winter. Ye'll be damp until April, and then the spring rains will come."

She laughed again, looking at his profile, the strong jaw, those blue eyes and all that blond hair. And his mouth. What was she thinking? he'd asked. Nothing she could tell him. She smiled.

"You have a gift, both of you," she said, "of making me

feel like I will heal. You've seen me in many of the worst moments of my life. And yet, somehow, you make me believe I will survive."

"Ye will, lass, I swear ye will get past this," Rory said, those impossibly blue eyes serious now. "Are ye sure Rachel will take ye in?"

"No, I am sure of nothing. But I hope she will, at least for a while, until I can find a way to make a living. It will be far better than waiting in an inn in Newcastle for my father. What if he never came for me?"

"Yer father?" Rory's eyebrows raised. "I thought he was dead."

"I . . . I did tell you that. I apologize for my lie. It was simpler. For years I thought he was dead. I only discovered who he is a short time ago. I do not know the man. I do not want to know him."

Rory and Kieran exchanged a look.

"My father's name is Lord Lonsby. He fathered me in London, but he had a wife and children already and never married my mother. Who, as you saw, is quite bitter. She wrote to him nonetheless, asking him to find me in Newcastle. But I won't be there, so he will not find me, even if he does come."

"What will ye do then?"

"I can sew. I shall become a seamstress. I will find work somewhere, even if I have to sweep the streets."

"No one sweeps the streets in Berwick," Rory said. "A'right, then, we'll get off in Berwick as well, aye?" He looked at Kieran for agreement.

Kieran's smile was wide. "Aye. There's a lass there, serving ale, whose name I do remember."

They laughed together. Isabel smiled, although she was not sure why.

"You do not need to, sirs. I will find Rachel's family myself."

"Lass," Rory said. "Kieran is almost as anxious to see Rachel as ye are. We'll get off in Berwick and stay a bit."

"Thank you," she said, then looked at the port city. "I wonder how many people in this place have their own sad story. Surely many of them have tales much worse than mine."

Rory leaned against the railing and followed her gaze. "I havena told ye about my family, have I?"

"A bit," she said.

"Aye, well, whenever I'm feeling put upon, I think of what they went through. It all started in the summer of 1263."

She listened raptly while he talked of how his parents had met, of the slaughter of innocents at Somerstrath. Of the battle his father had fought against the Vikings. Of his and Kieran's aunt Nell, and all she'd been through.

And then Kieran told her of his father's abduction as a boy and eventual rescue by Rory's father, Gannon. How his father had in turn rescued Kieran's mother from captivity and brought her back to the Isle of Skye, where now he was building her a castle to live in.

They were wonderful stories, and, in comparison, her struggles seemed insignificant. Perhaps life was meant to be full of struggle. Perhaps those whose life was untroubled could never know the real joy of peace.

"And they're happy now, your parents?" she asked. "Your aunt Nell and uncle Liam? All of your family? Do they never think of the past?"

"I'm sure they do," Rory said. "But, aye, they're happy. And ye will be again, Isabel. I swear it. Life willna always be like this."

She was allowed out on deck as they sailed up the River Tweed, and looked up at Berwick's earthenworks and the wooden stockade that rose above it, enclosing the city. This would be her home, she told herself. She was relieved when she stepped ashore again, but suddenly the enormity of the changes in her life struck her, and the squalor and crowded streets just within the city gates did nothing to relieve her anxiety. Whores called to Rory and Kieran from open doorways and yet, mercifully, a short distance later, respectable homes lined the narrow streets. The castle rose high on the hill above the town, and she took a moment to look at it, then shut out the memories of her life at court. That was the past.

"Here it is," Rory said, stopping before an older building.

Over the door a freshly painted sign bore the name The Oak and The Ash. The steps were wide and clean, and a window jutted into the street, allowing her to see a room crowded with people. The inn stretched high above the street, its shutters painted and white walls clean. The door opened and two men left, delicious aromas following them into the street.

"Come, lass," Rory said and picked up her case again.

The inn was warm, for which she was grateful. The foyer was neat, a tall table in the corner, behind which Jacob de Anjou stood, talking with a customer. To her left was a large room filled with tables covered with food and cups, the air filled with the conversations of the patrons. At the far end a large fireplace roared with flames, and women bustled through the crowd with trays laden with food. A blond girl turned with a smile from serving ale to a dark-haired man, and she looked at Isabel, her eyes widening.

"Isabel!" she cried, drawing the attention of all in the room. "Father, look, Isabel de Burke is here! Rachel! Someone get Rachel! She will not believe this!"

Jacob looked up then, his expression going from surprise to welcome. "It is you! Isabel, what are? . . ."

And then Rachel was there, shrieking, her arms open wide as she rushed forward, her mother at her heels. "Isabel! I did not believe them, but it is you!" She clasped Isabel to her, laughing and crying at the same time, then leaned back. "What happened to you? Why are you here?"

"Oh, Rachel!" Isabel was sobbing now. "I need your help!"

"Anything," Rachel said, then spun around to Jacob. "Father? Mother?"

"Anything," they said together. "Welcome, Isabel."

"Only for a few days," she told Rachel's family. "Until I can find lodgings of my own. And a position. I can sew," she said with a rueful smile. "If you will help me to find a place to live, I will be grateful."

"Isabel," Jacob said. "You may stay with us."

"No. I thank you, but no, I cannot. I have made enemies of powerful men. If they were to come to Berwick, looking for me, and find you . . . it is unthinkable that I would put you in danger in such a manner. I cannot."

Rachel's mother laughed. "We are no longer in England, child. And look around you. Does this look like the sort of place kings and bishops visit? We are invisible in Berwick. Stay here, with us. We could use your help."

"But—"

"Isabel," Jacob said. "We have been talking. If you are willing, you could help us solve a problem. We need someone to serve and to help Gilbert attend to the patrons when we have our Sabbath. I'm sure you understand how loath we are to bring strangers into our midst. You need a safe place to stay. We need another pair of hands. You may stay, of course, even if this plan does not please you. But we would prefer that you worked for your bread."

"But the danger—"

"If it exists, we will face it when it comes. Are you willing to help us?"

"I am more than willing to work! Simply tell me what I must do. And how long I may stay."

"If you will smile," Jacob said, "just once, for us, you may stay forever."

Isabel smiled tremulously, looking from Jacob to Rachel's mother, who leaned across the table to take her hand.

"You have been a good friend to our Rachel, Isabel. Let us now be a good friend to you."

"I thank you," Isabel said, dangerously close to tears. "And I will stay."

"No thanks are necessary, but it's always nice to be thanked." Rachel's mother folded the edge of her shawl. "Your grandfather helped us. Did you know that? He owned the house we lived in. Jews could not own property, as you know. He let us live there all those years and never once raised the rent. Your grandmother never failed to say hello to me. She encouraged your friendship. This is rare, Isabel, and we were grateful. We still are. So if there is thanks to be given, it is ours, and we are glad to repay the debt."

"I did not know that," Isabel said, her smile wistful. "What good people you are. You are good people."

"We are." Rachel's mother rose to her feet. "Now, let's find you something more practical to wear. You look like one of the queen's ladies, not a tavern wench. Let's change that."

"I'm ready," Isabel said, rising as well.

Rory and Kieran stayed for four days. They spent their days talking and spending time at Berwick Castle, where William Douglas ran a well-managed fortress. Many of the young Scots assembled there, doing just what Rory and Kieran had set out to do—gather information. It was there that they learned of the Scottish people's continued dissatisfaction with the Guardians and the nobles who could not agree on a course for their country's future. And of the sporadic violence between Balliol and Bruce factions that was spreading, leaving no part of Scotland untouched.

At night, when the patrons were settled, the tavern was empty, and their time was their own, Rachel, Sarah, and Isabel joined Rory and Kieran there, listening to what they'd learned that day, then talking of every topic that came to mind. They were merry, which helped dispel Isabel's overwhelming sense of sadness and loss.

During the day she watched Rachel and Sarah and their parents joke together, and help each other, with no cross words exchanged, no accusations. No distrust. Gilbert, the previous owner of the tavern, was a surprise. She'd expected him to be a doddering old fool when she'd first heard of him, but while he was aged, he was far from feebleminded.

She felt she learned slowly, but everyone encouraged her, Rory most of all. Every time she turned, she found him carrying mugs of ale to a table, or taking a heavy tray from her hands with a smile. Or running to the cellar to fetch another pitcher of ale.

On her second night at the inn, a tall, gaunt, man with lean, windburnt cheeks, entered the foyer, a cold wind following him. Isabel had been standing in the corner with Rachel, watching the room for patrons who needed anything, and turned at the sound of the man's greeting. A Highlander, she could tell, both from his accent and his dress. He stood next to Rachel for a moment, surveying the tavern room, then whirled to face Gilbert.

"Are ye the innkeeper, sir?" he asked.

"I am," Gilbert said. "Which do you need, a meal, or a room, or both?"

"Neither." The man pushed a coin across the desk to Gilbert, keeping his finger atop it. "I'm looking for a man who might be staying here. Highlander. Tall. Very blond hair. Wears a golden brooch with a circle of jewels on it. He's often with one of the MacDonald lads. Easily angered, he is, and said to be somewhere in Berwick. Have ye seen anyone like that?"

"Several over the last month," Gilbert said, turning as if to move an object behind him. He caught Isabel's gaze and rolled his eyes toward the man, then turned back. "Do you have a name, perhaps?"

"Rory MacGannon."

Gilbert tapped his chin, then shook his head. "I've not heard that name. Have you checked the inns down by the water? They would be the sorts of places you might find a man such as that. We do not welcome ruffians."

The man nodded.

"If I do see him," Gilbert said, "where would I find you?"

The man smiled, revealing several missing teeth. "Just look outside yer door. One of us is watching for him."

"How will I know which to tell?"

The man laughed. "I'm not the only one looking for MacGannon. There's an English knight paying good money to hear of his whereabouts."

"Is there? What has this MacGannon done?"

"He's a murderer, sir." The man stepped to the tavern doorway again. "Ye have a Highlander there, the dark-haired man in the corner, playing dice. Who is he?"

"Him?" Gilbert shrugged. "I have no idea, sir. We only ask their names if they take a room. And sometimes not even then."

Isabel gave Rachel a glance, then, while the man was talking with Gilbert, crossed the room to where Kieran sat, engrossed in a dice game with Edgar Keith.

"Kieran," she whispered to him. "You need to listen to me!"

He looked up at her with a smile. "Isabel, lass, it had better be important. I'm making my fortune here."

Edgar snorted. "Losing everything is more like it."

"Don't look past me, but listen! There is a man, talking with Gilbert, looking for Rory by name and offering money for information. He knows Rory could be with a MacDonald. He says Rory is a murderer! No, don't look at him! Where is Rory?"

"Just coming down the stairs," Kieran said softly. "He's

standing in the dark, there, listening to the Highlander. Dinna worry, lass, I can tell by his expression that he's hearing it."

"The man is leaving," Edgar said. "He tossed Gilbert a coin and left."

Isabel turned to look across the room and met Rory's gaze. He looked angry. She turned back to Kieran. "Is it true? Did Rory kill a man?"

Rory told her late that night, as they sat with Rachel and Kieran, all that had happened before he'd gone to London. She listened, watching his eyes and the way Kieran nodded. Rory's tone was matter-of-fact, as though things like this were commonplace.

"Kieran told me all about it," Rachel said.

"He did?" Isabel looked from Rachel to Rory.

"And ye've seen the brooch Rory wears on his cloak," Kieran says. "Given to him by the MacDonnell's lady to thank him. She said he was the champion of all women, and I'm thinking she was right."

Rory shook his head. "And ye see the good that's come of it."

"Ye got a jeweled brooch out of it," Kieran said.

"And a price on my head."

"How can you make light of this?" Isabel demanded. "You said that John Comyn would stop it. Why has he not?"

Rory's expression sobered. "I'm sure he tried, lass, but the truth of it is that Scotland is ready to explode. My family has come out for Balliol and made no secret of it. The MacDonells have done the same, but this could be a way to divide us, could it not, to have one part of Balliol's faction distrusting another."

"So you think the Bruces are behind it?" Isabel asked.

Rory shrugged. "I may be reading too much into it, but does it not seem strange that I'm the object of such a search? John Comyn has spread the truth of what happened."

"But, as ye say," Kieran said, "Scotland is ready to explode. Could be ye're right. And if not the Bruces, then ye ken who it is."

Rory and Kieran exchanged a look.

"Who?" Isabel asked.

"My father has enemies," Rory said. "The Rosses. My mother's mother was one, but my father killed the king's cousin—ye remember the story I told ye, about our aunt Nell and all, and every so often the Rosses have a hothead who tries to kill my da, or Liam, or my brother, Magnus, or me. It's been years, though."

"Four since the last time, but that was soon settled," Kieran said.

"Let me understand," Isabel said. "There are men trying to kill you in Scotland. It might be MacDonells, or Rosses, or men after the reward."

"Not just Scotland," Kieran said. "They were in London, too. And dinna forget yer friend, de Boyer, who's now paying for information. Ye must have made quite an impression there."

"That's different. He's trying to find something foul about me to tell Isabel. There's nothing more to it than that."

"Damn, lad." Kieran slapped Rory's shoulder. "Aren't ye the popular one?"

The others laughed, but Isabel found no humor in it.

Rory turned to her with a grin. "It's not that dangerous, Isabel. I'm careful. I have Kieran to guard my back. I'm leaving soon, and when I get home I'll have a whole clan to protect me."

She nodded, pretending to agree. But that night she dreamt of Walter Langton chasing her and Rory on horseback. Behind him were faceless men dressed in Highland clothing, brandishing swords. And next to Langton was Henry.

Rory continued to make light of the price on his head, although she noted that he often looked outside at the street and scanned the tavern room before he entered it, and more than once he tensed when the door opened. And Kieran did the same.

On the night before Rory and Kieran were to leave, Rory found Isabel in the hallway. He carried a tray of empty cups, leaning into the kitchen to hand them to the girl there. "My excuse to come and find ye," he said with a wide smile and pulled her around the corner, where they could be alone.

"Ye've hardly had a moment for me, lass. It's busy tonight, but at least no battles yet, aye?"

"You are good to help us, Rory. Not your usual duty, is it?"

"No, and if ye tell anyone of this, Kieran and I will take grave offense."

"Grave offense. Then shall I take that warning gravely, sir?"

"I'm dead serious, lass."

"Are you plotting something, sir?

"Ye have not a ghost of guessing." He leaned over her. "But I like yer spirit."

She laughed and pushed him away, but he moved closer to her, putting a hand at her waist.

"Do you help serve food at home as well?" she asked.

"Och no, lass. At home we pound on the table with our daggers and demand to be fed."

"I'm sure you do."

"I'm sure we dinna do it at all. Ye have not met my mother. There's no pounding on her tables."

"She must be very proud of a son like you."

"How could she not be?" He laughed, then stepped even closer. "Ye ken we're leaving in the morning. We have to be going in order to be home by Christmas, else I wouldna leave ye. Will ye be all right here, Isabel?" He lifted her chin and looked into her eyes. "Ye can come with us, lass. We'll take ye to Stirling. My aunt and uncle are there, and Nell could keep ye safe. Or ye could come to Loch Gannon, to my home. I ken ye'd be welcome."

She could not speak for a moment, then tried to smile at him. "I thank you, Rory MacGannon, for this as well as everything else you have done for me. It is you I worry for now, riding across Scotland with men hunting for you. They know what you look like, Rory!"

"Whist, lass, d'ye ken how many Highlanders are tall and have blond hair? Let them look. I'll be careful, but I'm not really in danger. I'm going home. It's ye I'm leaving in a strange city. Will ye not come with us?"

She kept her tone light. "And share the dangers of the road with you?"

He raised his eyebrows. "And perhaps more. But seriously, Isabel—"

"I cannot. Rachel and her family have made me welcome, and there is work here that I can do to earn my keep."

"A far cry from what ye're accustomed to."

"Then I will learn to become accustomed to this life. My past is over. I will never go back to London. I am dead, remember?"

"And this is yer afterlife?"

She shared a smile with him. "You have been so kind, Rory. I do not know how to thank you for caring for me, for enduring that hideous voyage, for all your small kindnesses. You came back to London for me. How can I thank you?"

"This way," he said.

His kiss was gentle, but demanding. He claimed her mouth with an ardor that was impossible to mistake, his fingers stroking her cheek, his eyes closed. She closed hers as well, savoring the feel of his lips on hers, of the promise of more.

"Rory," she said breathlessly, wrapping her hand around his neck, pulling his mouth back to hers. "Again."

He took possession of her mouth again, lunging into her with his tongue, exploring her fully. She returned the kiss with all the passion she possessed. Just one kiss, she told herself. But as the kiss deepened, she pressed closer to him, wishing to meld with him, to be one, as she'd never felt before. As she knew she would crave the rest of her life. He lifted his head.

"I forgot something upstairs, lass," he said, his eyes dark. "Come with me, will ye no'?"

She knew she should refuse, knew he had not forgotten anything, but she let him take her hand and lead her up the stairway the family and staff used, down the empty corridor and into the room he'd shared with Kieran. He closed the door and pulled her into his arms without a word, and she clasped him to her, raising her mouth to meet his, letting his hands roam from her throat to her shoulders. When he cupped her breast she leaned into his touch, and when he slipped a finger under the edge of her bodice, she was lost.

"Take this off," he said, his voice hoarse. "Let me feel yer skin against me, Isabel. Just this once, before I leave, let me touch ye."

She did not hesitate, but pulled her outer tunic over her head, letting it fall to the floor, then fumbled with the laces of her chemise. She looked up to see him shedding his shirt and reaching for her, his hand already pushing down the cloth of her bodice, his fingers finding the soft flesh of her breast.

He pulled her against him and she melted at the feel of his skin on hers, the warmth of his chest, the brush of his chest hair against her breasts as he moved. His skin was silken beneath her touch, smooth and firm and wonderfully male. She stroked her hand along the muscles of his shoulders, then along his side, marveling at his tautness, at his strength. She kissed the base of his throat and inhaled.

"Rory," she said breathlessly, and felt his body respond.

He lifted her chin and kissed her deeply, his tongue probing her mouth while his hands continued to bare her flesh. And then his mouth was gone, enclosing on her nipple, the flicks of his tongue bringing her exquisite pleasure.

"Rory," she said. "Don't leave me."

He lifted his head and met her gaze. "I'll come back, Isabel. I shouldna want ye so, but God's blood, I do, Isabel! I ken better. There should be nothing between us,

I ken that, and I have nothing to offer ye, but ye make me hunger for ye, lass." He pulled her closer, leaning his cheek against the top of her head, her face nestled into the hollow of his shoulder. "It's more than just yer body, though that would be enough to make me travel to the ends of the earth. It's yer courage, and yer humor, and yer willingness to work hard. And yer loyalty. Truly, lass, there has never been another like ye. I will never forget ye, Isabel de Burke. Dinna be forgetting me, lass."

"Impossible," she said.

"Good. This will hold ye until I come back."

He kissed her again. And again. And still again.

In the morning he was gone. A month passed with no word from him. Then another, and another. By the spring she was convinced he would not return. By the summer she told herself to forget him, and she tried, and tried. But she failed. And still no word from him.

PART II

. . . If a lion in pride and fierceness,
he is a panther in fickleness and inconstancy,
changing his word and promise,
cloaking himself by pleasant speech . . .
The treachery and falsehood by which he is advanced
he calls prudence . . .
and whatever he says is lawful.

THE SONG OF LEWES
EDITED AND TRANSLATED BY C.A. KINGSFORD, 1890

ELEVEN

JUNE 2 1291, NORHAM-ON-TWEED

W e're in England, lads," Gannon said as their horses
stepped on the south shore of the River Tweed.
"Keep yer hand near yer sword and yer wits as sharp."

Rory nodded at his father, then at Kieran, who was beside him, and glanced around. Just behind him, his uncles
Liam and Davey were doing the same. As were most of the
scores of Scots crossing the river, arriving wary and watch-
ful, distrustful of this gathering that King Edward had
called. Highlanders in their summer saffron shirts and kilts
mixed with bejeweled nobles from the Borders and Lothian, and men who, though Scottish in blood, wore the garb
of mighty English landowners, for that is what they were.
Above them, on a rocky bluff, lay Norham Castle, its square
Great Tower gray and forbidding against the blue summer
sky. And within its walls, Edward of England waited.

"I dinna like this conclave being held in England,"
Davey said, glancing at the scores of Scots who, like them,
had been summoned.

"Nor I," Gannon said. "But remind yerself that this

castle was captured twice by our own King David. If we need to, we'd do it again."

Liam grunted but was silent. He didn't need to say what they were all thinking: that Scotland had had a king then.

"Makes ye wonder what Edward's about," Davey said, with a pointed look at the encampments of Edward's archers and crossbowmen they passed.

"What choice did we have?" Gannon growled. "Edward's summoned all the Guardians and Competitors and all clan chiefs. Every nobleman in Scotland is here or on his way."

"True," Davey said.

There were few smiles among the men who now paraded up the road to Norham Castle, and little conversation—only the jingle of bridles and halters, and the dull clunk of mailed gloves against armored breastplates. Weapons were kept within reach and voices muted. There was not a woman to be seen.

Even the birds flying high above seemed to feel the tension, silently dipping down as though to choose a meal from among the men who lumbered up the hill. A raven screeched through the sky, drawing glances upward and causing the hair on Rory's neck to stand. A raven, an omen of ill at the start of a journey. Not an auspicious beginning.

They crossed the moat, their horses' hooves sounding like thunder on the wooden planks of the bridge, and rode through the gate, into the Outer Ward, where throngs of Scots waited for admittance. Walking only from here on, they were told, and handed the reins of their horses to young men with English accents who would not meet their eyes.

The Outer Ward was lined with knights on horseback, their bright banners flapping above them in the breeze and the cheerful sun overhead. Rory wondered, fleetingly, if Henry was among the knights, but he thrust the thought from his mind. The atmosphere seemed more appropraite for a tournament than for this travesty of a gathering. There should be chanting, dirges, monks in mourning, keening women, rather than this silent collection of Highlanders and Lowlanders, grim-faced and anxious, filing past complacent English knights flying their banners.

Gannon and Davey exchanged glances with Liam; Rory and Kieran did the same as they followed the others through the stone arches to the Inner Ward, filing one at a time into the Great Tower and up the stairs to the Great Hall. It was cooler within walls, the damp of the stones mitigated by the crowds of men who stood silently in the chamber. The walls were lined with Edward's armed soldiers, their pikes reaching well above the heads of the Scots, their bright jackets a reminder that this was not a meeting of allies. The reminder was not needed, for one look at the end of the hall let Rory know what was to come. A raised dais stretched from one side of the hall to the other, wide enough to accommodate a score of men. And in the middle of the dais, a throne, a golden canopied chair, with purple hangings, ornate, as though to symbolize Edward's power and wealth. And above it, the banner of England.

The room was crowded now with new arrivals pushing through the door. The hall was relatively quiet, with only the sounds of shuffling feet and men talking quietly as they made room for others.

"MacGannon."

The voice was barely a whisper, from somewhere behind Rory. He turned, as did his father and Kieran, hearing it again, this time from a different direction, in a different voice.

"MacGannon."

Rory met Kieran's gaze, then Liam's, knowing that they both were remembering a dead horse in a stall at Stirling Castle. His father put a hand on Rory's shoulder and looked across the men gathered behind them, his gaze sharp. Liam and Kieran moved to stand behind Rory. Gannon stayed on his left, and Davey on his right. Rory looked straight ahead, but he could feel the gaze of someone behind him, and the hair on his neck rose again. He rested his hand on the hilt of his sword, realizing that his father had done the same.

"Bastards," Davey whispered, his lips drawn back in a sneer. "And more up there. Look who's arrived. Bastards, every one of them."

Rory followed his uncle's gaze to the dais, where six men had arrived, halting to stand in a row facing the crowd. The Guardians of Scotland, the men who had pledged to keep Scotland safe for the Maiden. A misnomer, Rory thought, for all they guarded were their own interests. And sadly enough, Black Comyn among them.

"Look who else has come," Rory said, as the eldest Robert Bruce appeared on the other side of the dais, his hands folded together before him like a priest, his expression patronizing.

And there, coming to stand next to him now, seven of his fellow Competitors, those who would be king of Scotland, wealthy men, well-dressed and impeccably groomed, who sought out familiar faces in the crowd or looked above the heads of the men who watched them.

"Sell their souls for a crown, the lot of them," Gannon said.

Liam nodded. "Or their mothers'."

Still they waited. Rory controlled his own impatience by noting the restiveness of the men around him. His father had learned years ago to school his expression to reveal nothing, but Rory knew that his father was angry by his stance, the rigid way he held his shoulders. He almost smiled, recognizing that his own stance was the same as his father's. And probably his anger matched Gannon's as well.

Several men filed out onto the dais now.

"Roger Brabazon," Liam said, pointing at one. "One of Edward's justiciars."

Brabazon held up his hands for silence, then raised his voice. "Edward, King of England, Lord of Ireland, and Duke of Aquitaine."

The hall fell quiet. Then, with a blare of horns from above, Edward arrived.

Longshanks once again, Rory thought. Still tall, his back ramrod straight, his limbs long, his manner assured. Edward moved like a warrior, his dark eyebrows drawn together as he gazed across the Scots, his lips forming a quiet smile, as though he was pleased by the scene. His clothing was simple, a long dark tunic and breeches, the simple golden circlet crown on his head the only sign of his rank. Edward waited until the horns were silenced, then sat on the throne, his movements spare and sinuous. A man who was accustomed to command. And obedience.

Edward looked to his left, where the Guardians stood,

then to his right, at the Competitors. And smiled slightly. He nodded at Brabazon, who held up a scroll and began to read in a sonorous voice.

"Last winter, King Edward authorized a search of all the records of all the monasteries and abbeys in his kingdom, looking for any entries that mentioned the relations between England and Scotland. He found many, one most significant, and will now share his findings with the Scots, so that they might understand as well."

Rory listened, mystified at first, at Brabazon's words. "In ancient times, Dioclesian, the King of Syria, had thirty-three daughters by his queen. Dioclesian arranged a mass marriage for his daughters, but on the night after the marriages, the daughters killed their new husbands and fled across the sea to the island of Albion. They stayed in Albion, mating with demons, and mothering a generation of giants, who ruled the island until Brutus, the descendant of Aeneas of Troy, arrived on Albion. Brutus killed all the giants and renamed the island Britain. After his death, his three sons inherited the island and divided it into the kingdoms of England, Scotland, and Wales. Humber, the king of Hungary, invaded Britain, and killed the son of Brutus who had ruled Scotland. His brother, the king of England, killed Humber and thus became king of both England and Scotland. His successors were kings of both England and Scotland. Which gave Edward Plantagenet the same right. Edward," Brabazon intoned, "is the rightful Lord Paramount of Scotland."

The room erupted with roars of protest.

"Shite!" Gannon shouted. "It's all shite!"

Davey, who leaned to listen to the man next to him, turned to them with a wild look. "He says Edward's serious about this. He's sent the same argument to the Pope, asking for his support in taking the crown of Scotland."

Rory stared in disbelief. How could Edward think anyone would swallow this as a legitimate argument?

Brabazon held up his hands, but the Scots still protested. Edward watched with a stony expression, looking from Brabazon to the men who opposed him. His face slowly flushing. At last he leapt to his feet.

"You have heard the story which explains our rights! From the earliest times of this land the king of England has had the right to rule Scotland," Edward roared. "By Holy Edward, whose crown I wear, I will vindicate my just rights, or perish in the attempt!"

"Then perish, Edward!" a Scot called out.

Pandemonium broke out as men shouted at each other and at Edward. The Guardians and Competitors exchanged wary glances. The men who lined the wall shifted their weapons, and scores of Edward's soldiers rushed into the room, weapons at the ready.

"We have never heard this outlandish tale before," one Scot shouted.

"You have not studied the records as we have," Edward said.

There was a movement at the side of the dais that drew Rory's attention. There, almost in the corner, in shadow, stood John Balliol. There could be only one reason for that, and Rory's heart sank at the realization of what it meant.

"It is my intention," Edward said firmly, "to rule Scotland until such time as Scotland has its own king." He let the rumble of comments fade. "To further that aim, we will convene hearings, with a court of men chosen to weigh the evidence, and hear the arguments of all the Competitors. At the end of those hearings, the succession of Scotland's throne will be announced. Until then, I am Lord Paramount of Scotland, and as such, demand your fealty. In addition, I demand the surrender of all the royal castles of Scotland into my control. Two months after Scotland's king is chosen, I will return those castles to the new Scottish king."

Edward paused again, then continued, louder now, to be heard over the murmurs of the Scots. "And now listen, men of Scotland, as your leaders acknowledge me as their Lord Superior." Edward took a deep breath, visibly controlling his emotion, then nodded to his men, once again calm.

The Guardians came as a group, kneeling before Edward, each one resigning his authority in tones that varied from wavering to proud. When it was done, when all had relinquished their Guardianship of Scotland, Edward asked each to swear an oath of loyalty to him. And each did. Rory watched, his contempt for them growing, as the Guardians knelt before Edward and swore their fealty. Rory looked at his father, who had tears in his eyes. Their gazes met, then fell away.

Brabazon came forward then, announcing, "The most serene prince, the Lord Edward, by God's grace illustrious King of England and Wales, Lord of Ireland, Duke of Aquitaine, and Lord Protector of Scotland, appoints each of you as Guardian of Scotland, subject to his rule."

Like puppets, Rory thought, the Guardians stood in line to sign that they acknowledged Edward of England as the sovereign lord of their land. And then the nine Competitors, along with the younger Robert Bruce, who somehow had appeared on the dais, came forward to kneel before Edward, one by one swearing their oaths of loyalty to him as Lord Superior of Scotland, then signing as well. Rory felt the bitter taste of bile in his throat.

When it was done, Edward shook back his hair and smiled slightly, as though careful not to let his triumph show. He raised his voice. "Hear this, men of Scotland! You have seen your leaders swear their fealty to me. As will the king we choose at the end of the hearings. As will every Scot swear his loyalty to me, by July twenty-seventh. I mean to calm your land. I will do it with your help or without. If you value your lives, your homes, and peace, you will do this without violence. And if you oppose . . . it will still happen."

There was silence.

"Never!" Gannon shouted, and Rory joined him. "Never!"

Edward's expression did not change. "Then pay the price, Highlander. One more or less of you does not change a thing. A score more or less of you changes nothing." His voice grew louder. "I will have this! It is my right!"

"Never," Rory shouted.

He followed his father as Gannon made his way through the crowd, Kieran, Davey, and Liam at their heels as they strode from the Hall, from the Tower, from Norham itself. None of them spoke as they crossed the river, though all around them Scots were shouting their anger and disbelief at what had just happened. They rode like madmen for a mile. Then the talk began. The five of them expostulating on all that had happened, and all they feared would happen now. The road was well known to them, and they paid little attention to their route, nor to how far ahead of their men they had ridden.

"He means to do it," Davey said. "Edward. He means to take Scotland."

"He has done it," Gannon said. "Our own leaders gave Scotland away today. We watched it."

"I dinna believe they would all do it," Rory said. "I kept thinking one of them would refuse."

"What?" Liam asked. "And lose his lands in England? And in Scotland? They have always acted in their own interest. Nothing changes."

They rode into the trees atop a hill, the silence in the shadow of the trees stopping their conversation. The very air seemed to withdraw, the creatures of the forest gone from sight. The men slowed, their horses' hooves quiet on the soft dirt of the road, with its dusting of green leaves. It was cool here, welcome after their hours in the sun, and Rory pushed back his hair with a sigh, realizing where they were. Just on the other side of this copse of trees lay the crossroad, where he would stop and tell them that he was off to Berwick, not Stirling. He leaned back in the saddle to stretch, imagining Isabel's expression when she saw him.

He did not hear the first arrow but saw it instead, as it embedded itself into the trunk of the tree next to him. Then another, closer, but still missing him. If he had not stretched at that moment . . . He whirled to call a warning, but the attackers were already upon them, and the others busy defending themselves and shouting to each other. There were a score or more Scots attacking them. Young. A few Highlanders mixed with Lowlanders. Mercenaries, perhaps, for some of the words they spoke to each other were unintelligible.

"MacGannon! There he is!" one shouted, and two of them set upon him.

Rory fought them off, Kieran rushing to his aid.

"Ye'll pay for yer sins, MacGannon," one man shouted, his eyes blazing with fury. "Ye'll die for them."

But the man was the one who died instead, as Kieran's blade ran through him. It was chaos for a moment, then over as their own men arrived, making short work of the attackers. They killed several; the others rode off, whooping loudly as though they had been victorious. Rory and his father, on horseback, a little removed from the others, watched the attackers leave.

"They kent yer name," Gannon said. "It was ye they were after, Rory."

Rory nodded, catching his breath. "Aye, Da. Aye, I ken."

"Ye'll no' be going to Stirling, lad, where they could pick ye off in a crowd. I'm getting ye somewhere safe. Ye'll go to Magnus."

"Da, I'm going to Berwick."

"God's blood, dinna argue with me! I'll not be the one telling yer mother that ye're . . ." Gannon stopped. When he continued, his voice was quieter. "It's Isabel ye're wanting to see, aye?"

"It has been a verra long time since I saw her."

"Aye. And since ye let it go this long, I'm thinking the lass doesna mean as much to ye as ye first thought."

"She means more." Rory glanced at the now empty road before them, then back at his father. "I tried to forget her, Da. What have I to offer a lass like her? She's English,

I'm a Highlander. We're either about to be occupied by the English, or we're going to war with them. We have little in common, and little of worth between us. I am a younger son."

"Ye'll have the Ayrshire lands one day."

"Aye, sir. One day, and I'm not in any hurry for that day to come. We're too different, she and I, our lives have been so verra different. It would never work. She's happy at last in Berwick with her friends, and I could never live there."

"And ye've been telling yerself that since ye saw her last?"

"Aye."

"D'ye believe it yet?"

"I'm trying to."

"But ye still want to see her?"

"I do."

Gannon moved the reins back and forth, then looked into Rory's eyes. "I'm asking ye not to go to Berwick. For me. For yer mother. And for the lass herself."

"For the lass? Why?"

"If ye love a lass, ye have a responsibility to keep her safe, aye?"

"Aye." Rory saw where his father's argument was going and felt his heart sink. "Ye're thinking I'd be bringing danger to her."

"There are men willing to follow ye and kill ye and whomever ye're with. Today we fought them off. Could she? And after ye're gone, they'd kent who she is. They could reach her any time and ye'd be far away. Is that what ye want?"

Rory looked out over the road for a long moment,

remembering his fine eyes filled with fear when Walter Langton had talked to them that day at the Tower. Isabel in jeopardy. He sighed, then nodded. "I'll go to Ayrshire."

STIRLING CASTLE, SCOTLAND

Nell MacDonald Crawford heard the riders pound into the courtyard, heard the greetings and the excitement in the voices of the men who welcomed them. She longed to hurry to the window and see who had arrived, and whether Liam was among them, but Nell kept her gaze on the priest who stood before her with a somber expression. She folded her hands at her waist, trying to appear not only attentive but also contrite.

"I'm sure you understand why I had to speak with you, milady," the priest said. "It is not the first time."

Nell swallowed her irritation. He was a good man, if entirely without humor. But then, she reminded herself, how could he possibly understand? He had never been a lass. Of course the priest was correct. Her girls should not be stealing looks at the lads during the sermon, even an interminable one on the duty of a dying Christian to clear his soul of sin. But Meg was fifteen and Elissa only thirteen.

"I am sorry, Father. I will speak to them immediately," she said, glancing at her daughters who were standing out of earshot against the wall.

Meg was tall, like Nell's sister, Margaret, after whom she'd been named. Elissa had not reached her full height, but she already had a penchant for getting herself in trouble. As Nell had had at that age. And sometimes still did.

The priest shook his head sorrowfully. "It cannot happen again."

"No, Father," Nell said apologetically. "I will speak to them, be assured of that. But ye ken that such young lasses may find it difficult to be thinking of their own deaths."

"They are very young." The priest nodded, as though realizing their youth for the first time.

Nell bit her tongue, anxious to go downstairs and see who had arrived. She could hear the voices outside, some raised in anger. But none of them Liam's. The noise quieted and the knot in her stomach loosened. Nell bobbed a curtsy and made her escape, motioning for her daughters to follow her down the stairs.

"Well, Mama? Are we to face death?" Meg asked.

"Ye'll not take that tone, young lady," Nell said. "I am weary of making excuses for the two of ye. Ye'll mind yerselves next time or I'll tell the priest he needs to spend time instructing ye on how to save yer souls. God kens ye need it."

"But, Mama, ye've said ye were just like us when ye were young," Elissa said, clattering behind her. "Tell us again what it was like."

"Ye came here during the reign of King Alexander III and Queen Margaret . . . ," Meg prompted. "Scotland was at peace. That's how ye always start it."

Nell sighed. She could never stay angry at her girls for long. "Aye. It was a marvelous place to be. The court was filled with music and laughter, and the king seemed to prize his people. I was verra young. I thought Alexander's court was the center of the world. Davey came occasionally, and Gannon and Margaret—"

"Were favorites of the king," Meg finished. "Until Gannon—"

"Was banished," Nell said. "For saving my life. We will not speak of that." But all these years later she still thought of that dreadful time, followed by the lonely years. And then, at long last, Liam.

"So what will we do, Mama? Will we stay after the new king is chosen?"

"Depends on who it is," Nell said. "I canna see the Bruces wanting us to stay on. And I canna see the Balliols letting us go. We'll have to wait and see."

Below them the wooden door to the stairwell banged against the wall, and they heard the sound of boots on stone.

"Nell! Nell, is that ye up there?"

"Aye! Liam, we're here!" Nell lifted her skirts and ran down the stairs like a young girl to meet him. He was not alone. He'd come up several steps, the space behind him filled with his men, but she saw only the foremost man, into whose open arms she threw herself.

"Liam!" she cried, kissing him soundly, heedless of those watching.

Her husband's face was weary, his clothes dusty from his journey. But it was the look in his eyes when he met her gaze that made her heart leap, and her excitement at his return fade. He was angry. Beyond angry.

"My love," she asked, "what is the news?"

"They swore their loyalty to him, Nell. Every damned one of them."

"What did ye do?"

"We left. Many others did the same, but many more did not. And Edward is demanding that all the royal castles be given into his hands. He's sending troops to occupy them. Stirling will be one of the first." He nodded at her gasp. "And there's more. He's called for a court to be set up, of auditors who will decide who should be king, overseen by Edward, of course. They'll start next month. In Berwick. Now come, yer brother and Gannon await."

Liam threw the door open to their rooms and swept her into her brother's embrace. Nell turned from Davey to Gannon.

"Nell," Gannon said, embracing her. "It's good to be back."

"It's good to have ye back. I ken ye'll hurry home to Margaret, but at least ye're here tonight." She stepped back to let her girls embrace their uncles, then poured a cup of wine for herself and sat down with the men.

They told her again what had happened in Norham. Nell studied her brother while she listened. Davey never seemed to age. His hair was still dark, his demeanor always cheerful, despite all that had happened in his life. Davey had his lands on Skye, his wife Maureen at his side, and his castle almost completed. Nell had Liam and their wonderful girls. God had been good to them.

And to Margaret as well, she thought, looking fondly at her brother-in-law. Or perhaps Gannon was the fortunate one there. Her sister was a prize beyond value. How all their lives had changed. And now . . . would it be war again? She glanced at her daughters—she would bargain her soul to keep them safe. She turned to find Liam watching her and knew he'd guessed her thoughts.

"Will you sign the oath?" Nell asked the men.

"I willna do it," Gannon said. "I'm not a Scot."

Liam snorted. "Ye married one, produced several, and ye've owned and lived on Scottish land for decades. Ye're one of us now, and the king may send men to the Highlands to convince ye of just that."

"I'm thinking the king has better things to do than send men to Loch Gannon or Skye to ensure we swear fealty to him."

"But Magnus is in Ayrshire, and easily reached," Nell said.

"Aye," Gannon said. "Which is why I told Rory to tell his brother to swear to Edward, and why I want Rory to stay with Magnus. I want my lads safe."

"Kieran wants to go to Berwick for the hearings," Davey said, "and to see this Rachel. She's captured his fancy something fierce. Maybe it will pass. He's young."

"And how old were ye when ye met Maureen, lad?" Nell asked him.

"Nine. But that was different."

"Aye. Ye were captives together. But ye remembered her, even when ye were sold to the Danes and went to Jutland. And ye went back for her, young as ye were."

Davey gave her a half smile. "That was different, Nell."

She sighed. "So we'll be getting English soldiers here, at Stirling?"

"Aye," Liam said. "They'll use Stirling as a base to monitor the countryside. And then, of course, Edward will be coming here himself."

"I'm glad I live on the edge of the world," Davey said. "Our Comyn cousins are already telling me I should have signed the oath."

"We need to be invisible now," Gannon said. "Lay as low as ye can. Perhaps all this will pass when the king is chosen. Balliols and Bruces will still hate each other, aye, but the rest of us can get back to our lives. Let us not draw attention to ourselves. Let the madmen fight between themselves."

"What is it ye've seen in yer dreams, Gannon?"

"Nothing I can say for certain. But we need to be careful."

"I think we learned that well," Davey said. "Ye're not staying here, Liam?"

Nell heard the odd note in her brother's voice. "Davey, what else has happened? Liam. Tell me. What is it? What has happened that ye're all looking at each other like lads with a secret?"

"A'right," Liam said. "First, love, ye can see we're all alive and whole."

"And was that ever in question?"

"For a moment or two," Liam said.

"Tell me all of it, if ye would. And now, before I faint."

He told her of the attack, of the men knowing Rory's name.

"Margaret and Maureen will be sick about this," Nell said. "And ye have no idea who they are, the ones who attacked ye?"

"No," Liam said. He looked at Davey and Gannon. "Highlanders, or dressed like them among them. But now, when there's fighting in the streets and on lonely roads, when Edward of England is looming on the horizon and everyone's watching what will happen next . . . now is a good time for a murder, or two, or four, that will barely be noticed. They want revenge and they kent we would be there, and returning. We're not staying here in Stirling, love. We're going home." Liam glanced at their daughters. "We'll keep out of the thick of it, aye?"

Nell nodded. "We'll stay out of it. Let Edward and the Competitors fight their battle without us. We'll keep safe in Ayrshire."

In that, she was wrong.

Ayrshire. Nell took a deep breath of the fragrant air. Summer in Scotland was magnificent, the hills alive with heather and the trees bright green. It was hard to remember that winter would come soon. And so might Edward of England. The king had declared that he would make a progression through Scotland, visiting Dumfermline and St. Andrews, Edinburgh and Perth. And Stirling. But they would not be there to greet him. They'd be here, in peaceful Ayrshire, far to the south and west of Stirling.

Below them, in the verdant glen, lay the town of Paisley, where they hoped to find lodging at the abbey. One more day and they'd be home. The trip south had been an easy one. They had set a leisurely pace, enjoying, for once, no set schedule. Liam had sent men ahead to tell the staff to prepare the house for their arrival, but there was little to be done there. The house Liam had been born in was a simple structure, two stories of rambling whitewashed stone surrounded by a high stone wall and a belt of trees that had stood for centuries. And farther on, the pastures and fields tended by Liam's tenants, whose rent was generally paid with their crops.

In the good years Liam's family ate well. In the lean, he kept a tally of what his tenants owed, which was often forgiven. In all the years Nell had known him, he'd never forced anyone off his land. Perhaps it was that he had been without a home for so many years. Perhaps it was simply the goodness of his character, but he was an indulgent landlord and was content with that. As was she.

Her childhood home had been destroyed when she was twelve. She'd spent some years at her sister's home at Loch Gannon, many more years in royal castles, Stirling most of all. But Liam's home was her home as well. They would spend the next few months here, they'd decided. Or perhaps forever. If they were fortunate.

The news was unsettling. Edward had begun his progression through Scotland, stopping, along with a huge entourage, at every city that could house him. He would go to Berwick last, where he would begin the hearings that would end in his choosing the next king of Scotland.

"Ranald will join us in Paisley," Liam said, looking up from the letter he'd been reading. "He's doing his rounds and says he'll stay until we arrive."

"Good." Nell was pleased. She was very fond of Ranald Crawford, Liam's uncle and the Sheriff of Ayrshire. He was a powerful but temperate man, who had been good to Liam through the years.

Liam's mother had died when Liam was very young. When, just a few years later, his father had died as well, Ranald had stepped in to care for the orphaned boy. Despite losing his parents, Liam had had a happy childhood, surrounded as he had been by Ranald and his sons, William and Ronald, both close in age to Liam, and their cousins Malcolm, William, and John Wallace.

"Ranald has my cousin William with him," Liam said. "Enjoy the quiet we have now. We'll not have it tonight."

"Not if William Wallace is as I remember him," Nell said. "He was never alone. He always had a group of lads with him and was coming up with something to keep them all busy."

"I dinna think ye'll see a change in that," Liam said. "Last I saw William he had about ten companions."

Nell smiled. Liam's cousin William had always been a favorite of hers. He, with her daughters, would make for a lively evening.

Ranald was waiting at the Abbey for them, his smile wide, his arms open. He embraced Liam and Nell and told their girls that their beauty was a sight to behold. Meg and Elissa giggled and blushed.

"And ye remember this one," Ranald said, gesturing to the young man with him. "My sister's son William Wallace."

Liam shook his hand, and William greeted them warmly as Nell hugged him.

"Look at ye, William!" she said. "Ye've grown again! I dinna think it possible."

"Nor did I." William smiled. "I dinna do anything to cause it but eat."

"Aye," Ranald said with a laugh. "Exactly. Ye dinna do anything but eat."

"My da says that's why he lets me travel with ye, Uncle," William said, his grin wide, "so ye can feed me for a change."

Nell laughed with him, this giant of a young man with the bright smile. She'd not seen him in years, and the change in him was remarkable. He'd been a boy the last time; he was grown now, or at least she hoped so, for he was extraordinarily tall, well over six feet. His hair was brown and wavy, his eyes bright. He'd always been a charming boy, and she was pleased to see that William's bright manner and winning ways seemed not to have been changed.

"You've heard that every Scot must swear fealty by July twenty-seventh?" Ranald asked. At their nods, he continued. "They're to report to Ayr, or Inverness, or Perth, or Dumfries. Every Scot. Or face severe penalties. And I'm to enforce it."

"And if they dinna?" Liam asked.

"I'm not sure what will happen. You know many won't do it."

"Gannon willna," Nell said. "And I doubt Davey will."

"No," Liam said thoughtfully. "And will Edward enforce it, d'ye think?"

Ranald sighed. "He's told us, the sheriffs of Scotland, to enforce it, and he's sending his soldiers to see that we do. Which means I am asked to oversee my fellow Scots paying homage to an English king."

"What a mockery this makes of the hearings Edward will hold in Berwick," Nell cried. "What use is there in even holding them? If we have all sworn fealty to Edward, is he not the lord of Scotland?"

"Exactly," Ranald said.

"What will the Crawfords do?" Nell asked, slanting a look at her husband, for Liam had always been loyal to his family. Whither the Crawfords went, he would go. And she and their girls. "Will they sign it?"

"Most will. I have, unpleasant as that was," Ranald said.

"My da won't," William said.

"I have warned him that refusing to sign puts my sister and their sons in jeopardy," Ranald said.

"But I agree with him, Uncle," William said. "My father should follow his heart. You know what my other uncle says."

Ranald frowned. "Aye, I've heard it enough times."

Nell and Liam exchanged a mystified look.

William smiled. "My uncle the priest told me 'No gift is like to libertie. Then never live in slaverie.' "

"Fine words," Ranald said, "but sometimes difficult to live by when ye have a wife and sons."

Nell met William's gaze, saw his intensity and earnestness, and smiled. "To have liberty, William, is worth all the riches in the world. Never forget that. Freedom is not a word. It is a passion."

William's eyebrows rose, and he grinned at her. "Aye, it is!"

Liam looked from William to Nell and reached for her hand.

Ranald drummed his fingers together. "This is too serious! It's been far too long since I've seen you, Nell. Look at your daughters! You are a most fortunate man, Liam Crawford. Each one is a beauty."

Liam laughed. "I know that well, Uncle! And each one is as much trouble as she is bonnie!"

It was a merry evening, the first of many, Nell hoped,

now that they were back in Ayrshire. They set out for the last leg of their journey in the late morning and arrived at midday to find all in good order. Liam took the horses off to the stables, and Nell and the girls unpacked. The world and Scotland might be in an uproar, but here, on this quiet bit of land, there was peace. She said a prayer that it might continue, then made up their bed, smiling as she heard her daughters' laughter in the other room. They were home. All was well.

TWELVE

Rory wiped the blade of his sword on a handful of leaves, then looked at the man on the ground. He felt ill, but at least he'd not lost his meal, as Kieran had. Not that he blamed his cousin. The scene they'd come across on their daily ride of Magnus's lands was stomach-turning. Two men dead. A woman, who'd died just as they'd found her. And one man alive, but barely, his stomach torn open. He'd cried like a bairn when Rory had leaned over him, and asked Rory to be merciful and end his suffering.

And Rory had. Which had, no doubt, ensured him a spot in hell, if he'd not already been headed there. He sighed and looked for a soft bit of ground in which to bury the four. This murder was unnatural, and unsettling.

There was no easy way to know who had killed them, for their belongings had been stripped from their bodies, leaving only the weathered woolen clothing most Scots wore on the road—long tunics and lined cloaks. That their cloaks were lined indicated that the victims had not been vagrants. He cut a piece of hair from each head, and a square of cloth from each cloak and took their belts and a brooch that the attackers must not have noticed. And yet he did not believe this had been simple robbery. It had been murder, the kind that had been happening all too often, and far too close to his brother's home.

"Come," he said to his brother's men, gesturing them forward. "We'll bury these poor souls and then get home. Two of ye, get yerselves to the road and watch. We dinna want to be set upon unawares."

He looked at the bodies on the ground and swore. This was the second unexplained attack in a fortnight. The roads were dangerous, as they'd learned on their return from Norham. They'd heard that Scotland was in turmoil, both from the increasing discord between the Balliol and the Bruce factions, and from the invasion of English soldiers, but they'd not been prepared for this kind of attack.

With so many helping, it did not take long to dig the graves. When a cairn had been laid atop the graves to keep the animals out, Rory said a few prayers over the dead, then washed with the others in the burn nearby before returning to their horses. He pulled a cloth out of his pack to dry his hands; as he did so, he dislodged a circle of branches, which fell to the ground.

It was Isabel's crown, dried and brown now, most of the needles gone. But still he kept it with him. He should discard it, he knew, for it would not last much longer, and he might never see Isabel de Burke again. But he wrapped it carefully in the cloth, ignoring Kieran's crooked smile as he watched.

He was the Oak King and this was the symbol of his reign. He was glad the story of the Oak King was just an old tale, a way to explain the world to those too young to know the yearly rhythms of growth and death. For if not, he would be dead by now, at least symbolically, for it was well after midsummer. And this was Henry de Boyer's season. Rory leapt onto his pony and lifted the reins, leading the others away, then turned, for one last look at the four graves under the sheltering oak.

His time in London seemed very long ago.

Magnus's men welcomed them back, telling them that Magnus had a guest. Ranald Crawford, Sheriff of Ayrshire, was within. Rory, wet through from the rain that had caught them as they'd neared the coast, nodded. They'd been expecting this visit, for none of them—not Magnus, nor he, nor Kieran—had sworn their oath to Edward yet. And Ranald was a relative of sorts, their uncle Liam's uncle. Not a blood relative, but still kin. In their seven months here, they'd seen much of him, and much more of Ranald's other nephews, the Wallace lads, with whom they played dice frequently.

He tossed his reins to the waiting lad and crossed the yard. Someday Magnus would return to Loch Gannon and Rory would live here in Ayrshire. The house had originally been a small fortress overlooking the sea, not much more than a lookout station, but over the years it had been enlarged and walls had been erected around it. The original rough gray stone building was still visible, serving as the entrance to the hall their father had built here, a comfortable if not grand space with a large fireplace dominating the room. Their mother had plastered the walls and hung tapestries and placed rugs on the floor. Jocelyn had made her own improvements when she'd married Magnus several years ago.

Rory and Magnus had been close when they were younger, but since Magnus's marriage to Jocelyn their lives had been very different. This visit had both reinforced their affection for each other and highlighted their differences. Rory wondered how his wild older brother had turned into a man who pondered with his wife whether to repaint the beams of the ceilings. Jocelyn's doing, of course.

The house was warm, and welcoming. Rory and Kieran stripped themselves of their wet clothing in the kitchen, waiting by the fire while new clothing was brought from their room.

Magnus found them there. "Ranald's here," he said. "And William is with him. We thought ye'd be back earlier. Was there trouble?"

"Aye," Rory said, telling him what they'd found. He handed the bundle to Magnus. "I took these, locks of hair and bits of clothing, to see if anyone recognized any of it. Someone must be missing them or expecting them."

Magnus opened the bundle. "I dinna recognize any of this, but Ranald might. Look, dinna tell Jocelyn about the murders just the now, a'right? I'll send runners out with the word." He tucked the bundle away and led the way to the hall.

Ranald and William greeted them warmly. Jocelyn rose from her seat at the long table near the fireplace. Rory had always thought she looked like one of the fey, the fairie people who had once ruled this land, displaced by the Picts. Her hair was very light, almost white, and her eyes were the palest blue. She did not walk; she floated, which enhanced her fragile appearance. Until she opened her mouth. Her voice was a whine, and her face was most often set in lines of dissatisfaction. Rory had never heard her laugh aloud, nor sing with joy. What his brother found in Jocelyn he had never understood, but Magnus was mad about her, always had been.

"Rory," she said. "Kieran. I will have more food prepared." She sighed, as though their return had been unexpected, and went to the kitchens.

Rory and Kieran thanked her, then exchanged a look. They'd talked about Jocelyn many times and were in agreement on her charms. Magnus, as always, seemed to notice nothing disagreeable about her manner and simply watched her walk away.

"Sit," Magnus ordered. "We've ale and wine ready and food on the way. Tell Ranald what ye found."

Ranald listened to their story, then nodded. "It's getting worse." He held up the buckle. "I think this belonged to one of the Irvine lads. If it's the one I'm thinking of, he and two English soldiers had some words last week over swearing the fealty." He shook his head. "It's getting uglier every day. I'm here to convince ye three to swear and get it over with."

"William," Rory asked his uncle's cousin, "have ye sworn yet?"

William Wallace grinned. "I've been swearing about this a great deal, aye. I'm not a landowner, so I'm not required to swear. My father is. And yours is, but Magnus can swear in his stead."

"Liam is a landowner too," Kieran said.

"Which is where I'm going next," Ranald said. "They've

returned from Stirling, no doubt because English soldiers are on their way there. Liam must agree to swear fealty. I cannot have all my family in jeopardy. It's bad enough that the lot of you got into it with the Bruce's men."

Rory nodded. That had not been wise of them. He, William, and Kieran, accompanied by several of William's Crawford cousins, had been involved in a brawl with some of the Bruce men at a tavern in Ayr. No one had been seriously hurt, but the incident had caught the attention of the English soldier garrisoned there.

"And now Malcolm!" Ranald said. "I tell ye, this is not wise!"

Rory looked from Ranald to William. "What? Which Malcolm, yer father or your brother?"

"My father," William said. "He's refusing to swear fealty. He said he could not do it. He's leaving Ayrshire with my brother Malcolm rather than swear."

"He's refusing?" Rory shot a glance at Magnus, who nodded.

"Do not think to follow his example," Ranald said sternly. "Aye, Malcolm's gone, abandoned his family." He silenced William's protest with a raised hand. "You're young, William, and I'm glad you defend your father, but his actions are not wise. Principles are one thing, but he's left your mother, my sister, to face the consequences."

"She was in agreement," William argued.

"Which does not matter," Ranald said. "He left her to fend for herself. We've taken Margaret and the youngest, John, in, for now at least. I'm here to convince you to be wiser, and off to your uncle Liam next to do the same."

"What will you do?" Rory asked William.

Ranald answered. "William's off to Dundee to study

to be a priest, and that will keep him out of trouble. But, lads, think of how much better off my sister would have been in her own home."

"So ye're doing it, aye?" Rory asked William. What would it be like, to be that tall, that strong, and choose to be a man of God? Of course, William had had little say in it. His father was a knight. His older brother, also named Malcolm, would inherit his father's lands—assuming he'd not just lost them by refusing to swear fealty. It was traditional that second sons became priests, and younger ones became soldiers. Which meant that had his own parents thought the same, he'd be off with William to learn to pray for the rest of his life. He was grateful that they did not.

William nodded and shrugged. "I like the study . . . we'll see how godly I become. But rest assured, I'll say an extra prayer or two just for you, for I'm thinking you'll be needing them."

Rory grinned. "Better make it more than two. I intend to deserve whichever I get, heaven or hell."

"I'll make it several then."

"Ye could spend yer whole life praying for him. I ken our mother has," Magnus said, his laugh so like their father's that Rory was startled. How was it that he'd never realized it before?

"What will happen to Malcolm Wallace now?" Rory asked Ranald. "We've all heard that the penalties for not swearing will be severe. But what does that mean? Death? A fine? Flogging?"

Ranald's smile faded. "I do not know yet. Maybe all three. Maybe they simply take his land, which means the Wallaces lose everything."

"What I dinna understand," Kieran said, "is how we got here, swearing fealty to a king that is not ours. If we do it, we acknowledge him as our overlord, which means he's ruling Scotland already. So why do we need to go on with the fiction of choosing a Scottish king?"

"We don't, remember?" Rory said. "We dinna get a vote in this. We were sold to Edward."

"Given is more like it," William said, his tone angry now. "I don't like what's happening at all. We have English soldiers in Ayr, and Irvine, and they're moving into every castle and manor house. How can that not be called an occupation?"

"It should be," Rory said. "And the Balliols and Bruces fighting over the scraps. And ye," he said to William, "on yer knees, praying for the lot of us."

"I'll be a busy man," William said lightly.

"We'll all be busy," Ranald said. "Pray that the hearings in Berwick find us a king soon."

"I'm thinking of going to see for myself," Kieran said.

"Think again, lad," Magnus said, handing him a letter. "From yer da. Calling ye home. Rory, I'd like ye to stay until things settle around here, if ye would. It will make me feel better, kenning that Jocelyn has the both of us protecting her."

August 1291, Berwick-Upon-Tweed, Scotland

Rachel stood next to her father on the riverbank, watching her sister and mother arrive on the ferry that crossed the Tweedmouth estuary. Behind her the city hummed with activity, for Berwick was preparing to host a king. And perhaps see another king chosen. The weather was clear now, but the thin clouds and the look of the sky promised rain later, not unusual for August. She'd learned to predict the weather in this strange northern city that was now their home; she'd also learned to predict her father's mood. The second was the easier of the two tasks.

She didn't need to ask her father if he was worried. Jacob rubbed his chin and sighed occasionally, and she knew his mood was somber. Small wonder. The inn had been doing very well, so well that her father had bought the building next door and broken through the wall to join the two. So well that her father had hired four more people and Rachel's days were so full that she hardly noticed the months passing. So well that they'd put Isabel to work on her second day with them and she'd never stopped, and it was a delight to have her with them. So well that she'd almost forgotten what had brought them to Berwick.

But now . . . Edward of England was coming—bringing an army, they'd been told, and why did a king need an army except to wage war? It was difficult to acknowledge the possibility that once again they might be driven from their home. Should they flee to the Continent? But where? Jews had been driven out of Anjou and Gascony—by Edward Plantagenet himself. Gilbert, the former innkeeper, had told them to stay, saying that the king would not come to the inn, nor would his courtiers, who would be housed at the castle or in grander places. The less important members of the royal entourage who might come to the inn would not even notice the Angenhoffs as long as the rooms were clean and the food palatable. If anyone asked, Gilbert said, he'd claim to still own the inn.

And so they'd decided to stay. But still they all worried, and once again Mama sewed coins into their hems.

And now . . . now, of all times, Sarah had announced that she would marry Edgar Keith. Rachel had not quite believed Sarah would go through with it. But Sarah was returning now, with Mother, from meeting Edgar's parents, the last obstacle to the match.

"It will be good to have them back," Rachel said.

Her father merely nodded while he watched the ferry land.

"I hope it went well, " she said.

"How could it not?" Jacob asked. "How could any mother not want your sister to marry her son? The boy is smitten."

"He is, isn't he? And very handsome. Your grandchildren will be lovely."

Jacob's smile was weak. "My grandsons will be handsome, child, not lovely."

"What if you have granddaughters?"

"Then they will be beautiful, like their mother, and aunt, and grandmother."

"Oh, Papa! Mama and Sarah are beautiful, but I am not."

"Both my daughters are beautiful," Jacob said firmly.

Rachel kissed his cheek. "Thank you. I wish they would live closer. She'll be two days' journey away."

"She'll be safe. No one will notice her there."

"We'll miss her."

Jacob rubbed his chin. "We will. We will. Isabel will help. She's been a godsend, Rachel. Always cheerful, always thoughtful. I would not have thought she could work as hard as she does. I don't know what we would have done without her. Or she without us. Still nothing from her mother?"

"Nothing. Her grandmother writes once a month, but no word from her mother. Not one letter."

"What kind of mother sends her only child, an innocent girl, to travel alone and wait for a father who might never come? I ask you, Rachel, what kind of woman does that? Your mother wouldn't. Look, look at her there, a bright smile on her face." He met Rachel's gaze. "She hates this match as much as I do. But you'd never know it, would you? And Sarah will not either. You'll not tell her."

"No, Papa, I wouldn't. I want her to be happy."

"So do I. But she won't be. It can't work." He rubbed his chin again.

Rachel sighed and followed her father to the ferry. Sarah's wide smile let her know that the trip had been a success, and Rachel buried her own shameful hope that it would have failed. She would be happy for Sarah. And like their father, never let Sarah know otherwise. How strange life was, she thought, for the Almighty to have given her Isabel just when Sarah was leaving them. And for Edward of England to have followed them here.

It wasn't until late that night that the sisters had a chance to talk. They'd returned to the inn to find it suddenly full of travelers and Isabel overwhelmed because she'd been serving alone this evening. They had immediately plunged into the many tasks that awaited them and had not had a moment to sit together. When the kitchen had been cleaned and the last of the patrons had left the tavern room, Rachel and Sarah huddled together in the small bed that they shared in the attic and whispered so that Isabel, in her cot across the room, would not hear them.

"Well?" Rachel asked. "How was it? Tell me, tell me!"

"His mother was so very nice. You should have seen her and Mama, like two cats watching each other. But no claws. It was all very polite."

"So it's settled? You will wed?" Rachel felt a pang of sorrow. She should not be so selfish. She wanted Sarah to be happy—but it would never be the same without her.

"Yes. At their Yule celebration. Edgar will come and get me. We'll be wed here with a rabbi, then there with a priest."

"You will have a Christian wedding too? For Edgar?"

Sarah lowered her voice. "When I am married, I will become a Christian."

"How can you . . . ?"

Sarah's expression hardened. "How can I not? I will convert, Rachel. What has God done for those of us who keep our faith? He's let us be driven out of every land on earth. We are not the Chosen People; we are the forsaken people."

"Do you believe it? All the Christian teachings? Do you believe it?"

Sarah shrugged. "It is not so difficult. I will learn it."

"Do Mama and Papa know?"

"It was Mama's idea. We're not going to tell Papa, until after we're wed."

Rachel's mind raced. "But—"

"Mama says we need to survive, and if this is what it takes, then I should do it. She says that our God has not protected us, He's abandoned us. And so I will abandon Him. Edgar loves me, Rachel. He is a good man and I will be the best wife I know how to be. I will have my own home and I will never be forced out of it in the middle of the night."

"What about your children?"

"They will be raised as Christians. When they are grown I will tell them the truth and they can decide for themselves."

"Will you let them visit us?"

"Of course! I'm only changing my name, Rachel."

"And your religion. And where you live. And who you are. And have been."

Sarah smiled a tight smile. "Do not judge me, Rachel. Where has God been in all our travails? Where was He for Isabel? She did no wrong, but she was once a lady-in-waiting to a queen, and now she serves ale in a tavern in another country. And her own mother has abandoned her. There is no God, Rachel, just our own idea of Him. Which I no longer believe. We decide, ourselves, whether to do right or wrong, whether to be good or evil. For some, it is fear that keeps them within the law, but for others it is a greater sense of good. I do not think any religion can make a bad person good. Or protect a good person from bad happening to them. It was chance that brought Edgar to me, and I intend to hold him. He is a good man, and in our house religion will take a second place to love. I will worship where he worships, and truly, there is little difference between the two. Wish me well, Rachel, please." Sarah pulled the cover over her shoulder and turned to face the wall. "It's your turn now. We'll see who—and what—you choose."

Or who and what chooses me. Rachel stared into the dark.

Isabel was wonderful, Rachel thought the next day, watching, from the shade of the tavern wall, as her friend brought in a tray loaded with food. What a transformation in her. Isabel had arrived pale and thin and with a heart so heavy that she'd cried every day. The time she'd spent here in Berwick with Rachel's family, Rachel was proud to say, had healed her.

Isabel was full of ideas for improvements for the inn. This summer had been very warm. The tavern room, which faced west, had been uncomfortably hot. Isabel had suggested that they serve food on the flat terrace behind the inn, where patrons could sit outside in the shade. The terrace was so popular that they'd enlarged it, then enlarged it again. And still new patrons came, waiting to be fed.

Her mother's food, always wonderful, was partly responsible. As were the comfortable rooms upstairs that were seldom unoccupied, and never more so than now, when half of Scotland was expected in Berwick. Edward had established a court of auditors to make the choices of who would be king.

The new court, along with everyone else who wanted to be here for the momentous decision, had already begun to fill the castle and now the town. Thus far Gilbert had been correct in predicting that none of the courtiers, nor anyone that Isabel knew would come to the inn. And those Englishmen who had come had paid no attention to Rachel or her family. Everyone at The Oak and The Ash sighed with relief. They all hoped that finding Scotland a new king would prove to be a simple process, but with so many involved in the decision, few believed that it would.

"One hundred and four auditors," Isabel said, coming to stand with Rachel.

"You have to stop reading my mind," Rachel said with a laugh. "I was just thinking of them."

"We're all thinking of them and the man who will accompany them. Who needs a hundred and four auditors? And why that number?"

"Forty are Balliol's nominees. Forty are Bruce's nominees. The rest are from Edward's council."

"Ah, at least they will represent the common man," Isabel said caustically.

"What court does, royal or otherwise? It's absurd. But who are we to care? We're making money from them for a change."

Isabel nodded. "How strange that King Edward is now responsible for refilling your coffers. Who would have thought that?"

"Who indeed?" Rachel laughed.

Isabel glanced around them. "Rachel, I heard you and Sarah talking last night. I couldn't help but hear. I know you don't want her to marry Edgar."

"It's not that. I knew she would marry someone. But she's changing everything about herself. She's becoming a completely different person."

"She loves him, and he loves her. Does it matter what God she prays to?"

"It does to my father. It is who we are, the rules by which we live. But, then I listen to her and what she says makes sense. But still . . . how can our heritage matter so little? And yet, I do want her to be happy. Is she right?"

Isabel frowned slightly. "There is merit in what she says. Why should there be just one road to God, or to good? Why, Rachel? Look at what has happened to your family, to your people."

"Look at the history of man, Isabel. What I fear is that the sister I have always known, who has shared our history, and our people's history, is willing to walk away from all that. Just walk away into a different world."

"And leave you behind. That's what you fear, that the bond between you will be changed forever. And it will. Nothing stays the same. Just look at me."

"It feels like she cares more for him than for us."

"She is in love. She does not see it like that. She still loves all of you."

"My father is convinced their marriage will fail."

"I hope not," Isabel said, then shrank back against the stone. "Rachel, hide me! Oh, dear God, he's here!"

Rachel spun around, expecting to see Walter Langton, but the man who had just stepped through the inn door was far from the monster Isabel had described. He was extraordinarily handsome. He wore the uniform of a king's officer, the badge of a knight. She whirled back to Isabel.

"Is that Henry de Boyer?"

Isabel's eyes were huge. "Yes. Here. What do we do?"

"He is even more handsome than you said!" Rachel whispered, admiring de Boyer's even features and long limbs, his dark hair gleaming in the sun, curling just over his collar. "No wonder you found him memorable."

"He must not see me!" Isabel whispered. "What do we do?"

"I will distract him so you can make your escape."

Rachel stepped forward quickly, rounding de Boyer and drawing his attention to her when she asked if he needed her help in finding a seat.

"Yes, mistress, if you would," he said.

"Of course," Rachel answered, drawing him to a table at the other end of the terrace while Isabel darted through the door. She brought de Boyer a cup of ale and talked to him about food, then hurried inside to find Isabel.

She found her in the kitchen, deep in conversation with Mama, who wiped her apron and started for the door. "I must see this young man for myself. No one can be that handsome. No one."

"Mama! What about Isabel?"

"She must hide. Go upstairs, Isabel. If one of the king's knights has found us, more will follow. You will hide until they are gone, no matter how long it takes. Welcome to the world of the exile, child. Don't look so startled. We knew they would come, just not when. Rachel, get back outside and feed our guests."

"This could endanger your family," Isabel said concerned.

Mama laughed harshly. "Oh, yes, you are far more dangerous to us than a city full of King Edward's soldiers. Go, child."

Isabel watched him from the room just under the attic. It was Henry. She'd had a moment of doubt after she'd darted up the stairs, wondering if she had lost her wits entirely and it was some other man downstairs. But of course it was not. It was Henry, looking even more appealing than he had in London. He was alone, which was curious, for surely he had tasks if he was here for the king, and of course he must be, for what else could have brought him to Berwick? She should have realized some of the king's courtiers or knights would find the inn, with its reputation for serving the best food in the city.

What if he was staying here? She knelt beside the open window and peered out. How long would it take to choose a king? Days? Months? She watched while he ate his meal, laughed with Rachel, and ordered more ale and a cup of wine. Her heart sank. He was waiting for someone.

She sat down on the floor, her back to the wall, then leapt up again as she heard Alis's voice. Alis de Braun, of all people. Here, of all places. Her heart pounded. Why was Alis here? The king had not yet arrived. Why was a lady of his court here before him?

She peered out again. Yes, Alis sat with Henry, wearing a blue silk gown and cream underskirt and wimple. Her neckline was low and she leaned forward often, as though she did not know how much of her lovely bosom she revealed. Her headdress was unadorned but elegant. Even her shoes were exquisite. She sat across the table from him, simpering, smiling. Ignoring Rachel, who served the food. And then there was a shrill cry, a scrape of wooden chair on stone, and Rachel's clear and calm voice.

"I'm so sorry. Here, let me dab at it and try to get the stain out."

"It is fine," Alis said with annoyance. "Truly."

"I insist that you come to the kitchen. My mother will know just what to do."

"That's hardly necessary," Alis said.

"I insist," Rachel said smoothly, smiling at both Alis and Henry. "I do insist that you come with me."

"Very well," Alis said and rose to follow Rachel.

Isabel could see Rachel's smug smile and laughed quietly to herself. Rachel was wonderful. Isabel knew just what her friend would do next, and a moment later she was proved correct, for Rachel returned and talked quietly to Henry. Rachel laughed at something Henry said, then left him to serve the other patrons. Henry looked around him.

Then, as though he knew she was there, he looked right at Isabel.

THIRTEEN

For a moment, just the briefest breath of time, she stood frozen, then pulled back into the shadow of the room, her heart pounding. Had he seen her? Of course he had. But, no, she was in the dim room and he was in the bright sunlight. But she had seen his expression change. He'd seen her. He knew she was here.

She threaded her fingers together and paced the room, then stopped, knowing her footsteps could be heard below her. She sank to the floor, where she sat while the long rays of evening came and dimmed, while the noise below increased with the amount of ale and wine served. She was still there, in the gloaming, when Rachel came to her at last, sinking wearily on the bed.

"What on earth were you doing spying on him?" Rachel demanded.

"I just wanted to see if it was truly him! Do you think he saw me?"

Rachel sighed heavily. "Yes. He was still staring up here when I went back to him. I asked him if he was well, and he said he'd just seen a ghost. Then he asked me if we had a girl named Isabel de Burke staying here. I said no. And then he asked if we knew of anyone named de Burke. Or Lonsby. He saw you, Isabel."

Isabel covered her mouth.

"What were you thinking?" Rachel asked.

"I was not thinking. I just wanted to see him. Did he say anything else?"

"No."

"Is the whole court here?"

"No, only a few."

"Is Langton here?"

"I've not heard of him, but I will ask. Isabel, my parents say you should stay hidden while they're here."

"And what of the hearings?"

"The king is collecting all the petitions but saying nothing. Some of the men said they would not be here long, but others said even if the king leaves, his soldiers will remain here."

"If King Edward takes over Scotland, what will you do?"

Rachel shook her head and looked into the distance. "I don't know. If we have to leave, it will kill my father. He is so proud of what he's built here. I don't think he has the heart to do it again. Perhaps Sarah is right, to marry a Gentile and never have to worry about being forced out of your home."

"That would kill him, Rachel. He's so unhappy about Sarah and Edgar."

"I know. He calms himself by saying if she's a Jew, her children will be Jews."

"Not if they do not practice your religion. They'll be what they're taught."

"No. They'll be what their blood is."

"Do you want me to leave, Rachel? Ask your parents. I do not want to bring attention to them."

"Where would you go?"

"I don't know. But ask them, Rachel. Maybe I should go to Newcastle."

"No. You're not leaving. We'll hide you."

"And if I'm found?"

"You've done nothing wrong, Isabel. You keep forgetting that."

"But I have, Rachel. I questioned a king. And one cannot do that."

Isabel crept downstairs once the terrace was empty and the tavern room quiet. No knights or courtiers remained, and she breathed a sigh of relief and joined their efforts to get everything prepared for the next day, which was Friday. Shabbat would begin at dusk, when the third star was visible, and Rachel's family would do no work until the following evening.

Isabel was fascinated by all the rules that Rachel was supposed to adhere to, like the thirty-nine things that Jews must not do on the Sabbath. No sowing, plowing, or reaping or binding sheaves, all of which was easy for Rachel's family to avoid.

But there were other things on the list that made life at The Oak and The Ash far more difficult: no kneading or baking, sifting, or kindling a fire. How was one to run an inn under such constraints, when the rest of the world rested on Sunday? Which was why, Rachel's parents told her often, Isabel's arrival had been a gift to them, for she could work while they could not. Gilbert helped, of course, for he knew everything about running an inn, even if he was no longer able to do it all himself. They had hired townspeople to work. But Sabbaths were still difficult, and Isabel's efforts helped immeasurably.

By the next evening, the weather had turned cool, and Isabel helped bring in the tables and benches from the terrace. When the third star was visible, Rachel and her family retired to say their prayers and eat their Sabbath supper. Isabel and Gilbert tended to the last of the patrons.

Close to midnight, just as it was beginning to get dark this summer evening—dim, actually, for the light never seemed to go completely away this far north—they were finishing their tasks. Gilbert went to the kitchen, and she was wiping down the tables when the door opened, then closed quietly.

"Isabel."

She turned and met Henry's gaze.

She stared at him, unable to speak. She let the cloth fall from her hand and bent to retrieve it, trying to think of what to say. When she straightened, he stood before her, his expression so severe that she caught her breath.

"I knew it was you," he said, his voice low and harsh, full of suppressed fury. "The serving girl tried to laugh it off, but I knew I'd not seen a ghost."

He caught her wrist and held it between them, his eyes flashing. "What happened? And it had better be good, for I do not understand why you let me think, all this time, that you were dead. I mourned you, Isabel! I lit candles in churches all over England in your name. I paid for prayers for your salvation. I was sick at the thought that you had thrown yourself from a bridge into an icy river and had not come to me for help. Whatever it was, I would have helped you. And all this time, you were here. Alive. Well. And even when I arrived, even when you saw me on the terrace, you did not send word to me. No, you had them lie to me, and you hid from me. From me! What have I ever done but be kind to you? What have I ever done to deserve such treatment from you? Tell me!"

"I will, Henry. I will. Please let me go." Tears welled in her eyes and spilled down her cheeks. She rubbed her wrist when he released it. "I never meant to cause you pain! You were gone from London. I could not come to you. You were riding north with the king."

"No. First you refused to travel."

"I never did! Alis invented that. I was told to stay behind, and then that I'd been dismissed. I wanted to go, Henry. You must believe me!"

"Why?"

"Because I am telling the truth! Why are you so angry with me?"

"Because I care for you, Isabel! Because I was sick with worry."

"Miss Isabel?" Gilbert stood in the doorway. "Do you need help?"

"No." She took a breath. "No, we are fine, Gilbert, thank you."

Gilbert looked from her to Henry. "Are you sure? Sir, she—"

Henry stepped away from her. "I will do her no harm. You have my word."

"We're fine, Gilbert," she said. "I will call you if I need you."

"I will be near," Gilbert said and left them alone.

Henry paced the room. Isabel watched him, rubbing her wrist and brushing tears away. At last, with a sigh, he sat at one of the tables and looked at her.

"Tell me," he said. "All of it."

And she did.

When she was finished, he nodded. "I had no idea. Why did you not seek my help?"

"I didn't feel I could trust anyone, Henry. My own mother had lied to me, and Alis, and Lady Dickleburough. I no longer knew what—or who—to believe. Even my grandmother had kept things from me."

"You trusted MacGannon. He brought you here."

"He and his cousin were traveling north at the same time."

"On the same ship. I know. I was told that the two of them were accompanied by a young woman."

"Who told you that?"

"The man I hired to watch Rory MacGannon while I rode north with the king. He sailed with you."

She thought of the voyage, of the silent man who had traveled alone. Of what she might have said in front of him. She had spent most of the trip hanging over a bucket, but still . . .

"Then you knew I was here."

"No. I thought you were dead. I knew MacGannon and his cousin had a woman with him, but that did not surprise me. He's the sort to have more than one woman."

"Like you. Lady Dickleburough said you fathered the child of the girl that I replaced at court. Is it true?"

"No."

"Did you . . . ?"

"Yes, I slept with her. But I was neither the only one, nor the last. The child is not mine. Why would you believe Lady Dickleburough over me?"

She looked down at the table, trying to compose her thoughts, then back up at him. "But it could be yours."

"No. The timing is not correct. And what if it were, Isabel?"

"Then you would have abandoned her and the child."

"No. If the child had been mine, I would have married her and we would have been legally tied, but desperately unhappy. She was a whimpering, clinging sort."

"But you dallied with her."

"Dallied. I bedded her. Like every other knight and half the royal household. We used to joke that she was determined to have us all. The child is not mine, Isabel. Whatever you've heard is wrong."

"Alis has a child."

He leaned back as though she'd struck him.

"A girl. Her name is Miriam. Alis left her behind in Gascony and has not seen her since the child was two years old. I believe she is in a convent now."

Henry nodded, as though he was piecing information together in his mind. "And who told you this? Lady Dickleburough?"

Isabel nodded. "But I believe her."

"Because it is about Alis, who you despise."

"And who despises me."

"If she does, she keeps it well veiled from me. She has only the most kind things to say about you."

"Ask her again how I refused to travel with the king."

"Why? She thinks you're dead. Is it not better that she continues to think so? Would you have me draw attention to you now? Here? Langton does not believe that you are dead. He has questioned your mother. And your grandmother."

She put a hand to her throat.

"Both are fine. I've not talked to your mother, but I visited your grandmother and she is well. She did not trust me enough to tell me anything, but she played her part well, as the aged woman in mourning."

"How is she?"

"As I say, she is well. She misses you, that much seemed genuine. But so much of this did not ring true, and now I understand why."

"Langton."

"Did you think to evade the snake? You, pitted against one of the country's most powerful men? If you had trusted me earlier, I might have been able to stop him, but I cannot now. Apparently you still do not trust me. When I came here, Isabel, when you saw me, why did you not have them tell me you were here?"

"I thought of it. I almost did. But then I saw Alis."

"Ah. Still jealous?"

"No."

"Don't lie to me. You do not do it well. You should not be jealous. Alis is lovely, yes, and willing. And I am her current favorite. It is nothing more than that."

"A willing favorite."

"Yes. For now." His eyes grew darker. "Yes. I'm not a monk, Isabel, and I make no excuses for what I do. I will never lie to you. I have never made promises to you, and I break none now. She pleases me for what she is. When I return to Berwick in June, we will talk, you and I."

"About what, Henry? What do we have to say to each other now?"

He watched her for a moment. "Do not pretend there has not been something between us from the first. In June when the King returns we will know what will happen in Scotland and I will be in a better position to know my own future."

"Why?"

"If the king decides to take Scotland, his territory will increase. I am one of his household knights and can be assigned to any place where he has a household. London. Gascony. Wales. He is struggling with France and there may be war there. Or not. It seems to change with the wind, and I am not privy to what is planned. If there is a war, anywhere, then there are means by which I can receive advancement, a title, perhaps, which would bring lands and increased wealth. Now I have only a small holding in Essex, but I would like to increase that. My future is as undecided as Scotland's. So when the decision has been made, I will know if I will live in London or in Stirling. I will return in June and we will talk then."

"I could be married by June."

"But you won't be." He rose and looked down at her. "Don't be any more of a fool than you have been, Isabel. I could have protected you from Langton. With one well-placed word the story would have gotten everywhere."

"I could have told Lady Dickleburough myself," she said, standing.

"She is not the only purveyor of news. Keep yourself well, Isabel. I will see you next summer."

"And I am to wait here, alone, while you are entertained by Alis?"

"MacGannon has abandoned you, then? I would not have guessed that. It seems the Oak King has died after all. Until June, Isabel."

He put a hand on her arm and pulled her into his embrace before she knew what he was about. His kiss was tender, then over.

He strode away looking as if he was well pleased.

Isabel closed the door behind him. "You can come out now," she said.

Gilbert, Rachel, and Jacob sheepishly came around the corner.

"We wanted to be sure he did not harm you," Rachel said.

Isabel leaned her head back against the wood and sighed. "I cannot tell you if he did or not."

It was not quite a month later that she received a letter from her grandmother, who told her how much she was missed, and small bits about those who lived nearby.

And then this:

"I write to tell you two things. Your mother has written to Lonsby, asking how you fared. He wrote back to her that you are not with him. So now she knows. It will not be long before she realizes, as I did, where you have gone. Continue well, sweet, and give my best to those who shelter you."

Life went on in Berwick. The inn continued to be busy and the days flew by. Isabel and Gilbert joined

Rachel's family in the Rosh Hashanah meal, their new year celebration, and learned about Yom Kippur, the Day of Atonement. Isabel was intrigued by the tradition of atoning for sins or wrongs done to another in the past year. But she and Gilbert still went to Mass on Michaelmas, at the end of September. And the weeks passed.

FOURTEEN

Is he dead?"

Nell kept her voice to a whisper as she held the candle higher. Liam bent over one of their men, who had been carried, bleeding and unconscious, to their barn by the others. His breath had been loud, rasping. And then he'd stopped breathing. Nell looked at Liam who appeared shocked.

"Aye," Liam said. He sighed and closed the boy's eyes, pulling the blanket over the boy's head.

Nell looked at the others, the four young men who stood before them. One was the dead boy's brother, the others his cousins. All were Crawfords who had lived on Liam's family's lands for as long as anyone could remember.

"He was a child!" she whispered.

"He was seventeen, madam," the boy's brother said, his voice on the edge of tears. "He was verra proud of it. His birthday was not three months ago, on Michaelmas."

"God in heaven, I cannot believe this!" Nell cried. "How could the English soldiers simply have murdered him?"

"Well . . . we were burning their barn, mistress. And they found us."

"Ye were burning down their barn?" Nell asked. "Have ye gone mad?"

"Are we to simply let them do all the things they're doing? The soldiers burnt four families out of their homes near Kilmarnock, madam!"

Nell shot Liam a look. "Is this true?"

Liam nodded. "Aye. I've been keeping the news from ye, love, but aye. Four in Kilmarnock. One in Kilmaurs. Two near Elderslie. The soldiers say they're looking for William."

"And no one's stopping it!" the boy cried. "They're killing people all around us and we're doing nothing, just waiting for them to come and burn us out."

"They've been looking for William," Liam said. "We kent that."

"I'd not heard," Nell said. "Why? I thought he was studying to be a priest?"

Liam met her gaze. "He is. But he's been irritating the English soldiers occasionally. What good would it have done ye to ken it, love? It would only have worried ye, and where else are we to go? D'ye wish to go back to Stirling?"

"No."

"Nor do I. It'll pass." He looked at the boys. "I told ye all to stop yer harassing of the Englishmen. It led to this. Yer brother is dead! Is that not enough?"

"I'll avenge him! I'll kill the whole of the English army!"

Liam grabbed his arm. "Ye'll do nothing of the sort. Ye'll keep yer head down and ye'll not bring them here."

"Who's to say they're not coming for us now?" one growled.

"We'll set sentries to watch for that. But this is over. Ye willna do it again!" Liam's voice was quiet but forceful. "It's not a game. People are dying."

"Scots are dying," the brother said.

"Aye! And I'll not have ye bringing the English here after ye."

"And if they come, sir, will ye give me up?"

Liam sighed. "If they come here, I'll help ye kill every last one of the bastards. But dinna go looking for them, lads. It leads to this. And if they follow ye home and touch one hair on my family's heads, I'll kill ye all myself! No more!"

"It's over thirty Scots that have been killed in Irvine area, I've been told," the brother said. "Thirty, sir, and now him. And it's not all young lads causing trouble. It's everyone. What about Sir Malcolm Wallace, dead these two months, slain by Sir Fenwick, the English bastard, and nothing done in answer? And now my brother's dead and ye tell us to do nothing. Our own are being killed, and ye tell us to simply watch it?"

"Just be patient, wait until June, when the new king is chosen."

"And if not then? What if it takes even longer?"

"Then we'll all be on the brink of rebellion. Look, lads, I ken how angry ye are, how much ye want to avenge the killings. But I'm telling ye, put yer heads down and stay away from the English and we'll get through this."

Their sullen faces told Nell what they were thinking.

Liam ran a hand through his hair, the coppery strands catching the candlelight. Nell felt her throat tighten. She knew what it was costing him, this fiery man of hers, to tell these lads to be passive. They'd talked of it enough, the anger that was building in him, in all of them, as the soldiers garrisoned in Irvine grew ever more bold.

At first it had been simple things—a cask of wine confiscated from a landowner, a horse taken from a field. An innkeeper who had gone without pay in Irvine for all the meals the soldiers had eaten there. And then the beatings and the floggings started. And more. It was only a few of the English soldiers who were wayward, but they'd gone unpunished, and as the months passed the abuses had intensified, and so had the local people's resentment. And then there had been the rape of a young wife left alone in her home. Then the murder of an English soldier. And the reprisals from the English, the search for the soldier's killer, who, not surprisingly, had been the woman's husband. And who had left in the night for the wilds of Lennox, abandoning his farm and livestock. And now this.

"A'right," Liam said. "We'll bury him, aye? And then . . . lads, let's have Christmas in peace. And Epiphany as well. Three weeks is all I'm asking. And then we'll talk with everyone else. But no more of having a bunch of ye with a bellyful of whisky going after armed soldiers. No more."

"What will we do, sir?"

"We'll be effective. If ye want to make them suffer, there are ways."

She saw the light in their eyes, saw the glimmer of respect for Liam there, and her heart leapt with fear. She looked from them to her husband, hoping to see in his eyes that he was dissembling. But all she saw there was his own desire for revenge. And she began to pray.

They had a week of quiet, of Rory stopping by to tell

them all was well, lingering to laugh with her girls, the cousins' merry voices cheering her. And then, one wild and windy evening, there was a pounding on the door. She rose, letting the mending she'd been holding slip from her hand. Liam moved to answer the pounding on the door.

"What is it?" Meg asked. "Is it the soldiers come for us?"

"Meg, Elissa, go in the kitchen," Nell said softly, surprised to hear how calm her voice was. "If I scream at ye, go out the side door." When they did not move, she raised her voice to a harsh whisper. "Do it!"

They scrambled to obey her. She watched them go, then went to join Liam, expecting to see English soldiers. But it was Ranald Crawford who stood there, his face gray. Liam held the lantern high, and by its light Nell could see that Ranald was not alone. A woman stood at his side. She moved forward, revealing herself to be Ranald's sister, Liam's aunt, Margaret Wallace. And behind her were two hooded figures—men, she assumed, by their size.

"Just the night, Liam," Ranald said. "Or two. Not more. I swear I'll find a place for them soon."

"Aye, Ranald," Liam said. "Come in, come in."

"Margaret, come in!" Nell cried.

Margaret hurried into the house, followed by the men. One threw back his hood and embraced her.

"It's me, Nell," Rory said.

"Rory!" Nell cried. "What are ye doing here? What . . . ?"

Ranald interrupted her. "You know Margaret, of course. And my nephew, her son, William?"

"Aye, of course. But I thought ye were at Kilspindle, by Dundee," Nell said to Margaret.

"We were," Margaret said breathlessly. "We had to leave."

William pulled his cloak off, his rugged face weary, but his voice calm. "I've been outlawed. I killed a constable's son in Dundee, and they're looking for me."

"Outlawed!" Nell put a hand to her throat. "But why?"

"I killed a man. We got out of Dundee, but ye know they'll come looking for me in Ayrshire soon."

"Tell us what happened," Liam said, leading the way. The story came out over the meal Nell and her girls hastily prepared. William had been attending the church school in Dundee, where his mother, and younger brother John lived with their uncle. Dundee Castle had been handed into the care of an English baron, Brian Fitz Alan, whose constable was a man named Selby. Selby's twenty-year-old son and his friends had roamed Dundee for months, causing trouble, gradually becoming more bold.

"They accosted William," Margaret Wallace said.

"I let my temper go," William said. "They wanted my dirk, and they wouldna stop coming after me. They were armed, and they would not stop. We struggled for it. And I killed him. Selby's son"

"We left Dundee at once," Margaret said, "and made our way to you. I did not know where else to go. I knew Ranald would take us in, but he's the sheriff, and we put him at risk by being there."

"My house will be the first place they search," Ranald said. "Which is why we've come. I need a place to put them until I can make other arrangements, Liam."

"Of course they can stay here," Liam said, looking at Nell for agreement.

She nodded, ignoring the knotting of her stomach. "Of course. But how did Rory come to be with ye?"

"I was in Ayr," Rory said, "getting the news, when the word came that William had been outlawed. The city's full of English soldiers, and no one would even notice me, so I went looking for William for Sir Ranald instead of him."

"And found my sister and nephew for me," Ranald said. "I must get back to Ayr. You know they will come looking for me, hoping to find William. I had hoped one of my nephews could aid another and am pleased that you will."

"Aye," Liam said. "What else would we do?"

"I'm grateful," William said. "It's not everyone who would shelter me."

"Wait 'til ye hear the whole of the story," Rory said, his eyes shining. "After Selby's son was killed, his friends chased William through the town. He went to his uncle's town house, and the housekeeper took him in and gave him one of her own gowns and wimple."

"Russet it was," William said, grinning. "Suited me."

"She set him to spinning," Rory continued. "And then the English came, to search the house."

"I kept my head down and tried to look small," William added.

"And they never realized the big lass in the corner was him." Rory laughed, joined by the others.

Nell smiled tightly, glad that William had escaped, but filled with dread as she looked at her daughters, at her husband, seeing the light in his eyes. It was here, the shadow of the violence that she feared, that she'd sensed was drawing closer. Brought here, to her house, by Liam's earnest and handsome cousin, a young man named Wallace. She would remember the moment all of her days. Liam reached for her hand and held it tightly.

Nothing happened for a month.

Meg crowed with delight. "I won, I won!"

Rory shook his head, laughing. "It's only that we let ye win, ye twit."

"How can ye let someone win at dice?" she demanded.

Nell laughed and exchanged a look with Liam. "Show her, love."

Liam rose from the chair in which he'd been sitting and joined Rory and the others. Rory and William had brought eight of their companions this time, mostly young men William had known in his childhood, many his cousins. It had been a merry evening.

Through the last of December, and into January, Rory and William had spent a great deal of time here, talking with Nell and Liam, playing games with the girls, or just eating. Rory told Nell that there was always better food in her kitchen than in Jocelyn's, and Nell said that he and William would one day eat them completely out of house and home, but that she was glad they were here.

William loved to laugh, and tease, although since his father's death his mood was seldom jovial. In his darker moments he talked of killing Fenwick, the English knight who had killed Malcolm Wallace on Loudon Hill. In his lighter moments, he tricked Meg with the weighted dice he'd brought back from a trip to Glasgow.

"Here," Liam said, "look, Meggie. The dice are weighted on one side, so they fall a certain way. That way the player who kens what they are can predict the number shown. And win."

"Ooh!" Meg gave William a glare, and everyone laughed.

"What's that?" Rory said.

"Dice, Rory," Meg said.

"No. Listen! I hear something."

They were all still for a moment, but the night was quiet. Liam went to the door and stood on the step, listening. Rory stood behind him. An owl screeched. Then another. And a third, and the hair on the back of Rory's neck stood up. He and Liam exchanged a look.

"Nell," Liam whispered. "Get my sword."

Nell handed Liam the sword.

One of Liam's stable lads came running from the barn, his arms flailing.

"Sir! Sir! There are soldiers outside the gate! With torches!"

"How many?" Liam asked.

"About twenty, sir. What shall we do?"

"Tell the lads to get weapons if they have them, pitchforks or scythes if they dinna. Get the horses out of the barn and yerselves as well."

Behind Rory, William, whispered, "Are they coming for me?"

"Dinna ken yet," Liam whispered. "Nell, get the girls out the back of the house, but not out of the gate. They may have put men out there as well."

Rory turned to the lads with them, putting his finger to his lips. "Liam, they willna ken we're here. We can take our lot out the back and circle round."

"Not yet," Liam said. "Wait. Let's see what they'll do. Maybe they're just here for a visit, aye?"

"Most likely they heard about Nell's food."

"Rory, let's go," William said.

"Ye take them, William," Rory said. "I'll stand with Liam. If there're two men here, maybe they'll back down."

"Twenty soldiers? They're coming to burn Liam out. We'll go over the wall."

Rory nodded, turning to watch as Nell and the girls hurried out the back door, with William and the lads behind them. He heard the click of the door.

Then silence.

And then the night erupted. The gate was battered down, and soldiers, carrying torches, streamed into the yard. They whirled their horses and shouted into the air. One howled like a wolf.

Rory drew his sword. Liam did the same. Liam pulled the door shut behind them. The stable lads came running from the barn with knives and pitchforks and stood uncertainly on the side of the yard.

The soldiers were still riding in circles, but slower now. One stopped in front of the door, holding his torch high, lighting the space between them and his own face. Rory sucked in his breath. It was Fenwick, the knight who had killed William's father.

"Crawford! We hear you have been harboring William Wallace," he said to Liam, his voice thick with drink. "He's outlawed."

Liam nodded slowly. Rory counted eighteen men on horseback. And on their side, Liam, William, their eight companions. Three young stable lads. And himself. But green lads were no match for trained soldiers, which meant the odds were not in their favor.

"We've come to search for Wallace," Fenwick said.

"He's not here."

"Who is that standing with you?"

"My wife's nephew."

"Another MacGannon, then?"

"I am," Rory said.

Fenwick's horse danced under him. "I have no argument with you, MacGannon, unless you are keeping company with Wallace. Your brother is peaceable enough."

Neither Rory nor Liam answered.

"Search the house," Fenwick told his men.

Six men dismounted and moved toward the door.

"I told ye that he's not here," Liam said.

"We're searching the house. Move him out of your way." When his men hesitated, Fenwick shouted at them. "Move him aside!"

They stepped forward, but they stopped as Rory raised his arm. There was silence for a moment, then one of the men in the back ran his horse straight at the doorstep, at the same time tossing the torch he held onto the thatched roof. It bounced off, landing at the corner of the house, where it lit the empty branches of the trees with an eerie light. The horse turned at the last moment, its hooves flying. Rory and Liam dove to the side, leaping back to their feet in time to face the swords of the soldiers who now advanced.

Rory parried his first blow, from a soldier with a grizzled beard and missing teeth. He dispatched the man in three blows. Liam fought by his side, and he could hear shouting. The torches waved wildly as the soldiers fought, some still on horseback, some on foot now. One of the stable lads darted between the horses and thrust a scythe in a man's side, then raced away.

With a war cry, William and the others poured through the broken gate.

Fenwick whirled his horse around, shouting orders. Then, seeing William, he shouted again. "Wallace! It is Wallace!"

William fought his way toward the knight, but there were others he had to deal with first. Rory leapt to grab a soldier by the waist, to yank him off the horse. The man resisted, slicing at Rory, who ducked, then lunged, and the man was unhorsed.

The fighting was slowing around him. Several soldiers, on foot and on horseback, ran for the gate, fighting their way out. Fenwick, rearing his horse, followed them. And William followed Fenwick.

Liam dispatched the man he'd been fighting, then went to the aid of one of the stable lads. Men littered the ground. One of William's cousins lay mortally wounded, his brother leaning over him. One of the stable lads was dead.

Rory had no time to look more. He faced his opponent, a knight, younger than Fenwick, but trained. And fast. His swordsmanship was excellent. Rory pushed him toward the center of the yard, realizing that they were the only ones left in combat. The knight fought Rory back a few feet, then forward again.

A blow hit Rory's blade but glanced off, the shiver of metal on metal loud in the now quiet yard. He could hear his own labored breathing, and that of the knight. They were both tiring.

Rory battled forward, back three steps, then lunged. And hit flesh. His blade sank into the man's neck. Rory pulled it back and struck again. The knight's eyes opened wide. He stared at Rory. Raised his arm.

Then fell.

Rory stood over him, his emotions tumbling as the man died.

"Jesu," he said, throwing his head back and looking into the trees.

It was over. The soldiers were dead, or gone. They'd killed four. Two of their own were dead.

Rory let his sword arm fall.

"They meant to do it," Liam said. "They would have burnt us out this night."

"Aye," Rory said woodenly.

"Liam! Liam!" Nell raced through the gate, her hair flying and skirts billowing behind her. She threw her arms around her husband, holding him to her, tears running down her cheeks.

"Oh, dear God, love. Dear God!" she cried, then stepped back as Meg and Elissa flew at their father.

Liam embraced them, assuring them he was fine.

"Get the gate back up," he told the stable lads. "Rory, are ye hurt, lad?"

Rory shook his head.

William and the others came back through the gate. "They got away," William said, then saw the man on the ground in front of Rory. "Well done."

Rory nodded.

Liam, his chest heaving, pulled Nell to him. "Ye're going to Loch Gannon, love. I'll not have ye here any longer."

Nell lay her head on his shoulder and nodded. And sobbed.

* * *

A week later Rory was outlawed.

Magnus held his hands up. "Aye, I ken they brought the battle to ye. But why didn't Liam let them search the house?"

"Would ye have?" Rory asked.

"Aye. It's not our battle, Rory. William's battle is not ours! Now ye've killed an English knight and ye have a price on yer head! They can kill ye on sight, Rory! Tell me what ye think will come of this!"

"We had no choice, Magnus! They brought the battle to us."

"No! Ye could have let them look through the house. Aye, it wouldna have been comfortable, but they wouldna have found William and they would have been on their way."

"It wasna like that."

"Listen to me!" Magnus roared. "Have ye made Ayrshire more peaceful? Or have ye made it so we'll all be having English soldiers riding to our doors? Did ye think of the danger ye were placing us in? And not just me and Jocelyn? Nell and Liam and Meg and Elissa. They're in danger, too!"

"That's not my doing!"

"It's not our battle!"

"Nell and Liam are our aunt and uncle, Magnus. It is our battle!"

"Ye damned fool! And that's just what ye are now, Rory, damned! Ye should have let the knight live."

"Why? He would not have let me live. And how is this not our battle, Magnus? Malcolm Wallace was not a wrongdoer. All he did was refuse to swear fealty to the king of another country, even when all around him were willing to do so. That was his crime, that he wasna ready to give his oath to Edward of England. And when he refused—"

"And when he refused he offered up his wife and sons to those in authority to do with what they would. Ye've seen Margaret Wallace. She's a ghost of who she was a year ago. Her life is altered forever. And yer friend William is making sure she has nothing. He's become more than an outlaw, Rory. He's no more than a ruffian with a price on his head. As you are now. What have ye done?"

"So ye would not raise a hand to aid Liam? Ye'd let their house burn?"

"Ye dinna ken they would have burnt him out. And aye, I would think twice before killing a knight."

"So what would ye do, cower behind yer door and let happen what happens?"

"If it would keep Jocelyn safe, I would."

"Yerself safe, ye mean. It's men like ye who allow the English to continue abusing our people."

"And what can one man do? Rory, be honest with yerself. D'ye think ye and Wallace and his brothers, and a handful of friends and cousins, can defeat the whole of Edward's army? D'ye think the lot of ye have a chance of driving English soldiers out of Ayrshire even? If ye did, if I thought it would change the tide, I would join ye. But it will only make things worse for the rest of us and ye'll find yerself living in the bracken wearing filthy clothing and eating acorns for your supper."

"Ah, so it's about comfort, is it, Magnus?"

Magnus pounded the table next to him. "No! It's about being sensible."

"I'd rather be alive, and try to change the godawful way things stand, brother, than hide in my comfortable bed and pretend I'm not hearing the screams of my own people."

"So I'm a coward?"

"What do ye call a man who refuses to look at the bloodshed happening just beyond his door? Does that make him a warrior, Magnus? Would Da do that?"

"Da would be sure he kept Mother safe."

"Not letting the English kill our own knights is a step toward doing that."

"It's a step toward yer own death, Rory."

"We all die, Magnus. But I'll not ask ye again to join us. Ye stay here, safe and warm. I'm off, to live my life before I die."

"Dinna come back."

Rory stopped at the door and faced Magnus. His brother's face was pale, his eyes very dark.

"I mean it, Rory. Dinna come here again. We're trying to live in peace. You're trying to set Ayrshire aflame."

"It is aflame already, Magnus. But ye canna see it over the top of yer walls."

Rory hated that he and his brother had argued. In all their years they'd never talked so to each other, and he regretted his accusations. Magnus was right. In taking on William's cause, he'd put those he loved in jeopardy.

He went back to Liam and Nell immediately after and told them. Nell, packing their things, preparing to go to Loch Gannon, was saddened. And disappointed in Magnus, Rory could tell. She did not put it into words, but he saw her press her lips together.

"I dinna ken what will happen now," Rory said, "but I canna stay with Magnus. I'm sure the English will come looking for me here, which is why I came to tell ye farewell. And safe journey."

He looked at Meg and Elissa, his lovely young cousins, who watched him with wide eyes. "I am sorry this happened. Tell my parents, and Kieran and the rest of the family on Skye, the truth of it, not the garbled story they're sure to hear."

"We will," Liam said.

Nell shook her head. "Oh, Rory! Thank ye for doing what ye did here!"

"I'm glad I was here. And now what, Liam? Are we to sit on our hands while men are killed around us?"

"No."

The calm in Liam's voice made Rory take notice. He saw the glance that Liam and Nell exchanged.

"There are other ways, lad."

"What are they, Liam? I'm ready."

"Not now. Not yet. I'll get my lasses safely away first."

Rory nodded. "I'll go now, before anyone sees me."

Nell cried, embracing him. His cousins hugged him, but he knew they did not know what to make of all this. And to tell the truth, neither did he. Liam walked him outside, where they talked for a moment. Then Liam gave Rory a handful of coins.

"This will help ye a bit. Let me ken where ye are. I dinna tell ye in front of Nell, lad, but we're not alone in this. There was another lass raped, over in Dunlop, and some of us are going to find out who did it. But we'll wait until June."

"Do ye think having a king will change anything?" Rory asked. "Will it help?"

"Depends on who it is. The three Robert Bruces are already sleeping with the English. The youngest Robert is with King Edward, playing courtier. Who's to say any of them even remember they're Scottish? Would Balliol be any better? I dinna ken. All I ken for sure is people are dying and being maimed while our leaders do nothing, and it canna stay like this. So off ye go, with William, and for God's sake keep yerself safe, aye?"

"Tell Kieran—"

"No." Liam held up his hands. "Dinna send any word to Skye, or Kieran will be joining ye and I canna do that to his parents. It's bad enough that ye are where ye are. Ye dinna ken the fear a parent feels, Rory, when yer child is in danger. God keep ye safe, lad. And send for me if ye need me." He embraced Rory, then clapped him on the shoulder. "Get ye gone."

Rory leapt onto the horse. "Tell Magnus I'm sorry."

"I will, lad," Liam said. "Now get ye gone."

Rory thanked him and rode away. He had no idea where he would go.

At Loch Gannon, Margaret MacMagnus woke from a sound sleep to find she was alone in bed. Gannon stood at the door to their bedchamber, looking out at the last of the night. Already the morning light, dim as it was, had lit the earth once more, allowing her to see the set of his shoulders, the weariness there. And more.

"What is it?" she asked, clasping the bedcover to her as she sat up.

Gannon turned to her with haunted eyes. "I had a dream of Rory."

"Oh, dear God, Gannon, dinna tell me he's hurt. Or

dead!" She leapt from the bed, pulling her night robe closer as she went to him. "Tell me it's not that."

"No," he said slowly. "I'm not thinking he's dead. But that something has shifted. Something has changed in his life, something unalterable."

"And Magnus?"

"It's like a storm has centered on our sons, Margaret. But it's not Magnus at the center. It's Rory."

"Are ye sure, love, are ye sure that Rory's in danger?"

Gannon pulled her against him. "No. The dreams are not that clear, and I can never tell exactly what the whispers are saying. But it's Rory, that much I ken."

"Ye'll go to him."

"Aye."

"Shall I go with ye?"

He thought for a moment, then shook his head. "No, stay here, lass, if ye would. I'm not sure Rory is where I think he is. What if he comes home, in need of us and we're both gone?"

"Aye," she said. "When will ye leave, then?"

"With the change of the tide."

Which he did.

She waited impatiently for his return, not climbing to the top of the headland as she usually did, because of the continual storms that battered the coastline. She wrote to Nell, but the messengers who had regularly carried messages from clan to clan were no longer reliable, and Gannon would be there by ship long before her letter could possibly arrive—if it ever did. But it gave her something to do.

So many losses in her life. And now . . . but no, she would not think of the summer when she and Gannon had met, when all she'd known had been taken from her.

Nor of the children they'd lost, each one a blow that she'd thought she would never be able to bear. But she had; each time she had continued to live. And each time Gannon's strength had helped keep her alive. It was more than their love for each other that kept her going. It was the growing realization that this was the path on which she had been placed, on which she was to travel, and learn.

But now, as so many times in her past, she was afraid to step forward for fear of the next loss she might suffer. She prayed, repeating the words so often they sounded like the chanting of monks. *Please, God, not my sons. Not Gannon. Not Nell or Liam or their girls. Or Kieran, who Davey had tried to keep home, or Davey and his family. Or Jocelyn, whom my son loves.* There were so many she could not bear to lose. She prayed to find strength to endure the waiting.

She went to the small stone chapel Gannon had built to celebrate the birth of their first child, a boy they'd named Alexander, as King Alexander had requested. The first child that she'd buried, the prayers for his soul uttered here, in the chapel where he'd been baptized. This had been her place to find comfort over the years when she could not go to the sea, a sheltered spot where she could think.

It had taken years for her to find this peace. She'd been angry with God, and bitter. And numb when death had raised its head again and claimed another of her own, her second son. And the next. She'd raged at God then, at all the gods, for they were here too, the spirits who guard springs and pools and trees and the sea itself. She'd compared herself to other women, who bore children who lived, who had never known the suffering of placing your own in the ground, and while she did not covet their children, she wondered why she had not been chosen to be among them. Some days she had lived only because others had expected her to, but as the years had gone on, she'd seen things differently. Magnus and Rory, living to be grown men, so different and yet each so wonderful, had helped to heal her. Time had helped as well, and Gannon, whose love and own suffering had made her realize she must be stronger to comfort him.

There was some solace in knowing that she was part of an eternal chain of women who had traveled this path, who had survived without cowardice, who had waited for their men or their sons to return, accompanied by the knowledge that they might not. Knowing that other women knew this kind of suffering did not comfort her. Their survival did.

Or was she wrong? Was the world nothing more than a series of mishaps strung across time, and was a woman who tried to make a pattern from it all nothing more than a fool?

A week passed, then a day and another day. And on the tenth, a runner came with news. Rory had been outlawed for murder. Margaret questioned the man over and over, but he knew no more than the bare bones, that Rory had killed an English knight in Ayrshire.

On the eleventh day, Gannon returned on *Gannon's Lady*, her sails billowing in the winter wind. When the men told Margaret that his ship was in the loch, she waited for him, standing in the cold at the end of the dock. Each moment seemed an hour, but at last the ship was nearing. Gannon stood alone amidships, his back straight and arm raised to wave at her, but his movements were not buoyant, and the band around her heart tightened.

When he arrived, he drew Margaret into his arms. "Rory is outlawed."

"Aye. They say he murdered an English knight."

"No. He killed an English knight who was attacking Nell and Liam's house."

She gasped.

"No, lass, all are well. Rory and the others fought them off, and none of them were hurt badly. But the knight is dead and some fool of Liam's told the English Rory and William's names, so they're on the run. We dinna ken where Rory is. He was alive a fortnight ago, but no one's seen him since."

"He's not with Magnus?"

"No, and Magnus doesna ken where he is. Apparently neither do the English, for they've searched Magnus's house three times now."

"How is Magnus?"

"Heartsick. Our lads argued, and Magnus told Rory not to come there again, that he was endangering Jocelyn if he came. Which, of course, he would be. Magnus is doing the best he can, but he's worried. With good reason, Margaret. It's getting worse by the day over there."

"Oh, Gannon."

"Aye."

"And Nell and Liam?"

"They're well. John Comyn sent word that the Crawfords are not to be touched. And it seems the soldiers are listening. Nell says now she has a debt to repay the Comyns, but it's worth it to have peace, aye?"

"Gannon! They should come here, all of them! Did ye talk of it?"

"Oh, aye, until I had no breath left. They intended

to, but now none of them will. Nell sends her love and told me to tell ye she's got a pot of pitch on the fire at all times. And that Liam is still the most infuriating man in the world."

Margaret smiled briefly. "And here I thought ye were." She sighed. "I'll write to her and tell them to come here at once. But, Gannon, where's our Rory?"

"With William Wallace is all we ken."

"I canna believe this has happened. This is what ye dreamt."

"Part of it."

"And what else, Gannon? What else did you see in your dream? Tell me what else is coming!"

"I dinna ken for sure, Margaret. But I saw our lads in armor. And me with them. And Liam. But where we were, and when, I dinna ken any more than that."

She took a deep breath. "A'right. Then Rory is still alive. If ye dreamt he was with ye in war, he's alive now. And he and Magnus will repair the rift."

"Or my dream is nothing more than a dream."

"And neither of us believe that."

The next day a contingent of English soldiers arrived at Loch Gannon, looking for Rory and William, saying that they had orders from King Edward. Gannon let them search the fortress and the village outside. The men were polite. Friendly even, interested in hearing anything Gannon MacMagnus had to say. On the third day, Gannon told them they had to leave. He did not raise his voice, but he let them know that the only way they could stay at Loch Gannon was to be buried there. They left then but warned that they would not be the last to visit him. And so he stayed home all the rest of the winter and into the spring, loath to leave Margaret and his people unprotected.

And all that time, they heard nothing from Rory.

It was Nell who sent the news that Rory and William were in Riccarton, in Ayrshire, at the home of William's uncle, Sir Richard Wallace. Gannon sailed at once, finding Sir Richard blinded and disabled after a skirmish with English soldiers.

Sir Richard welcomed Gannon and confirmed that Rory and William had been there with him. But they'd left, in the night, warned of a visit from Edward's men. He'd heard they'd gone to stay in the forests of north Ayrshire.

But when Gannon went there, he discovered that William, and Rory, and about twenty others, had gone to the eastern Highlands to discover the mood of the people there. Gannon returned home disheartened. Margaret wrote to Nell of their worry.

And they waited.

FIFTEEN

Sarah Angenhoff married Edgar Keith at The Oak and The Ash on a gray and wet afternoon near the end of May 1292. It was a simple ceremony with few in attendance. Their parents, of course, and Isabel and Gilbert and the others who worked at the inn. And the rabbi who performed the marriage. A handful of Jews from Berwick had made their disapproval known, but still they'd come and wished the happy couple well. Rachel was sure that Sarah never suspected the comments that were made out of her hearing.

Edgar's family had come as well, his father composed, his mother's plump face sagging with obvious anxiety. She never said a word against the marriage, though, smiling when appropriate and toasting them with a cheer afterward. But Rachel stood close enough to hear her sighs and saw the looks she gave Edgar's younger brothers, whose wary eyes and stiff manner let Rachel know that they'd been warned to behave.

The party that followed the ceremony was a quiet one,

but Sarah glowed and Edgar beamed with pride. They saw only each other, Rachel was sure, and she tried to keep a smile on her face through it all—even when Mosheh, the butcher's son, told her he'd offered for her hand in marriage that very day. She stared at him, trying not to laugh, for he made it obvious that he was very much in earnest. He nodded, telling her they would speak more of this later, then spent the rest of the evening trying to catch her eye. And she trying to avoid his.

It was not that there was anything wrong with the man. He was pleasant looking, and kind, and certainly attentive. But she had not spoken more than a hundred words to him in all the time she'd been in Berwick. How could he possibly know her, or she him?

And, more importantly, she admitted to herself, he was not Kieran MacDonald. She could not promise herself to another man until she knew whether Kieran cared for her. He'd written twice. And then nothing. She'd written two letters, knowing neither might ever reach him, and then waited. And waited.

It was both a delaying ploy and a denial, for nothing could come of her attraction to Kieran. She knew that, knew that she could not deal the blow of marrying outside their faith to her father, could not be the second daughter to disappoint him. Jacob had done his best to hide his discontent, just as Edgar's mother had, but they all knew he was unhappy with this match. How could she do the same to him?

And yet . . . Sarah was radiant. Edgar burned with passion for her. How could that be wrong? What did it matter that they were not the same faith, that their families had different traditions? Was everything meant to always be the same, or could love inspire new traditions, as cherishable as the old?

Isabel wept during the ceremony, smiled during the meal after, and now hurried to help clear the tables. Rachel rose to help her, carrying the trenchers to the kitchens to be broken in two and handed out to the poor who had already gathered at their door. When all the work was done, they sat together in the silent tavern, sipping cups of wine and talking about the day. Outside, the rain had increased and the streets were empty.

"Aren't you glad your father closed the inn for this day?" Isabel asked. "I could not serve a meal now if my life depended on it."

"Oh, yes," Rachel said. "It was a good day. I've never seen Sarah so happy. She was radiant."

"Wasn't she? As you will look on your wedding day to Mosheh," Isabel said.

Rachel laughed and shook her head. "If you had asked me, I would have sworn that the man did not even know my name."

"Apparently you were wrong."

"Apparently I was wrong. Or it is not my name he is after. At least you don't have a father breathing over your shoulder to be sure you pick a Jewish man."

"At least you have a father."

"So do you." Rachel was surprised by the sadness in Isabel's voice. Isabel rarely spoke of her family, and she certainly had not spoken kindly of her father since she'd discovered he was alive. "Do you ever wonder if you should have gone to Newcastle and waited for him to come for you?"

"Sometimes. But I wonder what I would have done if he'd not come. What would I have done, Rachel? I'd be living on the streets, selling myself perhaps, or sewing some Newcastle woman's clothing for a pittance. Your family is good to take me in. But I cannot stay here forever."

"Why not? Sarah will leave in the morning to live with Edgar and we need you more than before. I will be here forever and would be glad of the company."

"What will become of us, Rachel? Do you think we'll ever marry?"

"You will catch the eye of some wealthy nobleman and go to live in a castle. And I will marry Mosheh, the butcher's son."

"At least you will always eat," Isabel laughed.

"And you could always write to your father. I have nowhere to go. And if the king comes back, things might be very different."

Isabel put her chin on her hand. "I'm hoping so. Henry will be here."

"With his vague promises."

"You don't like him, do you?"

"It's hard for me to trust a man who is so self-assured. He assumes you will wait for him to return. And he's too beautiful."

"He is beautiful, isn't he? Too bad the inner man does not match the outer."

"What has he done?"

"What has he done? He wooed me, led me to believe that he cared for me, and then he pursued Alis. I was correct from the start not to believe him. I have learned not to believe anything a man says."

"What about Rory? He's not lied. And he is beautiful as well."

"But where is he? Rachel, I have waited for a year and a half and nothing from him! Nothing! Kieran has written to you."

"Yes. Not often, but yes. Although it's been months. Perhaps he's forgotten me as well. Perhaps they are dealing with something important."

"I've told myself that, but it's time to face the truth. He has forgotten me completely, and I should do the same. But when I think of him . . . sometimes . . . sometimes I can still feel his kiss. I dream of him, and I wake and feel as though he's there, with me. It's like a melding. He takes my breath away, Rachel. My whole body feels alive when he touches me."

"He is very handsome."

"Handsome doesn't say the half of it! Henry is handsome, but Rory . . . Rory glows, like there is a flame within him. When I am with him, I forget the world—" Isabel was silent for a moment, then shook her head. "As he seems to have forgotten me, it is time to do the same." She raised her wine cup high. "To beautiful Rory MacGannon, who has abandoned me. Good riddance!"

"You don't mean that."

"I think I do. I thought he would come back, Rachel. But he hasn't."

"Kieran's gone, too. Perhaps I should marry Mosheh after all. But how could I?"

Isabel wrinkled her nose. "How could you sleep next to a man who killed animals for a living? Your house would smell of blood, and dogs would follow you everywhere. He a nice man, but there will be someone else. And perhaps it's for the best that the Highlanders have forgotten us. You know what your father thinks of Kieran."

"Yes." Rachel sighed. "When Henry returns, please ask him if any of the knights are Jewish. It would solve so many problems for me."

They laughed together.

Berwick began to fill with Scots. Word came that Edward had sent a force of men to camp just outside the city, and that Edward himself was approaching. Jacob and Rachel created a tiny room with a hidden door in the attic of the building next door for Isabel, in case she needed to hide while the hearings were held at the castle.

Gilbert helped them, and of course Mama knew, but they told no one else. They'd had to hire more people to work at the inn, and every new person meant greater risk of discovery. Sarah had invited Isabel to come to them while the hearings were on, and Isabel, they all agreed, might do just that.

The butcher's son Mosheh came to see Rachel almost every day. Jacob joked that if Isabel would find a fisherman to woo her, they'd be doing well. He was pleased with Mosheh, who was serious, and quiet, and told Rachel he planned to marry as soon as he could afford living quarters of his own. Rachel was polite to him, laughed at his infrequent jokes, and told Isabel she was going to discourage everyone from eating meat so that Mosheh's preparation would take longer. But she was beginning to feel as abandoned as Isabel, and as the weeks passed, she looked forward to Mosheh's warm smile and his open admiration.

Until the first day of June, when a man arrived late in the evening, after almost all the patrons were gone. He stood just inside the door, dripping with rain, then he shook the water from his cloak. He looked at Isabel, who manned the desk in the foyer, then across the tavern room, where Rachel was wiping tables.

"Kieran!" Isabel cried.

Rachel turned, her heart pounding. Kieran pushed back the hood from his dark hair, leaving it wild and wet. His cheeks were ruddy. He looked wonderful. Rachel clasped her hands before her as Kieran crossed the room.

"I'm sorry for coming so late," Kieran said. "The city gates were closed, and I had to bribe the guard to let me in. It took some time."

"Kieran," Rachel said. "How are you?"

"Better now that I see ye before me, Rachel. It's been so long."

"Are you hungry, Kieran?"

"Oh, aye. Food would be grand," he said, with a wide smile. "How are ye, Rachel? Ye look . . . splendid."

Rachel tried to smile. And resist being drawn under his spell again.

"And Isabel," he said, "ye look splendid as well. How is everyone? Yer parents, Rachel? And Sarah? And Gilbert?"

"Sarah is married. A fortnight ago."

"So they did marry. Well, good for Edgar, and Sarah, too, of course. I hope they're happy." He glanced around them and lowered his voice. "Is Rory here?"

"Rory?" Rachel asked. "No. Why would he be here?"

"I'm looking for him."

"You are looking for Rory? You have not been together?"

He shook his head. "No. I've been on Skye, with my family, trying to get the fortifications done, in case they're needed. It's taking all of us to do it. Rory has been in

Ayrshire, with his brother at first. But now . . . there's been some trouble . . . and we dinna ken where he is."

"What happened?" Isabel asked, grabbing Kieran's arm. "Is he all right?"

"We think so, but we dinna ken. Here's what we do ken." He told them of Rory killing the English knight. "And now he's been outlawed and we dinna ken where he is. He was with William's uncle in Riccarton, in Ayrshire, but they were discovered and went to the forest, and no one's seen them since. We thought perhaps he'd come here."

"No," Isabel said. "He's not been here, nor have I heard from him since your last visit."

"Nothing? In all this time?"

"Nothing."

Kieran let out a huff of air and shook his head. "The English are looking for him. The MacDonnells still want his head. What a mess. Look, if he comes here, will ye tell him to go home, to Loch Gannon? Tell him the English mean to hang him."

Rachel and Isabel nodded.

"If he has not come to see me by now," Isabel said, "he'll not be coming."

"Ye dinna ken that, Isabel . . . I ken him better than ye do. He still has that wreath, the crown ye made in London. He keeps it with him. I think I ken why he's not come here. It's most likely that he's afraid to bring the trail to ye. He kens they're looking for him, and he would keep ye safe."

Isabel nodded but said nothing. She did not need to. Rachel saw the hope flash in her eyes, then dim. Jacob arrived with ale and food, and joined them, asking the news. Between bites of the savory stew and crusty bread, Kieran told him the story.

Jacob nodded. "Killing a knight is serious business. He'll hang for it."

"Aye, sir," Kieran said. "Which is why we're all out looking for him. His father is in the north. Our uncle Liam has gone to the east, and my father is in the south. We have men everywhere, searching for him and William."

"Dangerous," Jacob said.

Kieran nodded, but Rachel gave her father a sharp look, knowing his comment was meant for her.

Kieran took another swallow of ale. "What is the news here?"

"King Edward has set the auditors to decide which Scottish laws apply to the succession," Rachel said, "and whether the rules for succession that Edward laid down in England last year can be applied here. So far all we've heard is that there is disagreement among the auditors."

"Not surprising, with that lot," Kieran said.

"Who can tell what will be next?" Jacob shrugged. "Do you need a bed?"

"One night, sir, if you have room for me."

Jacob stood. "I'll get the room ready."

"I'll do it, Jacob," Isabel said, rising with him. "It's wonderful to see you again, Kieran."

"Thank you both." Kieran watched them leave, then looked at Rachel. "Have I done something wrong?"

Have you done something wrong? Rachel thought, looking at the way his blue eyes, surrounded by those long lashes, studied her. At the way his mouth moved, making her body tingle at the vision of it on hers. Or on her body. At his long fingers stroking the cup and the thoughts that brought. At the slant of his cheekbones and the width of his shoulders and the way he moved, sinuous and wild and male, so very male. Had he done something wrong? Yes. He was beautiful, long and lean and far too tempting. And all wrong, everything about him all wrong for her future. But she wanted him so. She longed to reach across the table, to take his hand in hers, to look into those eyes and tell him to make love to her that moment, to make her forget all her responsibilities to her family, to her people, to make her forget that she would break her father's heart and betray his trust if she accepted the promise in Kieran's eyes, if she acknowledged the way he looked at her, as if he would devour her. But she said none of that.

She looked away from him, moved her hand out of reach of his touch, ignored his gaze on her mouth.

"What do you mean?" Rachel asked.

"Yer father. His manner is different. We were welcomed before. Now I have the feeling I'm being tolerated. And Isabel. Is she angry with me?"

"Isabel? No, of course not. But she's hurt that Rory has not come to see her. Nor has he written. You did, I was so glad to hear from you each time."

"I wish I could have sent more, but the runners dinna come regularly, and it's not always wise to put things in writing. But yer father, Rachel. Is he angry?"

"Oh. That." Rachel smiled ruefully. "He wants me to marry the butcher's son, Mosheh, who has asked for my hand."

"The butcher's son, aye?" He took another drink of ale. "What's he like?"

"He is a good man. Dependable. He seems to care for

me, though the truth is we're just becoming acquainted. He hardly knows me."

"He likes what he sees, Rachel. What man wouldn't?"

"He is Jewish. He lives in Berwick. He comes from a good family. My father thinks it's a good match."

"I see. And ye, Rachel, what do ye think? Are ye considering it?"

"Not yet."

"Not yet." He turned the ale cup in his hand. "But ye might?"

"I have no plans to marry now."

"But ye might in the future?"

"I might in the future."

Kieran leaned back and studied her. "How good are ye with a knife?"

"Very good," she said slowly.

"Ah, then perhaps ye'd enjoy cutting meat all day?"

"Never!"

"We have meat that needs butchering in the west as well, lass. I could buy ye a sharp knife and let ye have the run of the place."

She laughed.

He smiled and finished his food. "I missed ye. That's why I wrote, ye ken. I'm glad to see ye again."

"And I you, Kieran."

"Good. And I'm sorry that I have to leave in the morning. I wish I had more time to stay with ye."

"Must you leave?"

"Aye. But I'll come back when I can."

"Truly?"

"Truly. Did I ever tell ye about my da?"

"A bit. He was abducted—"

"Oh, aye, all that. But what ye need to ken is not just about him, but about my mother as well. They were both captured and sold as slaves. They were at the same place for a while, but then my da was sold to a miller in Jutland, far away, and he dinna see her for years. But he never forgot her. He kept her in his heart. And when my uncle, Gannon, Rory's da, rescued him, my father wouldna go home without going back for her, so back he went, and got her. And they married, and had me, at seventeen, the two of them."

Kieran gave her a brilliant smile. "So, ye see, I'm like my da. I dinna forget a bonnie lass. I canna stay this time. But I will come back. And I hope ye'll be waiting here for me."

She smiled. "Then I will wait."

"Keep those wits sharper than the butcher's knives, aye?"

She laughed. They talked most of the night.

When at last Rachel was in her bed, she tried to reason with herself, that she should tell Kieran not to return, that she could not wait for him, that while it had been marvelous to meet him and that she would never forget him, nothing could come of it, and they'd both be better off if they faced that now.

And then she should marry Mosheh, the butcher's son, whose eyes lit when he saw her. Who would not tempt her to break her father's heart. Or, if she could not marry him, she should find another Jewish man in Berwick who suited her better. She decided then that in the morning she'd tell Kieran that there could be nothing between them.

But the morning came and she said nothing of the sort.

Kieran stood before her, his expression so dejected, his words so earnest, his eyes so full of regret that she could say nothing. He held her hand and told her he would come back. And then he kissed her, his lips surprisingly soft, his desire for her tangible. His mouth lingered on hers for a moment, then his hand slid to the back of her neck and he claimed her mouth again, his kiss fierce and deep and hungry. And then he released her and rushed away, not looking back. She watched him leave, her tears streaming down her face, knowing that whatever was between them was stronger now.

She turned to find her father behind her, watching Kieran as well. He said nothing, but his eyes told her all she needed to know.

King Edward came in June, as promised. But Henry de Boyer did not. He was not among the knights who visited the tavern, and when Rachel asked about him, she was told that he had stayed in London. With his wife, Alis. Isabel nodded and pressed her lips together when Rachel told her, then retreated to the room that they had prepared. She spent the days of the king's visit staring at the ceiling, watching the shadows move along the wall. And thinking.

Edward did not stay long in Berwick. The Scottish auditors had been unable to determine which laws should govern the proceedings, and applied to the English auditors for assistance. Edward postponed the hearings yet again, this time until October 14, and all of Scotland groaned at the delay. Tensions mounted. The friction between those backing Balliol and those supporting Bruce had intensified, and skirmishes were frequent, almost as frequent as those between the Scots and the English garrisoned at every castle and manor house and town of any size. Abuses went unpunished, as before, but now the Scots were retaliating.

In England, Edward's mother, Queen Eleanor of Provence, died, and the people muttered about the deaths of three queens, wondering if God himself was abandoning their lands. First the maid of Norway, then Edward's wife Eleanor, and now his mother. All gone in such a short time. The mood in Scotland was sour. The people chafed under the English yoke. For every insult or assault revenged, there were five that were not, and the Scots vowed to even the score. Tempers were growing ever shorter.

In Berwick, Rachel and Isabel served ale and thought of Highlanders.

And in Ayrshire, Liam Crawford and a band of men attacked the supply trains that resupplied the garrisons. And Nell worried.

Rory stopped his horse at Magnus's gate. Magnus's men had prevented him from entering the yard. There were only one or two he even recognized, and they did not call him by name but threw wary glances at those Rory had not seen before. Something was amiss. Obviously he was not welcome, but there was more. One of the men he did know came forward. "I'll tell Magnus ye're here," he said, as though greeting a stranger. "Ye'd be best to wait just where ye are."

Rory nodded, his concern growing. He should have gone to see Nell and Liam first, he thought, debating whether to go in at all, whether Magnus would welcome him. No matter. He'd come to do one thing and he would do it, welcome or no. He'd talked to no one on his ride back, avoiding towns and villages and any place he might be recognized, although he did not worry overmuch about that. The number of outlawed men was growing by the day, and although he was somewhat known here in Ayrshire, there were as many who would not recognize him.

He was here because he'd missed his brother. Worst of all, despite his best efforts, he had endangered his entire family. And Fenwick was still alive.

Magnus hurried out of the house, his expression, when he saw Rory, pleased, quickly replaced with something else. He stopped with his back to the others, then put a finger to his lips.

"Magnus . . ."

"Liam," Magnus whispered.

Rory frowned at him. "Magnus . . ."

"Thank ye," Magnus said, raising his voice a bit. "I'll see ye in Ayr, then. Good to ken ye've decided to sell the land." Magnus mouthed the word "Go."

"Thank ye, sir," Rory said, seeing the relief in Magnus's eyes. "I'll see ye anon."

"Aye." Magnus closed the door.

Rory grabbed his horse's reins and left without a word. He waited for hours in the copse of trees on the road to Liam and Nell's home, thinking Magnus would be right behind him. He waited until the gloaming, then continued on to his aunt and uncle's. It was quiet within the high walls, but when he walked around the outside of the enclosure, he could hear Liam's deep voice rumbling and Nell's lighter one answering, and Meg's and Elissa's voices joining in. And then laughter. He stood for a moment, for the first time in his life realizing that he, too, wanted this—a home, a woman who loved him, children, a house full of laughter.

Isabel. He pushed her out of his mind, as he did every time his thoughts turned to her. Not now. He was outlawed, and penniless. A younger son with few prospects. When he had his life sorted out, then he would find her. Until then . . . until then it was still the season of the Holly King.

He circled the walls again, found the gate, and pounded on it until Liam's man came, opening the small window and asking who was without.

"Rory MacGannon," he said, not sure if it was wise to give his real name.

"Och, lad," Liam's man said, swinging the gate wide. "We thought ye'd never come. They'll be so glad ye're here."

And they were. Nell cried, his cousins laughed and wept, and Liam embraced him, too, demanding to know where the hell he'd been.

"With William, aye I ken," Liam said, then held up a hand. "No, never mind. It's best ye dinna tell me. Then I canna reveal it under torture."

"Torture!" Rory looked from Liam to Nell. "Is it as bad as that, then?"

Nell shook her head. "Dinna listen to him. It's his idea of humor. But, aye, it's been a bit tense."

"I went to Magnus's."

They both stared at him.

"I dinna give my name," he said and told them what had happened. "What is happening there? Is Magnus a'right?"

"Aye," Nell and Liam said together, then stopped. Nell

sighed and told him to sit at the table, that she would bring him food and wine while Liam told him.

"Magnus has English soldiers billeted with him," Liam said. "They've been waiting for ye to come home. He told them ye wouldna, that the two of ye had argued that bitterly. And then he sent word to everyone we trust to stop ye before ye went to him."

"Soldiers living in his house?"

"Aye, eating his food, drinking his wine, and watching his wife. He wants to send Jocelyn to her family, but she'll not go."

"Jocelyn willna go?"

"She says she willna leave him here alone."

Rory sat back, trying to take it all in—Magnus's worry for him, Jocelyn's worry for Magnus. "I did this. I brought danger to all of ye, and for it I am sorry."

"Ye should be sorry for worrying us all," Nell said. "But ye dinna place the soldiers throughout the land, laddie."

"They are in my brother's house because of me."

"Aye, they are. And ye could hang for it, Rory." She sighed. "I still don't know how we got to this spot, with soldiers in our homes."

"Our leaders did it to us," Liam said. "Now it's up to us to change our leadership."

"Which is what William is trying to do," Rory said. "He's meeting with the Balliol people all over, talking to clans and Lowlanders. And I've been with him."

"How have ye been received?" Liam asked.

"Well. They've agreed to wait until the end of the year. If we dinna have a king then, we'll take matters into our own hands."

"Ye're talking war, lad," Nell said.

"Aye."

"Magnus is here," Meg said, pointing at the open door.

His brother was not alone. Rory waited on the step while Magnus handed the horses to Liam's stable lad and crossed with Jocelyn to the house.

"I'm sorry," both brothers said at the same moment, then laughed.

"I'm sorry, Magnus," Rory said. "I came to apologize for the things I said. Ye were right to protect Jocelyn and yer home. I was wrong to say such things to ye. I'm sorry. And I'm sorry, Jocelyn. I ken how hard it must be for ye to have soldiers living in yer home."

She did not answer, but nodded her head.

"Ye were right, Magnus," Rory said.

"Aye, I was," Magnus said. "But ye were as well. I thought I could live my own life without taking a stand." He extended his hand. When Rory took it, he pulled him into an embrace. Jocelyn watched without expression.

"Come in, the both of ye," Nell said from behind Rory. "Dinna be standing here, where anyone could see ye. Have neither of ye a wit of sense? Come!"

Nell bundled them into the house, where she placed ale before each and then sat with them, Liam, Meg, and Elissa watching. "Now talk, we dinna ken how much time we have. How is it ye're here, Magnus, when ye had soldiers all over yer house?"

"We told them we were off for a wedding in Ayr," Magnus said. "We've been on the road since ye came. I told them we'd be back in the morning."

"I am sorry for what I said," Rory said. "I wondered if we'd ever speak again. I hoped we would."

Magnus nodded. "It wasna good, us tearing at each other like that. We'll not do it again, aye? But dinna fear— the tie between us is stronger than that, younger brother. I can argue with ye and think ye a fool, which ye are and always have been. And no doubt always will be."

Rory smiled and shrugged.

"But," Magnus continued, "let anyone else say a word again' ye, and I'm offended on yer behalf. And when they threaten ye, they have me as their worst enemy. When the soldiers came to my house, moving in like they owned it, I kent that I was the bait to draw my brother into a trap, where he would be arrested, or killed. And I'll be damned if I'll do that. It's Fenwick behind it. He wants William's head, and now he wants yers as well. The Comyns want ye to ken that they're with ye. The English still listen to John Comyn, thank God. It's him that's made Fenwick and the others back off Nell and Liam."

They talked all through the night. Jocelyn curled up in a chair before the fire and slept like a cat while the others sat at the table. In the morning they broke their fast, then Rory left with promises to return, or send word more often. He'd written a letter to his parents, which Nell promised would get to them; after giving it to her, he said his good-byes.

Magnus rode out with him. The brothers said their farewells at the top of a rise.

"Dinna go home, Magnus," Rory said. "They'll discover where ye were."

"It'll buy ye some time to find William."

"They'll slit yer throat as soon as they look at ye."

Magnus shook his head. "I dinna think they will. They may suspect, but if they kent anything, they would have been here by now. They'll continue to watch me. I am their link to ye and to William."

"Ye're gambling with yer life here, and Jocelyn's. What if ye're wrong?"

"Laddie, am I ever wrong? I'm not a fool. We'll see what the next few months bring. Perhaps things will calm down if we have a king, but while we have soldiers living in our houses, there will be no peace here."

"Magnus, thank ye. I've missed ye."

"And I ye, ye halfwit imbecile." Magnus stuck out his hand. "God keep ye safe, Rory. Send word to Liam and Nell, or Ranald, if ye need me. I'll be there as soon as I hear."

Rory smiled. "No. Take care of yerself, Magnus, and Jocelyn. That's what ye can do for me, aye?"

"When will we see ye next?"

"I dinna ken. We'll see what the hearings bring us." *In Berwick,* he thought. *Isabel.*

At Loch Gannon, Margaret and Gannon were relieved to hear from Rory and delighted that the brothers had mended the rift, but still they worried. Every ship that entered the loch, every runner that approached, made them look at each other and wonder if this was the day they would hear of the death of their son.

The summer passed, although not without news of skirmishes and more deaths. In the north Andrew de Moray was making noise about the soldiers billeted there. In the east Gilbert de Umfraville refused to surrender the castles of Forfar and Dundee and was punished for it. But nothing came of all the uproar.

In Ayrshire, things had quieted. The English soldiers continued to be billeted with Magnus, but there were no incidents from it. Gannon traveled as far north as the Orkneys, and south to Carrick and Solway, learning of the mood of the clans. He had an interesting meeting with the Bruces, who received him graciously, and he was far more impressed with the youngest Robert than he had been when he'd met him before.

"He's young," Gannon told Margaret when he returned. "And as rash as our lads, but he's intelligent, and no fool, and not Edward's lapdog, as I've thought. His father and grandfather are telling him to go this way, and right now he's listening. But we'll see what happens. If the Bruces get the throne, at least he'll be in line."

"But we'll still back Balliol?" she asked.

"Aye. Robert the Younger has potential, but he's also borrowed a great deal of money from Edward. And he's off to London again soon." Gannon sighed. "I just wish Balliol were stronger. But it's out of our hands. What's to be is what's to be, aye, lass? There's no hope of us changing it."

"Is it all mapped out for us, d'ye think? Life?"

He smiled and reached for her hand. "D'ye think our meeting, and all that happened the summer that we met, was just chance? I think I was meant to be with ye, Margaret."

"Then this was destined as well, this endless waiting?"

"I dinna ken, lass. And maybe it's just as well that I dinna. I'm not sure I would have had the stomach to face all that life has handed us."

"I've never seen ye shrink from life. Are ye having any more dreams?"

He shook his head. "Nothing. So we wait."

She sighed. "At least we wait together."

"Aye."

September came, and October was on the horizon.

All eyes turned to Berwick. King Edward was said to be traveling north for the hearing, scheduled to begin on October 14. The Scots once again went to meet him, and once again the roads were clogged with travelers. Isabel listened carefully for news of the king's arrival. She was loath to spend more time in the tiny room, but she was afraid to be seen. She'd heard nothing from Rory, or Henry, and contented herself with keeping busy.

And then the word came: Edward had arrived.

SIXTEEN

The king had been at Berwick for four days, but all was quiet. Isabel was hidden away in her tiny room in the attic, and Rachel and her parents were busy every moment. Soldiers who had heard of the good food at The Oak and The Ash filled the tavern, and courtiers filled the rooms above. Rachel and her parents smiled at their patrons, not revealing how frightened they were that one of their staff would talk, that someone would reveal Isabel's hiding place.

The hearings had begun at last, but there was little news there—only that every one of the 104 auditors would speak. It would be a long process, their patrons told them. Rachel smiled and tried not to think.

And then Henry de Boyer arrived.

It was evening, the gloomy day shortened by the heavy, overhanging clouds. Henry came alone, and sat alone, his manner quiet. Rachel did not serve him but let one of the others bring him food and wine. He watched her but said nothing to her, not even as he left. The next evening he came again and ate. And watched her. And again on the third night. But this time he found Rachel in the hallway outside the kitchen and blocked her passage.

"Is she still here?"

"Who do you mean, sir?"

"Do not play the innocent with me, Rachel de Anjou. Isabel."

Rachel started at his use of her real name. She looked into his eyes, trying to see into his heart. She could see his intensity, his anger, but not his motive. "I don't know who you mean, sir," she said and saw the flicker of his eyes.

"I know, and you know, that she was here. All right." He took a deep breath. "Tell her this. She was right about Alis. I was played for a fool, and know it well. She told me there was a child, and I married her. The child was a phantom, but the marriage is real. I cannot change that. But I know her now for what she is, and am paying the price for my own part in the deception. That is why I did not come back. None of that matters now. Isabel continues to be in danger, as do you all. If she is here, get her out of Berwick as soon as you can. If she has gone, tell her not to return. I will come back and tell you when I learn more."

Rachel shook her head, but Henry stopped her with an impatient gesture.

"Do not even say it, that you have no idea of whom I speak. Listen! Just tell her that Langton is here. Ah, I see that gets your attention. It is true. Walter Langton has come to Berwick with the king. And he is looking for her. He has discovered that she came here with the Highlanders. Langton is a powerful enemy. He says she is sought for plotting against the king, Rachel. Which is treason. And those who shelter her . . . Tell her to stay hidden. Tell your father to keep his head down. Do nothing to attract attention to the inn. Let the drama stay at the castle, at the hearings."

"How does that go, sir?"

"Slow. Tedious. I do not know how anyone stays awake through it."

"When will it end?"

"God's blood, mistress, it looks to never end. I don't know. I will return."

He came again two days later, stopping her as she passed him in the tavern. She smiled, pretending to take his order.

"The man in the green cloak," he whispered. "By the window. He is Langton's spy. The soldiers are as well. They intend to leave without paying."

"Then I will serve them very slowly," she said.

"Tell Isabel that the talk at the castle is not about her and that I am doing my best to distract Langton." He gave a harsh laugh. "I have convinced my devoted wife that I will have no advancement without her assistance. And that Langton is the key to our future. I am pleased to say that she has applied herself diligently, which has solved two problems for us. It has taken Alis's attention from me, and Langton's attention from Isabel—and you. Keep your wits about you. Tell Isabel I am doing my best to protect her."

Rachel said nothing.

"I know you do not trust me," Henry said. "Nor do you need to. Just do it."

He left a short time later.

When no one would miss her, or notice her creeping up the stairs to the attic, Rachel went to Isabel and told her all that had happened. Isabel wanted to leave immediately, but Rachel told her to stay where she was, that Papa said it was best. And then she locked Isabel in, to make the small door look like nothing more than a closet.

They came that evening.

The soldiers arrived first, a squad of them lining the road before the building. More, Gilbert said, were in the garden, and on the terrace. No one was to enter or leave the inn. And now they waited—Rachel, her mother, Gilbert, and the rest of the staff—lined against the wall like children, while her father answered questions.

Langton. It could only be Walter Langton, Rachel thought as he entered and sat at a table the soldiers pulled into the middle of the room, his hands folded before him. He was dressed richly, the material of his clothing finely woven, but the color muted. He wore gold, and much of it, but few jewels. But one could tell from his every movement, his every gesture, that this was a powerful man.

"Bring him," Langton said, and Jacob was motioned forward.

Langton spoke so quietly that Rachel could not hear his words, but she saw their effect on her father, who stood like a criminal, listening.

Isabel was right. Langton had no neck. Rachel fought a wave of nervous laughter. And he walked strangely, his chest and stomach reaching his destination before the rest of him. Like a goose or a duck, with that same rolling motion of his body. She put a hand over her mouth lest she laugh aloud. There was no humor in this, for, while no one had said so, she was sure it was Isabel for whom they searched.

Her father was told to stand with her mother. Jacob nodded to Rachel as he passed, his eyes haunted, and her heart sank.

"Now the girl," Langton said.

He motioned Rachel to stand before him, his eyes hooded, but not missing a detail as he looked her from head to foot and back. She stood still under his scrutiny, not speaking, her urge to laugh gone now. Isabel was right about him: there was something evil and furtive about the man, a darkness that oozed from him, that no amount of fine cloth could disguise.

"Isabel de Burke."

"No."

His annoyance was immediate. "No, what?"

"I am not Isabel de Burke, sir. I am Rachel Angenhoff."

"No. You are Rachel de Anjou, formerly of London. Are you not?"

"Yes."

"And now you live in Berwick."

"Yes."

"And you have a friend, named Isabel de Burke."

"I did. When we lived in London, we were friends."

"So much so that when your family decided to leave . . ."

Decided to leave. Rachel did not comment.

"When your family decided to leave London, Isabel ran down to Aldgate and wished you well."

"Yes, sir."

"And then she came here."

Rachel shook her head. "I have not seen her since London, sir."

He leaned forward, his chin upthrust. "She came to Berwick on a boat last December, in the company of two Scotsmen. One is named Rory MacGannon, now outlawed for murder. The other is Kieran MacDonald, whom we now seek. Where is she?"

"I don't know, sir."

"Sit here, next to me."

"I prefer to stand, sir."

"Good. I can see more of you when you stand. Where is Isabel de Burke?"

His smile was slow, and pleased, and she realized, as she watched him watch her, that he loved to terrify. And that he was very good at it.

"Search the inn," Langton said, "all of it, from the cellars to the attic. Clear this room of everyone but the Angenhoffs. Keep their staff in the kitchens."

The soldiers did as he said, some ushering their patrons into the street, others pushing the rest of their staff into the kitchen, and still more pounding up the stairs. Gilbert protested and was struck to the ground. He lay there, his face bleeding and a soldier standing over him. Mama cried out and bent to help Gilbert, but she was shoved against the wall.

Rachel began to pray. When all the patrons were gone and only the soldiers, her parents, and Langton remained, he smiled and rose to his feet.

"Hold her!" he said, and two men came to grab Rachel's arms. He circled her, then looked at her father. "Where is Isabel de Burke?"

Papa shook his head. "I do not know."

"Strike him!"

The soldier did, clouting Papa on the head with the

hilt of a knife, drawing blood. It ran down Papa's face.

"Where is Isabel de Burke?" Langton demanded.

No one spoke. Langton put one hand on Rachel's breast. With the other he tore her bodice open, revealing her body. He reversed his hands and did the same to the other side. He kept his hand on her breast and looked at Rachel's mother.

"Shall I take her here, now? While you watch?"

"No, please no!" Mama cried.

Rachel closed her eyes.

"Where is Isabel de Burke?"

"Gone!" Mama wailed. "She left us when we heard the king was coming! You must believe us!"

Langton looked at her for a moment, then scratched his chin. "But, you see, I don't. Beat him!"

The soldiers fell on her father, beating him to the floor. He did not cry out, but Mama did, her eyes wild. She flailed at the soldiers, who shoved her against the wall and struck her across the face.

"Enough!" Langton said. "Keep him alive." He turned to Rachel. "I can feel you shivering. Are you cold?"

He did not wait for her answer but leaned to take one of her nipples in his mouth and sucked, hard. Then bit her, drawing blood. She cried out in pain. He straightened and wiped the blood from his mouth, taking his other hand from her.

"You taste like a Jew." He kept her gaze but spoke to his soldiers. "Watch them. I need a bath. And a decent meal. I will come back. And we will continue."

Isabel closed her eyes and prayed. She'd heard the boy cry "Soldiers!" and had been terrified since. She paced the room, then stopped, realizing her footsteps might be heard.

The room was tiny, a corner of a corner under the attic, not more than five feet wide, the only ventilation the small opening at the roof beam. There was a narrow bed, a chamber pot, and a chair, nothing else.

She could hear the soldiers' booted feet on the stairs, their muted voices, male, rough, determined. She could hear more outside through the thin, unplastered wooden walls. They were in the garden, on the terrace of the inn next door. And here, on the floor below her. She sat on the corner of the bed, determined to be calm if they found her. When they found her. She had no idea who'd sent them.

Henry? Would he betray her this way? Was Henry capable of such duplicity? No, she would not believe it. But . . .

What if it was not her that they sought but Jacob and Rachel's family? What if there had been another expulsion order? What if she cowered here, like a small trapped animal, while they faced horrors below? What if, when at last she left this room, the Angenhoffs were gone, removed to face God knew what fate? What a coward she would have been.

The boots were closer now, slower, as the men climbed the narrow stairs to the attic. Two men, then a third, circling, stopping near the small window in the larger attic space. Knocking on the wall, talking in heavy Northumbrian accents to each other. These men, from the borderlands, would be no friends of the Scots, nor those who found refuge in their cities.

She opened her eyes, staring at the wall that held the small door to this room. This had once been a closet in the attic, stretching across one end of the garret. Jacob and Gilbert had divided it into three spaces, this the smallest and only accessed through the other two.

Now the soldiers were in the closet, knocking on walls. If they moved the chest that hid the door to this room, they would find her. She held her breath.

The boots stopped moving, as though they studied something, or were gesturing to each other. And low whispers, and a laugh, low and guttural, that chilled her. And another, full of the sound of men telling each other bawdy stories.

And then they were gone.

Her tears came then, pouring silently from her eyes while she lay on the bed, trying to stay calm. She watched the shadows change on the wall, the sun setting so much earlier in these days of autumn, and she remembered that this was Samhain, the ancient marking of the night when evil spirits roamed the earth at will.

It was hours before anyone came.

She heard the footsteps on the stairs, then the slow moving of the chest, and the unlocking of the door. She stood. It was Gilbert who opened the door. He put a candle on the floor and shoved it toward her with a tray of bread and cheese, but he did not come into the room.

"They're still here," he whispered. "The soldiers. But Langton is gone."

"Langton was here! Oh, dear God, what have I done?"

"Langton went back to the castle. All the guests were made to leave."

"What did he do, Gilbert? What did they do?"

There was silence, then Gilbert moved forward and turned his face so she could see. His cheek was ripped open, a jagged tear that was already turning purple and a deep red. "They beat Jacob. He has marks all over his body."

Isabel moaned. "And Rachel? And her mother?"

"Her mother was struck, but not hurt badly. But Rachel . . ." He told her then what Langton had done to Rachel. "Do not come out. Rachel will come when she can. She is badly shaken, and they are watching her."

Isabel felt a rage unlike anything she'd ever felt. "The man is a monster! Their only crime was protecting me!"

"He wants to know where you are, Isabel. He says he will come back tonight. When he returns, it will get worse."

She drew in a shuddering breath, then made her decision. "They must leave! They need to escape his clutches. Tell them I am so sorry for having brought this on their heads after all their kindnesses. They must go!"

"Yes. They are planning to do just that. We have already made plans. They want you to come with them."

"No. I cannot endanger them further. Tell them to go without me."

"What will you do?"

"What I must. Do not lock the door. And, Gilbert, leave your knife."

Staring into the distance, she waited until his footsteps faded, then picked up the knife Gilbert had left on the floor and slid it under her garter.

She crept down the stairs, stopping every few feet to listen, but there was no sound from any of the rooms. She continued, reaching the ground floor, standing in the dim light that spilled from the inn next door. She leaned against the door that linked the two buildings. All was silent.

The door to the outside creaked when she opened it and she froze, fearing discovery. But no one cried out, no soldiers leapt at her out of the dark, and she slipped outside and up the hill. She shrank against the wall of the inn, leaning forward to look into the large window that faced the street. Then farther, until she could see shapes. The glass, thick and mottled, did not allow her a clear view, but she could make out Rachel sitting alone on the floor in the center of the room, and there, by the hallway to the kitchens, two shapes on the floor. Soldiers walked across the floor, talking cheerfully and lifting cups of ale.

There was no sign of Langton.

She lifted her skirts and hurried up the hill.

She paused outside the gates, trying to find the courage to do what she must. For a while, as long as it lasted, she must become another person, stronger, fiercer. She must not waver from her goal. She went over her plan again. It was madness.

The gates were open but manned, the causeway full of men who hurried to and fro. Overhead torches lit the scene, their flames dancing in the light wind, casting shadows across the stones of the castle and on the yard below. She said a prayer, then another, then squared her shoulders and walked forward. The guards gave her a quizzical look as she neared them.

"I am Isabel de Burke. Tell my lord Bishop Langton that I await."

A few moments later she was shown inside, through the portcullis and into the yard. The men who passed her threw curious glances her way, but no one spoke to her. She was jostled by two whores, who laughed at her, their breath foul with drink. They continued on to the group of soldiers standing on the far side of the yard, distracting them with simpering looks and a vast display of cleavage.

Isabel closed her eyes, saying a prayer that her courage wouldn't fail her.

"I had to see it for myself."

It was Alis's voice. With a feeling of inevitability, Isabel opened her eyes.

Alis leaned from a balcony above, her hair tousled, as though she had just risen from bed, her low-cut bodice as revealing as the whores'. She held a crystal glass in her hand and sipped from it, then smiled down at Isabel. "It is you. I knew you were alive."

Isabel smiled in return. "How could I have not known you would be here?"

Langton hurried up behind Alis, clutching his open robe to himself. He peered over her shoulder at Isabel, then grunted. "Bring her up," he said.

Langton's apartments faced the river below. Isabel followed the guard up the narrow and spiraled stairs. She could hear music from the Great Hall, and laughter floating up the stairwell. The king was entertaining his guests, and apparently most in the castle were with him. They passed the balcony from which Langton and Alis had leaned, then down a long corridor lit by torches held in sconces on the walls. It was quiet here, with no one about and all the doors closed. The guard knocked on a wide door.

"Come in," Langton said.

The guard opened the door. Isabel lifted her chin and stepped inside.

It was a large room, comfortably furnished, one end

dominated by a large stone fireplace, carved with biblical scenes, in which a fire crackled. There were two windows, one open slightly to the night air. The breeze rippled the flames of the candles that stood on the low table before the fireplace and the higher one next to the tall bed. The bed itself was of carved oak, the pillars of its canopy stout and roped, the canopy above carved with Langton's crest.

Langton stood near the closed window, his face in shadow, his form, in dark clothing, blending into the heavy draperies behind him.

"Leave us."

The guard bowed and retreated. The door closed with a solid thud. And then there was silence. She stared at him, but she could not see his face.

"A bold move, Isabel." His voice was calm.

She did not answer.

"An unexpected treat, to have you come to me. I am glad the Angenhoffs sent you."

"They did not."

"Oh, come, Isabel. I was so persuasive. I know they were eager to assist me in my search."

"They do not know I am here."

"And pigs fly."

"What do you want with me?"

His laugh was amused, but cold. "Is it not obvious? I was concerned when you left London so suddenly. That was not wise, to tell the world that you were dead. Your mother tells me it was your idea, and that she begged you to come to your senses. Your grandmother played her part well. I felt terrible, having my men tear her house apart. We found nothing, of course. And no, she was not harmed. You may think me one, but I am not a monster.

The captain of a boat that runs the coast remembered you and the Scotsmen. And here we are."

He stepped forward into the light. His robe had been hastily donned. It was still askew, and not properly fastened, revealing dark hair below his throat. He crossed the room and locked the door, pocketing the key.

"Why did you come here, Isabel?"

"I heard you were looking for me."

"Ah, your friend Rachel told you."

"No. My benefactor."

His eyebrows raised. "Your benefactor? Jacob? The old devil! And all this time I thought it was the daughter you were fond of."

"Not Jacob."

"Then?" He moved to a table, pouring wine into two crystal glasses. "Tell me more about your mysterious benefactor."

"He is not mysterious. I was at the inn. He visited and offered me . . . a different position."

"A different position." He stood before the couch before the fire. His robe fell open, giving her a glimpse of his rounded stomach, matted with dark hair. "Yes?"

"I am under his protection."

"Of course you are. Who is this man? And do not tell me it's de Boyer. I know he cannot afford a mistress. His wife takes all the coin he has."

"No. Not de Boyer."

"Then the Scotsman. MacGannon."

"No. He is French. He visits Berwick on business. He is a wine merchant."

"And you service him here?"

"Yes."

"His name?"

She pulled a name out of the air. "Gaston de Vezelay."

Langton moved closer and handed her the wine. "And all this time I thought you a virgin. I am pleased you are not. It is tedious, deflowering."

She smiled then and took the wine, draining it. She would need its strength.

He laughed and took the glass from her. "More, Isabel? Shall we become quite debauched?"

"I believe you are already."

He laughed again and poured the wine. "I am delighted that we can agree on something. Now tell me the truth. Why are you here?" He handed her the wine.

"Why do you look for me here?"

"We had unfinished business."

"What is left to say?"

"I offered you my services and you ran. I can make it all go away, Isabel. The accusations against you can dissolve." He snapped his fingers. "Like this. The king will be told it was all a dreadful mistake. You will not have to hide in a sewer like Berwick. You will be able to return to London again with no fear."

"In return for?"

"You. Your body. When I want it. How I want it."

"And if I refuse?"

"I cross the room and call the guard. Do you know what a traitor's death is?"

"Yes."

"I would hate to have to watch you suffer." He pushed his robe open farther and rubbed his hand down his chest, then lower. And laughed. "What does de Vezelay like you to do?"

"The usual things."

"Does he like you to touch him?" His hand moved up, then down. "Does he ask you to put your lips around him?"

She felt faint. "Yes," she whispered.

"And do you?"

"Yes."

"Come here, Isabel." He put his wineglass on the table.

She moved to stand stiffly before him. He took the glass from her and placed it next to his, then, keeping one hand still in his robe, he reached for her with the other, his hand circling her neck, drawing her mouth to his.

"Kiss me, Isabel. Prove you are not dissembling."

She leaned closer, pressing her lips against his. He tasted of wine and garlic, and when his tongue probed her she thought she would gag. He pulled back.

"You are not wholehearted in this. You tremble, Isabel. Do you fear me?"

"Yes," she whispered.

She saw the flash of pleasure in his eyes and felt a thrill of triumph. She could do this. She would do this.

"I can be most generous. To those who please me."

"What do you want me to do?"

"Put your hand here."

He guided her hand into his robe, to wrap her fingers around his penis. He was very hard, his erection jutting forward. He shrugged out of his robe and stood naked before her. His body was as she'd thought—formless. His shoulders and his waist were the same width. His chest and stomach were covered with thick dark hair, and lower . . . He smiled.

"Yes. You excite me. You have from the first moment I saw you. I wanted you. I still do. Will you be wise, Isabel? Or will this pretty neck be stretched on the gallows?"

She was silent.

"Look at your hand on me. Look!"

She did.

"Now move your hand. Slowly. Up. Down. Your Frenchman has not taught you much, has he? This is only the beginning. Does he like you to do this?"

"Yes."

"And what else? Does he like you to move faster? Like this?" He guided her hand. "Yes. Tighter. Again. Again." His smile was sly. "I don't believe you are practiced at this. But you will learn. Now let me go. I am not ready for this to be over. Take off your clothing."

"I . . ."

"Shall I cross the room and call the guard?"

"No."

"Then?"

She removed the long tunic she wore, then turned, as though she were being modest, fumbling on her leg for her garter. She stepped out of her shoes, rolled down her stockings, and dropped them on the floor. He reached from behind and caressed her breast through the material.

She took a shuddering breath. She could not do it. He pressed against her, his erection firm through the cloth that covered her.

"We will do this as well. But not yet. Here, let me help you."

She dropped the garter from her leg, Gilbert's knife with it, and put her foot atop it, then her long tunic. *Dear God.* But no, she could not ask His help in this.

Langton lifted her undertunic over her head. She stood naked before him.

He studied her, tilting his head and turning her to face the light. "Yes. Yes. You are perfect." His smile was slow. "Do we have an agreement, Isabel? Your body for your life?"

She nodded, trembling. *Dear God.*

He ran a hand from her shoulder to her breast, lifting it, then along her waist, to rest between her legs. "Not yet," he said as though talking to himself. "Touch me again. Hold me."

She reached for him. "Do you want my lips on you?"

She felt his surge of blood under her hand and felt her own surge of power. This was what Alis knew, how to make a man do what she wanted. She thought of Alis with Langton. With Henry, then banished that vision from her mind. She would be Alis. She stroked the length of him. She needed him to believe her.

"Sit down." He pushed her roughly onto the couch, pushed her back against the cushions and leaned forward, his erection almost touching her. "Take it."

She wrapped her hand around his penis and squeezed.

"Take it in your mouth."

She licked her lips and opened her mouth. The tip of his penis pushed past her lips, but they were dry and she pulled back. He hit the side of her head.

"Take it!"

She did, letting him press into her, his sigh almost a moan. He pulled out, then thrust in again, and again she thought she would gag.

"Move your tongue."

She leaned forward, moving her mouth and her hand

at the same time, reaching for the floor. He pulled out and thrust again, and her fingers closed around the hilt of the knife. She tightened her lips, and he leaned his head back.

She struck him between his legs, feeling the point of the knife penetrate soft flesh.

He screamed. She pulled the knife back and thrust it in again. He struck her head and staggered back, blood gushing from his scrotum. He looked down at himself and screamed again. Then lunged for her, bent over, but she darted out of his way, holding the knife between them. He was stronger, she knew, and faster, and if he caught her, she would die. Blood streamed down his legs, and he clutched himself and stared at her. Then fell to his knees.

She did not wait. She grabbed her clothing and darted for the door.

It was locked. He was trying to stand again. She whirled around, grabbed the stone wine bottle, and struck his head. Again. And again. He fell forward with a sigh and lay prone.

Her breath was ragged, and her heart pounding. But she found his robe and fumbled in the pocket for the key, then wiped the knife on his robe. Langton did not move, but his blood crept across the floor. So red, so very red. She thrust her hands into the basin of water, watching the water turn a pale red, and fighting her roiling stomach. She threw her undergown on with jerky movements, slid her feet into her shoes, then unlocked the door, closing it behind her. With her clothing bunched around the knife, she ran down the corridor, toward the stairs. She rounded the corner.

And saw Henry, hurrying forward.

He was alone. He stopped when he saw her and stared.

"Isabel? What in hell is happening?"

She held her clothing before her. "I killed him. Oh, dear God, Henry, I killed him. Or perhaps not. He might still be alive. Dear God, dear God, dear God."

He grabbed her arms. "Langton?"

She nodded.

"What did he do to you?"

She shook her head. "He harmed Rachel and her family."

"Alis told me you were here . . . wait, I'll go see if he's dead."

"No! I have to get out. Henry, help me get out of here!"

"Not like this. Here, put on your clothes." He pulled the tunic from her hands and shook it out. The knife fell to the floor. He looked from it to her. "You cut him?"

She nodded, shivering now. He draped the tunic over her and helped her get her arms through the sleeves. She was shaking so badly that he had to steady her. He held up her stockings, splattered with blood, then shook his head.

"No time." He grabbed the knife from the floor and thrust it in his belt. "Come."

He took her hand, rushing her down a corridor she'd not seen before, then down a long and dark stairwell, the light so dim here that she had to hold the wall so as not to misstep. They emerged at last onto a kitchen garden.

"Wait!" he said and dashed through a door.

She stood, trembling. "Dear God, dear God, dear God."

He was back then, with a cloak that he threw around her shoulders. He took her hand and ran with her toward the walls. She was not sure how they got there, down stairs and through tunnels or corridors, passing a few servants and soldiers, who threw them looks, but said nothing.

Henry held her close against him and laughed to one pair of soldiers. "Worse for the drink, she is, and better for me!"

Their laughter rang against the stones.

They were through a gate then, out in the night air, hurrying headlong down an immense staircase. And suddenly she knew where she was. Breakneck stairs. From the castle to the river.

Henry pushed her into a round tower at the foot of the stairs.

"Say nothing!" he hissed and yanked the hood over her head.

He talked quietly to a guard. She heard the clink of coins, and then Henry pulled her through the tower, to the dock outside. And into a waiting boat, small, a river craft. He handed the man who waited in it some coins.

"Get her away now!"

"Where to, sir?"

"Anywhere! Across the river! Get her somewhere safe. And keep your silence!"

"That will cost more then."

Henry swore but handed the man more coins. The man bit them, then picked up the oars and pushed away from the dock.

Isabel looked back as they left. Henry stood, his arms at his sides, watching her. Then he pulled the knife from his belt and tossed it in the river.

And then the darkness closed in and she could not

see him—only the castle, lit by torches, and the flag that waved from the topmost tower. The royal banner of Edward, king of England.

Rory paced again. Twelve steps. That was how wide this glade was where they hid—he, Kieran, William, and William's brothers. And two dozen others, most outlawed, most for murder. He paced again.

"Sit down, Rory," William called to him. "Your walking will not make the decision in Berwick come any sooner."

Rory nodded, as though he agreed, but he could not sit. Isabel was there, in Berwick, in the thick of it. With King Edward. And worse, terrifying news: Walter Langton. Rory cursed himself for a fool. Why had he not gone to her in all this time?

He'd thought himself noble, to stay away and let her forget him. And perhaps, if he was honest with himself, to forget her. It had not worked. She haunted him. He saw her smile in his dreams, sometimes sweet, sometimes so rawly sexual that he woke, throbbing with need, to roam the night.

And now, to be just twelve miles from Berwick, in this makeshift camp with thirty other men, waiting for pampered nobles and harassed lawyers to plead their cases to a king who already knew the answer he wanted. It was torture.

William laughed at him. "Sit down, Rory. You're making us all nervous."

"One day you will love a woman," he said, "and I will laugh at ye."

Which made William laugh all the more. And Kieran

stare at Rory. And then he heard it, his own words. He loved her. And he did. There it was. Wrong time. Wrong place. Wrong woman, for God's sake, an Englishwoman instead of a warm Highland girl who would understand his life, and he hers. But there it was.

Kieran had gone to Berwick earlier that day to hear the news. And see Rachel. The story he had returned with had chilled Rory to the bones.

He looked at the sky. Two hours at the most until darkness came.

"Tell me again what Rachel told ye," he demanded of Kieran. "All of it."

His cousin sighed but repeated it. Rory listened, hearing different things now.

He had to see her. Had to talk to her, to know she was alive, that Walter Langton, curse the man, had not touched her. It was madness, he knew, to cover his hair with a dark hood, to change his trews and plaid for an English soldier's tunic and cloak, to leave the magnificent sword, given to him by his father, behind, and bring the short and inadequate one they'd taken from a dead man.

But that is just what he did.

The ride was not bad, even when he passed the English army, their campfires lighting the bottom of the low-hanging clouds with an orange glow. Closer were the minstrel camps, where vagabond musicians and jesters and tumblers waited for one chance to perform before a king, or lacking that, a group of nobles who would pay well for entertainment during this tedious process. Closer still was the collection of tents, each a bit away from the next, where traveling whores met their customers and exchanged their talents for coin.

And then the gates, closed, but not well guarded, for what madman would try to enter Berwick with an army inside as well as out? The king's knights were there, in the castle, and some in the town. Those who had wives and the coin to bring them to Berwick paid high prices to house them in the inns nearest the castle.

The guard hardly glanced at the bent man who fumbled with coin to hand him, too busy arguing playfully with the whores who were begging admittance. A second coin and Rory was through. He walked quickly up the hill, past the Flemish church, where music sounded from within, then around the corner.

And there it was, The Oak and The Ash. And somewhere, within those walls, was Isabel. But wait. The inn stood quiet. The door was closed, the large window that faced the street dark. The window above was shuttered. Silent.

He felt the hair on the back of his neck rise.

He climbed the steps and tried the door. Locked. He circled the inn, going to the alley behind it, where the kitchen garden was, and found the gate there that he remembered. He waited, listening, then found a dark corner and watched. Nothing moved. There was no light, no noise in the inn. He tried the door.

It was open and he entered, expecting to be challenged at any moment, but there was no voice raised in protest. The inn stood empty. He roamed the rooms, his boots sounding loud on the wooden floors. Beds were neatly made, waiting for occupants. The kitchen was cold, but food still stood on the shelves. There was ale in the cellar, but their clothes were gone. Jacob's books and Bible, all gone. In the attic he found a tiny room with a bed—a hiding place.

And in the tavern room, near the wall, bloodstains on the floor.

He asked at several inns, but no one would tell him what had happened at The Oak and The Ash. They shook their heads and shrugged.

"They're gone."

Rory turned to face the old man who spoke to him.

"Jacob, all of them. They left after Langton's visit."

"Do ye ken where they went?"

The man shrugged.

"Was there an English lass? Isabel de Burke? Was she with them?"

"Ah. She's the one who stabbed Langton, aye?"

"What? She stabbed Walter Langton?"

"She got away is all I heard."

"She got away? Did he die? Did she kill him?"

"No one has said."

"Where did she go?"

The man shrugged again. "The inn is closed and they are all gone."

PART III

Dico tibi verum, libertas optima rerum;

Nuquam servili sub nexu vivito, fili.

(My son, I tell thee soothfastlie,
No gift is like to libertie;
Then never live in slaverie)

LATIN PRECEPT OF WILLIAM WALLACE'S UNCLE,
PRIEST OF DUNIPACE

SEVENTEEN

Nell Crawford put her finger to her lips and pulled her nephew quickly into the room. "Kieran! What are ye doing here, and at such an hour? What's wrong?"

Kieran planted a kiss on her cheek and gave her a grin. "Whist, Nell, isn't that the very thing I've come to find out from ye?"

Nell closed the door. "And ye thought that the middle of the night was a good time to visit and get caught up on all our news?"

"I was hoping that some of the English spies will be abed. Ye just left attending the queen, Nell. I sent word. Did they not tell ye I was here?"

"No, but that's more the case these days than not. I may be her lady-in-waiting at the behest of John Comyn and John Balliol, but Isabella de Warenne and I will never be close."

"Because she's English?"

"That doesna help, does it? And because her father is the Earl of Surrey, one of King Edward's closest advisors and no friend of any Scot's. Is Rory here with ye, lad?"

"No. Just me. Rory's with William, meeting with some of the barons."

"At least he's not off looking for her. Has he conceded defeat yet?"

"No. Ye ken Rory."

"Aye, I do. What can I get ye—ale? Wine? Food?"

"No, I'm a'right. I ate with the others, just one more worried Scotsman coming with those who are attending Balliol's council. For what it's worth."

It was John Balliol who had been named the rightful King of Scotland by King Edward in Berwick, and King John Balliol who had jumped every time Edward of England called, hurrying down to Newcastle or London or wherever Edward told him to go, sitting silently or with token protest as Edward took over lawsuits and properties, saying these were his legal rights now. The Scottish nobles were silent through it all, but the Scottish people were most vocal in expressing their disapproval.

"I was listening," Kieran said, "to the others talk while I was waiting to see ye. Is it true, Nell? Does King John mean to defy Edward at last? Edward's sure to have noticed that Balliol missed the deadline to have troops in London to fight in Edward's invasion of France."

Balliol had not officially refused, but neither had he done as told. Instead, he'd summoned his council, and the nobles were gathering at Stirling.

"Of course Edward noticed," Nell said, "but then again, with the Welsh staging a rebellion at the same time, he's been a bit engaged. Very neighborly of them, is it not, to distract him so nicely?"

"Aye, it is. So . . . how are ye faring here?"

"Lonely." Liam had been gone for so long, off in France, with the barons and bishops from Balliol's council, arranging a match between Balliol's oldest son and King Philip of France's niece. She was very weary of being without him for the good of a king or two. "I miss Liam fiercely, and Meg and Elissa. But my girls are safe with Margaret at Loch Gannon, and Liam's better off in France than being with the lot of ye, living on the road."

"Ah, so ye did send them off."

"I did, though it broke my heart. But when King John ignored Edward's summons, I was afraid to keep them in Stirling."

Kieran nodded. "They are safe there. I'm glad my mother and sisters are on Skye and not here. And, I confess, I am weary of the road. Maybe I'm ready for a wife of my own. D'ye think Liam will help arrange my marriage as well?"

She smiled. "Not unless yer da turns out to be a king."

"Does it count if he thinks he is?"

"Be good, or I'll tell my brother what his oldest son is saying about him. Now, d'ye want some wine, or do I drink alone?"

"I'll have some wine."

Nell poured each of them a glass. "Strange to think that we can drink French wine from crystal glasses and the English cannot."

"They have crystal. Some of them."

"I meant the wine and ye ken it. What did King Edward expect when he argued with Philip of France? It's been a boon for Scottish merchants that the English are banned from trading with France. I hear Newcastle's wool merchants are making arrangements with Scottish merchants to get their goods to the Continent. I imagine they'll be paying a pretty price for the privilege."

"No doubt," Kieran agreed. "Edgar Keith says he's making more money from the English in a month than he makes from the Scots in a year."

"Rachel's brother-in-law? Tell him to enjoy it. That will end if war comes. Has Rory heard anything new from his father?" Nell asked. Gannon was gone as well, Magnus with him, off with a party of Scottish nobles in Norway, talking with King Erik there. "Margaret heard from him earlier in the month."

"We've heard nothing since then. Nell, d'ye not think it's a waste of time, Gannon being in Norway? Does Balliol think to win Erik of Norway back to our side? I would think, after Robert the Bruce the elder married his daughter to Erik, that John Balliol wouldna be thinking too kindly of him."

"It's not a waste of time," Nell said. "Erik is already talking to Philip of France. There's a rumor of a treaty between France and Norway, not made public yet. But France and Philip are Edward's enemies. If Philip and Erik are allies—"

"An enemy of my enemy is my friend?"

"It's happened before," she said. "How is Rachel?"

Kieran's smile was rueful. When he had found Rachel a year ago, living with her sister, he'd been elated.

But Rachel had quickly disabused him of any hope. Her manner had been distant, polite, as if she'd not ever kissed him, as if the fire that had been between them did not still burn. But it did, he could see it in her eyes, see it in the way she refused to meet his gaze and would not be alone with him. In front of Sarah and Edgar, she had told him she was pleased to see him.

"Pleased," he'd said, hoping his teasing tone would draw more from her.

"Pleased is all I can be, Kieran," she'd said. "And all I will ever be. I can feel nothing more than that."

He'd ignored the others watching them. "Canna or willna, Rachel?"

"I feel nothing more," she'd said, turning her back.

"Rachel? Can we at least talk?" he'd asked, hearing the pleading in his tone.

"There is nothing to say, Kieran," she said, walking away. "Nothing."

He'd watched her, feeling his cheeks burn and his temper flare. She was lying. He was sure of it. He'd tried once again, but she'd refused to even see him. And so he left her alone. For a while. When he visited yet again, he told her he'd accepted her decision and this time he did not say more. They had had an uneasy truce since. At least he could still see her, and he visited as often as he could. It was not enough.

"She's well," he said. "She's back in Berwick. Her father has reopened the inn and they're doing well. She hears a lot, with all the ships going to and from France and the Continent. She says the French are crowing about Edward having to fight the Welsh yet again."

"He'll soon solve it," Nell said. "He'll be ruthless and he'll crush them as he did before. And Rachel's heard nothing from Isabel?"

"Nothing, in all this time. And Rory says her grandmother in London has heard nothing. She's gone from Berwick is all we ken."

"Tell me that Rory didna go to London looking for her."

"That was only part of why he went."

"Is he mad? He's outlawed!"

"Aye, he kens. We all ken. For the most part he's staying in Scotland, meeting with the clans and the nobles. Even the Bruces. He met with the younger Robert Bruce when he was in London. Bruce invited him to dine with him in his castle just north of the city, and to come to a fine party there."

"Young Robert Bruce was here last summer, when our Parliament confirmed him as Earl of Carrick, and Rory talked at length with him then. Gannon liked the lad when he met him two years ago. Maybe this Robert is not the schemer his grandfather is, or maybe the Bruces are trying to woo people away from John Comyn, one cousin at a time."

"Oh, aye, that will happen," Kieran said. "Especially after John Comyn called the English soldiers off ye in Ayrshire and ye kept yer house when so many others were burnt out."

"Notice the Bruces are not wooing me." Nell sipped her wine. "But . . . if they do decide to, I just may listen. I paid my debt to the Comyns when I agreed to come and serve Balliol's queen."

Nell did not say the rest of it—how much she disliked Balliol's queen. The woman was haughty, accustomed to servility, and she expected her household to run itself. Nell had soon learned that she was expected to be little more than a well-dressed housekeeper, which suited her fine. She distrusted the Englishwomen with whom the queen surrounded herself, distrusted even more the many letters that came to the queen from England. They were a constant reminder that Scotland was under Edward's scrutiny at all times.

"I thought I was finished serving in a court," she said. "I'm weary of it all. I keep reminding myself that just a few months ago I was worried the whole countryside of Ayrshire would have been murdered or burnt out of their homes. And I think of all those I ken who had nowhere else to go, while I have Stirling and could be taken in by Margaret or yer Da. I'm the fortunate one, lad, and while I may be bored, I've a roof over my head, and that's better than where we were before Balliol became king. But what a disappointment he has been. He looks the other way while the abuses continue, and it's men like ye who keep the people safe."

"Aye, we've been trying to. And now Edward's drawing his soldiers home to fight the Welsh and then the French. It is better out there now, Nell."

"Tell me true, Kieran, are any of the stories I'm hearing close to what ye're doing? I've heard ye've cleared half of western Ayrshire of English soldiers, and Andrew de Moray is doing the same in the north."

"We've been busy."

"So it's more than just talk ye and Rory are doing these days."

"Perhaps."

"Ye willna tell me more?"

"I canna, Nell, for the truth of it is we're all waiting to see what's next. If Balliol does defy Edward, we'll have war and we're sure to be in the thick of it. Right now all we're doing is getting promises of men and aid from the clans. William's not a Highlander like us, and he doesna have the same ties to some of the families, so Rory and I are doing the talking. That's all we're doing."

"I willna even ask ye if ye're both being careful. I ken what ye would say."

"And what would that be?"

"Ye'd say, 'Aye, Nell, whenever we're in a dangerous pinch, we just explain to the others that we canna get hurt. It does wonders to calm things.' "

He laughed. "I hope I wouldna be so rude. But d'ye think it would work?"

"Just tell me ye'll be mindful of all of us waiting and worrying, aye?"

"I am. We are." He rose to his feet. "I have to get back to the others."

She stood. "Already?"

"Already. Dinna worry so much, Nell. We're sensible."

"Ha! That is the one thing none of ye are." She placed her hand on his cheek. "Ye are very dear to me, lad. Keep yerselves safe. And tell madman Rory that there are other lasses in the world."

He kissed her cheek. "I'm trying to remember it myself."

Nell watched him go down the hallway. At the corner he waved and then was gone. She laid her head against the door, saying a brief prayer for Kieran, for Rory, and all those she loved. *Liam, come home to me. I need ye here, love. I am afraid.*

"Rachel."

Mama's voice was low. She pulled Rachel to the door of the kitchen.

"Come. Look outside."

Rachel followed her mother to the foyer, where she stood in the shadow and looked out into the street before the inn. Her heart began to pound.

Henry de Boyer.

He stood alone in the middle of the pathway, staring

impassively at the inn, as though deciding whether to enter. He wore the uniform of the king's own, his clothing even finer than she remembered it. His head was uncovered, his dark hair gleaming in the last rays of this late September day.

"Pray that this does not mean the English are returning," Papa said as he came to Rachel's side.

"I do," she whispered. "We've not heard anything of that, though."

"But would we? We will have nothing to do with these people, Rachel."

"Perhaps he has news of Isabel."

"If she had wanted us to know where she was, she would have written."

"How could she, Papa? She did not know where we would have gone."

"Where else did we have to go but to Sarah? She would know that."

Rachel was silent. They'd had the same conversation dozens of times in the last two years.

"I will not have this family endangered again." Papa looked into her eyes. "Isabel knows her presence here harmed us and that's why she keeps away."

"I just want to know she is alive, Papa, that's all. Just that she is alive and has not paid a price for what she did."

"Of course she's paid a price. As we have. Here he comes."

They stood where they were as Henry climbed the stairs to the door. He hesitated when he saw them, then gave Rachel and her father a smile.

"I am glad to see you both well. Sir, Rachel, I bid you good day."

"And you, sir," Papa said. "It has been a long time."

"Two years," Henry said, looking past Rachel. "Is she here?"

"Isabel?" Rachel asked. "No. Do you not know where she is?"

"I've not seen her since I helped her leave Berwick Castle. Truly, she is not here? Please, tell me if she is."

"You helped her leave the castle?"

"Stop," Papa said. "Sir, come to another room. Rachel, take him away from those who may be listening. I will get someone to man the tavern. We cannot be talking about this here."

"No," Henry said. "Of course you're right."

Rachel led Henry to the suite of rooms she shared with her parents. She offered him food, which he accepted, and drink, which he did not.

"You've heard nothing of her since?" Henry asked.

"No," Rachel said. "I hoped perhaps you had some news."

"She's not been back in London that I can tell you. Neither her mother nor grandmother told me anything. But she cannot have vanished in air. How has she lived, these two years? She had nothing with her, only the clothing she wore."

"She had coins sewn in her hems. Not enough to live well for a long time, but enough to feed her."

Her father entered then, closing the door behind him softly.

"Where would she have gone?" Henry asked. "Have you heard from MacGannon? Perhaps she's with him."

Rachel ignored the sharp glance her father threw her.

"No. His cousin has been here, but not Rory. And they'd not heard anything the last time he was here."

"Why are you in Berwick now?" Papa asked. "Is King Edward returning?"

"Not now, but who knows what's to come? I'm sure you know how high tensions are. I am part of a group . . . We are seeing whose loyalties lie where. I am glad to find you well and safe. I had worried that you had suffered as well."

He rose to his feet.

"Do not go yet, sir," Papa said. "Tell us of that night, if you would."

Henry sat again, telling them a story that made Rachel's skin crawl. How had Isabel been close enough to Langton to stab him? What had happened between them?

"That's the last I saw of her," Henry said, spreading his hands wide. "I cannot believe what she did. And, of course, the worst of it is that Langton lived."

"I've always wondered how she got away," Rachel said. "We'd heard she'd been aided by someone within the castle, but did not know who it would be."

"Who else would aid her? My wife? The king? Only a few of us even knew who she was," Henry said. "I'm just grateful that no one else was around. If Alis had not told me that Isabel had arrived . . ." He shook his head.

"How is it you've managed to avoid suspicion?" Papa asked.

"I did not avoid it." His laugh was bitter. "Alis even told them that I went in search of Isabel. I told them that I did but had not found her, that my knock on Langton's door went unanswered."

"No one saw you?"

"A few did. But the castle was full of men and many women, and I was dressed simply that night, a brown tunic and leggings, like half the men there, so those who did see me might not have known who I was. I was questioned several times. It was fortunate for me that Langton lived and he absolved me of attacking him. And I had a bit of revenge on my dear wife. I told them that Alis had been with Langton when Isabel arrived, and that she and Isabel had been close friends when they were in London. I hinted that perhaps she had aided Isabel. She added her own twist, that she had talked with Isabel that night, that Isabel was in a rage of jealousy about Alis's affair with Langton. They loved it in London. They're still talking about it."

"And Langton? What does he say about it all?"

"Very little. He is back at his offices, although I'm told his voice is higher than before. Isabel said that Langton harmed you all. When I could, I came to see you. But you were gone and the inn closed. No one knew where you had gone."

Papa nodded, and Rachel could see he'd made his decision to trust Henry, at least a little. "Langton came that night, looking for Isabel. He searched the inn . . . and . . ." He looked into the distance. "We were here, under guard when we'd heard the news that Langton had been stabbed. As soon as the guards left us, we left Berwick. We came back a year ago, and all has been quiet since then."

"Langton is still looking for her. If you see her, if you have any way to get word to her, tell her that he has many men searching for her. If they have not already come here, they will. Please be on guard, for her sake and for your own."

He held out his hand to Rachel's father. "I thank you for your hospitality, and for protecting Isabel. I hope you will pay no further penalty for your charity."

Papa rose. "Isabel was a good friend to my daughter."

Henry nodded. "Farewell, sir. Rachel." At the door he turned. "If there is war, and I suspect there will be, we will be on opposite sides, you and I. You should know that there is no chance of Scotland winning against Edward's army. The Scots will be annihilated. If you have any means by which to get word through to the Scottish leadership, tell them to reconsider their defiance."

"I have no means to do so," Papa said.

"Then tell everyone who comes here to this inn. Spread the word. The Scots need to know the odds they face. Edward is invincible. He will wreak a terrible vengeance upon those who defy him."

Papa nodded. "I will tell those who listen."

"Tell Kieran MacDonald. Tell him his cousin and I will be enemies as well as rivals. Tell him to tell MacGannon that I will look for him on the field of battle. And God help us both, for one of us is sure to die. And if you see Isabel . . . tell her I was here. And that I wish her well."

Rachel listened to her father say the Sabbath prayers and read from the Book of Prophets, today from the Book of Micah, with its promise of hope, its message that a new king would be born of the line of David and replace the weak king now on the throne. Fitting, she thought, for the current situation in Scotland, for both Balliol and Bruce claimed to be from the line of David of Scotland. But it seemed that the wrong man had been chosen. Few were happy with Balliol thus far. Hardly a day went by without someone in the tavern room complaining about King John, and others defending him. Often it led to violence.

Rachel looked at the bruise on her wrist, where last night a man had held her against her will, trying to get her to agree that someone should kill John Balliol. She'd twisted away from him, but she had been shaken by the experience. It was not unusual these days, for feelings against the king ran high. Two years ago Berwick had been waiting to host King Edward, hoping that the search for a Scottish king was over. Now Berwick chafed under English laws while King John of Scotland did nothing to change that. The mood was once again sour.

She'd tried to keep her spirits up through it all, through the months when she'd thought Kieran would return, when she'd gently refused to marry the butcher's son. Mosheh had listened, his head down, as she'd talked. He'd nodded once and left. She'd felt dreadful about hurting him, but she'd been sure Kieran would return, at least to argue with her. She'd told Kieran she could never marry outside her faith, that she could not do to him what her sister had done.

They saw Sarah less often these days. She had accompanied Edgar in the early days of their marriage, when Edgar had come on business, but she was with child now and travel was not wise. Mama would go to stay with her when she was near her term, they'd decided, although Rachel was not sure how they would manage the inn without her. She could serve, but neither she nor her father could cook. A baby, though, her own niece or nephew to hold, a new life in their family—it was marvelous beyond words and almost made her forget what had happened the night before.

Yesterday had been Martinmas, the day the Christians

celebrated the life of St. Martin with a feast, usually with a goose. Mama had learned to make all the side dishes the Christians expected, and the tavern had been filled with patrons. Advent would begin soon, and the festivities had reflected the upcoming days of reflection and penance. The last of the harvests had been brought in, and the autumn slaughters had been finished. Mosheh, days of hard work behind him, had been in a festive mood and joined the others in the tavern.

Ale had been the favorite drink of the night, and the mood had changed when most had been fed and drinking had begun in earnest. The families had long been gone, and the only women left had been whores when the inevitable fight had begun. It was Mosheh who had waded into the center of it, Mosheh who'd thrown the men out into the street and who'd wrapped his arm around Papa and laughed about it. He'd thrown Rachel a look of triumph, and she'd realized that, despite her words to him, and his verbal acceptance of them, Mosheh had not given up hope of marrying her.

Mama would leave on Sunday morning to attend to Sarah during the birth of her child. She would be gone for two weeks or so, to return by November 30, the feast of St. Andrew, the patron saint of Scotland. Strange, Rachel thought, to have spent so much time in a Christian city that she now measured the years by their saints and holy days as well as her own.

Her father led them now in prayer and she bowed her head, praying for Scotland and for the end of the uncertainty that had kept her adopted country in turbulence. And kept Kieran from her. He'd written a few times, not often, and never a long letter.

Rachel's parents had never commented on the letters, nor had they forbidden her to write back. Each letter took months to arrive, and she knew that one day they would stop arriving. And then they did. It was her fault. How could she expect him to continue when she'd told him so plainly that nothing would come of it? Now the letters had stopped, and she could only believe that he'd finally accepted her decision. Or had found someone to replace her. Martinmas, the feast of the harvest. Hers was a bitter one, but the only one that should be.

It was time to make her decision. That night she lay in the dark and thought. And the next day, after the Sabbath had been observed and the tavern was quiet and empty of patrons, instead of letting Mosheh talk to Papa alone, she joined them, smiling at Mosheh's simple jokes, laughing at his more clever ones. He was a good man. She could do worse than to choose him.

But still she waited. Just in case Kieran would write or come to her.

Mama sent word that Sarah had given birth to a beautiful little boy; named James Jacob Edgar Keith. Papa was delighted and told everyone who would listen about his grandson. Mama returned, after three weeks away, and they resumed their normal lives.

Hanukkah came, and Christmas, and 1295 arrived with a fierce snowstorm. When Papa shoveled the snow from the steps, Mosheh came from nowhere, took the shovel from Papa's hand, and finished the job. She watched the two of them laughing together. And that night she let Mosheh kiss her.

Candlemas came, Lent began, Passover and Easter came and went. And still no word from Kieran. On the first day of May, when Berwick was celebrating Beltane, or May Day, or both, Mosheh asked for her hand in marriage. She thought about it for two days. Then agreed.

They were married in a solemn ceremony at the end of the month. Sarah and Edgar came for the ceremony, and sweet little James slept through it all. Mama wished her well, and Papa beamed with happiness.

Rachel cried on her wedding day, thinking of Kieran, and of Isabel, who should have been here with her. And on her wedding night, when Mosheh lay snoring at her side, when she was no longer a virgin, she cried again, her tears soaking the pillow.

She continued to work at the inn, often spending more time there than necessary, sometimes even forgetting that she had a husband waiting for her at home. She and Mosheh lived with his parents behind the butcher's shop. His mother did all the household tasks or hired them out, and often made comments about Rachel working in a tavern. Rachel never answered them. She never fought with Mosheh, or his mother, and the weeks, then months, passed.

One Saturday evening in August, she was at the inn with her parents, saying the prayers that ended Shabbat before they went upstairs to work for the rest of the evening, when they heard a thumping noise coming from the tavern. They stopped praying, all of them, and looked up at the ceiling. No doubt, she thought, there was another argument over the merits of the king. It was early for that, but some men drank to excess regardless of the hour. Her father sighed, closed the Bible, and removed his prayer shawl.

"We'd better go upstairs," Mama said.

"Three stars," Papa said. "Shabbat is not over until we see three stars."

Mama smiled. "Three stars it is, Jacob. We'll stand on the terrace and wait for the stars while they tear down our inn."

"Three stars," Papa said.

"Let's go look," Mama said, leading the way outside. She pointed at the dim sky. "One, two, three."

"That's not a star, that's the moon," Papa said.

Rachel laughed and went inside. She'd counted at least five stars. It was time to go to work. She tied an apron around her waist and went to find the source of the noise.

It was a Highlander, dancing on a table, his arms upraised and much more of his legs visible than should be. The men watching him were clapping in time, and one pounded his hand on a bohdran, an Irish hand drum. She shook her head. It would end in a fight. It always did.

"Not again," Papa said, then turned to Mama. "Go get Gilbert and the lads. We're sure to need help getting this one out."

Rachel stared across the room as the clapping and the drum stopped and the Highlander laughed and bowed.

"Ye owe me that drink, sir," he said. "I danced like a fool. Now I'm going to drink like one."

She hardly heard the roar of laughter that followed. She watched the tall man leap from the table and run his hand through his hair. His black hair, tied in a knot at the back of his head. He turned, still laughing, and saw her. And her heart stopped. Kieran.

"Rachel!" he cried, coming toward her. "I told ye I would return!"

He came closer, laughing, even more handsome than she'd remembered. He seemed taller, bigger as he leaned over her.

"I told ye I would return," he said. "And here I am."

Without looking to see who watched, he wrapped an arm around her waist and, leaning her over, kissed her until she was dizzy.

"Well," he said, his grin wide. "Are ye not glad to see me, lass?"

"Yes. No. Oh, Kieran!" She burst into tears.

It was the hardest thing she'd ever done. At first she could not speak, could not do anything except stare at him while her mind both raced and went numb. Three months. If she had just waited three more months. She told him, in rushed words and with many tears, of how she'd despaired of his return and had finally married Mosheh.

He listened, his head down. When he looked at her again, his eyes were ablaze. He turned from her and, without a word, left the inn. She cried most of the night. Mosheh did not ask her why.

Kieran came back the next day, looking worse for the night. She did not ask where he'd slept; he did not offer the information. He sat with her at a table on the terrace, his long fingers toying with the cup he held, while he told her of his life. She told him about Langton and that horrible night, that they had never heard from Isabel, and all that had happened in his absence.

"I'm still with William Wallace's lot. De Boyer is right that there will be war. Unless some miracle happens and Edward of England falls dead. But de Boyer is wrong about who will win. We will be the victors. That's what Rory and I have been assuring our people. Rory's done great things, helping to unite the clans, getting them to forget their differences." He pulled a packet of letters from his shirt. "From him, to Isabel. He wrote her all the time but had no way of getting these to her. If ye ever see her . . ."

"He never came, Kieran, never wrote. Isabel left here thinking he'd forgotten her. I know she was distraught about it. As I was that you stopped writing."

"He never forgot her. He still has that ridiculous crown she made. He was coming to see her when he was outlawed. And when we heard King Edward was here, and Langton was with him, Rory came to Berwick like a madman, risking being an outlaw in a city full of English soldiers, to find her. But she was gone, ye were gone. He heard about her stabbing Langton, but no one kent where she was, or where ye were, and the inn was shut. No, he's still thinking of her, Rachel. As I have been thinking of ye. All this time, I thought of ye constantly."

"Why did you stop writing?"

"I joined William's troop. When I was home, I could send letters through the runners and on the ships that come by. But living in the forest as we do, there's no easy way to send a letter. We get messages out, aye, and they come to us, but none of it is reliable."

"I thought you had forgotten me."

"Never. Did I not tell ye, lass, that I would come back?"

"It's been over a year, Kieran."

"I thought ye'd wait."

"I thought I'd been abandoned."

"Never. Not by me. Not even now. If ye ever need anything, I'll be here."

She smiled sadly. "How will you know? How could I tell you?"

His smile was rueful. "Aye, that's the thing. Is that him?"

She turned, her stomach in a knot, to see Papa and Mosheh standing together near the door, watching them. "Yes."

"He's coming over, lass."

Kieran stood, and Rachel did the same. Mosheh moved slowly past the tables, his face impassive, but his fists clenched. Kieran stuck out his hand.

"I'm Kieran MacDonald, sir. Congratulations on marrying the bonniest lass in the city. I wish ye well in yer marriage."

Mosheh did not take Kieran's hand. "And I wish you gone, sir. Or dead."

"Mosheh!" Rachel cried.

Kieran's eyes flashed. "I dinna deserve that, sir," he said. "I'm trying to be civil to ye and I expect the same in return. She's yer wife now, not mine, as she should be. Ye should be generous in yer victory. I'll leave now, but ken this. If ever she needs anything, I will come to her aid. Not yers. Hers." He looked at Rachel. "I wish . . . I wish ye the greatest happiness."

She cried for most of the night and for days afterward.

EIGHTEEN

"Miriam!"

Isabel had barely taken a step away from the house in which she rented a room when she heard the voice.

"Miriam!"

She stopped. Even after almost four years, she sometimes forgot to respond to the name, often covering her blunder by pretending she was somewhat deaf. She turned to face her neighbor Florine, an inquisitive older woman. Or rather, Miriam turned, for she'd renamed herself.

Isabel de Burke no longer existed. She was now Miriam, which she found particularly apt. The biblical Miriam had been the sister of Moses and Aaron. When Miriam had opposed Moses, she'd been stricken with leprosy by God, which was how Isabel felt. Like a leper, she hid from the citizens of Newcastle, and the world, shielding her face and showing no one her true self. The biblical Miriam had been healed seven days later, after Moses had appealed to God. Isabel was still waiting for God to forgive her.

The name Miriam itself meant rebellion, which she still had in her heart. Her sins might be many, but she repented only for a few. She'd been too timid, too fearful in her former life, and it had cost her much. She would be afraid no more. The name also pleased her because Miriam was the name Alis had given the daughter she'd abandoned. Isabel, too, had been abandoned by her own mother. And betrayed by Alis. She thought it very fitting.

"It's Michaelmas. A holy day of obligation," Florine said. "Are you not coming to mass?"

Isabel cursed herself for a fool. If she'd waited only a few moments more before leaving the house, no one would have seen her. She paused, deciding. She could lie and pretend she would be going later in the day, but she knew she would be found out.

"Oh, yes, mistress," she said, smiling tightly. "That's where I was going."

"We'll go together then."

Isabel nodded. There was no hope for it now. Instead of the quiet day she'd anticipated, she would go to mass, as she did every holy day, ignoring her feelings of being a charlatan in the church, pretending to pray to a God she no longer believed in. And doing her best to fend off Florine's endless questions.

"Where will you have your Michaelmas feast, dear?"

"With my charges."

"Does the man think his daughters will learn Latin and French between Mass and a feast? He abuses you, Miriam. You must demand more time for yourself."

"I don't mind, madam. It keeps a roof over my head."

"Ah, yes, of course. Rents are due, accounts are settled

on Michaelmas. Are all your accounts paid?" The older woman laughed.

"Of course," Isabel said, but in truth her accounts were far from paid. She had attempted murder, and failed. Langton had lived, and thrived, curse the man.

The rumors of who had stabbed him varied widely. A madwoman. A spurned lover who had taken her revenge upon finding Langton with another. A political enemy, and apparently Langton had many, perhaps a paid assassin, who had used the gathering at Berwick for his own ends. A French wine merchant had been questioned about his mistress. And the worst one: a jealous husband, one of the king's own, outraged to find his wife in Langton's arms. Had Henry taken the blame himself for her deed? Over time the story had taken shape. The attacker was a woman, once a queen's lady, who was sought throughout the land. Her name was Isabel de Burke.

She'd failed in her goal to prevent others from becoming his victims. As she had failed in London to withstand Langton, failed to see Alis and Lady Dickleburough for what they were. And failed in Berwick, where Rachel, her parents, and Gilbert had been harmed because of her, their lives shattered because they'd protected her. Her accounts were far from settled.

"I cannot imagine that you have anything to worry about," Florine said.

Isabel blinked to stop herself from staring. The woman had an uncanny ability to sense Isabel's turbulent thoughts.

"Your merchant seems pleased enough with your efforts," Florine said. "I saw him just yesterday, you know, and asked him how you did at your tasks."

"Did you?" Isabel asked icily. The effrontery of the woman! "And what was his answer, mistress?"

"That you acquitted yourself well. I knew you would be pleased to hear that, Miriam. You are, of course?"

"Of course," Isabel said.

"You were fortunate to find such a position."

"Yes," Isabel said, and in truth, she had been extremely fortunate.

That first night, left on the southern shore of the River Tweed, she'd not thought about it at all, simply followed the road south, fleeing Berwick and what she had done. When snow had begun to fall the next day, she'd found sanctuary in a church. A kindly priest had fed her and brought her to a convent, where she'd stayed for two months, until the new year had arrived and her sanity with it.

She'd not told the abbess who it was that she'd served in London, only that she had been in service. Nor that she'd been in Berwick. But the attack on Langton was much discussed, and Isabel suspected the clever abbess had guessed the truth. She'd attempted to employ Isabel in the convent kitchens, but it had soon become apparent that she had no talents there. Instead, Isabel had earned her keep by repairing the altar cloths and mending the nun's habits—simple tasks that had pleased the abbess. So much so that the abbess had asked her if she would like to stay at the convent, if she had a calling to God. To which Isabel had firmly said she did not.

They had discussed her skills, the abbess's eyebrows rising when she discovered that Isabel spoke and wrote Latin, French, and English. It had been those skills that had brought her to Newcastle, where she taught the three pampered daughters of a merchant, and where she lived quietly, keeping to herself.

She had debated whether to stay in Newcastle, whether to stay in England or return to Scotland. Each had its hazards. In England, she had been outlawed, which, while sobering, also amused her. Isabel de Burke, wanted by the crown for attempted murder. But in Newcastle she could hide among the people who crowded into this ancient and most northern of the English ports. In Scotland her accent would give her away, and with English soldiers billeted in every castle and town, the English were most unwelcome. But Rory was in Scotland, somewhere. He would never find her in Newcastle. But then, he'd not come to find her in Berwick.

And if she did not stay here in Newcastle, where would she go? Not to London, obviously. Not back to Berwick. Not to some small village, where a newly arrived woman with a London accent would be sure to draw attention. And so she had stayed, living quietly, keeping to herself.

It was simple to be invisible in the merchant's household, for it was a noisy place, with seven sons and three daughters. She had declined their offer to live within their walls, preferring her freedom. The sons were at church schools, or taught at home by monks. The daughters were being groomed for successful marriages. The better she did her job, the sooner it would end, but still she applied herself, and the girls were eager students. Isabel steeled her heart against them, was reluctant to care about them or mourn that she would never be a mother or a wife. Life was as it was, she told herself, and she should be content. Some days she had to repeat that several times.

The older woman was now complaining about the

arrivals expected in Newcastle. Soldiers, the woman said, due to arrive this day.

"Why are they here?" Isabel asked. She pulled her cloak tighter, suddenly chilled. The king's soldiers in Newcastle.

"Why to protect us from the Scots, of course. They continue to defy King Edward, fools that they are. We're to have some of the king's own knights arriving soon, I've heard. Perhaps you could find a new husband among them."

Isabel looked at the woman. She'd let the world think Miriam was a widow, the better to confuse those who would be seeking a virgin named Isabel de Burke. New name, new past. She'd even dyed her hair darker with walnut stain.

"It would be good for you to have a man in your bed again."

Rory.

It was far too easy to imagine him in her bed, long legs and wide shoulders and his golden hair sweeping across the pillow. Four years and she still could not forget the man, nor his touch. His kisses. His lean body pressed against hers, ready. His smile, that mouth that made her knees buckle and her will weaken. *He never came to see you.* She remembered watching Rachel open Kieran's letters, happy for her friend, but sick for herself at being so quickly forgotten by magnificent Rory MacGannon. Who had never been in her bed except in her dreams. The past was past. And just as well. Better to be an aging virgin than the bastard mother of a bastard.

Florine nudged her. "I can see that brought on some memories, eh? Well, wipe them from your mind, lass. We're here at the church, and it will do you no good to walk inside thinking of a man between your legs." She chuckled and walked through the open church door, crossing herself with holy water.

Isabel followed more slowly. This time, she told herself, she would try to pray. This time she would ask for forgiveness and listen for God's answer. But she knew she did not deserve His absolution, for she did not repent her sins; she only regretted that she'd not been more successful. And so, sinner that she was, with full knowledge that she was only visiting the house of God and would spend eternity in Hell, she went inside.

When they left the church it was sunny, rays of light slanting through the clouds. The streets were wet, but it did not hinder the parade they found in progress. A troop of the king's cavalry had arrived in Newcastle. Hundreds of them, it seemed, riding gaily through city streets, waving to the citizens, then disappearing into the Black Gate, the entrance to Newcastle's castle.

She told herself not to look for a handsome, dark-haired knight among them, but she did nevertheless, searching through the faces for Henry's, hoping that he would not be there. And yet, that he would. She would like to thank him, to ask him what had happened after her departure. Whether he'd been discovered and punished for his part in it. Just to see someone who knew her, who knew the truth. But there lay danger as well, which made standing here watching those who might be seeking her madness in itself. If Edward's troops were here, could the king himself be far behind? And Newcastle, though a thriving city, was not large enough in which to hide if Edward or Langton sought her here. But where to go?

"I wonder if I'll see the one who came to talk to me the other day," Florine said. "I thought I could point him out to you. In case he came back, to talk to you this time. He was looking for a young woman. From London."

Isabel tried to keep her expression calm. She unclenched the fist that she had brought to her waist. "Really?"

"Yes. Her name is Isabel de Burke. She was lady-in-waiting to Queen Eleanor."

"The queen has been dead for years. Why is he searching for her now?"

Florine laughed softly. "You remember, my dear. There was that attack on the king's Steward of the Wardrobe. In Berwick. A woman stabbed him. It was just before you arrived, maybe a month or two earlier. Didn't you come from Berwick?"

"What else did the soldier tell you?"

"That this woman was about your height. Her hair was a little lighter. Like the shade yours is in the new growth around your temples. He told me Walter Langton is looking for this Isabel de Burke in every city in England."

"And he thinks she stabbed Walter Langton?"

"So he says."

"What did you tell him?"

"That I knew no Isabel de Burke. He offered money for anything I could tell him. I imagine that Isabel de Burke, wherever she may be, might be willing to pay more for my silence." She waved at the soldiers, then threw Isabel a glance. "You look pale, dear. Does talking about stabbing a man make you feel ill?"

"Yes," Isabel said.

"Then we won't talk about it again. Shall I tell you if the young soldier comes looking for more information?"

"Yes. Please."

"I shall then. Are you off to your feast at the merchant's now?"

"Yes."

"Tomorrow I would like you to come with me to mass again. You will, won't you? Before you go to the merchant's. And again on Sunday. It's so much nicer to go with a friend than to go alone. We can talk. You do understand, don't you, dear?"

"Yes," Isabel said. "I understand."

She bid farewell to Florine and made her way to the merchant's house. She had to pause once, to calm herself. It was bound to happen. Walter Langton would not willingly let her live to tell the tale. It made no difference that she would remain silent. While she lived, there was a risk that she would talk.

She'd known this might happen, that one day someone would come looking for her. She was fortunate that Florine had chosen to warn her. And all she'd asked in return was for Isabel to attend Mass with her. And pay her. Isabel took a deep breath. She could do this. For now. Until the demands grew greater. Dear God. She could do this. She continued on to her Michaelmas meal.

Today she would dine with the girls' parents and their guests. Normally on feast days she was alone, but this day Isabel was to translate for the visiting merchants, Frenchmen. Simple enough. She'd done this sort of thing before, sitting quietly while the men talked of horses and ships and wine. The merchant spoke French of a fashion, but his wife spoke none and would question Isabel afterward as to what had been said.

She was early, but better than spending more time

with Florine. Here no one cared about her past, or her life outside these walls. She refused to think of Langton, thinking instead of the images of Rory brought on by Florine's comment about a man in her bed as she waited while the girls' maids dressed them for the meal. Glorious man. But best forgotten. If all went well she would teach these girls until they were ready to marry, live in her small room, and save her money for the day when she could not earn her food. Or needed to flee.

But now . . . if Edward's troops were here . . . Where would she go? Her mind ran in circles.

When at last all three girls were ready, she accompanied them down the stairs to the second floor, where the spacious dining room faced the street. The Frenchmen were already there, two of them, seated with her employer at the small side table. Her plump face serious, the merchant's wife drew Isabel aside, and Isabel knew she was about to be given her orders. The merchant rarely talked to her directly.

"Our other guest will be here momentarily," his wife said. "A wool merchant. You and I will, of course, refrain from speaking unnecessarily during the meal, but I would like you to assist my husband without seeming to do so. He sometimes gets confused in his French, though he will never admit it. Please see that he gets the sums correct this time." She smiled and patted Isabel's arm. "It will be a tedious meal, but I will see that you are compensated for your efforts."

Isabel nodded. She hated this, the part she played, of the deferential servant. But she would play it well, for she had few other choices. Who would have guessed, all those years ago, when she'd learned French as a child, that her very bread would depend upon it? She sat in one of the window seats, nearest the door, her hands folded in her lap, while the three girls, seated in the other window, giggled into their hands at some silly thing. She looked up at the gray sky, remembering being as silly with Rachel, in a different world.

The door opened. A man hurried in. He was of medium height, with lank brown hair.

"I'm sorry to have kept you waiting," the man said.

He greeted the others, bowing to the Frenchmen, shaking hands with his host and kissing the hands of the three delighted daughters and their mother.

"And Miriam here," the merchant said, "will translate for us."

Isabel rose to her feet, a sudden roaring in her ears.

The man turned to her. His mouth fell open.

Isabel looked into the eyes of Edgar Keith. Rachel's sister's husband.

"His name," Edgar Keith said with pride, looking past Isabel, "is James Jacob Edgar Keith, named after his grandfathers and his father. My wife, Sarah, is delighted with him. He is fortunate to have two grandmothers who adore him and his aunt Rachel, who visits often since her return to Berwick with her parents. She and her husband, the butcher's son, visit us when they can, but it is difficult to leave a thriving inn. Her parents need her there." He sipped his wine and looked at Isabel over the rim of the fine crystal. Thus far he'd not given her away.

"It is a shame that you cannot trade directly with France, sir," Edgar told the merchant, "but I am happy to be the joint that connects you. Tell me, sirs," he said in

French to the Frenchmen. "How was the harvest? I have heard the summer was very warm and dry. How did your vines do?"

The topic turned to wine then, and Isabel spent some time translating. Her charges grew restless and were dismissed. They hurried out of the dining room, their laughter resounding in the hallway. One of the Frenchmen smiled and talked in English of his own children, and Isabel was able to let her mind wander. Rachel had married Mosheh, and was once again in Berwick. The stab of longing she felt was tangible. How she'd missed her friend. And what of Kieran? If Rachel had married Mosheh, had Kieran not returned?

Edgar's manner was winning, and he proved popular with her employer's guests. Their business was conducted quickly, terms decided on with few quibbles. Outside, the afternoon ended and the rain pounded on the side of the building. The candles burned low. And still they talked.

At last the meal was over. The Frenchmen made their farewells, bowing low over the merchant's wife's hand, then doing the same honor to Isabel, who nodded and politely refused their offer of a ride to her lodgings. Edgar said good-bye then, as courteous as the Frenchmen, and strode off down the lane, where his coach waited. Isabel assumed she would go over the discussions with the merchant's wife, but she was relieved to be dismissed.

"And tomorrow I will not need you until evening. We will be attending a gathering at the castle and would like you to help me keep my daughters in check."

Isabel began to protest, but the merchant's wife placed her hand on Isabel's arm and smiled.

"They listen to you, my dear," she said. "Please, I need

your help for this event. I would be most grateful if you would attend with us. It should be a short evening."

Isabel gritted her teeth and agreed, eager to make her escape. Outside, she stood under the shelter of the porch for a moment. Edgar's coach still stood at the corner, as she'd suspected it would. She pulled her hood far over her head and ran toward it. Edgar opened the door and helped her in.

"Good God, Isabel, it's wonderful to see you!" he said and embraced her lightly. "We have much to say to each other."

She hugged him back, all of her suppressed emotions coming to the surface. How foolish she had been, to think she could leave Isabel behind.

They talked all evening and well into the night, sitting in the tavern where he was lodging, hidden in a dim corner. He had been astonished to find her at the merchant's house and demanded that she tell him all that had happened since she'd left. She did, omitting nothing but the intimate details of that night with Langton, telling Edgar simply that he had been trying to make love to her and she had stabbed him.

"An evil night that was," he said. "Rachel and her family are all well now, even Gilbert, though they all have scars from that night. Rachel has missed you. We have all missed you, Isabel. But you should not go back. You would be recognized, even with the darker hair, and Berwick is still talking about what you did."

"I could not go back, Edgar. I brought the horror of that night to the Angenhoffs and I will not risk their safety again. I was afraid even to write, for fear of bringing reprisals upon them, upon you all."

"And you were wise. Langton sends men to stay at the inn. They think we don't know why they are there, but they always ask about you. Jacob always tells them you left and they do not know where you are, nor do they want to know."

She felt her lip tremble, and she controlled her sadness. She was not Jacob's daughter. She'd endangered his family. How could the man want her back in their lives? "I don't blame him."

"I don't think he means it, but he is protecting his family."

"Yes, of course. I would ask you not to tell him then, and not Rachel, that you saw me."

He laughed then. "And risk her killing me slowly were she to find out that I saw you? No, I will tell Rachel at once. It will be her decision whether she tells her father."

"I am so grateful to you, Edgar, for not giving me away here. And so happy to hear that they are all well."

"Aye, Rachel is well, but Sarah says she is not happy. Three months after she married Mosheh, Kieran came back."

At Isabel's exclamation of surprise, Edgar nodded.

"Poor Rachel! If only I had been there!"

"What could you have said that would have changed anything? She said she'd given up on Kieran returning. I know she regrets her decision. I know Kieran regrets it as much. He comes to see me now. And Rory."

"Rory?" Isabel could hear the catch in her voice. It was suddenly hard to breathe. "How is he?"

"He is one of Wallace's captains now, acting as a liaison for the Highlanders. He has been looking for you since you left, Isabel. In every city in Scotland. He has scoured the country." He told her of Rory's trip to Berwick. "He went to Lonsby, to see if you'd gone to your father's."

She put a hand over her mouth.

"Your father said he knew nothing of you. I'm sorry."

"No. Do not be. I meant nothing to the man."

"Rory even went to London."

"Oh dear God, Edgar! How dangerous that was! He could have been captured! What was he thinking?"

"Of you, Isabel. He was thinking of finding you. He's different now. Harder. Seasoned. I'm helping them, bringing messages back and forth from the Continent when I travel. And messages from here. I am trusting you to be silent about this, for now we both hold secrets about each other that could destroy us. I will take a message to Rachel, if you'd like. I know she will be so relieved to know you are alive and well."

Tears sprang to Isabel's eyes. "Yes, Edgar, if you would . . . tell her everything I have told you. And that I love her, that I've missed her so very much." She wiped her tears away. "I cannot go there, nor can she come here, but tell her I think of her."

He nodded. "I will. And any message for Rory?"

She looked at him, her mind whirling. "Tell him," she said, "that I wish him well."

"Anything else?"

"No." She shook her head, ignoring the tears that spilled from her eyes. "There is nothing more to say."

Edgar sent her home in a coach. She ran from its shelter to the stairs to her room, hurrying as quietly as she could. At the landing before her room, she fumbled for her key. And heard Florine's door close. *Let her think what she will,* Isabel thought, and closed her own door behind her.

Rory. Rachel. The past kept her awake the rest of the night.

"Newcastle Castle," the guard told the merchant's wife and daughters, "was built upon the site of an ancient fortress built of wood. A hundred years ago Henry II rebuilt it of stone and added the curtain wall. Fifty years ago Henry III added the Black Gate through which we just passed. Step carefully, ladies, the bailey here is full of horses, and the grooms have not tidied up yet."

Isabel lifted her skirts above the muck, following in the wake of the merchant's family. It was a formidable entrance, but to one accustomed to the Tower in London and the royal palaces and castles, not as awe-inspiring as it obviously was to the others.

"We will ascend the staircase to the Great Hall. If you feel the sudden need to pray to our Maker, there is a chapel below the Hall. And if you need to escape," he leaned low over one of the girls, his smile meant to be charming, "there are two postern gates around the grounds, and a sally port through the storage chamber below, by which the soldiers could sally forth to fight the invaders. But you lovelies will want to stay for the dancing, I warrant, aye?"

"Will there be dancing, sir?" one of the girls asked.

"I hope so, else why all the musicians arriving, eh? We need to keep those knights and soldiers on their toes." He laughed at his own joke. "Here we are, ladies. No escaping, now. Enjoy yourselves."

The Great Hall was spacious, with a vaulted timbered ceiling, several passages leading from it, a large fireplace in which a fire roared, and steps up to a window alcove.

It was there, in the window seat, that Isabel sat with the merchant's daughters, their merry chatter keeping them occupied. The floor of the Hall was full of tables, laden with every sort of food. The newly arrived knights sat there. Henry, mercifully, was not among them, and Isabel saw no one she knew. As the hours passed, she relaxed her guard, enjoying the music and watching the dancing. Her charges were too young to join in, but their parents were in the middle of the festivities.

Rory. She could not get him out of her thoughts. Rory, searching for her. She should have sent a warmer message with Edgar, one that would have let Rory know she was willing to be found by him. But no, how could she lure him here, where he was certain to be captured as soon as he entered the city? She should have told Edgar to tell Rory not to come here. What if he did? Was there no end to the people who faced hazards for her sake? What a fool she had been not to think this through.

She calmed herself with the thought that her message had been cold and perhaps Rory would take it as an end to whatever had been between them. She'd not meant it to be as meager as it had been, but how could she have bared her soul when he'd not come for her in Berwick? All those months of waiting, only to discover now that he had searched for her. She closed her eyes for a moment, praying that Edgar would return, that when he did she could tell him . . . what? That she'd never been able to forget Rory MacGannon? Yes. Exactly that. Let the world be mad around them. Perhaps she and Rory could at last speak freely to each other. She opened her eyes and felt better.

The dancing was continuing and the merchant's daughters were discussing who was the fairest among the men who were on the floor. One liked the blond man, another the dark-haired younger one. She studied the two and realized that the younger one, the dark-haired one, who now danced with the bailiff's daughter, his smile wide . . . was Henry de Boyer's squire. Or had been, years ago, in London. She shrank back against the wall, her heart constricted. The world seemed to be closing in on her.

"Ask your mother which one she thinks the most attractive," she told the merchant's daughter. "And find out who they are."

Perhaps, she told herself, she was not remembering the man correctly. But when the girl came back, it was the same name, the same man.

"He is a knight," the girl said. "Newly made, just in time for the war with Scotland. Look, he is looking at us!" She waved gaily, and the knight returned the wave, his glance passing over Isabel, then returning to her face. His brows drew together. For a long moment he held her gaze, then his attention was diverted.

She would, she swore to herself, never step foot in this castle again. And perhaps she should leave Newcastle. But where could she go?

NINETEEN

Rory tossed the shredded bits of leaves into the fire, watching the tiny flare as the flames engulfed them. It would take more fuel to hold off the night, but there was no wood left. He reached for more of the leaves bunched at his feet. These had blown in with the last gust of wind, and he, one of those nearest to the cave's entrance, pulled his clothing tighter, trying to stay warm. His thoughts chilled him even further.

He could no longer count the number of men he had killed. Surely he would spend eternity in Hell. He hated taking another man's life. Every time, he hated it. And, God help him, he'd gotten very good at it. There were the wild ones, dangerous, who flailed away, their eyes frenzied. He'd learned to wait for the moment when their energy slowed. That was the moment he took. There were the terrified ones, who almost wanted him to end it. Those were difficult. But the worst were the brave green ones, the young lads who no more wanted this war than he did, who fought bravely and cleanly, whose faces haunted him in his dreams.

Killing a man with an arrow, shooting it from a protected spot behind a stone wall, that was simply a task of aiming correctly. You did not see the surprise when a thrust hit home, did not look the man in the eyes and see his soul for a moment before it left his body. Did not feel the difference in your hand when a blade left the air and sank into flesh. Did not have to face the night. There were some, of course, about which he had no remorse, men who had lusted after his death and who had died instead. Foul men, ardent men. Those he did not mourn. And there were the others, who had never become men to him, but simply were the enemy.

But more than the men who had come to Scotland to kill, to burn people out of their houses if they complained about the deaths of their friends or loved ones; more than the simple fact that his country was coveted because it was prosperous and peaceful and had the misfortune of being situated on the same isle as England. More than anything, he hated the man who directed it all—Edward of England.

King Edward Plantagenet, whose riches could not be counted, who owned lands and men in England, Wales, Ireland, and France already, and still lusted after Scotland. Who sent men to do his bidding, to steal, and rape, and kill in his name. Who sacrificed those men, did not care if they lived or died in their pursuit of his aims, for there were always others to send. Who, with his queen, had not bothered to attend his own young son on his deathbed but had left him to die with neither of them near. Who humiliated John Balliol simply because he could. Who kept a man like Walter Langton in his employ and looked the other way while Langton did as he wished. Edward, who directed it all, was the one Rory hated, almost as much as he hated his own part in Edward's plan. He knew that by killing the men Edward sent to subjugate Scotland he was reinforcing the hatred the English now felt toward the Scots, adding to the fury with which their comrades would retaliate.

Scotland had not invaded England, nor had its people invited Edward to occupy its castles and towns, but Edward would not recognize that in his ache for conquest. Edward knew that the best, the bravest, the boldest, and most responsible of Scotland's men would oppose him. And that many would die in the process. Which would make the next generation that much easier to control. The tactic had served him well elsewhere, and Edward had honed his skills with it.

Rory remembered Isabel championing Edward, telling him her ridiculous story of Eleanor sucking the poison out of Edward's wound in the Holy Land. Of her telling him, her eyes so serious and lips so tempting, of their devotion to each other, of the overwhelming grief Edward had shown at the death of his lady. How could a man mourn his wife and turn around and sentence other women to die or to live as widows? How could a man occupy another country and cause tens of thousands of deaths and also build twelve crosses celebrating God in his wife's honor? Or was it all of one piece, the vainglorious Edward constant through it all, brilliant in war, ruthless and insensible in all he did? Was that the explanation?

"D'ye think it was always so," Kieran asked, "men killing men? D'ye think there was ever a land or a time when men just lived together without war?"

Rory shook his head and shredded another brittle leaf, adding it to the pile at his feet. Oak leaves, he realized now. And almost midwinter. The men around them slept or talked quietly. Somewhere, out of sight, a man sang softly, a sad song of lost love.

"We're living in a cave," he said to Kieran, "freezing our arses off."

"Ye've just discovered this, aye? Ye're that brilliant, ye are."

"This was not how I thought I'd be living now." He picked up another leaf.

Kieran poked at the fire. "At least ye still have a house to go to when this is all over. Think of all those who were burnt out before we drove the soldiers out."

"Aye, ye're right. But ye ken why they went so easily?"

"I'm not remembering that a lot of that was easy," Kieran said.

"No. But they're gone," Rory said. "Edward's pulling back the last of them."

"Because he's planning to invade."

"Aye. Ready for war at last?"

"Better than the waiting. I feel like we've been waiting for years."

"We have been. What did Edgar have to say? Any news?"

Kieran looked into the distance. *Rachel,* Rory thought. More bad news of the lass. Kieran had been inconsolable when he'd learned she'd married the butcher's son after all. Wages of war. They were far from the only ones whose wives or lovers had drifted to another. He waited. Kieran would talk when the time was right. They needed information and Edgar was a good source of it, but seeing him, as Kieran had today, always saddened Kieran.

It usually took days for his mood to rise. Wages of war.

"I was going to tell ye in the morning," Kieran said, his voice low.

Rory raised his eyebrows. "Why not now? How bad is it?"

"It's not. But I thought it could keep until daylight."

"Kieran . . ."

"She's in Newcastle, Rory. Edgar found her there. She's changed her name and dyed her hair and is teaching a merchant's daughters French."

Rory's hands stopped moving. "Isabel?"

"Aye. He talked with her. Told her all that has happened in Berwick, and where ye are. And that ye've looked for her. She sends ye a message."

Isabel.

"What is it?"

"That she wishes ye well."

"And?"

"There is no more."

"Nothing?"

"No."

"What else did he say?"

Kieran told him all Edgar had told him. Rory listened without comment, then threw the last of the leaves in the fire and reached behind him for his pack.

"What are ye doing?" Kieran asked.

"Going to talk to Edgar myself."

"Now?"

"Now." Rory stuffed his clothing into the pack and stood.

"Wait until morning."

"I've plenty of light. It's almost a full moon."

Kieran sighed and rose to his feet. "I'm going with ye."

"Ye dinna have to."

"Aye, I do. Because I ken what ye'll do next."

"I'm going to Newcastle."

"Of course ye are. Which is why I was waiting until morning to tell ye."

"No. I thank ye, lad. But this one I do on my own. Ye can come with me as far as Berwick is all."

"That's far enough for me."

"Aye, I thought so. Ready?"

He heard all Edgar Keith had to say. He'd eaten the good food at The Oak and The Ash and talked with Rachel, whose delight that Isabel had been found was tempered by her fear for her friend. And her awareness of Kieran. Jacob made it plain that he wished them both gone. Rachel's mother was the only one who welcomed them without restraint, feeding them copious amounts of food and letting her daughter spend time with them. But not alone. Jacob was always in the room.

"Tell Isabel," Rachel told Rory as she sat at the table with him, "that I've prayed for her and wondered so many times where she was. Tell her to be careful. She shouldn't come back here, but I would love to see her."

"Ye canna go to England, Rachel," Rory said.

"No." She looked close to tears. "Tell Isabel I love her."

"I will."

"And Rory, she thinks you forgot her. If that is not true, make sure she knows it now. Please?"

"I intend to do just that. Rachel, I'm sorry to hear that ye have moved back to the tavern with yer parents."

She sighed and looked across the room, where Kieran and Gilbert stood talking. Kieran met her gaze for a moment. She looked away first. "I could not forget Kieran. There were three people in my marriage, Rory, not two. And Mosheh is too proud to be one of them. I cannot blame him. I only blame myself for letting this happen."

"No more than I blame myself for not being here when Langton came. Ye all lived through it, Rachel. Sometimes that's all we can ask."

She nodded, but her eyes were shadowed. Even more so when she looked at Kieran, who looked nowhere else but at her.

"Ye need to be on yer guard, lass. War is coming and ye need to prepare."

"We will," she said. "But Berwick is strong. We will be safe here."

"It will be war, Rachel. No place is safe. Be careful, aye?"

She looked at Kieran, her longing for him visible, then back at Rory.

"And you."

They stayed just the one night, leaving in the morning with the dawn, late on this December day. They parted outside the town. Kieran would ride north, to find William and tell him where Rory had gone.

"Tell William I will be back when I can," Rory said.

"Aye. And I'll send word to yer da."

"No, dinna. They'll just worry. And if I'm not back, go home for Christmas as we'd planned."

"If ye're not back by then, the lads and I will come and find ye."

"No, Kieran. Dinna go to England after me. Promise me."

"I'll do nothing of the sort. Nell calls ye Madman Rory, ye ken. Do yer best not to live up to the name. Are ye sure I canna come with ye?"

Rory grinned. "I'm off to woo a lass, Kieran. I dinna need help doing it."

"Ye're off to woo a lass. That means ye need me there surely."

"Safe journey, cousin. I'll see ye anon."

"Make it sooner than that."

Rory waved his hand in farewell and turned his horse to face south. Forty miles from Berwick to Newcastle. And a world away.

The road was dry and the travelers few. He spent the night at a roadside inn that had neither the charm nor the cook that The Oak and The Ash did. But the food filled him and the bed did not need to be shared, so he was content.

He rode slowly into Newcastle just before dark, telling the guards at the gate that he was visiting his cousin. The guards exchanged a look but let him pass. He should have changed his clothing, he realized much too late. Everything about him said Scot and Highlander, and Newcastle was full of English soldiers preparing to invade his land.

The first thing he needed was a place to stay. He went to the inn that Edgar Keith had mentioned and got a room. He ate alone in the tavern, his back to the wall and his guard high. In Scotland his being outlawed no longer meant anything, with Balliol on the throne and the English soldiers gone. In Newcastle it could mean death.

He thought he recognized one or two of the knights and squires who shared the tavern with him. He watched as they talked quietly, which might have meant they had recognized him as well, or only that they were watching the Highlander closely. He finished his meal. And found a room in another inn for the night, not as clean, but mercifully not shared.

He did not sleep well and was awake much before dawn, washed and dressed. He broke his fast with three other men. None spoke, which suited him. When he left the table, they did the same. And when he left the inn, they did that as well. It took some doing, but at last, when he was confident that he was no longer followed, he walked toward the street where the coachman had told Edgar that Isabel was living. If she was here, Rory would find her.

He waited in the dark recess of a doorway while the sun rose and the streets began to fill with people. And still no one moved in the houses he watched. Another hour, marked by church bells. Another bit after that. And a door opened. He straightened but slumped again as he saw two men greet each other and walk the other way. Then a woman came out of a doorway, followed by another, taller. Younger. Walking slowly with the older woman.

He would know her anywhere. The set of her shoulders, that lift to her chin, the way she held her hands. *Isabel.* He was filled with longing, with the need to rush to her and take her in his arms and this time keep her there. To fill her body with his seed and his life with her presence. If he'd had any doubt why he was here, it was gone in that moment. But she was not alone, and so he waited.

They went to a church, a small parish church, a chapel really, joined by the other faithful this Advent season. He watched her enter, then found a spot where he could watch the church door. He'd not thought her devout, but perhaps she had changed. Or, more likely, he'd not known this about her, as he did not know so many other things.

He waited nearby, wrapped in his heavy, dark cloak, fading into the shadows of doorways. He did not move, not even when he saw two men take their positions and realized he was not the only one watching Isabel de Burke. When Mass was ended, the faithful left the church, hurrying off to their day. Isabel walked outside with the older woman. They spoke for a moment, then, with a wave, Isabel walked quickly away.

One of the men followed Isabel, and Rory was about to do the same when the older woman waved at the second man in the shadows. He looked in the direction Isabel had gone, then stepped forward to greet the older woman. They talked quietly. The older woman shook her head and held out her hand, saying something that displeased the man. She said something else and he nodded, pulling a coin purse from his waistband. He counted coins into her hand. She counted them on her palm. And smiled. Then left him.

Rory waited another moment for both of them to disappear, but when he went after Isabel, she was nowhere to be found.

* * *

She was being followed. Isabel did not turn to see who it was that dogged her steps, but she could hear him on the quiet street. When she moved forward, he did the same. She hurried to the more crowded areas, where perhaps she could lose him, glad to reach the merchant's street, bustling with the morning's activities. She paused a few doors down from the merchant's house, as though to readjust her cloak and hood, and turned to look behind her. She could see no one watching her, no one waiting in a shadow to resume the chase. But she could feel his presence. For the first time since she'd come to Newcastle, she was afraid.

Should she return to her lodgings? But no, if he'd followed her here, he would follow her back, and there would be no chance of assistance there. Her best chance was to go about her day as though she suspected nothing, to spend her day with the merchant's daughters. And think of what to do next. And where to go.

This morning Florine had pressed her for money. Isabel had given her a tidy sum, but the woman had not been pleased, and she knew that unless she could pay more, Florine would report her presence here. The woman might take her money and still expose her.

This would be her last day in Newcastle. Only a fool would not heed the warnings. On her way to the merchant's she had reviewed her choices and found no answer. But perhaps, as the hours passed and she concentrated on French verbs and Latin declensions, something would come to her. And that is just what she did, spending her day as she normally would, correcting the girls' small errors, pleased to see how much they had learned. It would have to suffice.

She ate her midday meal alone, in the warm kitchen, chilled to the bone. The merchant's nephew, a soldier in Edward's army, now billeted in Newcastle, as well as two of his friends, had joined the family for their meal. The merchant's wife had been kind enough to invite Isabel to join them, but she had refused, feeling the noose of danger tighten around her. Soldiers dined above in the dining room, and here the talk was all of the king arriving.

She would leave in the morning, she determined, as soon as the city gates were opened at dawn—which, since it was December, would be late. But at least there would be daylight when she determined where to go. She dared not book passage on a ship, for if she was being watched, the harbor would be one of the first places she would be sought. No, it was best to slip through the city gates, simply dressed, and melt into the crowds passing the guards. How long, she wondered, did she have, before the old woman took the money Langton's men offered? Had she been a fool not to offer more money for the woman's silence, if even to buy only a day? But if she was correct, if someone was following her, it was already too late.

As she left the merchant's house at day's end, she told his wife that her own cousin was among the soldiers, and begged the next day to visit with him. The merchant's wife, her mood softened by the wine at the midday meal, granted Isabel's request, saying she could make up the time by attending another event at the castle. Isabel left then, smiling, taking one last look at the house where she had found refuge, thanking the merchant's wife more profusely than she should, knowing that when she disappeared the merchant's wife would remember this conversation.

She was not good at subterfuge and lies, she decided as she stepped outside. But she would have to do it all over again, have to create a new person, a new past, a new name for herself. No more French or Latin. Few people—fewer women—in England spoke and wrote both, and she was convinced that using her abilities there had led to her discovery.

Unless it was Edgar. But surely Rachel's brother-in-law, kind Edgar, who had been so careful not to give her away . . . surely Edgar had not betrayed her. But had he told someone, who'd told someone . . . ? He had been going to Berwick straight away, he'd said, to tell Rachel. It had been more than two months, plenty of time for the message to reach London, for Langton to send men to Newcastle. What if it had been Edgar, inadvertently revealing her whereabouts? That meant she could not even dream of going to Berwick. Nor London.

One step at a time. First, leave Newcastle. No, she corrected herself, first leave this doorstep, where the merchant's page watched her as though she'd been behaving strangely. It was dark already. The lanterns at the door of the merchant's house shed some light into the street but not beyond, and she stepped down into the street knowing that she was visible to those who watched, the ones she could not see.

She heard no footsteps behind her, and took a very circuitous route to her room, pausing often to look around her, to wait in a doorway, or just within an alley, to see if someone also paused. She saw no one. And at last she reached her street, then her house, where all was quiet.

She could see a line of light under the older woman's doorway and hurried past, keeping her steps as light as she could as she climbed the stairs.

She paused again outside her door, her heart pounding as she fumbled for her key. In the morning, in the morning, she told herself. She put the key in the door and heard the latch click. And a noise from behind her, where the stairs continued to rise.

She turned, staring into the dark. Nothing.

Then a body, big, moving quickly, burst from the shadows. One large hand covered her mouth, the other wrapped around her waist, and she was bundled into her room. She struggled, but he held her fast, his chest hard against her back. He released her waist and quietly closed the door, then pulled her to him again. She kicked at his legs and clawed at his hand, trying to scream. His head leaned low, his mouth next to her ear.

"Isabel. Lass. It's me. Rory. I've come to take ye home."

She spun in his arms and faced him, putting a hand on his cheek. "Rory! Oh, Rory! Tell me it is really you!" Tears streamed down her cheeks, and her vision blurred. She threw both arms around his neck and pulled him closer. "I thought I'd never see you again!"

"Whist, lass, shhh! It's me, true enough."

He wrapped his arms around her waist and pulled her up to meet his mouth. One kiss, sweet and short, then another, longer this time. His lips were warm and she closed her eyes, savoring the feel of them on hers, of his arms holding her against him, his body long and hard. She could feel the moment he abandoned his restraint, lifting her higher against him, leaning her back over his arm, demanding that she open to him. She did, the feel of his tongue dancing with hers filling her with yearning, with a need she had suppressed for so long. His thigh pressed against hers, his chest meeting her breasts. His desire for her was obvious. And she melted, pulling him closer, devouring his mouth. His lips left hers, traced a line of kisses down her neck, then back to meet hers for another long moment. He pulled away far too soon.

"Isabel, ye are in danger. We have to get ye out of here."

"Rory, how is it ye're here?"

"I came for ye, lass, as soon as I heard where ye were. Edgar told Kieran. I would have been here sooner, but we've been in the north and only just came back to Lothian. Isabel, I thought I'd lost ye forever."

She strained to kiss him again, but he shook his head.

"Not now. But later, lass, and we'll make up for the time we've lost. We have to get ye out of here."

Her mind started to clear. She looked around the dark room, then stepped back from him, searching for the candle and flint she kept near the door. Her hands were shaking, but at last she got the candle lit and looked from it to him. He filled the small room, his head almost to the ceiling, his shoulders wider than she'd remembered. Edgar was right; Rory had changed. There were lines at the edge of his eyes and around his mouth. His lips were thinner, his jaw more defined. He had been lean before, but he was honed, like steel now. His hair, that glorious mane of gold, was braided at his temples and flowed past his shoulders, and pale stubble was just making its appearance on his cheeks. He looked dangerous.

She tore her gaze from his. "Rory, are you still outlawed?"

"Aye."

"It's dangerous for you to be here."

"Aye."

"I was followed today."

"Aye, ye were. I was one of them, lass, but yer neighbor, the one ye went to Mass with, she sold ye today. After ye came out from the church, she took money from one of the men who was watching ye."

Isabel put a hand over her mouth. "I didn't think she would do it yet."

"Yet?"

"I knew she would." Isabel told him of the conversations she and the older woman had had. "I was planning to leave in the morning."

"No telling what could happen before then. Hurry. Get yer things. I was followed as well. Come, lass, what d'ye need?"

She threw a look around the room. After the first conversation with Florine, when the soldiers had arrived in Newcastle, she had begun to prepare. Her clothing, what little there was, was folded in readiness. Her hair combs, the boar bristle hairbrush her grandmother had given her when she was a child, her cloak, and the few small treasures she had were already inside the leather satchel. She had spent the day thinking of what she needed to do.

There was cheese and bread on the board, quickly wrapped in cloths. A stone bottle of wine, thrown into the satchel. She left the rest. The sheets, threadbare and patched many times, were not worth taking. She'd found the rug on the floor at the side of the road; the same with the cloths she'd sewn to cover the shuttered window. One candlestick, made of wood. Nothing to mark her time here, nothing to tell anyone who she was.

She picked up her satchel. "I'm ready."

He took the satchel from her hand and leaned to kiss her again. "I love ye, Isabel de Burke. Let's get ye out of here and start to ken each other someplace where it's safe, aye?"

She smiled, her heart singing. "And I love you, Rory." She put her hand on his cheek and stroked his jawline. "I cannot believe you are here."

"Nor I, lass. Now blow out the candle. I'll go first."

He led her through the streets as though he had been the one living here, his pace quick, but not so quick as to draw attention. The churches were full, and they passed many revels. It was Yuletide, and Newcastle was celebrating both the season and the arrival of so many of Edward's men. He led her close to the castle, down a narrow street and then into a dark corner across from a squalid inn.

"Stay here," Rory said. "I have to get my horse and my things."

"But it's dark. The city gates will be closed already."

"They open with the right number of coins, lass. Shhh."

The night seemed to close in as soon as he was gone. She shivered, both from the cold and from her awareness of the danger they were in. Two men lurched out of the inn, obviously well into their cups. One staggered to the side of the building, and a moment later she could hear the sound of urine hitting the wall. They left at last, telling each other disgusting jokes and bragging about their prowess in bed. And still Rory did not come.

Three soldiers, still in uniform, came down the street, stopping not far from where she hid, arguing about which tavern to enter. The argument intensified and one left, still shouting obscenities to the others, who laughed and went inside. The street grew quiet, but she could hear laughter and voices from the inns around her. A rat ran across the street, disappearing into the shadows not far from her.

And then, at last, Rory rode out of the darkness, riding a tall bay, and leading a smaller dark horse. He dropped to the ground and without a word helped her atop the horse, strapping her satchel onto the rear of his horse, then returning to her, gesturing her to lean close to him.

He kissed her, then let her go, his hand cupping her cheek for a moment. "Say nothing, lass, if ye can help it. We're going to bribe the guards at the gate. I want ye to hide that face best ye can. If they see how bonnie ye are they'll remember ye. We want to be forgotten, aye?"

She nodded. He leapt atop the horse and led the way.

At the city wall the gate was closed. Rory slid from the horse and knocked at the gatekeeper's door, talking in quiet tones when the man answered. She saw Rory fill his hand, and a moment later the gates were opened and they were outside Newcastle.

He gave her a wide grin and danced his horse in a circle, giving the city a mock salute. She laughed, throwing her head back and taking a deep breath of the cold night air. They had done it. And now it was time to face the future. Together. She laughed out loud and he grinned again.

They rode northwest, riding quickly as soon as they were clear of the city. They rode for what seemed like hours, and might well have been, for she watched the moon cross the sky. Her ebullient mood had faded with the moon's progress. She was exhausted and aching from the cold and her fear. Rory seemed unaffected, cheerful even. At last he slowed their pace, gesturing to her to be silent.

"We're almost there, lass. I've been there before, but it's been a long time. There's a place I'm thinking we can try. A'right with ye?"

She nodded.

It proved to be a cluster of small cottages atop a small hill overlooking the river below. Rory woke the owner, who grumbled but, wrapping his nightrobe about him, led them to a cottage a bit apart from the others. He unlocked it, disappeared inside, and lit a candle, the light glowing from within. He handed Rory the key with a nod. And was gone.

Rory pushed the door open and looked inside. "He said I can put our horses in the stable, lass. I'll be back."

She nodded and watched him walk away, then she went into the cottage. It was clean, a box bed in a corner, a fireplace, a flint nearby, two chairs, and a table that held the candle and a vase with a sprig of holly stuck in it. *Holly.* But she would not think of Henry now.

There was a door in the rear of the cottage that led to a small lean-to full of stacked firewood. She carried wood in and lit a fire, then roamed the room, trying to put her hair to sorts. One bed. Two people. There was a barrel of water in a corner and a basin nearby, with thin cloths in it for washing. She filled the basin and set the kettle on the fire to warm some water.

"It looks right, ye ken," he said as he closed the door behind him. "To see ye thus, Isabel, waiting for me. I have dreamed of this." He pulled off his cloak and tossed it on the chair.

She straightened with a smile. "And I as well. Now tell me everything."

He shook his head. "There's time for that later." He crossed the space between them, holding out his arms. "Come to me, lass."

She did, sliding into his embrace and raising her mouth for his kiss. He took possession of her mouth, lunging into her with his tongue, exploring every portion of her. She returned the kiss with all the passion she possessed, pressing closer to him, wishing to meld with him, to be one.

He lifted his head and stared into her eyes. "I was afraid ye wouldna want to see me, that ye'd tell me to leave ye alone."

"Never," she said breathlessly, reaching to pull his mouth back to hers. "I want you, Rory. Now. Forever." She slid her hand along his collarbone and under the opening of his shirt. "Take it off. I want to see you."

He held her gaze as he unpinned the brooch that held his plaid over his shoulder, then unbuckled his belt and let it slide to the floor with the plaid, a puddle of wool at his feet. He smiled.

"There's only the shirt left."

"That too," she said and put her hand on the triangle of skin below his neck.

He did not move as she pulled the laces apart, moving her hand lower to caress each inch of skin newly revealed. She could feel his pulse quicken as she touched him, and leaned close, to put her lips where her fingers had been, inhaling his scent. His quick intake of breath made her bolder, and she spread the material wider, pulling the last of the laces apart. She looked into his eyes, then pushed the cloth over his shoulders, baring them, and his chest, savoring the sight, then letting the shirt fall to the floor.

He stood, his stance wide, without moving, letting her look her fill. Which she did. He was magnificently made, his wide shoulders tapering to a lean waist and hips, the muscles of his chest and stomach defined, a dusting of blond hair on his chest. His legs were long and muscled, and his body was ready. She touched his side, running her fingers lightly along his ribs, then lower. And lower still. He was very ready for her. His hand clasped around hers before she could touch him.

"Not yet, lass. If ye touch me it will be over."

"Then I could just look at you, Rory. I could look at you forever. You are beautiful, sir."

His laugh was low. "No. But I am verra willing, as ye can tell."

She traced the tip of her finger along his collarbone, following it to the tip of his shoulder, then back. "I had dreams of doing just this, Rory. I would wake in the night and think of touching you. Of how your skin would feel under my fingers. Warm, just as I imagined. I can feel your strength."

"Isabel, is this what ye want? Ye need to tell me now, because soon I willna be able to stop."

She slid her hand down his side, feeling the contours of his hip, the concave surface of his stomach. "I am ready, Rory. I want to feel you next to me. And inside me."

"Jesu," he said and kissed her again, his lips arousing her even more.

His hand slid her bodice off one shoulder, his lips doing as hers had done, following his hand along her skin. She shivered at his touch. He lifted her overtunic over her head and threw it across the room, then the undertunic as well. He pulled out the last of the pins that bound her hair and let it tumble to her shoulders. And he smiled.

"There has never been a woman more beautiful, Isabel. Never, in the history of man has a woman been so splendid."

His hand cupped her breast, kneading it softly while his lips found hers, then her neck. Then her breast. She closed her eyes, letting her head fall back at the sensation of his lips on her nipple, of his hand caressing the curves of her waist and hip and back again. He groaned softly, blowing against her nipple.

"I want ye, lass. I want every inch of ye."

"Yes," she said breathlessly, her mind focused on his touch, on the tingling of her skin wherever he touched her.

He ran a hand from her breast to her waist, her hips, the swell of her buttocks, the top of her thigh. And then between her thighs, his touch gentle, but still she jumped.

"I'll stop," he whispered.

"No. Don't."

He moved his hand back and forth, pushing his finger

between her folds, then finding the opening. She shivered again, with delight, and made a sound that surprised her, almost a purr.

He took his hand away and looked into her eyes. "Isabel?"

"Yes," she said, and let him lead her to the bed.

He tossed the coverlet aside and pushed the pillows to the floor, then swept her into his arms and lay her down on the cool sheets, stretching that long, lean body next to hers. They did not speak as they explored each other.

He kissed her shoulders, lingering over her collarbone and neck, then feasted on her breasts. She held his head to her, threading her fingers through his hair, memorizing the moment. She'd waited so long to have him in her arms.

She let her hand run down his spine and his arms and shoulders, feeling his muscles ripple under his skin as he moved. He slid his hand along her waist, to her ribs and down to her hips.

"Feel how beautiful ye are," he whispered. "How perfect ye are."

She held him in her hand, feeling the pulse of his blood under her fingers.

"You feel like silk," she said, running her fingers along his length.

He laughed and kissed her stomach, then moved lower, pushing her legs apart and making her cry out with surprise as his tongue touched her. She arched to meet him.

"Now, Rory," she said.

"Are ye ready for me?"

"Yes, and yes, and yes!"

He moved above her, then closer, his erection just

touching her. Then inside her, slowly thrusting, withdrawing, then thrusting again. With a moan he thrust inside her, then pushed himself up on his arms.

"Isabel, I thought Langton—"

"No," she said. "Let's not talk of him."

"Let's not talk," he said.

They didn't. He taught her well. Once. Then again, more slowly. She enjoyed it more this time, and even more the third. And as she closed her eyes, sated and warm, his arms wrapped around her, she realized she felt safe for the first time in a very long time. *I am a woman,* she thought, and smiled.

He kissed her neck and sighed. And slept.

TWENTY

They made love all night, then slept wrapped in each other's arms, waking to talk of all that had happened during their time apart, then feast upon each other again. He was surprised and charmed by her passion. When he said that to her, she laughed, saying the Isabel she used to be was gone forever.

"I was afraid to live, Rory. Now I'm afraid there won't be time to do it all."

She listened while he told her of the abuses committed by Edward's troops in Scotland, of his time with William Wallace and his men. Of the negotiations he'd conducted between clans, the alliances that had been formed but not yet tested.

"Will they hold?" she asked. "If it does come to war, will they hold?"

He sighed. "I dinna ken. Memories are long in Scotland. Some will find ways to hate each other again no matter what they've promised. Others may at least find peace between their clans, if not between Scotland and England."

"Then it was worth being without you."

"No, lass, not even that was worth being without ye."

He gave her Rachel's message of love, which brought tears to her eyes. And he talked of his loneliness and his longing for her. And his guilt for not being in Berwick when Langton arrived. She soothed him, reminding him that he would have had no way of knowing Langton would arrive, but he knew the guilt would never leave him.

"I should have been there. It should have been me protecting ye." He trailed a finger down her arm. "Ye've not told me of that night. Tell me now."

He listened while she told what had happened with Langton, and Henry's part in helping her escape. And he knew her story would haunt him all his days.

"He could have killed ye, lass. Or had ye killed. I could not stop thinking of it, a woman like ye, with a fiend like him. It set my blood on fire. Still does."

She put a finger to his lips. "Hush. It was my decision to go there, Rory. And believe me, as hard as it was to actually live through it, it was much harder to be in that tiny room at the inn and wonder what was happening to Rachel and her family. I can never make it up to them for what they suffered because of me."

She talked of her childhood, and her dreams of her father, of being a girl in London with one dear friend, who was then torn from her. Of being chosen to be a lady-in-waiting to a queen, and how that had come to be. Of her time in Newcastle, and her loneliness and longing for him.

He told her of his visit to Lonsby, of her father's displeasure at his arrival, her father's wife's dismay, and her father's children's wide-eyed curiosity at learning they had a half sister.

"Charlotte is yer age," Rory said. "She sent you greetings."

"And the rest of them?"

"Nothing."

She nodded. She'd expected as much.

They made love again. She laughed, saying she would not be able to walk, and he showed her things they could do to satisfy each other. They agreed they would go to Scotland—but not to Berwick, where Langton's men were watching for her, but to Stirling, where he would leave her with Nell and rejoin William. And then he kissed her again, feeling the silkiness of her breast against his rib, the softness of her leg along his.

"Lass, we need to talk about this. About us."

She smiled. "It was wonderful, Rory. But we do not need to talk. I chose what I did. I gave myself to you freely and do not expect anything from you."

"Ye should. And I want more from ye than this. I dinna want this to end, lass." He took a deep breath. "Marry me, Isabel. Today. Now. We'll find a priest and pay him well. I am only a younger son, aye, but we willna starve. I'll work so verra hard the whole of my life. I canna promise ye jewels, but ye'll have a roof over yer head, and food each day, and a man who loves ye with every part of his soul. And his body. And often, if I have a say in it."

"I love you, Rory," she said, beginning to cry.

"First tell me, lass. Will ye have me?"

"Yes and yes and yes, and in every way possible. Now kiss me."

She wrapped her arms around his neck. He kissed her, thoroughly, pulling her against him, her willingness making him desire her even more. She kissed him with abandon, leaving him unable to think, her mouth and hands creating sensations that made him forget time. She was more adventurous now, exploring him and letting him do what he would. They lay, sated at last, listening to the wind in the trees outside.

"Shall we find a priest?" he asked. "Or wait until we get to Scotland?"

"I think we both need to get out of England. And we'll find a priest when we're safe. We need to leave here, don't we?"

"Aye. We're too close to Newcastle. I dinna ken how far they're patrolling, but we're too close and we're on the main road. But I thought we could be safe for one night."

She pulled herself from his side, giving him a view of her breasts. He cupped one, smiling at her, then climbed out of the bed, rummaging through the clothing he'd tossed on the floor. She watched him move, enjoying the long line of his leg and where it met his hip, the muscles under the skin of his arm flashing and then gone, his lean body sinuous and inviting.

"Rory," she said. "What are you doing? Come back to me."

He grinned and held up something, then came to sit on the side of the bed. "It was given to me by Lady Mac-Donnell," he said, handing it to her.

The brooch was a golden circle, set with jewels and engraved on the back in a language she could not read. The pin, long and golden as well, was engraved with a raven and what looked like Norse runes.

"It's beautiful," she said. "I remember you wearing this in London. What did you do to please the Lady Mac-Donnell so well, sir?"

"A small thing. But I'm giving it to ye as a way of giving credence to yer words. That's my name, in Gaelic, and the date, and the thanks of Lady MacDonnell. The story and the brooch are well kent in Scotland. Show it to anyone who kens the Highlands and they'll give ye hospitality and send word to my parents, who will take ye in."

"But we'll be together, won't we?"

"It's just in case, lass. And I will have to rejoin William and the others. Kieran's no doubt already on his way to Newcastle, looking for me."

He turned, staring at the door as they heard the sound of horses outside and voices calling orders. They exchanged a look. He folded her fingers around the brooch.

"Get dressed, lass!" he whispered, and leapt from the bed.

"Are they soldiers?" she asked, pulling her undergown over her head.

He listened through the door and cursed himself. Soldiers. English. Many of them, from the sound of it. And well known to the innkeeper, who was welcoming them and inviting them in to eat. Rory lifted the latch as quietly as he could, then slid the door open a crack. There were at least twenty of them, wearing the uniforms of the king's household. And there, in the shadow of the door of the innkeeper's lodge, a knight, only his back visible. The others were watering the horses and following the knight inside.

Rory closed the door, leaned against the wall, and told her. Her eyes were huge, but she was calm. She opened the door to the lean-to, where the wood was stacked, and pointed. At the side of the lean-to was a narrow door. He nodded.

He threw his clothes on, strapped on his sword and dirk, and grabbed her satchel as she finished dressing. He hurried her out to the lean-to, then inched the door open. The way to the trees was clear.

"I dinna think I'll be able to get to the horses," he said softly.

"No," she whispered and slipped through the door.

"Run, Isabel. I'll be behind ye." He watched her disappear into the trees, then turned to push the door to the lean-to closed.

The door to the cottage burst open. Three men rushed in with swords held high, spotting him at once. Their shouts rang out, and he knew it would be no more than a moment until the others arrived.

One rushed forward, swinging wildly. Rory parried two strokes, then struck at the man's thigh. He went down with a scream, holding his bleeding leg. Another came forward and fought well, his strokes quick and varied. Rory wounded him in the arm. The man slowed but did not falter.

The third circled him and Rory pushed back, trying to get near the lean-to door. Then a fourth and fifth came in, and another through the door from the lean-to. They charged him at once.

He fought madly, forcing them back and gaining the door. He burst through it, into the yard, to find the knight waiting, his sword raised in anticipation. Rory darted to the right, then whirled and charged, striking the knight with the flat side of his sword, knocking him to the ground. Rory kicked the knight's weapon aside and turned to face the others.

The soldiers formed a ring around him, their weapons

drawn, bloodlust in their eyes. It would take just a word from the knight for them to hack him to pieces. There was no way he would get through them, but if he delayed them a little longer, perhaps Isabel would escape. The knight rose clumsily to his feet.

"Sir," he shouted to the knight. "On what grounds do yer men kick open the door and assault me?"

"You are outlawed, MacGannon."

"I do not ken ye, sir. How is it ye ken me?"

"I saw you in London and learned your name. There are not many blond men wearing outlandish clothing, wooing one of the queen's ladies. We knew who you were. The inn-keeper said there was a Highlander here and a woman with him. So tell me, sir, where is Mistress de Burke?"

Rory watched the men who were closing in on him. "Ye burst in here on that alone, sir, that there was a Highlander and a woman? Is it now a crime to be a Highlander? Is Mistress de Burke the only woman who might be traveling? Is she the only woman in the world, sir?"

"You do know there is a bounty on her head? A princely sum. Or should I say a stewardly sum? Do you not want a share? Or do you plan to have the lady's favors and the bounty as well? When we find her, we may all sample her favors."

"Skewer yourself, sir. Or rather, let me."

The knight leapt forward, his arm raised, letting Rory know exactly what sort of blow he intended.

Rory parried it, and again, and knocked the sword from the knight's hand.

The knight, on his back on the ground like a turtle, flushed scarlet. "Take him," he said to his men. "Alive."

They closed in. Rory fought, but there were too many.

His last view was the ground rushing to meet him. His last thought was of her.

Isabel stood in the trees, in a muddle of indecision. Should she come forward and appeal for clemency from the knight? Or would he only arrest her and take both of them to Newcastle?

She could think of only one thing to do: ride for Scotland and find Kieran, or someone who could get a message to him, that Rory had been captured. She moved slightly, to feel the coins still sewn in the hem of her skirts, and blessed Rachel's mother for teaching her that. She would find a way.

The soldiers left not long after beating Rory to the ground. They tied Rory, unconscious, to his horse, and led him away. The knight disappeared inside the innkeeper's lodge for several moments, then emerged, alone, watching the others take to the road. He stooped to retrieve Rory's sword from the ground and studied it for a moment, then, with a vicious thrust, drove it into the ground, where it wavered and stood, the hilt looking like a cross marker on a grave.

He leapt to the saddle and whirled his horse in a circle, staring into the trees. She dared not breathe, knowing that any movement might draw his gaze. And then, with a splatter of gravel from the horse's hooves, he followed the others.

She waited for what seemed forever, then crept out of the trees. No one stopped her as she pulled Rory's sword from the earth with great effort. She hurried into the cottage, grabbed Rory's pack, his cloak, and her satchel, then ran with it all to the stable, hoisting herself to the horse's back. She took a deep breath, deciding what to do, then kicked the horse into motion.

She rode as quickly as she could, finding a village, and in it a villager who told her where to find what she needed. She rode carefully, unwilling to catch up with the knight and his men, and with full knowledge that she would be noted by those who saw her. Women did not travel alone. She was tempting the fates; she could be killed for her horse alone or she could simply disappear and no one would even notice that she was missing. She retraced their journey of the night before, asking several times before she found the route that brought her to Hulne Priory near Alnwick.

The friars were able to provide her with vellum and ink and tell her where she could find a reliable messenger, who assured her he would take both of her letters immediately and return in time for Christmas. She wrote to Rachel, just a few words, in case it was intercepted by others: "English have RM. Newcastle." And signed it simply "I." The other was to Nell Crawford at Stirling Castle: "Rory taken. Newcastle. Isabel." She tucked the brooch Rory had given her into the pouch with the letter to Nell, wondering if she was being foolish to entrust it to the messenger, but knowing that Nell or someone at Stirling would recognize it and believe her words. She paid the messenger well and turned her horse south, praying as she rode, the words forming a chant that matched the rhythm of the horse.

In Newcastle she found a room near the Black Gate, not realizing until she had secured her room that the house was full of soldiers. She told the woman who rented it to her that she was a widow, visiting her brother, a soldier. The woman winked and said that happened all the time, and that as long as they were quiet, she and her "brother" were welcome.

That night she sat in the room, listening to the soldiers below talk and laugh and occasionally sing. Rory's pack lay open before her. In her hand she held a brittle circle of wood, hardly recognizable. But she knew it was the circlet she had woven that night, so long ago, in her grandmother's house. A crown, they'd called it, and bantered about the Oak and Holly kings. He'd saved it, all this time, just as Kieran had said. She held the crown to her lips and wept.

The next day, Isabel stood in a crowd near the entrance to the Black Gate to watch the prisoners held at New-castle paraded as a Christmas treat. She watched while four men, accused of theft and rape and murder, were led past, and then, the people were told, the Highlander was next.

Rory was tied to the front edge of a cart, his arms spread wide, his legs bound with chains. He was naked, his hair wild and his body bruised. On the cart with him a soldier read out a list of Rory's crimes, and that these crimes held a penalty of death. "Treason," the man said, and the people cheered.

They pelted him with refuse and rocks, shouting threats and epithets at him, swearing vengeance on all Scots, reminding him that King Edward was coming to punish his countrymen. He did not flinch when he was hit, did not look at any of them, but into the distance, his jaw clenched and his eyes glacial. The crowd followed the cart, jeering and throwing more at him, but Isabel stood where she was, her hand over her mouth to stop from crying out. When the parade was finished, he would pass by here again, and so she did not move.

It seemed to take forever, but the prisoners were returned to the castle. The four who walked were coated with filth, but they at least were clothed. Rory's skin was blue with cold. His eyes were closed and he did not react when a rock hit his head. But she could see his ribs move with his breathing. She looked after the cart as it went through the gate. Then, as the crowd cleared, she looked across the road.

And into the eyes of Henry de Boyer.

He nodded but stayed where he was. As did she, until all around her were gone. And then he crossed to her, stopping before her. His expression was impassive. He took her arm.

"Let us talk," he said.

He took her for a meal. He said nothing to her, ordering food for both of them, and mulled wine.

"And plenty of it," he told the serving girl. "My companion is chilled."

He ate heartily while she watched. She sipped the wine, grateful for its warmth, and avoided his eyes. He drained his cup of wine and poured more.

"I was there when he was brought in," he said at last. "There are many here who would have killed him on the spot. Many have lost comrades in arms, and Rory is known as a murderer of English soldiers."

Rory, she thought. *He's calling him Rory, as though they are well acquainted, as though they are friends.*

"When I heard the story," he said, "I knew you must have been there at the cottage. I'm glad you were bright enough to stay out of sight. But this, Isabel, coming back to Newcastle now, is by far the most foolish of all the foolish things you have done." He leaned forward and grasped her wrist, looking into her eyes. "Why are you here?"

"Because he is."

"Fool! I have been searching for you."

"Why?"

He released her wrist and sat back. "God's blood, but that is a good question! I cannot answer it!"

"Why? We can be nothing to each other now. We have never been anything to each other."

"But you wished it. There was a time that you wished there to be."

"I thought you handsome, Henry. There was nothing more to it than that."

"No, there was something between us from the start."

"No. And even if there had been, you were able to abandon me easily."

"Not easily. I've tried to dislodge you, but still you stay in my heart."

"You chose Alis, Henry. You married her."

"No. Alis chose me. I was fool enough not to see what she was doing. And yes, I married her, but because she lied and convinced me there was a child, not because I loved her. But none of that matters any more. Alis is dead."

"What?"

"She died. In childbirth. And no, it was not my child. It might have been Langton's, but I think you put an end to that. She is dead, and the child with her."

"Do you mourn her?"

"I mourn the death of my idea of her, but I have had years to do that."

"I'm sorry."

He nodded. "So am I. I wish I had never met her."

"I remember the day you did."

"So do I. I should have stayed at your side. Rory would never have had a chance to creep into your heart."

"He did not creep. He roared into it, like a lion."

"Well, he's a caged lion now."

"And that's how he's been treated, Henry. He was paraded through the city like an animal."

"That is what they do to traitors. The parading is the easiest part. The rest of it is far worse. And while I'm sure he was discomforted—"

"Discomforted! He was naked in December. Horrid things were thrown at him. He had bruises all over him."

"He is alive! Is that not what you wanted? He is not being hanged and disemboweled at this moment because I insisted that he should not be given a merciful death here, but be brought to trial in London. Do not give me that look. Think, Isabel! The other choice was instant death. Tell me, which would you have chosen?"

He tore off a chunk of bread and chewed it, then followed it with more wine. He put the cup down with a thud. "I sent word to John Comyn that Rory was arrested. And to Berwick. I have done what I can."

She was close to tears. "Why did you do that?"

"For you. For the man he is. If we were not enemies . . . But we are enemies. And rivals. And I remember both."

"Why are you so angry, then?"

"Because he won you."

"You never tried to win me."

"I meant to."

"But Alis . . ."

"Yes. Alis." He drained the cup again and once again refilled it. "If he does not live, and I do not think he will . . . could there be anything between us, Isabel? I have lands in Essex. You could live there, far from Langton's reach."

"As your mistress?"

"Or my wife. What difference does it make? You would be safe."

"I do not understand you, Henry."

"I do not understand myself."

He finished his food and his wine. "If you had shown yourself, they would have arrested you as well. Or done things . . . You are being sought for attempted murder of a high-ranking government official. A bishop, for God's sake! Do you have any idea of what they would do to you, a woman, one who tried to cut a man's testicles off? Do you not know that there are men who want to dominate you for your insolence? How can you be so imprudent as to put yourself back within their grasp?"

"Rory is here."

He shook his head and sighed heavily.

"When will he be taken to London?" she asked.

"I don't know. Not before Christmas, perhaps as late as Epiphany. I do not know. Do not cry, Isabel. God's blood, I did what I could by sending those messages, and I may be discovered for it. It's only that war is in the air that I might escape notice. War is a grand time for advancement. My career could soar."

"How wonderful for you."

"I knew you would not thank me."

"I do thank you, Henry, for sending those messages. But you should know that we are pledged to each other, Rory and I."

"I thought as much. How long has he been here with you?"

"We had one day."

He laughed quietly. "One day. So had I found you a week ago—"

"Nothing would have changed. He has my heart, Henry."

"And I hold your life in my hands. Remember that, Isabel."

"I do. And I hold your career. And possibly your life. Langton will kill me, but what will he do to you for aiding me, Henry?"

He blinked, then threw his head back and laughed. "So. Sweet Isabel is gone and leaves me with a vengeful woman who seems to forget that I risked all I am and have for her safety, not once, but again now."

"I forget none of that, Henry. I owe you my gratitude, and you have it for that night in Berwick. I have often wished to thank you."

He finished his wine, then threw coins on the table and pushed his bench back. "Do you want to see him?"

"Is it possible?"

His smile was sardonic. "I am one of King Edward's own knights. Of course it is possible."

Isabel tried to remain calm as they entered the Black Gate. She refused to look up at the portcullis, nor at the guardrooms, full of men, on either side of the passageway.

A guard led them across the outer bailey and up the stairs to the Great Hall, passing them on to another guard, who took them through the hall and to the spiral staircase. The ground floor was a storage room lit by flickering torchlight that did not penetrate past the casks and barrels filling most of the room.

"He's in the cell at the end," the guard said.

Isabel and Henry followed him down an aisle between the stacked casks of wine. The air was colder here, and still, as though the world were very far away. In the first cell were the four men who had been paraded earlier with Rory, watching them with sour expressions. The guard stopped in front of the next cell, gesturing to the wooden bars before them, some cracked and broken, some missing altogether. "He did this last night. We had to chain him up."

Henry took a step forward and looked into the cell, his face impassive. Isabel moved to his side and looked into the cell. Rory's arms and legs were chained to the stone wall at the other end of the cell. He wore only a long linen shirt, his legs bare below it. His jaw was tilted up, his eyes closed, his hair pale against the dark stone, his face in shadow, but there was enough light to show her that the filth thrown at him still coated his legs and throat.

"Rory," she said.

He did not move.

"Rory."

He was sure he was imagining her voice. He hoped he was. He did not want to believe she was here and not heading for Scotland, that somehow she'd been captured, too. And all that that might mean.

"Rory."

He opened his eyes. Isabel stood next to Henry de Boyer just outside his cell. He closed his eyes, his stomach roiling. Was there no end to this day? For de Boyer to bring her, to see him thus . . . It was suddenly all too much. She could not be here, not when they'd risked so much to get her out of danger. He closed his eyes, willing this to be a dream.

"Rory. My love, speak to me."

"Isabel," he said, his voice hoarse and strained. "Why are ye here?"

"I am here because you are here."

He was too weary to speak. All that effort and she was here.

"Henry," she said. "I need to go to him. Please have the door unlocked."

"You are joking," de Boyer said.

"No. You must have him unchained. He cannot stay like this."

"I cannot have him unchained," de Boyer said.

Her voice was calm. "I ask only that you have him unchained from the wall, not that you take all the chains from him, only that he be allowed to lie down or to sit. Look how exhausted he is."

"Isabel, he is in prison for crimes against the crown. We cannot—"

She cut across his words. "I must be allowed to take that filth off him. He was paraded like a beast. Do not make him live like one. At least let me wash the filth from him."

There was silence. Then the sound of a key in the cell door, and the creak of the door opening. Rory opened his eyes again. The guard was gone. De Boyer moved into the cell, and Isabel followed. She stopped before him and put a hand to his cheek.

"My love. Rory," she whispered. "I'm so sorry you have to suffer this. I cannot bear to see you this way."

"Isabel, why are you here in Newcastle again? Has he arrested ye?"

"No. I came back to find you."

She put a finger to his lips. At her touch his emotions flared. He should be protecting her, not chained like a mad dog, like an inadequate failure.

"I do not want to be where you are not," she said. "I do not want to live if you do not."

The guard returned, carrying a basin of water and a cloth. He placed it on the floor at Rory's feet and stepped back, watching, with Henry, as she immersed the cloth in the water and twisted it in her hands.

"Isabel, I am too filthy for ye to touch."

"Hush. It's cold, love, but you'll be clean."

Her touch was gentle. He closed his eyes, his emotions warring within him. He was unwilling to watch De Boyer and the guard watch her. She wiped the filth from his face first, with soft fingers pushing his hair back from his face, then from his throat. She pulled the shirt open, washing his neck and shoulders. Then open more, to clean his chest and sides, her hands moving behind him to his back. He could smell her scent, could feel her breath on his skin as she leaned close.

Rory willed his body not to respond as her hands roamed over him, but her touch brought back the memories of their lovemaking far too vividly. He opened his eyes to drive the images from his mind. Henry had turned away, his back to them, his stance stiff. But the guard watched with rapt attention, and Rory focused on the man, on hating him, on the way he watched Isabel's every movement.

She rinsed the cloth out again, then pulled the shirt all the way open. It fell to his sides and she put the cloth against his stomach. Then his hip, then slid it lower. She moved the cloth again and he could not speak for a moment.

"Ye dinna have a knife in yer hand, do ye?" he asked her.

She looked up, her eyes wide with surprise, then laughed. "No. That was a special occasion. But mind that you do not anger me in the future."

"I'll remember that." She smiled softly, pulling the shirt closed across him, then stepped back and let the cloth fall into the water.

"Thank ye, lass," he said quietly.

"I love you, Rory."

"And I ye."

"Right," Henry said briskly, taking her elbow. "Let us go, Isabel."

"Keep her safe, Henry," he said.

"I intend to."

Isabel let Henry lead her out, pausing to look back at Rory through the bars while the guard locked the cell door. She gave him a wave of her hand. And then was gone. He could hear her footsteps echo on the stone, in step with de Boyer's.

TWENTY-ONE

Rachel handed Kieran both letters. Her father stood, arms crossed, watching as Kieran read Henry de Boyer's letter first, then Isabel's. Kieran read both again, then lifted his gaze to meet hers, his beautiful eyes filled with grief.

"Ye were right to send word to me. I thank ye for that. I kent I should have gone with him." He looked at her father. "Sir, I ken ye dinna want me here, but Rory has been taken by the English."

"I know that," her father said. "And Isabel, fool of a girl, has no doubt gone back, thinking that she can do something about it."

Kieran and Jacob looked at each other for a long moment. Rachel's mother watched the two of them, then stepped forward.

"You'll be needing something to eat before you go," Mama said.

"I must get word of this to the others," Kieran said.

"You'll eat first," Mama said. "You'll think better on a full stomach."

Kieran almost smiled. "Aye. And I thank ye for it, madam."

"Will you go to Newcastle?" her father asked.

Kieran nodded. "I had half a mind to go before this, but now, aye, we will."

"If you find her, bring her back here," her father said.

Rachel looked at him in astonishment. Papa shrugged.

"She needs a home. We have one again. She should never have done what she did."

"You know why she did that," Rachel said.

Papa nodded. "I don't need a slip of a girl protecting my family. She needs us to protect her." He met Kieran's gaze. "Do you want me to go with you?"

Kieran's surprise was obvious. "I thank ye greatly, sir, but I canna accept yer offer. Ye risk death by going into England, and I canna ask that of ye. I would rather ye stayed here and make sure Rachel is safe. And all of ye, of course."

"Of course."

"If King Edward comes to Berwick, ye canna stay. I ken my family would welcome ye. My parents and brother and my sisters would make ye welcome, and Skye is far from England. Ye'd be safe there."

Papa pressed his lips together in the way he always did when he was trying not to show emotion. "Thank you, Kieran. We will keep that in mind."

He reached out his hand. Kieran shook it. Then cleared his throat and nodded to Rachel, then to her mother.

"Let's get you fed," Mama said. "All of you."

Rachel watched while Kieran and the others ate. The extraordinarily tall one was William Wallace, Kieran told her, the man who had made a name for himself by uniting the resistance in the south of Scotland. The man who had been ignored by the nobles but was followed by the ordinary people. The man who he and Rory had been with for years now.

Kieran was polite, nothing more. There was no undue warmth in his tone when he spoke to her, no words that could not be overheard. There was a heaviness in his manner now—because of Rory, of course, she told herself. But she knew there was more. He watched her every movement. He seldom looked away from her, even when others were speaking to him. Nor she from him.

And Mosheh watched it all. Her husband, for he still was her husband despite their living apart, stood quietly near the wall, speaking only to her father. Mama welcomed him calmly, but Rachel had only nodded, not sure of her emotions. Did he think she would break their vows? Here, in her parents' home? Surely he must know her better than that? But perhaps he did know her and knew how thoroughly she regretted marrying him. It was not his fault that she'd wished she had not. The only one to blame for her pain now was herself.

The door banged open and was shut at once by a big burly man wrapped in fur and leather. "Brutal weather. Is your wife still cooking that good food, Jacob?"

"Of course," Papa said. "Any news, sir?"

"Nothing new," the man said. "It's two months since King Edward ordered Balliol to relinquish Berwick, Jedburgh, and Roxburgh, castles and boroughs all, and two months now that Balliol has not done so. And you have heard that Robert Bruce the elder has been appointed governor of Carlisle Castle?"

"Yes," Papa said. "Some time ago. And the younger Robert is with him."

The man nodded. "But what am I thinking? There is news. Edward has just ordered two hundred of his tenants in Newcastle to form a militia by March. There are knights and soldiers from his army already there."

Kieran and William Wallace glanced at each other.

"Looks like he plans on coming north," the man continued. "They caught a Highlander and paraded him through Newcastle." He nodded at Kieran and the others with him. "Lots of folks traveling just now."

Papa nodded and turned his back to the man, glancing at Mama, and putting his finger to his lips. Rachel looked at the traveler more closely. He was dressed as a Scot, as a Highlander even, but he was certainly no Highlander.

"Let's get some food for our guest," Papa said, then turned back to the man. "We have fine fish today, and chicken and beef as well. Take your choice, sir."

The man nodded but did not move. Kieran glanced at him; then, fishing coins from the purse at his waist and tossing them on the table, he stood. William and the others rose with him, thanking her parents for the food.

"Safe journey, sirs," Papa said with a wave of his hand.

"Going north or south, sirs?" the man asked.

"North. And you?" William Wallace asked, coming to stand before the man. The difference in their height was noticeable.

The man took a step back. "West for me."

"Too bad," William said. "We would have looked for you on the road." He went out the door and the others followed him.

Kieran lifted his hand in farewell and nodded to

Mosheh as he passed. Ignoring her parents and Mosheh, Rachel hurried after Kieran. He was just outside the door, standing with the others as she hurried down the steps, stopping on the bottom one.

"Safe journey, Kieran," she said. "I will pray for your success. And for you."

Kieran nodded and looked behind her. She glanced back to see Mosheh coming to stand next to her, and Papa on the top step.

"Keep her safe," Kieran said to Mosheh. "If Edward comes, ye'll get her out of here, aye?"

Mosheh put a hand on her shoulder. "I will decide what is best for my wife and me, MacDonald."

"I ken ye are her husband, Mosheh, and I respect that. All I'm asking is that ye keep her safe from harm. Ye will not be safe here either if the English take over Berwick."

"I will decide what is best for us."

Kieran's eyes flashed. "If ye dinna keep her safe, I will."

Mosheh's hand tightened on her shoulder. "Do not come here again."

"Mosheh . . . ," Rachel said.

Kieran nodded at Mosheh. "Good to ken the war is not lost then, sir. Rachel, take care of yerself. Jacob, thank ye for the meal."

"Bring us news when you can," Papa said.

"Aye, sir, we will." Kieran gave Rachel a half smile and joined the others.

Rachel and Mosheh watched them out of sight.

"Rachel," Mosheh said, "you need to come home."

She gestured at the inn. "I am home, Mosheh."

"No," Mosheh said. "Your home is with me."

"I am sorry," Rachel said. "More than I can ever let you know, I am sorry."

"We are married, Rachel. We'll work this out."

She looked down the street, where Kieran had gone, then patted Mosheh's arm. "I am sorry."

"It will pass, Rachel. This feeling you have for him, it will pass. And I will be here, waiting."

Her eyes filled with tears. "From your lips, Mosheh. Would that it were so."

"Do you wish it, Rachel?" She did not answer at first, then nodded. "Yes," she said. And knew she was lying.

Isabel paced the small room. The day was almost over and still she had not decided what to do. Henry had brought her the word this morning: Walter Langton was coming to Newcastle. To find her.

The news was all through the court and the king's army that Langton had found the woman who had maimed him, Henry said. Langton had had men searching for her since Berwick. When they'd found her in Newcastle with Florine's help, they'd sent word to Langton. He had started north at once, using King Edward's troop buildup in Newcastle as his excuse for the journey.

It terrified her, the thought of being in his power. Here, even more so than in Berwick, he would be able to do what he wanted. And she knew he would want revenge of the most foul sort.

She should never have come to this inn, full of soldiers. She'd heard multiple versions of her attack on Langton, some so detailed that she'd wondered at the story. But someone, she'd realized, had had to repair the damage she had done, and although certainly Langton must not have wanted it known, the story would not have been held in confidence. Some of the versions were so extreme as to be amusing. Or would have been if she had not been one of the players involved. And, of course, there were myriad ribald comments associated with any version of the story. The men who talked within her hearing had no idea that she was the woman who had attacked Langton, and she was well aware that they would gladly hold her prisoner for him if they got wind of who she was.

She had to leave Newcastle. But . . . How could she leave Rory? But how would it help Rory to have her in Langton's clutches? She had asked herself the questions all day.

"Madam." Her landlady's voice was almost a welcome interruption.

"Yes?" Isabel called.

"Another of your 'brothers' is here. He awaits below."

Another?

She kept her voice calm. "Thank you," she said through the door and heard the sound of her landlady leaving.

Only Henry knew where she was, for he had accompanied her here after their visit to Rory. The landlady had snorted when Henry, who knew some of the men in the inn, had introduced her as his sister. And Henry had given Isabel a glance as though to say he'd known her idea would not work.

She'd told Henry of seeing his former squire, and of him recognizing her. Henry had assured her that the man had no interest in betraying her, but how could he know what was in another's heart? Money did strange things to people, and every new knight had many expenses, some unexpected. Had he told someone that she'd been in Newcastle? But so many knew that already, which was why Langton was on his way. She shook her head to clear it, knowing that she was on the edge of hysteria.

Dear God, let it not be Langton.

She leaned her forehead against the wooden door, trying to calm herself. There was no choice. She could not continue like this. She straightened and took a deep breath, making sure her dagger was tucked in the garter on her leg, and that the coins were still sewn in her hem. Fewer now, for she'd had to use some to pay for her lodgings and travel here. She wrapped her cloak around Rory's. She was ready to flee if necessary. She threw a glance at her satchel, never unpacked, standing near the door. She'd leave it if she had to.

She slowly crept down the stairs to the ground floor, looking into every dim corner, listening for every creak of wood. The sound of male voices floated up from below, the normal jovial chatter, which cheered her. She'd been afraid there would be silence there, while the soldiers waited for the infamous Isabel de Burke to be apprehended.

She paused at the foot of the stairs, in the foyer. The door to the outside was ten feet away, the door to the tavern room to her right, open. Was this her chance to escape? She took one step, then another, her heart pounding.

"Isabel."

The voice was a whisper. Male, but not Langton's voice, and she closed her eyes, breathing a prayer. She turned to see a figure step out of the shadow at the far end of the corridor. Tall. Dressed in a dark tunic and leggings.

She whirled around and ran for the door. One step. Two. Her hand on the door latch. And another, larger, male, placed over it.

"Isabel. It's me," he whispered.

For the briefest of moments she thought it was Rory, but she turned to look into the eyes of a man who was almost as welcome. Kieran MacDonald nodded.

"Aye, lass, it's me. D'ye have any things here?"

"Rory's sword. My satchel."

"Go and get them."

"Was it you, waiting for me?"

"Aye. We're getting ye out of here now. We'll talk later. Hurry."

She scurried back up the stairs and down again, hiding the sword behind her skirts when two men, far into their cups, passed her in the narrow hallway. One leered at her, the other just looked, but mercifully neither stopped. And then she was with Kieran again. He took her satchel and the sword, nodded to someone behind her, and opened the door. No one seemed to notice as they left, she, Kieran, and somehow two other men whom she had not even seen. A reminder, she told herself, that she was not good at this sort of thing.

They did not speak as they hurried down one dark street after another, turning so many corners that she became completely disoriented. At last, after what seemed like far too much walking to still be in the city, Kieran opened the door to a narrow house and walked into the dark.

There were eight of them altogether, Kieran said. He, William Wallace—the impossibly tall man who watched her silently—and Edgar Keith, who embraced her warmly, had come into Newcastle. Five others waited outside the city walls. She embraced both Kieran and Edgar, and shook William's hand.

"I am sorry for all your troubles," William said, his sincere tone undoing her.

She did not sob, but she could not stop the tears from streaming down her face. The men pretended not to notice, but Edgar handed her a handkerchief and she smiled ruefully at him.

"You are married, sir, and know to keep a handkerchief with you."

Edgar grinned. "True, indeed."

"How did you find me?" she asked, looking from him to Kieran. "How did you know where to find me?"

"De Boyer," Kieran said.

"He told you?"

"No. We dinna ken where ye were. We went to the inn Edgar uses, but they had no word of ye. We'd heard Rory was held in the castle, so we watched the troops come in and out of the gate. When we saw de Boyer, we followed him, and he came here. When we asked if there was a woman staying here, the woman laughed and told us where ye were. And here we are. Now yer turn. Tell us what has happened."

She told them almost everything, all about Rory's capture, and her journey back to Newcastle to be near him. And that Langton was on his way. Kieran told her of receiving the message from Rachel, and his visit to Berwick, although she could tell from his expression that there were things he left unsaid.

"I told Rory I should come with him," Kieran said.

"And now he's chained to the wall in a prison cell and Langton is on his way here to find ye."

"There has to be a way to get him out," William said.

"I do not think you can break Rory out of the castle with only the men you have with you," she said. "I've thought of all the things I might do to smuggle him out, but the castle is well protected, and to get inside the walls, free him, and get out would be nigh impossible."

"Tell us what ye know about the castle," William said.

She did, glad she'd paid such attention on her earlier visits. "What can we do? We cannot leave him there with Langton on the way! I'd thought to follow Rory south when they took him to London and find a way to free him, but now . . . We have very little time. Langton will recognize Rory. He'll remember that Rory was with me at the Tower, and I'm afraid he'll take the revenge he wishes for me out on Rory. Can you think of any way to get him out?"

The men all looked at each other.

"Perhaps we're looking at it wrong," William said. He paced the room, rubbing his chin, while the others watched. "It could be difficult—nigh impossible, ye said—to get Rory out with so few of us. But if they brought him out, we might have a chance, aye?"

"They will do that when they take him to London," Isabel said, "but not before Christmas, and perhaps not before Epiphany, and Langton will be here long before that."

William rubbed his chin again. "There is one thing we might do."

She was sure that she would be sick at any moment. She'd been unable to eat anything this day, knowing what was to come. She'd had to talk long and hard to convince the men to include her, but at last they had agreed. They'd had no choice. Without her, she was convinced, William's strategy would fail.

It was a bold plan. A desperate plan. And one which, if it failed, would surely end in all their deaths. And if she fell into Langton's hands again . . . but no, she'd run into a sword before she gave herself to him. If she died and Rory was freed, she would be satisfied. Not, she thought wryly, that she would know. But if their plan was betrayed and Rory died because of it, she herself would kill those who had betrayed them. There had been a time when she'd not been capable of such a thing, but now she knew she was very capable of it.

They waited in a small cottage near the river. There was little to say, not even when the men had returned with uniforms of the king's own guard, enough for all eight of them. She never asked how they'd obtained them, nor if men had died in the acquisition. But they lay piled next to the hearth, waiting. It was madness, this plan of theirs. But none wavered.

At last they heard the news that Langton was nearing. He rode with a large troop of men, over two hundred, which would swell the numbers of soldiers at Newcastle yet again. She sat on a horse, hidden in the trees, Kieran on one side, Edgar on the other, as Langton passed. He looked as he always had, his gaze intent, his back rigid, his self-satisfaction obvious.

Kieran waited until the sound of their hoofbeats died, then leaned to her. "Was that him? Langton? The one with no neck?"

She nodded, pushing aside the rise of fear just seeing

Langton had brought. The man had not changed. One could see his arrogance in his posture, in his every movement. How could they have thought for a moment to attempt this?

"Ready?" William asked. "We need to get within the gates before dark."

Kieran leaned to pat Isabel's hand. "Ye need not be part of it, ye ken."

She shook her head. "It will not work without me. I am ready."

"Are ye afraid?"

She nodded, and Kieran grinned at her. "So am I, lass. But there's always my da and Gannon and Liam to try and get us out if we're all taken."

She nodded again. They might be brave, these Scots, but they did not realize the might of King Edward and his armies. A handful of men, valiant as they might be, could not change the course of Edward's ambitions. All she wanted was this small group of men to be safe in Scotland and not in an ever-tightening noose of English soldiers—and not to widen the risk of loss.

"Nothing was ever accomplished by cowards," William said. "If we do not live through this day, so be it. But at least we will have tried."

"Yes," she said, raising her chin, somewhat comforted.

Kieran leaned close to her. Without words, he lifted her hair and cut a large lock from it. He held it up for her to see. "To convince Langton."

She nodded.

They rode in silence to the gates of the city. Their men were dressed in uniforms of the king's army, and entry was gained with no difficulty. She had pulled the hood of her cloak far over her face, and slumped, as though she were aged. Her ruse was not necessary. No one seemed to even notice the one woman riding in a troop of men.

Inside the city they stayed close to the market area, lively with a solstice fair, the merchants using the arrival of the soldiers to fatten their purses. It was a simple matter to mingle with the others who wandered through the crowds. Music filled the air and laughter with it. And somewhere there was dancing on the stones of the street, even in the December chill.

Darkness came early, on this, the shortest day of the year. In Scotland, they told her, those who practiced the old ways would be praying to the nature gods and the spirits of the land, would be chanting ancient words and dancing in the darkness. There would be special masses said this day in every chapel and church, to pray for the return of the sun, for the soul of the Oak King, sentenced to darkness until the summer solstice. The reign of the Holly King began this night.

She tried to pray, but the words rang hollow, and it was wrong to pray for divine assistance for such a task. And so she waited, numb, but unable to rest, while vivid images of Rory ran through her mind. Of the first time she'd seen him, in Westminster Abbey, the smile that lit his face, the halo of his hair and the amazing blue of his eyes. And that mouth, conjuring carnal thoughts. Rory, kissing her in a London alley, startling both her body and her mind, leaving her breathless. Stretched naked next to her in a cottage far too close to Newcastle. And now here, waiting in a cell to be taken to his death. She could do this. She would do this.

And then it was time.

She followed her instructions, staying silently in the house where Kieran had taken her before, four Scots below at the doors, protecting her, while Kieran, William, Edgar, and the five others went to the castle. She imagined their movements, a word with the guards, who might question their uniforms, but then through the gate, into the outer bailey. Up the stairs to the Great Hall. And finding him. Would he take the bait?

The waiting seemed interminable. Her hands shook, and she clasped them together to hide it, although there was no one to see the shaking. How had she thought to let them do this, to walk into the spider's web? It seemed an eternity, sitting in the dark, listening to the distant sounds of the solstice fair, of the nearer merriment in the inn down the street. She thought of Florine, who never ventured out after dark, and wished her a lifetime of loneliness.

And then the knock on the door. *Kieran,* she prayed, knocking in the rhythm they'd determined earlier. The signal echoed through the still house. Success.

She stood, crossing to the candle and striking the flint, fumbling for a moment in the dark, but at last the candle took the flame. She lit another, and a third, filling the room with light. There were sudden sounds, of struggle, of grunts and heavy things hitting the walls. And then silence. She stared at the door, her hands folding themselves as though in prayer, but her mind was numb. Men had just died below, she knew. But which? She took her dagger from her garter.

Footsteps hit the wooden stairs. Several men climbed, their boots ringing hollow in the narrow stairwell. Outside the room they paused, and she could hear voices, low, intense. And then the door was thrown open. She stood, hands hidden behind her skirts, staring into the darkness, knowing she was watched from the doorway.

Walter Langton stepped forward into the light. His hair was askew, but his manner was as arrogant as she'd remembered.

"Isabel. I wondered if they would truly produce you. Your hair is darker. I almost did not believe them."

She did not speak. For a moment it seemed as though he was alone and all was lost, but then Kieran came forward, other men behind him.

"I told ye that we had her, Langton. Here she is. Ye have two choices, sir. Die. Or write the orders."

"How do I know you will keep your part of the bargain?"

"Ye dinna."

"Then why would I agree?"

"Well . . ." Kieran showed Langton the long shining blade he held. "This might help to persuade ye. I might let her finish the job she started in Berwick."

Langton blanched, but nodded. "You might. But the entire castle knows where I have gone."

"No, they dinna. The guard ye gave the orders to was one of our own, not yers. No one kent where ye went this night but the men who accompanied ye, and none of them will be doing any talking. Ye have no other choices but the ones I've given ye, sir."

"I don't believe you. I told two guards where I was going."

"Aye. One was ours. And what did ye tell the other, sir? That ye were going to have a meeting with some Scots. Look around ye. See any Scotsmen? Or do ye see men dressed in the uniforms of the king's own? How would they ken which ones we are?"

Langton did not answer. He stepped closer to Isabel until he stood before her. His gaze raked over her body, and she began to shake. His eyes told her all she needed to know of what he would like to do to her.

"If I write the order . . . how do I know you won't keep her as well?"

Kieran held the knife up again. "I think ye misunderstood. If ye dinna write the order, sir, I will cut off a bit of yer body to persuade ye. The more ye resist, the more ye lose. And I assure ye, I will keep ye alive to enjoy every moment."

"You told me you would give her to me!" Langton circled her. "She goes to the castle before he is released."

"No," Kieran said. "She stays here, and ye with her, until I hear Rory's out."

"You cannot hope to succeed. Newcastle is full of English soldiers."

"Enough talk. Decide." Kieran stepped aside, letting the four Scots who had guarded her into the room. "I'll have yer answer now, sir, or they'll hold ye while I give her the knife."

Langton glared at her. "Very well."

"Good decision," Kieran said, nodding to one of his men. "Give him the parchment and the pen."

They watched while Langton scrawled out an order, then dusted the parchment with sand to dry it. He held it up and looked into the distance.

"No," Kieran said. "Put yer seal on it. Yer ring, sir."

Langton dipped his ring into ink and pressed it to the parchment. Kieran held it up, then showed it to Isabel.

"It needs the symbol," she said.

Langton glared at her. "What are you talking about?"

"You forget, my lord, that I have seen your orders before. This needs the symbol of your station or no one will believe it is from you."

"You risk your soul, madam," Langton said. "Do you forget that I am a bishop? You and these . . ." He gestured to the Scots. "You will not succeed. And I will enjoy every moment of my revenge."

"As I did mine in Berwick," she said. "Place the symbol on it, my lord, or risk another piece of your body."

"She is in league with you!" Langton said to Kieran. "You spoke falsely!"

"Aye," Kieran said lightly. "Learned it from the English. Place the symbol on it. Ye have one try, sir. My patience is gone."

Langton drew the symbol and handed the parchment to Kieran, who glanced at Isabel. She nodded, and the four men came forward. Langton was bound in a moment, trussed and laid on the floor, a filthy piece of cloth stuffed into his mouth.

"We're off now, sir," Kieran said, leaning over him. "I thank ye for the interesting time we had in Newcastle. Lass, see ye anon."

She nodded. Two men stayed with her, the others left with Kieran. They would stay below, to sound the alarm and stop any attempt to rescue Langton.

And they waited. Langton glared at her constantly and began to bang his feet on the floor. She held her knife before her, showing him the blade.

"Make any more noise," she said, "and I'll use this. You know I will do it."

He stopped moving. They waited.

The church bells tolled nine, then ten. Then eleven. Outside, the music quieted. Most of the revelers had gone, and Newcastle settled into the winter night. A stiff wind came up, rattling the doors and driving frigid air through the shuttered window. It blew out one of the candles, then another, and Isabel shivered and shielded the third. And prayed.

TWENTY-TWO

Rory lay on his back in the dark, running his fingers over the wall at his side, counting the stones for the thousandth time. There were still fifteen within his reach, as there had been each time. He closed his eyes, willing himself to sleep but knowing he would lie here, as he had every night, listening to the rustle of rats in the casks and muted sounds from the Great Hall above.

He'd overheard the guards talking among themselves and knew Langton had arrived. It was only a matter of time until Langton sought him out, and God only kent what that visit would bring. Langton would remember him, he was sure.

If only he knew that Isabel had left Newcastle. His own fate was in God's hands now. He would wait until his journey south to try to escape. And he knew that if he was ever free again, he'd rather face death than a lifetime of imprisonment.

He'd tried to stay strong, moving his body and mimicking sword play, to the amusement of the men who guarded him. He did not care what they thought. He had to stay fit. It would be easy to simply roll himself in the skimpy cover they'd thrown to him and sleep away both day and night, if only his thoughts would let him. But wiser to keep moving and wait for a chance. The door opened again and a shaft of light hit the ceiling. He could hear voices, several, then one clearly. "At the end. But mind yourselves. He's been violent before. Hold the torch high."

Rory rose to his feet as the sound of footsteps grew louder and the wavering light approached. Three men came into view, then two more. All were dressed in uniforms of the king's army, all armed. One held a pitch torch high, casting stark shadows on the walls behind him. Rory steeled himself as the men moved forward, and he looked from one to the other. These were the men who would take him to London. He looked at the last man, the tallest one, and found himself gazing, his heart leaping, into the eyes of William Wallace.

"Arms out," the guard said, coming forward with a length of rope.

Rory extended his arms, but not quite together, as the man wrapped them in rope. William's face betrayed nothing as Rory was led out of the cell. The men held in the next cell started shouting, one asking to be freed, the others jeering at Rory, but no one acknowledged them, and no one spoke as they moved down the aisle of wine casks toward the stairs.

As they cleared the last of the casks, Rory heard movement behind him and turned to see two men slumped on the floor, dead or dying. Kieran stood over one, Edgar over another.

William grabbed a guard—the one holding the rope—by the neck, pushing him against the wall. The last guard backed down the aisle of casks. Kieran disappeared after him, Edgar at his heels.

"You have two choices," William said. "Die now, or show us the sally port."

"You'll never get out of the grounds," the guard said.

"Not a good decision," William said and raised a long knife.

The man swallowed visibly. "I'll show you. But it's locked."

"Where's the key?" William asked.

"My commander has it. In the guardroom of the Black Gate."

"We'll not get through that," Rory said.

"No." William gave Rory a grin, then looked at the guard. "Strip, friend."

It took but a moment for them to take the rope from Rory's arms. He peeled his clothing from himself and took that of the guard.

"Back in the cell with ye," Kieran said and pulled the naked man down the aisle. He returned in a moment and handed Rory the cell key. "To remind yerself of yer stay in Newcastle, cousin."

Rory grinned and pulled the last of the guard's clothing on.

"Cover yer hair, Rory," Kieran said, "or it will give ye away."

Edgar led the way as they walked slowly up the spiral staircase and through the throngs in the Great Hall, sauntering as though they, too, were among the men who ate at the long wooden tables. No one spoke to them as they wove their way past the troops. No one even seemed to notice them. They did not look at each other as they passed through the tall door and down the stairs to the yard.

A group of knights was approaching the keep, pulling off gloves and removing cloaks as their horses were being led to the stables. Rory and the others stepped aside, keeping their heads down, as the knights passed. Rory waited until the knights were at the top of the stairs before he looked up. One lingered at the door, looking down at them, then stepped forward into the light, his face now visible.

"God's blood," Rory whispered.

Henry de Boyer met his gaze, then looked at the others with Rory, lighting on Kieran before returning to Rory. He did not move.

William's gaze followed Rory's. "Let's go. To the postern gate."

Rory stood a moment longer, looking up at de Boyer. He could feel his heart beat in his chest as their gazes held. Henry walked into the building.

"Jesu," Kieran whispered.

"Come," William said. "Walk. Now."

They crossed the yard and rounded the edge of the keep, passing other soldiers who glanced at them curiously but did not stop them. There was a bad moment at the postern gate when they were questioned, but Edgar laughed and handed the guard a coin. "More for you on our way back in if you keep your silence," he said in a Yorkshire accent. "I told them that it's the best brothel I've been to and they want to see if I'm correct."

"You'll pay for all of us if we're not," Kieran said, and they all laughed.

The guard joined their laughter. "The one near the church? That one?"

Edgar nodded. "Worth the coin."

"I was there last night, sir," the guard said.

"See?" Edgar turned to Kieran. "I told you."

"Best enjoy yerselves while you're here, lads," the guard said. "You'll only get Scottish tail when we move north."

"I think I'll go every night," Kieran said.

The guard was still laughing as he closed the gate behind them.

As soon as they were well away from the castle, Rory clapped the others on the shoulder. "There was never a man so happy to see such bastards as ye three! How can I thank ye for coming to get me?"

"Let's get out of Newcastle first," William said. "Then we'll accept your thanks. I thought we were done when that knight saw you. Is that de Boyer?"

"Aye," Rory said. "It is."

"All he had to do was say one word and we would have been taken right there," Kieran said. "I dinna understand the man."

"Nor I," William said. "But does it matter?"

"No," Rory said. But it did. And he knew that in Henry's place he would have done the same thing, for Henry had tried to keep Isabel safe. "Where is she?"

"In a house, not far away. With Walter Langton," Kieran said and told him of their plan as they walked. "We'll either get out tonight, or at dawn and she'll follow."

"No," William said. "She'll come with us. We have soldier's garb for her."

"And Langton?" Edgar asked. "Alive, or dead?"

"Rory's choice."

Rory shook his head. "Isabel's choice." He followed Kieran into the house. The men waiting there lowered their weapons as they saw him.

"MacGannon!" one said. "We thought never to see ye again, lad."

Rory grinned. "I thought the same, sir. Where is she?"

"Up there."

"Langton's still bound tight," another said, "but he's been quiet."

Rory took the stairs three at a time, being as quiet as he could. Outside the door to the room where Isabel waited, he paused. Then he opened the door, and the men inside greeted him. He answered them, but all he saw was Isabel.

She rose from the chair on which she'd been seated, opening her arms. He flew across the room, pulling her into his arms and kissing her.

"Rory," she whispered, then lay her head on his shoulder, crying.

"Whist, lass, dinna weep. We're together again," he whispered as she clung to him. On the other side of the room, Langton lay on the floor, bound securely. "Let's get ye out of here and away from that vermin. D'ye want me to kill him?"

She turned to look at Langton. "No," she said. "Let him live. I want him to remember this night, that once again we defeated him. Take his clothes. Leave him naked and bound and let them find him thus."

That is what they did.

It took only a few moments for Isabel to change into the soldier's clothing they'd secured for her. She refused to think of what lived in the foul-smelling wool, glad that the clothes were too large for her and she was able to stuff her own clothing inside it, next to her skin. The satchel had to be left behind. They dropped it outside a busy inn where it was sure to be found and closeted away. She salvaged a few things, but none of that mattered. Nothing mattered but escaping. Rory was delighted to have his sword back, and thrust it in the sheath of the uniform he wore. And then they were away.

Snow began to fall as they mounted their horses and started through the streets. The gates were opened wide and soldiers poured outside.

William turned to Rory as they approached the southern gate. "If de Boyer tells them we're dressed like this—"

"He willna have told them," Rory said.

"Do you know the man that well?"

"He willna do anything to risk Isabel. He kens she's here."

"You're sure of him?"

"I am," Rory said. But still his heart pounded as they came up to the gate.

The gatekeepers waved them through. And they were out.

He held her in his arms all night, mindful of the others sleeping nearby, but unable to stop touching her. She clutched him to her and told him of all that had happened while they'd been apart. He traced kisses down her neck and cupped her breast under the cover, whispering words of his love. And at last they slept.

He woke first, opening his eyes to see a cloud of her hair and the curve of her cheek. He would get her to Scotland and marry her the first day and never again would Henry de Boyer have a claim on her. Never again would she face the Langtons of the world. Never again would she be in danger.

She turned sleepily in his arms, and he felt his response as their bodies touched, even fully clothed as they were. He wanted to tear those clothes from her, to see her naked again, to thrust deep inside that luscious body until he could not move. Mixed with the physical need for her was his determination to get her out of England for all time. Edgar had sent Sarah north, near Inverness, to stay with his cousins, fearing Edward's invasion. Sarah wrote that she was happy in her new home. Edgar did not lie awake envisioning dreadful things happening to her, and Rory wanted the same sense of peace.

"I swear I will care for ye always, Isabel." He kissed her cheek. "I love ye, lassie. Wake now. We must be on our way again."

She smiled and opened her eyes. "I have never been awakened like that."

"It will be the first of thousands of mornings, if I have my way."

"You have already had your way with me, sir."

He smiled, his mood lifting at her playful tone. "Aye. And when we're alone I intend to have my way with ye again."

"Is there only your way?"

"Och, no, lass. There are dozens of ways. And I intend to show ye every one of them. Now, up, lass. We'll be in Scotland before another sunset."

"Nell! Nell, will ye hurry down, love?"

"Liam Crawford, stop yer roaring. I'm hurrying!"

Nell Crawford hurried down the last flight of stairs and threw herself around the corner and into her husband's arms. He kissed her ebulliently.

"Took ye forever to come down, love."

"For heaven's sake, Liam, I came as quickly as I could! I thought something was amiss with all yer noise! It's still early, ye ken. We've not even broken our fast." He kissed her again, drawing a smile from her. "Ye look fit, love. How was yer journey? Any news of Rory? Any news at all?"

"Aye, there is. Interesting journey. Edinburgh is always the same, thinking it's the center of the world when we all ken it's here, wherever ye are. Nothing new there. Edward Longshanks is bringing more men north, but we kent that."

"Aye. What of Rory? D'ye ken where he is? And where is Gannon?"

"Here! Come out," Liam called over his shoulder.

Nell watched in delight as the whole troop of them came around the corner—Gannon, Kieran, and William Wallace. And there, coming now, Rory and a lass.

"Oh, praise God!" She wrapped her arms around each of them to be sure they were real. "I thought never to see ye again," she told Rory, embracing him yet again, then doing the same to Kieran. "And William! Bless ye, sir, for helping to bring our Rory back!"

William smiled. "Had to, madam. We couldna do without him."

"What?" Liam said. "Nothing more for me? So soon forgotten?"

Nell laughed and threw her arms around her husband's neck, kissing him resoundingly. "As always, love, ye have my heart. And that should suffice."

Liam grinned at her. "It does."

She laughed. "Gannon, Margaret will be relieved to ken ye are here and safe. I just received a letter from her yesterday. She misses ye. And our lasses are well," she told Liam.

"No doubt making her glad she had sons."

Gannon kissed her cheek. "I'm sure it's the opposite. Sons make yer hair go gray before it's time," he said with a grin at Rory.

Rory laughed. Nell smiled at them all, then turned to the young woman who stood to the side. She was lovely, this tall lass, her dark hair lighter at the temples, her eyes bright now as she watched them all. A beauty. Which explained much.

"This must be Isabel," she said, holding out her hands.

"Aye, Nell," Rory said. "Meet Isabel de Burke. Isabel, my aunt Nell."

Isabel dropped a curtsy. "Madam, I am so pleased to meet you. I have heard so much of you."

Nell laughed. "I'm sure ye have. Believe only half of it, aye? Now come, the whole lot of ye, and get some food and tell me how ye came to be all together. And tonight we'll celebrate Christmas together with glad hearts."

The story came out over the meal, told mostly by Kieran, but some by Rory. Nell watched Isabel sit quietly, saw the looks she and Rory gave each other, and knew there was much more to the story. Liam and Gannon had found them, she was told, just inside the Scottish border, as they'd ridden south and Rory and the others were riding north. Liam, she knew, would tell her later, and in more detail, what he had learned.

"Are ye staying?" she asked them. "Or are ye off yet again?"

"I'd like it if ye would let Isabel stay here with ye," Rory said. "She canna go back to England. And I canna take her out to Loch Gannon just the now."

"But she will be going to meet yer mother," Gannon said.

Rory grinned at his father. "Aye, Da. She will." He turned to Nell again. "We're to meet with Balliol, all of us."

Nell nodded. "I was afraid of just that."

"Let's not even think of that now," Gannon said. "Get yer best clothes ready, Nell. My lad is getting married."

Nell looked from Rory to Isabel. "What, this morning?"

"As soon as we can," Rory said. "William's uncle is a bishop and with us."

"He'll waive the banns," William said, obviously pleased. "And perform the ceremony himself."

"Without Margaret?"

"There's not time, Nell," Gannon said. "We're off again at once."

"She'll have yer head for it," Nell said.

"Aye," Gannon agreed. "I'm safer with the English."

Rory and Isabel were married the next morning, just after matins, with the entire court in attendance. King John gave his blessing and ordered a wedding feast to be held in the hall in their honor. They spent their wedding night in a small room tucked in a corner of the castle, and Nell had to admit she'd never seen Rory so happy. Nor a bride more lovely. Gannon seemed pleased with Isabel, delighted that his son had been freed. All that was missing was her sister, Nell thought. Margaret would not be pleased to have missed this. But such was life in Scotland these days.

They met with the king—all of them, even Isabel, who was questioned at length. And then Rory, Kieran, and Gannon left to meet with the northern clans, and William went to Dundee and Perth. And Liam to Ayrshire.

Nell and Liam had two nights together. They enjoyed each other in every way, parting with regret, but no tears on her part. She would not send him away with the memory of her sobbing. It was difficult, but she smiled as he mounted his horse and gave her one last wave. Then they were all gone, and she and Isabel de Burke were left with King John's court and the strained mood there.

New Year's came, with a tepid celebration of Hogmanay. Nell toasted the new year of 1296 with Rory's Isabel, telling her of their customs. The girl was an eager student. The queen left, but Nell, not invited to join her, stayed behind. Her days would have been long if not for Isabel's company.

They were at first very polite and cautious around each other, but as the cold winter days passed, they started talking more, and more candidly. Nell talked of her life, of returning to find her family dead and home destroyed, and all that had happened when Gannon had come into their lives. She talked even of Tiernan, Gannon's brother, of her admiration of him. Of his death, and of the battles that had followed the raids, things of which she'd not talked in decades. After hearing some of Isabel's story, Nell even decided to talk of Lachlan. And finally of Liam and their daughters and the happiness they'd shared.

Isabel listened with rapt attention, sometimes crying with Nell at the stories, sometimes smiling that wistful smile she had. And Isabel talked, at first hesitantly, then the stories pouring out of her, her words moving Nell to tears and anger and sometimes to laughter, albeit laughter tinged with pain.

Nell enjoyed Isabel's company, but she missed her daughters terribly. She wrote to Margaret constantly, and her sister wrote back, as did Meg and Elissa, but it was not the same as having them with her, and her mood was always pensive when their letters came. The news from the south was alarming. Edward's fleet had sailed from East Anglia to Newcastle. Most of his army was massing on the border, and Edward himself was in Newcastle. Balliol responded by summoning all able-bodied Scottish nationals to come, armed, to Caddonlee, near Selkirk and the border, by March 11.

They watched, she and Isabel, as men poured through Stirling on their way south. The Highlanders were coming in droves, as were those in the south, knowing that they would be among the first to feel the wrath of Edward's fury should he invade. Not all came. The Earls of Angus and Dundee sided with the English, losing their estates when Balliol seized them in retribution.

The most noteworthy of those who ignored Balliol's summons were the Bruces. The youngest Robert, who had married the daughter of the Earl of Mar the year before, stayed in England, at Carlisle, where his father was governor. English nobles holding lands in Scotland were expelled, their lands confiscated and given to loyal Scottish nobles. Annandale, the home of the Bruces, was assigned to their old enemy, John Comyn. The insult did not go unnoticed.

Liam came back to Stirling as often as he could, and each

time Nell wept with joy to see him, and with sorrow that he would soon leave, but never in front of him. When they were at last alone, they found comfort in each other, but each time he left she wondered if that had been their last time together. She saw him off with smiles that hid her fear.

Isabel was grateful for Nell's warmth and affection, which soothed some of the pain she felt being separated from Rory yet again. Nell's stories, of her life, of losing her family and of Lachlan, were reminders that dreadful things could happen—and did—to anyone. And that the pain of the experiences could be overcome. Never erased, but diminished.

She resisted, as Nell did, being sent to Loch Gannon. Partly for the same reason Nell gave—that her husband could visit much more easily if she were at Stirling—partly for another reason, one she was loath to share with anyone. She had heard so much, and so much good, of Rory's mother, Margaret, that she was quite terrified of meeting the woman. What if Margaret disapproved of her? True, Margaret had sent a lovely and warm letter welcoming her into the family, and Isabel had sent one in return, telling Margaret of her love for her son. But still she worried. Rory was very close to his family, and Isabel wanted them to approve of her. Especially now. She missed her grandmother and thought of her often. And occasionally of her mother, wondering if she'd been too harsh in her judgment of her. It must have been hard to face being abandoned by the man she'd loved.

Rory arrived in the night, and none too soon, for she had news to tell him. Isabel embraced him with fervor and he returned her ardor, kissing her until she was breathless. He brushed the hair back from her face and smiled at her.

"How I have missed ye, lass. Ye've cast a spell on me. I canna stop thinking of ye, canna stop dreaming of ye. How have ye been?"

"Good. Nell has been most kind. She is quite wonderful."

"Isn't she? And I ken she's glad to have ye here just now, with her own lasses off with my mother. I want ye to go there, to Loch Gannon, at the first hint of danger here. It's war, Isabel, and I want ye far from it." He kissed her again. "Promise ye'll not be unwise."

She laughed softly. "Far too late for that. But yes, we'll leave if need be. Liam has asked the same promise from Nell."

"Good. John Comyn wants my father and Davey and their men to join his forces in Annandale. He's told us he means to march south into England."

"And start the war himself? Why?"

"He wants to take Carlisle and destroy the Bruces at last."

"Can they not let their feud fade?"

He shook his head in disgust.

"No. Even now, when they risk bringing Edward's rage upon us, they think most of harming the other. It is a kind of blindness, of stubborn pride that hurts my country more than anything else."

"What does your father say? Will he join John Comyn?"

"No. Which brings me back to ye, lass. Once word gets to John Comyn, ye can expect the Comyns to no longer support us here. Stay aware."

"I will." She put her hand on her stomach. "I cannot risk danger now."

His eyes widened. "Isabel? Are ye . . . ?"

"Yes. Two months."

He stared at her and she caught her breath, not daring to speak, terrified that he would be displeased.

His smile was brilliant. "A child. Our child. Two months. September, then. But why did ye not send for me the moment ye kent?"

"I did not know. I've never been with child before. And now, with war in the air . . . It's not a good time for this. Are you pleased?"

"We'll be fine, lass. I'll get ye home to my mother and she'll care for ye." He laughed and kissed her again. "A wee bairn. Our child. Aye, lass, I'm pleased! Ten thousand times over!" He whirled her around, then stopped, his eyes wide. "I shouldna do that. What am I thinking? Sit, Isabel. Ye need to rest."

She laughed. "I am fine. My stomach does not always agree, but I am fine."

"Come," he cried. "Let's tell the world!"

He told everyone at Stirling, and wrote to his parents and insisted that she write to her grandmother, saying she was safe now and this was news to share before the war began. And then he left her again.

Six days later the war began, but in a strange way. Englishman Robert de Ros, Lord of Wark in Northumberland, who was about to marry a Scottish woman, delivered his castle to the Scots. His brother, loyal to Edward, sent word to the English king, who immediately sent a force. Robert de Ros attacked Edward's troops, and soon thereafter Edward arrived to besiege—and take—the castle. He spent Easter, March 23, at Wark.

Three days later John Comyn took his army south and invaded England, besieging Carlisle, as Liam had predicted. The castle at Carlisle was defended by the Bruces, Robert the Elder and Younger, and Comyn's attack was successfully resisted. Those outside the walls suffered greatly, however, as John Comyn, in a frenzy of frustration, devastated the villages of Carlisle, then went west, attacking villages, monasteries, and churches, looting and killing as he went. In Hexham, it was said, he locked schoolboys in their school and set it afire, killing them all. And then he took his army, laden with booty, home to Scotland.

At the same time Comyn was attacking, Edward made his move. East. Toward Berwick.

TWENTY-THREE

Rachel was in the kitchen with her parents when Gilbert hurried through the door, his hair flying and eyes wide.

"Rachel," he said. "Kieran MacDonald is here and demands to talk with ye."

Rachel's parents exchanged a look.

Papa wiped his hands on a cloth. "I will speak with him," he said.

"He's asked for me, Papa," Rachel said quietly, pushing aside the food she'd been preparing and heading for the door.

"Not alone," Mama said.

They all went into the tavern room with her, Papa and Mama at her heels and Gilbert behind them. Kieran stood by the window, his back to her, his arms crossed. She could see the tension in his stance. She crossed the room, stopping a few feet from him.

"Kieran."

He turned, his gaze on her first, then flickering to her

parents and Gilbert behind her. "Rachel. Jacob, I must talk with ye all in private."

"No," Papa said.

Kieran gestured to the other patrons, who were watching closely. "What I have to say is not for them to hear, Jacob. But ye need to hear it. And now."

Papa nodded and led the procession back to the kitchen. Kieran waited until the door was closed, then faced them.

"Ye must leave, this day. Edward is coming this way with thirty thousand foot soldiers and five thousand cavalry. Whether or not ye believe he means to come to Berwick, ye must see how dangerous this is. Please, leave at once."

Papa shook his head. "I thank you for your concern, Kieran, but we've heard this before. Lord Douglas in the castle and all the city's leaders assure us our defenses are strong and that Edward will not besiege us."

Kieran's face flushed. "What defenses? Ye have none here! Ancient earthenworks, sir, not tall strong walls. And no army to defend ye, only a handful of guards at the castle. At the least ye must admit that Edward's forces are formidable. Close the inn, sir, if only until we determine Edward's plan. Dinna be more of a fool than ye need to be!"

"Kieran!" Rachel cried, seeing the anger in her father's face.

Papa's tone was cold. "I've been driven from my home twice, sir. Once in London, and once by Langton. We have made a new home here, a good home, and I have nowhere else to go. You exaggerate the danger."

"Go to Sarah's. Edgar assures me his cousins will take ye in."

"Sarah is in Inverness. We will not ask Edgar's family to shelter us as well," Papa said.

"Papa," Rachel said. "Perhaps we need to listen to him. We lived under Edward's rule and look what happened. We can leave—"

"No. I am finished running and letting others defend me. If war comes, I will face it here, in my home. Berwick may come under English rule, but we lived for years under English rule and came to no harm."

"Ye saw what Langton did here!" Kieran cried. "Now think of it a thousandfold, a thousand Langtons in Berwick. Is it defiance, or is it stubbornness that keeps ye here? I rode for two days to get here to warn ye. Ye must leave. Please. I beg ye to go, or at least let Rachel come with me."

"Which was your goal in coming here, was it not?" Papa asked.

"Of course it was! Like it or not, sir, I care deeply for her. I told ye, and Mosheh, and all who would listen, that I would keep her safe. That's what I'm here for. If ye love yer daughter, ye'll send her away."

"I do love my daughter, sir. And it's you I'm sending away. Leave now, if you will. I'm finished listening to your insults and empty promises. I asked you to bring Isabel back to us, and you swore you would, but did you? No. And now, using Edward as your excuse, you want to take my daughter, which you planned to do all along. I welcomed you before, but no longer, Kieran MacDonald. Get out of my house."

"Jacob," Mama said. "I know he's said it all wrong, but we should listen."

"No!" Papa said to her, his voice tight with control. "This man has done nothing but destroy our daughter. She would have been happy with Mosheh if he had not come wooing her again. Every time she starts to be happy, he arrives with something that makes her cry. King Edward may come close, and he may threaten, but do any of you believe he will do more than that? Why would he? Berwick is wealthy and prosperous. He'll not attack us. He'll tax us! Now get out of my house, Kieran MacDonald, and do not return."

Kieran spun on his heel and left without a word. Rachel looked at her father, his face scarlet with anger, and at her mother, shaking her head. And ran after Kieran. She caught him in the street, almost in front of the butcher shop, Mosheh's now that his father had died.

"Kieran! Stop! Wait!" she called.

He whirled to face her. "I'm not leaving ye behind this time, Rachel."

"It certainly looks like you are."

"Are ye coming with me? Now, this moment? Are ye coming with me?"

"No. I cannot simply leave. Let me talk with them again."

"Meet me tonight. In the square next to the church, lass. Say ye will."

"To talk. Only to talk, Kieran. Let my father calm down. You insulted him."

"He is easily upset. I dinna understand the man. Ye may all be facing a siege here and he's worried about me insulting him! What happened to the Jacob I remember?"

"He's been battered, Kieran. By King Edward, by Walter Langton. Even by Isabel, who thought she was protecting us but made him feel ineffective. Do you not see? Life has piled one thing atop another to defeat him! He did not want me to marry outside the faith, and I played the dutiful daughter, but not well enough to fool anyone. He wants me to be happy, but I am not. It is always between us."

He pulled her to him and kissed her fervently, then released her. "Tonight, ten o'clock, Rachel. Dress warmly, for we will stay outside. Promise me ye'll come."

"I will be there."

Papa said nothing to her when she returned, but Mama pulled her aside.

"I will talk to him," Mama said. "Perhaps, in a few days, he will see sense in what Kieran says. But right now, after all that has happened with you and Kieran and Mosheh, Kieran could tell him that the sky was blue and your father would not believe it. Give me some time, and I will make him see sense." At Rachel's nod, she continued. "Now go and see your husband. Tell him what Kieran says. And ask him if we should leave. If Mosheh thinks we should go, your father will listen."

Rachel sighed. "I will."

She ran down the street again, to knock at Mosheh's door. There was no answer. She lifted her hand to knock again, pausing as she heard voices within. Mosheh's, talking softly, his tone tender. A woman answering. Rachel stepped back from the door and stared at it, her emotions spinning. Then she went back to the inn.

At ten that night, she wrapped her heaviest cloak around her and went to meet Kieran. She waited, not sure where he was, relieved when he stepped from the shadows of the church, his horse's reins in his hand.

"Thank ye for coming, lass," he said. "Ye'll not regret it."

"I hope I do not."

"Walk with me to the city gates, aye? We can talk on the way."

She did, listening as he told her all that had happened in Newcastle, and that Isabel was now safely in Stirling with his aunt Nell. Of his certainty that King Edward was approaching.

"Stay a day," she said. "Two, perhaps, and my father may change his mind."

"We dinna have that much time, lass." He glanced at the gate. "Even now, kenning what could be on the way, yer city leaders dinna man the gate properly. Look, it lies open with no one around."

She turned to look, then turned back at the movement behind her. He had vaulted into the saddle and leaned down to her now.

"Kiss me, Rachel. Please, lass. It's time to go."

His tone was so intense that she did not stop to think but raised her arms to meet his, raised her mouth to his. He lifted her, almost into the saddle, then farther, onto his lap, his lips still on hers. The horse moved forward.

"What?" she gasped, turning to look.

His hand clamped over her mouth, and he pressed her against his chest. "Ye're coming with me, Rachel. Willing or no, I'm not leaving ye here."

She opened her mouth to argue, but he tightened his grip on her mouth and kicked the horse into a gallop. They flew through the gate and down the hill toward the harbor, veering sharply to take the road along the river.

He did not let her go, nor did he stop the horse until Berwick was an hour away, then another.

She'd stopped struggling long before, hanging on to his arms and the horse's mane and wondering if he'd gone mad. Or if she had as well, for she had not fought this abduction. She could think of nothing to say to him that would make sense. She loved him, but she was appalled at what he'd done. And much more so that she had let him do it.

"Stop," she said at last. "Kieran, stop. We must talk."

"We're going to Stirling, Rachel. Nell will take ye in. And Isabel is there."

"Kieran, stop or I'll jump off this horse."

He tightened his arm around her waist.

Her anger was late, but strong now. "As much as I'd like to see Isabel, I am not going to Stirling. This is madness. Stop the horse."

He did, slowing it to a walk, then stopping under the shelter of a large oak tree. She slid to the ground and walked stiffly as he did the same.

"You cannot do this!"

"It's already done, Rachel. Ye dinna understand! I've been on the borders. I've seen the might that Edward brings with him. I've heard of what he's done in Wales! What makes ye think he'll suddenly show benevolence to Berwick? It's madness to think that!"

"Then all the more reason I cannot leave! I must convince my parents to leave. And Mosheh. I must make them believe it. I am going back."

"That is madness!" he shouted.

"No! This is madness! I am another man's wife! And until I am not, there can be nothing between us. I cannot ride off to Stirling with you and pretend I am free of the past. If those I love are in danger, I need to convince them to take action! I am going back!"

She threw her hair over her shoulder and marched to the road. The moonlight was faint but strong enough to let her see the path, and she walked quickly, not sure whether to be angry or hurt that he did not follow. The moon lit her way, for which she was grateful. It crossed the sky and her pace slowed.

She heard the horse before she saw it, and was deciding where to hide when she recognized Kieran atop it. He slowed as he saw her, drawing near without speaking. She turned her back to him and continued to walk. He was silent for some time, then slid from the horse to join her.

"Ye are determined, then, Rachel?"

"I am."

"Ah."

She threw him a glance, not sure what his calm manner meant. "Are you coming with me?"

"I am. We should be at Stirling before long at this pace."

"I'm not going to Stirling, Kieran. I thought I'd made that clear."

She could see his smile even in the dim light.

"Ye're walking north, lass. Berwick is behind us."

She halted.

"I'll take ye back, Rachel, if that's what ye wish. But not to stay. Only to see if we can get the rest of them to leave. I willna let ye stay there."

"You cannot tell me what to do, Kieran."

He did not answer but leaned to kiss her, his fingers slipping around her neck, his touch gentle. "If ye willna leave Berwick, Rachel, I will stay there with ye. If ye are in danger, then I will be as well. And if we canna live together, then we'll die together."

She could not speak.

"There's a cottage nearby. We'll go back in the morning, aye?"

The cottagers took them in, fed them, and let them sleep on the floor. They were careful not to touch each other.

The next day, hampered by a drenching rainstorm, they made only a few miles, finding shelter in an abbey close to the border, hearing there that Edward's army had advanced on Berwick and demanded its surrender. The city's leaders had refused, taunting Edward, referring to the Scots' long-standing joke that all Englishmen had tails, calling them dogs of war. Rachel was adamant that they try to get her parents out.

But it was too late. Edward took Berwick in a day.

They continued south, the weather clear again. They could see the fires as they approached the city. The roads were clogged by those who lived near Berwick escaping north, who told them that Edward himself had led the attack, leaping his warhorse Byward over the earthenworks that had been meant to keep him out.

"They're killing everyone," one man said. "You could hear the screams."

His wife nodded, sobbing. "My sister is in there."

"He has thirty thousand infantry and five thousand cavalry," the man said. "No one has come out since he rode in. No one. And there is no escape by water. Four of his ships went aground on the river, blocking that route. The townspeople burnt them. They're paying for that now. It's a massacre."

* * *

The killing went on for three days. At least twenty thousand
died, perhaps more. The city was sacked. Merchants were
murdered, their goods confiscated, their homes set aflame.
The Flemish had held out the longest, barricaded in the
Red Hall, which was burnt to the ground with them in it. It
was said that Edward let the killing continue until he saw a
woman giving birth as she was being hacked to death. And
then it stopped. There was not a building left untouched
except the castle, which had been surrendered. Edward
moved part of his army into the town and announced that
Berwick was now English. He invited the Northumbrians
to come and claim a home there, saying that Berwick
would now be rebuilt as a fortified outpost.

Kieran and Rachel went as close to the city as they
dared. Rachel wanted to go closer, but Kieran refused,
saying that what they'd heard from all who'd passed made
it impossible to think her parents had lived through it.
They were not alone in their vigil. Hundreds had gathered, waiting to hear word of loved ones. On the fourth
day they heard.

The man had been an innkeeper in Berwick and well
known to Rachel and her family. He was trudging north
alone, his shoulders slumped and filthy, but answering,
with a calm manner, the questions of those who waited.
He did not know most of those who were asked after, he
said. But then he saw Rachel. He stared at her, his mouth
working. His chin trembled, and silent tears streamed
down his cheeks.

"They are all dead, Rachel. All. They left me for dead
and I was able to scramble over the wall and down Breakneck Stairs to the river. My wife is dead. My son is dead."

He stopped, his whole body trembling now. "Your father fought valiantly. He and Gilbert held them off the best they could. But they killed him anyway. And Gilbert. And your mother. Mosheh barricaded himself in the shop. He was burnt. They are gone, too. All dead. All of Berwick is dead. They were not men who did this. They were demons. I am sorry, Rachel. They are all gone." He shook his head, almost a tremor, then shuffled north again. He did not turn to look back.

Rachel did not speak but sank to the ground with a wail, huddling on the dirt. As spasms of grief washed through her, all her regrets bombarded her. Kieran patted her back but did not try to comfort her. There was no comfort. There was no God. The God that her father had prayed to, had relied on, had abandoned them yet again.

At last, when word came that Edward's army was moving north, she let Kieran take her to Stirling. She was numb for most of the journey. They spoke almost not at all.

Kieran gave his name at the gate, telling her through their long wait that Nell would be happy to see them. But the woman who greeted them, when at last they were admitted, was not happy. Tears streaked her face. She hurried forward to throw her arms around Kieran with a hoarse cry.

"I thought you were still there! Dear God, Kieran, I thought you must be dead. And you must be Rachel. Only you two? No one else?"

"No," Kieran said. "Only us."

She wrapped Rachel in her embrace. "I am so sorry, lass. I am so sorry. Come, let us find Isabel."

* * *

On April 5, 1296, King John renounced his fealty to Edward of England. The letter was polite and dignified, but weak, as the man himself was. It was a list of grievances that moved no one, not the Scots who had hoped for so much more for their king. And not Edward, who shot back one brutal sentence: "Be it unto the fool according to his folly."

Edward moved north, to Dunbar, taking it with ease, destroying much of the infantry and taking many of rank as prisoners. When he turned his army toward Stirling, Rachel, with Nell and Isabel, fled westward finding refuge with Rory's mother, Margaret, at Loch Gannon. And none too soon. Edward took Stirling with no resistance.

It was wonderful being with Isabel once again, Rachel thought as she walked along the shore of the sea loch. Fascinating to see the changes in her friend that being married and with child brought. But her happiness for Isabel was a reminder of her own losses. Her parents were dead. She was a widow. But she could not bear to dwell on that. She was at Loch Gannon, had been welcomed by Rory's mother with a warmth that seemed genuine, and she should look no further than that. She would not think of Kieran, or wonder what they would do, when this war was over, with whatever it was that lay between them. She observed Shabbat alone now, praying the prayers from memory. But the words rang hollow, and she was convinced that there was no one listening. She looked over the water and tried not to think.

"Here you are," Isabel said, coming to stand next to her.

Isabel's body was changing, the first signs of childbearing just beginning to be visible. Rachel watched her friend pick her way carefully over the rocks on the shore, and for the first time Rachel wondered why she had never conceived. All those times with Mosheh, and she'd not borne him a child. She'd not thought of it often, but it did seem strange now to contemplate. Perhaps it was just as well, for wouldn't that have altered everything? Or perhaps a child would have been just the thing to help her forget Kieran. But if she had borne a child, she and the baby would have been in Berwick. And dead now.

"How are you?" Isabel asked quietly.

Rachel shook her head. "I do not know. I feel like I have been transported to a different time. I cannot believe my parents and Mosheh are dead. None of the things we do after a death have been done, and there is only me to do them. Our traditions need people to do them with, Isabel, and there is no one."

"I am here."

"You are not a Jew."

"No. But I am a friend. Tell me what you need."

The words came first, spoken without thought, surprising her with their intensity. "I need to sit shiva."

"What does that mean?"

"Shiva means seven. For seven days we go out of the house only if necessary. We do not work. We think about the ones who have died, and their souls. And we pray. We sit low to the ground, sometimes on special chairs. And there is a candle . . ." She met Isabel's gaze. "I should have torn my clothes to show my grief. On the left side for my parents. But for Mosheh . . . I do not know all of it. I do not know all of it, Isabel! I should know my traditions, should know the prayers. I thought I did, but now, when I need them, I'm not sure! How can I not know? Why did I not listen?"

"You are too hard on yourself, Rachel! You never thought to be in this situation. If your mother were here, she would tell you the same thing."

"But she's not." Rachel was sobbing now. "Isabel, I am the only one left! Sarah is somewhere in the north—I do not even know where. She probably does not know yet! I need to sit shiva. Help me bury them in my mind."

Margaret was most accommodating, if mystified. She provided a chair that could have its legs shortened, and the candle that would burn for seven days and seven nights. And offered her company if Rachel desired it.

"You are not alone, Rachel," Margaret said. "All of Scotland is in mourning. We have all lost loved ones. Let us help you."

It was, Rachel decided much later, quite possibly the strangest shiva anyone had ever sat. But it helped. She spent the seven days almost alone, in a small room near the chapel Rory's father had built, praying. Crying. Remembering. Feeling isolated in a castle in the west, very far from home.

Time helped. It did not erase the pain, but it made her review all that had happened to her family since they'd left England. She realized, as she had not during it all, that in retrospect it all seemed so inevitable. So many pieces had had to fall a certain way for things to have come out as they had, and over and over she saw the same patterns. And no God in any of it.

But that belief, or lack of belief, was tested sorely the night that Isabel gave birth to her daughter. The labor was long, and exhausting, and after a day Margaret and Nell were exchanging looks that let Rachel know that something was amiss. She sat with Isabel, wishing they could change places so she could bear some of her friend's pain. She surprised herself by praying, and even, in the wee hours, when Isabel fell into an exhausted slumber, crossed the courtyard and found refuge in the chapel there, praying to a God she feared did not exist. For Isabel. For the babe, still facing the journey of birth. For Rory to come home. She could not bear it if anything happened to Isabel. Could not bear to think of Rory's pain if they lost her. And so she prayed again, aware of the irony of a Jew praying in a Christian church at the edge of the world.

But her prayers were answered. Rory arrived the next morning, haggard but driven, his father with him. Gannon told Rachel later that he'd dreamed that Rory needed to be home. And by that afternoon, September 7, 1296, Margaret Rachel MacGannon entered the world with a lusty cry. Rachel wept with joy, embracing Margaret and Nell and Gannon and finally Rory and Isabel when she could, seeing Rory's pride and tenderness, and Isabel's fierce and instant love for that tiny babe.

When she held the child she looked at all of them, and for the first time, felt like she had begun to heal and that perhaps life would go on. But she wondered, late in the night, when all was still, whether she and her sister would ever be reunited. And Kieran. She prayed for peace. But there was no peace outside Loch Gannon.

It was as Gannon had dreamed all those years ago. He was going to war with his sons. Margaret tried to come to terms with it, telling herself that Gannon had not dreamed of their deaths. Or had he, and not told her?

It was a bittersweet time, to have her granddaughter

come into the world and see her son go off to war. He looked so young, this tall and handsome man that her boy had become. A father himself now, a proud father, who she now had to share with Isabel and the babe. And she was pleased to do so, for she had grown to love this daughter-in-law of hers, beautiful on the exterior and as strong as steel within. And devoted to Rory—so different from Jocelyn, who had never looked at Magnus as Isabel looked at Rory. Who had never wept when Magnus had departed. Who had never borne him a child.

It was amazing to hold the baby in her arms and remember Rory and Magnus at that age. How long ago it seemed. And yet it was but yesterday.

And now war. For what? What would all this death and expense prove? Even if Edward defeated the Scottish forces, he would never tame Scotland. And while she was proud of the defiance of the Scots, she feared it as well. Loch Gannon might be far from Edinburgh and a world away from London, but it was not far enough to guarantee their safety.

She went to the chapel and prayed for the safety of her men, for Gannon, Magnus, and Rory. And her brother Davey and Kieran, and Liam, and so very many more, their faces passing before her in a steady stream. How many other women had prayed the same prayer over the centuries, and how many more would pray it after her, when all of this was only a distant memory? *Bring my men home safely to me.* There was no answer.

She was not alone in her suffering, she realized when she found Isabel crying one morning. Margaret sat with her and patted her shoulder.

"How do you go on, Margaret?" Isabel asked. "How

do you do it, find such strength? I thought I was strong, but this waiting, wondering, is too much to bear."

"Ye are strong, lass. But ye are a woman, and that means ye are not invincible. How does one go on? How does one get up and face another day? Another night in the dark without sleep? I have no answer, nor even a hint of how it is done. We women are doomed, by the sin of Eve we are told, but who could ever have fathomed such punishment for the sin of knowledge, this suffering the loss of those we love and no end to the suffering but death? Those of us who have others depending on us to be strong, to feed and clothe them, to lead them, to mother them, to protect them, we have not the luxury of finding oblivion. And so we rise each day, and find a way through the endless hours to put food on the table and clean sheets on the beds, and then we wait for the next dawn and do it all again. Here we are, the two of us, united by the love we bear for one man, both of us fearing that each day will bring news we canna bear to hear."

"Is this war worth the suffering?"

"Is any war worth the suffering, lass? I dinna ken. It is a wondrous thing to be free, and we Scots will never be free under the yoke of a king such as Edward."

She sighed. "The cruelest thing is to be the one who waits. We will go on, ye and I, if for no other reason than for the babe ye just bore. She is our link to eternity. And to the past. She is all of us and I welcome her. And no matter what happens, Isabel, I beg ye to stay here with us and make this yer home. It is all we have to offer, Gannon and I, our home and our hearts."

Isabel's tears streamed down her face. "Oh, yes, I will stay, and I will thank you with each breath I take."

Margaret laughed softly. "Oh, please dinna do that. There are so many other things we have to talk on." She drew Isabel into her embrace. "We will go on, lass. I dinna ken how, but we will go on. And God willing, they will be home soon."

Brave words, Margaret told herself in the night. *Brave words.* She rose from her bed and went to the chapel.

Within six months Edward had decimated Balliol's army, and at Montrose he humiliated Balliol once again, tearing his coat of arms from his clothing and saying that henceforth Scotland had no king but him. He appointed an English viceroy to govern. At Scone he pillaged the Stone of Destiny, where every Scottish king had been crowned for centuries, and stole the most sacred relic in Scotland, the Black Rood of St. Margaret. As Edward crossed the border into England, he was said to be pleased with his success.

"A man does good business," he was quoted as saying, "when he rids himself of a turd."

Scotland was now an occupied land, English soldiers in every city, castle, and port. There was no one to threaten Edward's control. For a while.

TWENTY-FOUR

She's dead," Kieran said.

Rory looked from his cousin to William, across the glade. "What happened?"

"We couldna stop him from going to see her again, even after what happened last time," Kieran whispered. "The English were watching her. When William arrived, they engaged him. He fought them and escaped, but when he went back for her, he found that they had slit her throat and burnt the house down around her."

"Jesu," Rory said. William had gone to Lanark to see his wife, Marion Braidfute, yet again, despite the danger. Only a short time before William had had to fight his way out of the town, and they'd warned him not to return to her. But he had, as Rory himself would have. He remembered William laughing at him, years ago now, for being in love with Isabel and his telling William that someday he, too, would be in love. He wished now that it had never come to be.

"It was Hazelrig."

"The soldier who was trying to marry Marion to his son?"

"Aye," Kieran said. "And tonight we're going after him."

Rory wiped his hand over his face and lay back, staring up at the ancient oak tree. Oak, he thought. It had been more than a year since Berwick had fallen, a year of fighting and losing. He had not been captured in the defeat at Dunbar, but many Scots had been. Some had been ransomed, but many still languished in prison, in England, in homes around England, or in the Tower. He thought of his time in Newcastle and sent strength to those who had lost their freedom.

His father had stayed closer to home, incensed that English troops were quartered all too close to his lands. Liam had gone back to Ayrshire to protect his home there. And Magnus, alone now, had done the same. Jocelyn had left him when Gannon had refused to fight alongside John Comyn. She'd given Magnus a choice: join her family or lose her, and when he'd refused, she'd left. His brother was bitter, saying she expected him to go after her and beg her forgiveness. And this time he wouldn't. It was hard to imagine Magnus without Jocelyn. Or himself without Isabel.

Or William without Marion.

It had been amusing at first to see the big man fall in love and celebrate with him when he'd married her. Rory had spent a great deal of time accompanying William to Lanark so he could be with Marion, and in return he'd enjoyed William's blessing when he'd ridden across the country to see Isabel. And his daughter. His little Maggie. Just her name brought him joy, and he conjured that wee face with the bright blue eyes. He'd been altered forever when he had held his tiny daughter for the first time. They were a family now, separated temporarily by the madness of war and defeat, but not forever, he swore. Not forever.

He'd been with William and Kieran since her birth. In Ayrshire for part of the time, close enough to occasionally go home to Loch Gannon and see Isabel. Kieran often came with him, for Rachel was there as well, but she was different now, withdrawn most of the time. Kieran had taken her back to Berwick a month after it had been taken, sneaking into the fortified city in disguise. Her parents and Gilbert were dead but not yet buried, and Kieran had done that, digging the graves himself in the yard behind the inn. Kieran had told Rory that bodies still lay in buildings everywhere, and that the inn had been too damaged to repair. They'd found Mosheh as well, and buried him, too. Rachel had been inconsolable, but she'd let Kieran bring her back to Loch Gannon. He hoped for more, but he told Rory he was content to wait.

The end of The Oak and The Ash, Rory thought, and of so many things and people. Scotland was a fiefdom under siege, and Edward was cruel in his victory. They had thought the earlier occupation had been harsh, but it had been nothing compared to this. There was no one to stop the abuses. Except them—he and William and Kieran and the others. And that is what he'd been doing since Berwick fell. They had raided forts, attacked supply trains, and ambushed troops coming to replenish men at outposts. Rory and Kieran had been all over Scotland, talking to clans and nobles, their visits welcomed but often fruitless.

"Where's their child?" Rory asked as the thought came

to him. He sat up. "Where is William and Marion's bairn, the wee lass?"

"With Marion's cousin, thank God, or she would be dead as well."

"Thank God indeed," Rory said.

"Tonight," Kieran said, "we'll go for Hazelrig."

Rory nodded. And they did.

William was never the same after Marion's death. In the past his moods had fluctuated, as all theirs had, from sadness over Scotland's plight, to anger at the king who had engineered it with the acquiescence of their own king and nobles, and fervent belief that this was only temporary. But after Marion's murder, William was a man possessed. No Englishman who came into his path, even those who had committed no act against him, was left alive. No one who supported the English went unpunished. William was driven. Relentless.

In the north, Andrew Moray—whose father had been a prisoner in the Tower since Dunbar—raised troops in rebellion, but few joined him. William had more success among the ordinary men of the southwest, who flocked to him. There were skirmishes and some routings, many more triumphs. And as their successes grew, the English ratched up the pressure to find William Wallace and his men and destroy them.

In April, 360 of the leading Scots of Ayr were summoned by the circuit court to a meeting at the Barns of Ayr, as the barracks there were called, Sir Ranald Crawford, Liam and William's uncle, among them. One by one the men were admitted. And one by one, hanged. Sir Ranald was the first to die. Kennedys, Campbells, Barclays, Boyds, Stewarts, Sir Bruce Blair, Sir Neil Montgomery, all murdered. William had been summoned as well, but he had refused to go. And lived to avenge the dead, attacking the Barns of Ayr and taking it and the castle in bloody revenge.

The next months were a frenzy of battles as William continued to succeed and men flocked to him from every part of the country. His cousins, both Wallace and Crawford, were with him, including Sir Ranald's sons. And Liam was there through it all. By June so were Gannon and Magnus.

They killed Lord Percy and threatened to take Bishop Bek. Edward of England raised the bounty on William's head, and the nobles of Scotland vacillated between paying homage to Edward and supporting William—but only with words. It was the ordinary men who fought with William at Glasgow and Ormsby, where Sir William Douglas joined him, among the first of the nobles to do so. And slowly the tide turned. With each success William experienced, more men joined him, and the greater the attention the nobles paid him. None more than Robert the Bruce, Earl of Carrick.

When Edward heard that Douglas had joined the rebels, he sent orders to Robert Bruce to take a force and seize Douglas's castle. Before Bruce was to leave, he was to swear, yet again, his fealty to Edward. Robert refused. Instead, he left Carlisle and rode through Annandale, summoning his father's vassals to join him in taking up arms. At an assembly of his knights, he said, "No man holds his own flesh and blood in hatred and I am no exception. I must join my own people and the nation in which I was born. Choose then, whether you go with me or return to your homes."

Many stayed with him, but not all. He had better fortune in Carrick, where they joined him almost to a man. He met the Scottish forces, led by a contingent of nobles, in Irvine. William, with his own troops farther west, was not among them; he welcomed Robert's newfound patriotism with wariness.

The army led by the nobles of Scotland enjoined Edward's troops on July 7. And were defeated. Many were forced to produce hostages to prove their good faith. Robert the Bruce was told to surrender his infant daughter, Marjorie, but he refused, and the die was cast. He would not return to Edward's good graces again. William did not surrender, nor did he agree to produce any hostages, and he and his men continued to defy Edward in Balliol's name.

And then, just when the Scots needed it, Edward left England, sailing to Flanders on August 22, to lead his troops there, leaving his army in Scotland under the leadership of the aging and infirm John de Warenne and Edward's treasurer, Hugh Cressingham, a brutal but effective leader. Warenne went north, to Stirling, to meet Cressingham.

Sir Andrew de Moray had joined forces with William earlier in August, and together they went to meet Edward's army. The north was at last free of English control. Their forces were now 40,000 strong, with 180 horse. Among the horse were Rory, Kieran, Magnus, and their fathers and uncles. The Scottish forces arrived first.

On September 9, 1297, Warenne camped his men in a bend of the river opposite the wooden bridge, the causeway below Stirling Castle, the only passage over the area called the Scots Sea, for the Forth was tidal even this far inland. The marshy meadows around the mount upon which Stirling Castle stood could be treacherous and had often been the only deterrent to armies taking the castle. Stirling was the key to the Highlands, and it was now in Scottish hands. And only William and de Moray's forces were left to hold it.

On September 10, John de Warenne dispatched two friars to talk with William.

"We bring you an invitation," the friars said, "for you and your men to come to the king's peace. Our lord Edward promises impunity for past offenses."

"Take back for an answer," William said, "that we are not here to make peace but are ready to fight for the freedom of ourselves and of our country. Let the English come on when they please."

The friars frowned and rode away.

"Freedom!" William shouted after them, the cry echoed by his men, Rory's cry among them.

On September 11, the battle was enjoined.

The Scots knew what was at stake this day. The common men were in the majority of the forces here, and they knew that the winner of this battle would rule Scotland, if only for a time. If they lost, they and their families would pay the price of the defeat in blood. There would be no hostages, no ransoms of these men. Yet if they won, the nobles would claim the victory as their own.

They faced battle-hardened soldiers, some of whom had fought with Edward in the Holy Land, many more in France and Wales. The English were well armed, well trained, and well fed. The Scots had few nobles among them. The leaders of the strongest families in Scotland either backed Edward or had been decimated by the defeats at Dunbar and Irvine and lay in prison in the Tower, or their actions were circumscribed by worries for the safety of the family members they had been forced to surrender into Edward's control.

William chose his spot well, on the flanks of the foothills near Abbey Craig. Below them lay a loop of the River Forth, crossed by Stirling Bridge, that linked to the causeway. To the north and east the majestic Ochil Hills rose from the plain; the river lay to the south, and beyond it, the village of Stirling, on the mound that rose high above the surrounding landscape. The wooden bridge was ninety or so feet long, only wide enough for two horsemen, and the causeway beyond it the same width. The marshland on either side was too swampy to hold an armored warhorse. With the foothills at their back, and on higher ground than the English, they could afford to wait for the enemy to come to them.

It was said that Warenne distrusted the English field position and delayed yet again. But Cressingham, clergyman though he was, and despised by his own men, urged immediate action in the most haughty and nondiplomatic terms. He led the English troops across the bridge, the column advancing most of the morning.

The men around Rory were restless, but he told them to be calm, to wait. He had been among those who had devised their strategy, but the final plan was William's. Rory waited for the signal and watched the heavily armored knights advance. Their huge warhorses were armored as well, some beplumed. Overhead the bright banners of the knights and barons flew, the colors catching the sun that glinted off the armor and weapons.

Like the others, Rory wore a breastplate, chainmail gloves, and mail over his arms and head. And a helmet of gray steel, made just for him, with a cluster of oak leaves at the crest. The nose guard impeded his view and made the world seem at the end of a tunnel, but he wore it, for he was determined to live through this day. Magnus wore a helmet that had once belonged to Rory's namesake, Rory O'Neill, long gone but with them in spirit, Gannon told them. They would need him this day.

"How many do they have?" Kieran asked.

"I've heard fifty thousand," Rory said. "And five hundred horse."

He did not tally the difference for his cousin. They waited. Rory battled his own impatience, reminding himself of their plan. And that these moments, spent in armor on the side of a hill, might be among his last. If they attacked too soon, they would wipe out the advance of the English army but leave the bulk of it intact. If they waited too long, their own ranks would be overwhelmed and outnumbered. So they waited, watching as the slow procession continued.

At eleven o'clock, the sun high in the sky, William sent the signal, one long blast of his horn, and the Scots moved forward with a roar of anticipation. Rory leaned low over his horse as they raced forward, his war cry joining the others. He raised his sword among the spears and battle axes around him. His father was at his side, Magnus just beyond. And there was Davey, and Kieran, and all the others, the friends and kin, swords lifted and battle cries loud. He said a prayer that they would survive this day. They would be among the first into the battle. The earth shook as they raced down the hill and across the soft ground to the head of the bridge.

They met the enemy with a clash of metal and a primal roar. The English were unprepared for the onslaught. It was a blur, of steel on steel, and men's shouts of triumph and screams of agony.

"On them! On them! On them!" William shouted.

They slashed their way through the knights to the head of the bridge. There was a stampede by those left on the wooden structure. Some panicked and whirled, causing the horses to rear and create even more confusion. Horses and riders were forced into the river. Most, weighed down by their armor, did not surface again. Some jumped into the water and were not seen again.

The fighting was vicious, but it soon became apparent that the Scots were pressing their advantage. Some of the English knights tried to retreat back across the bridge, hampering the advance of their own reinforcements.

Some fought valiantly, facing the Scots with measured strokes and sometimes successful thrusts, but it was in vain, for they were trapped. The Scots squeezed them together. As the death toll mounted and fewer knights were left to fight, there was more room on the bridge. Individual battles replaced the larger movements. Rory's horse was killed, and he jumped to the ground to fight on foot.

One knight, still on horseback, fought off every opponent, cutting a swathe through the Scots. Rory withdrew his sword from the man he'd just slain just in time to face that knight bearing down on him, sword raised. Rory flashed his sword before the horse, which reared, reaching for him with its hooves.

As he darted out of the way of the flailing hooves, he knew he should thrust his sword into the exposed belly of the horse and refuse to hear the animal's scream, but he could not kill this magnificent creature.

He waited for the horse to settle, then he leapt at the knight, dragging him to the ground. The knight staggered but did not fall, his sword raised and at the ready. Rory circled him, leaning back out of reach when the knight thrust forward, then slashing at the man's knees, and missing when the knight moved away.

They parried each other's blows, their swords clashing together in shivering metallic squeals, falling away, only to be lifted again. The rest of the world faded. Rory saw only this man, this knight, this opponent, who seemed to personify all of England's efforts, his persistence and refusal to yield earning both Rory's hatred and respect.

Finally, one of Rory's blows landed, and another, and the knight staggered backward, the wounds to his arm and leg forcing his sword to fall and he to lurch to the side. Rory waited while the man recovered and once again faced his sword.

The knight's blade tore a hole in Rory's arm mail. The wound was not deep, but it bled profusely, his blood streaming down to his hand, making his grip tenuous. The knight struck again, high, hitting Rory with the flat of the blade on his temple. The metal of his helmet dug into his skin, and blood gushed into his eyes. He smeared it away. The knight swung again, but too high.

Rory gripped his sword with both hands and swung wide, feeling his sword hit the other's side and sink into flesh. And then again, the same blow, this time hitting the knight's sword. It flew from the knight's hand. Rory leapt forward, his blade at the man's throat, forcing him to his knees. He ripped the knight's visor up.

Henry de Boyer looked back at him.

Rory froze, a roaring in his ears. He tore his helmet off and let it fall to the planks of the bridge. And saw Henry's surprise, heard his quick intake of breath.

"Rory MacGannon. Of course. How could we not meet here?"

"Henry de Boyer. How could we not?"

Rory shifted his grip on his sword, and Henry gave it a glance, then looked into Rory's eyes.

"Do it. Take your prize, sir."

Isabel's face swam before Rory, laughing, lifting the crown of pine boughs. The Holly King and the Oak King. All that had happened since.

He shook his head. "I cannot. Stand up, Henry."

"We are enemies, sir. Your side has won the day. Do it."

Rory glanced around then to see that Henry was right. The fighting was all but over. On the shore, the Scots were raising their voices in victory cries.

"I cannot, Henry. You will have to live."

De Boyer struggled to his feet. Rory almost reached to help him, but he did not, watching as the knight at last stood upright. They stared at each other. Rory sheathed his sword.

"Ye'll be a prisoner, Henry, as I was. I'm hoping we treat ye more kindly."

Henry opened his mouth to answer, then jerked forward, his body falling into Rory's from the blow to his back. His mouth worked, and he slumped heavily. Rory clasped Henry to him, looking over Henry's head and into the eyes of a young man—a boy, really, his eyes wild. The boy let out a triumphal shout and raised his ax to strike again.

"No!" Rory shouted, dragging Henry back with him.

He was too late. The blade fell, knocking them both to the bridge with the force of it. Rory pushed Henry off him, then leaned over the knight. Henry took a quivering breath.

"Our rivalry is over, sir. I yield to you," he said.

His eyes rolled up in his head. He exhaled, slowly. And then Henry de Boyer died.

"I'm sorry, sir," the boy said. "Did ye want to ransom him?"

Rory could not speak.

The world was celebrating their victory. The people, who had been noticeably absent earlier, came streaming from the hillsides and villages. Rory watched them join the Scots. Around him he heard prayers being uttered in several languages, priests, some of whom had fought with them, giving the Last Rites. The groans of the injured and dying mingled with the prayers. Victory.

Rory looked down at his hand, covered with blood. Some his, some Henry's, mingled in death as they never would have been in life. He saw his father, pushing through the crowd toward him, and Magnus on the far side of the river, bending over someone on the ground. And there were Kieran and Davey, a wounded man's arms over their shoulders. William, being lifted atop men's shoulders.

Alive. Victory. He felt nothing.

Few of the English forces were left. The Scots took no prisoners. Some of the foot soldiers threw off their armor and swam across the river to safety, and many still on the far side of the river turned and ran for their lives. In the castle, the English commander called for his men to retreat, and they abandoned the castle, riding southward instead of aiding the stricken army.

Rory rode with William and the others, harrying the English all the way to the banks of the River Tweed, greatly reducing their ranks.

And then they turned north. It was over.

He sat with the others that night, in the Great Hall of Stirling Castle, drinking the finest wine he'd ever had and tasting none of it. Victory was not sweet. It tasted like dust in his mouth.

William was dancing now, his long limbs moving like creatures themselves, his laughter mingling with the others'. Magnus was there with him, and Kieran. Liam was seated by the wall with Gannon and Davey. Somewhere a woman laughed, the sound merry and strange in the sea of men's voices. Outside men were still dying of their wounds, and the dead lay in rows to be buried. And Andrew de Moray battled yet again, struggling to stay alive after being badly wounded. The Scots had suffered few other casualties. Ninety thousand men and few Scots among the dead. He should be crowing with the others, but he could not stand any more. He left the hall, left the castle. He made his way to the bridge, standing at the spot where Henry had died, and stared at the water. Remembering.

"What brutes we men are, aye?"

His father's voice came from behind him. Rory did not turn as Gannon came to stand at his side. Around him men were dragging bodies from the battlefield, laying them in long rows and removing the valuables.

"I heard they flailed Cressingham's skin and are handing out pieces of it like prizes at a fair," Gannon said. "That his own men wanted to stone him alive for his many sins. We were fortunate this day that Edward was not here, for he would have seen through our strategy. He would not have taken this field against us."

Rory did not speak.

Gannon put a hand on Rory's shoulder. "The gods left ye alive, and for that I am grateful, and for our victory. But there is no glory in this or any other battle when men seek to kill each other. That's the revulsion and the grandeur of war, lad. Skillful men in both armies, intelligent men, who put all their effort into destroying the other side. There is an evil beauty about it, and a horror here that will never leave ye. Ye will never be the same, nor should ye be."

"Why are men like this? Why do we kill?"

"I dinna ken. Some of us seek it. The rest of us endure it, God willing. I'm glad ye lived through this day. I'm surprised I did."

"I'm damned glad ye lived through the day, Da."

"Leave it at damned, lad, for we all are. It's far from over, this war we're in. Come, have a cup of wine with yer ancient father. A wise man does not celebrate. He gives thanks that he's been given another day. And prays for peace."

Isabel could not bear the waiting any longer. Nor could Margaret, or Nell, who suggested the journey. Nor Rachel, who was finally coming back to the world. Isabel left her daughter Maggie at Loch Gannon, in the care of her nurse, with instructions to write to her grandmother in London if she did not return. They rode east, toward Stirling, joined by many other women. The ride was simple. And impossibly long. But at last they neared Stirling plain and heard the news. The battle had been enjoined the day before. Victory. There had been remarkably few injuries and deaths in the Scottish ranks, and the men were celebrating.

The plain was littered with the dead, laid in tidy rows awaiting burial. A pile of armor glinted in the sun, bright flashes of light amidst the russet and amber flowers that covered the ground, patches of green showing through, and of blue, where the soft ground gave way to water. Dead horses lay stretched on their sides, and overhead the vultures circled, waiting their turn. The women's horses shied from the spot, whinnying their fear.

Isabel looked into every face, learning early to recognize blond hair darkened with blood, or part of a face. None, God be blessed, was Rory.

She found Henry apart from the others, as though he had been different from the others who had died. She looked down at him from the back of her horse, the buzzing in her head louder now. Henry's eyes had been closed, coins placed over them, his hands folded across his chest. And she knew, as she gazed on him, who had done that.

They found Liam first. Nell screamed his name when she saw him walking toward her, slipping from her horse to throw herself in his arms.

"Margaret! Margaret!" Gannon called, not far behind Liam. "They are alive, Margaret. Our sons live!"

"Thank God! Oh, thank God!" Margaret cried, hurrying toward him, sobbing.

Alive. Rory is alive. Isabel took a shuddering breath.

"And Kieran. And Davey, lass!" Gannon called. "All well. We lost no one."

And there was Kieran, on horseback, raising his arm to wave at Rachel. Rachel put her hand to her mouth with a strangled cry. Kieran rushed to her side, then stopped, waiting. Rachel stopped as well. Then, with a trembling hand, she reached for him. He pulled her from her horse and held her against him, speaking softly. Rachel nodded. Kieran looked over her head at Isabel.

"He's there, lass," He pointed.

Isabel saw a man, riding north from the castle, his plaid thrown over his shoulders, his dark cloak flying over the rear of the horse.

Rory. Alive.

"Isabel!" he cried.

"Rory!" she called but could not say more.

He kicked his horse into a gallop, and she hers. The world disappeared, the sounds around them faded, and she saw only him, hurrying toward her, the colors of the field impossibly bright, the sky impossibly blue, and above them, Stirling Castle rising into the sky, a reminder of why they were here.

And then she did not think, only reached for him as he neared. He slid from the horse's back before it stopped moving and ran to her. She reached down, and he pulled her into his arms. And for a moment, all was right with the world.

EPILOGUE

The battle had been won, but the war raged on for years. William Wallace was knighted that Christmas, as were Rory and Kieran. Robert Bruce, now fighting for Scotland's freedom as well, did the honors. Scotland needed a leader, and Robert was quickly becoming one. William was named Guardian of Scotland, and the Scots revered him. He asked Rory and Kieran to stay with him, and they did, through most of the turbulent years of sporadic warfare. In 1299, John Balliol, held captive all that time, was released from the Tower. After three years in papal custody he retired to his lands in France, never again to claim the throne of Scotland.

On March 25, 1306, Robert Bruce was crowned King of Scotland in Scone with all the splendor the Scots could muster in such difficult times, with Rory and Isabel in attendance. And for once, the Scots united behind their new king. Edward died in Cumberland, on the Scottish border, in 1307, of dysentery. His only son, Edward II, led the English army to defeat in 1314, at the Battle of Bannockburn, which ended the war.

Scotland was now free, and a nation once again. And throughout the generations of MacGannons and Mac-Donalds the stories were told of the time of the rivalry for the crown.

AUTHOR'S NOTE

I have injected fictional events, places, and people into the history of late-thirteenth-century Scotland and England in order to tell this story. All of the towns, villages, and castles mentioned here existed then and many still do—except, of course, for Loch Gannon, which only exists within the pages of my books. I altered the historical facts only once, for the scenes that present the political meetings at Norham, which I compressed from nine days to two. Some of the meetings were large congregations of English and Scottish nobles and King Edward, others were much smaller gatherings of select groups. The various meetings had at least two venues—Norham Castle in England and the village green across the river in Scotland. Nonetheless, the various meetings' agendas were the same: Edward dictated them; the force of his personality and will was evident to all who attended.

I depicted Edward as my research revealed him, a brilliant, ruthless leader who dominated his own country, lusted after other lands, and often got his way. A trusted and loyal son, often a negligent father, but a devoted husband. To this day the mere mention of his name can still stir emotions in the English, the Scots, and the Welsh. He was fascinating to research. As was William Wallace.

Most people know the story of *Braveheart*, the movie that caught the imagination of millions and inspired changes in Scotland even recently, which shows the power of words and images to change the world. William was an inspired leader, a charismatic man who other men followed for years, who was loved by the common people, but underestimated and undervalued by the nobles of Scotland. His own journey, from an aspiring man of God to a war leader, is captivating and poignant. I chose to end this story on a high note, at the Battle of Stirling Bridge, but there is much more to William's—and the MacGannons'—story.

Walter Langton was indeed Bishop of Lichfield and Steward of the Wardrobe for King Edward. His reputation was that of a rapacious and merciless man; rumors flew about him, including the ones I have cited, that he strangled one of his mistresses, and that he worshipped the devil in secret. He was a most convenient villain, and I suspect he would not have forgiven nor forgotten Isabel's assault.

I very much enjoyed telling the story of the friendship of Isabel and Rachel. They are my inventions, but certainly women like them did exist. The Jews were expelled from England in 1290, not to return openly for more than five hundred years, and surely friendships and families were torn asunder because of Edward's edict. To be invited to be a lady-in-waiting to a queen was a high honor, but the younger ladies were often exchanged as political and personal situations changed. The factual dismissal of one of the less significant members of Eleanor's household was just the opening I needed for Isabel to take her place.

The years after this story were turbulent for Scotland, but fateful, because as William's and Edward's rivalry ended, a new challenger was growing in power. Robert the Bruce's story is as compelling as the earlier struggle. And the MacGannons andMacDonalds were there for that one, too.

ACKNOWLEDGMENTS

My thanks go to: Maggie Crawford, Louise Burke, and the Pocket team for all their help and encouragement. To Aaron Priest and Lucy Childs, for everything. To Paul Sandler, Jill Gregory, and Karen Tintori for helping me to get it right. To my wonderful family, the gang at REW, the Whine Sisters, and my marvelous friends who have stuck by me in sunshine and shadow. To Joe, Bill, and Michael K, for keeping me above water. And to those who went before us in the lands about which I write—the Celts, Britons, Normans, and all, who found ways to keep their freedom and integrity as well as their friendships. Thanks for leaving the path so well-marked.

Delve into a timeless passion…
Pick up a bestselling historical romance from Pocket Books!

Karen Hawkins
To Catch a Highlander
In this game of hearts, love is the only prize.

Johanna Lindsey
The Devil Who Tamed Her
He loves a challenge…and she is an irresistible one.

Jane Feather
To Wed a Wicked Prince
This prince has more than marriage on his mind…

Sabrina Jeffries
Let Sleeping Rogues Lie
Enroll in the School for Heiresses, and discover that desire
has its own rules…and temptations its own rewards.

Meredith Duran
The Duke of Shadows
Born an outcast. Raised to nobility. Only one dangerous
passion can unlock his heart.

Ana Leigh
One Night With a Sweet-Talking Man
He talked his way into her heart.
Can he do the same with her bed?

Available wherever books are sold or at www.simonsayslove.com.

Do you have a passion for the past?

Don't miss any of the bestselling historical romances from Pocket Books!

Never say never in this dazzling new series from **New York Times** bestselling author Liz Carlyle!

Never Lie to a Lady She'll play along with his wicked game…for her own pleasure.

Never Deceive a Duke Desire can never be deceived—or denied.

To Scotland, with Love Karen Hawkins
A handsome Lord has her *shaken*—and stirred!

Beware a Scot's Revenge Sabrina Jeffries
Revenge is a dish best served *hot*.

Madame's Deception Renee Bernard
When a innocent young beauty takes control of a bordello, can her seduction be far behind?

If You Deceive Kresley Cole
Can this ruthless Highlander ever learn to love?

Available wherever books are
sold or at www.simonsays.com

POCKET BOOKS
A Division of Simon & Schuster
A CBS COMPANY

POCKET STAR BOOKS
A Division of Simon & Schuster
A CBS COMPANY

16821

The past is heating up...
Don't miss these bestselling historical
romances from Pocket Books!

A Malory Novel!

Captive of My Desires ❖ Johanna Lindsey
On the high seas, love takes no prisoners...

A Wicked Gentleman ❖ Jane Feather
Someone wicked this way comes...

How to Abduct a Highland Lord ❖ Karen Hawkins
She took his freedom...He'll steal her heart...
How can two wrongs feel so *right*?

Indiscretion ❖ Jillian Hunter
A steamy reunion on the Scottish Highlands results in
desire, in delight, and indiscretion.

Caroline and the Raider ❖ Linda Lael Miller
She plotted a daring rescue—but never planned on a
dangerous passion.

The Perils of Pursuing a Prince ❖ Julia London
Some passions are worth the risk.

If You Desire ❖ Kresley Cole
How much desire can a Highlander resist?